JOSH PERRY

ON THE LINE

JOSH PERRY

COVER ILLUSTRATION BY BOOKS-DESIGN.COM
PUBLISHED BY JOSHREADSBOOKS
2024

First Printing: 2024

ISBN: 978-1-7770324-6-3

Josh Perry

www.joshperry.ca

TABLE OF CONTENTS

PREFACE

Initially released episodically as a fully voiced audio-book. This novel version of ON THE LINE is the *original* version; which the script for the audio-book was based off of. There may be minor differences in character dialogue and sentence structure as a result. The story — *in essence* — is the exact same.

ON THE LINE is inherently a story about video games and while it references a variety of genres across this medium it focuses *mostly* on the genre known as MMORPG. An MMORPG is a Massive Multiplayer Online Role Playing Game. This term can cover a wide variety of games even if itself is a specific denotation. The individuals who play MMORPG titles (commonly just referred to as an MMO) are themselves characterized by a degree of extremism.

In a *single player* video game it may be normal for a player to achieve 100% completion within fifty, to three hundred hours. This span of time varies between players and titles but is relatively common. An MMO may require *thousands of hours* of dedication to reach even fifty percent completion and even that is temporary. A common expectation of a living MMO title is an ongoing flow of content updates referred to as *expansions*. These expansions literally grow the world, add new content, things to do, places to go or abilities to interact with. As a result what may have been fifty percent completion at one point, could degrade to thirty, or less over time due to the growth of things which there are to complete. Accordingly, someone who plays and dedicates themselves to an MMO is inherently accepting an extreme dedication of their time. For some players, this may itself *be the point*.

For better or worse, in the modern world mental health issues are regularly disassociated with, or addressed through deferral. I myself have spent *thousands of hours* in video games and MMORPG titles. It is my belief that video games allow us to leave behind a world that we may not entirely enjoy, and pick where our mind resides. This ability to leave the regular world and go on an adventure, or be someone in a different set of circumstances is the core of the appeal of any video-game. We don't like the world we have built, and nobody can agree on what a perfect rendition of it would be. However video games let us pick our own worlds and dive into them. They offer a means of escape that is unbeatable, and thus, incredibly appealing the more you dislike the real world.

According to the above, when I have played MMO titles I get the sense a fair number of other players are catering to the same sort of void. A feeling of mismatching, or general dissatisfaction that cannot be dissuaded. It can only be dismissed, or ignored. Someone may be a IT professional or Carpenter but in an MMO they may be an Elf that roams the forest and protects against darkness. A video game fulfills desires not just challenging to satisfy in the real world, but those that are largely impossible. No matter how hard I try, or where I explore (as far as I know) I can never gain the ability to conjure fire from thin air, fly with the wings of a bird or defeat a dark lord hoarding corrupted power. Whereas in a video game, the question is not whether I can do those things it is *how do I want to do them*. This freedom makes the real world a somewhat bitter place to be. The rules are not clear nor are the rewards proportionate. There is chaos and horrors so ongoing they become mundane. Above all it feels like there is nothing to be done about it.

In a video game you can find the source of the issue, pick up your blade and destroy the evil. In the real world, you're just a dork with a sword. There is no easy fix, no singular evil. No quest to complete that resolves the problems of the world.

CHAPTER ONE
BEYOND THE TUTORIAL

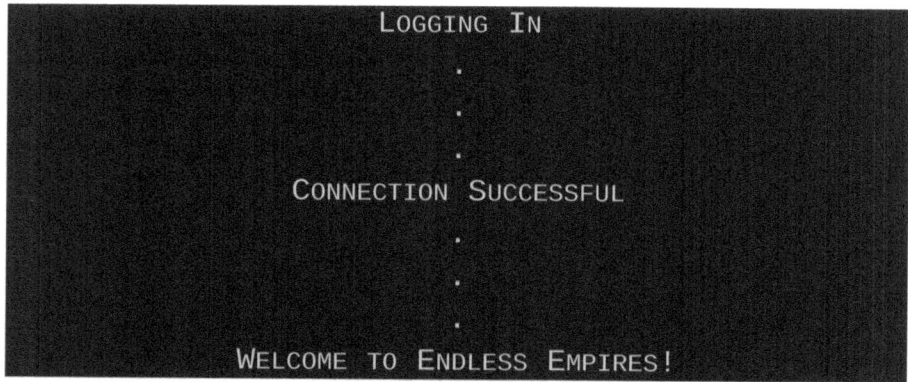

Blue light flushes around, swirling at the edges of each wisp as if it is ethereal flame. A soft *THUMP* sounds as *Kaan Kairo* logs into the game and lands on a bronze coloured cobblestone pathway. Around him in either direction are fleeting grasslands dense with gelatinous creatures bouncing about and various *warriors* roaming the open lands; engaging in conflict with such beasts.

"Slime Fields?" Kaan questions himself aloud. His avatar is tall, only a few notches below the maximum amount allowed on the character generation scale. Otherwise he's an androgynous looking man. His white hair is long in seven impossible braids down his back. His skin is as close to being grey as is possible while still being considered pale. Closer to beautiful then handsome; he's incredibly tone. Currently adorned with some common leathers and a great sword suspended in an implausible sheath on his back; he stares out at the grasslands. *"I must of been passing out at my desk to log out here."*

Soft music fills the background. A small band of travellers, mostly players; pass down the road near Kaan. They're higher level players, well armoured; each with a few notable weapons sheathed away. One plays a banjo; another a steel flute.

Green slimes burst as players challenge them and their *re-spawning* kin. In roughly thirty seconds after defeat; a slime will reappear a distance from where it was; born anew.

"Ping me if a blue one spawns!" A pink haired player shouts from the side-lines of the battle. They watch over a portable campfire, a small spit-roast and a few different pots and pans which bubble away.

Stoically, and *sleepily* Kaan opens his palm in front of him and a ball of light raises up, bursts, and in the expanding form of this light showcases a series of video game menus. Social information, information about Kaan as a character.

With a few simple flicks Kaan navigates right to the social menu, opens up his *guilds* tab and selects the one and only option on the page: *Velikaya Gil'diya*. A list of names appears, which he barely allows time to proliferate on the screen before selecting the bottom option. A system message pops up for him instantly:

> ILLKAT PROSOPHEROS IS .4KM SOUTH OF **VALD**

"I'm in the slime fields, you're not far outside that little mountain town." He laughs a bit to himself then smiles out at the artificial sky. "What *is it* that you're doing out there?"

A player approaches Kaan and waves towards him. The player is lower level, wearing a few pieces of the starting gear from the first series of quests. She's only a few levels lower then Kaan despite this. "Hi!"

"Hey." Kaan responds; his voice is deep, stoic and modified a fair bit from his real tone. "What's up?"

"Just looking for herbs so I can start levelling cooking a bit. Have you seen *Mint* spawn in this area?"

Kaan thinks for a moment. *"I think they're a rare spawn from the bundles under the light green trees."* He ponders for a moment longer. "At least in this area. I heard there is winterized mint southeast of Ilking that has a better spawn rate."

The player nods. She's picked a rather curvy avatar. The starting outfit for feminine players is a just above knee length skirt with suspenders, a white shirt armoured with a plate of steel over one shoulder and a portion of the chest. The matching gloves and boots look similar to real world construction safety gear; if it were constructed by hand with a thick leather stitching needle to finish the edges. "Thanks!"

Kaan nods politely. *"Good luck."* He turns away then looks around the area. The streets are mostly clear other then a few players walking about or travelling with groups. He yawns out-loud and stretches. In forgetting to mute himself before making a noise his avatar attempts to match the movement lips would require to make coffee slurping sounds; his voice modulator further modifying the sound to become bubbles in thick mud.

```
ILLKAT PROSOPHEROS HAS INVITED YOU TO JOIN A PARTY
                         .

                         .

                         .
              PARTY JOINED [2/10]
                    |H|
[ILLKAT PROSOPHEROS]
HEY, I SEE YOU JUST LOGGED IN.
                                          [KAAN KAIRO]
                    HEY, YEA. JUST WOKE UP. YOU SLEEP?
[ILLKAT PROSOPHEROS]
A BIT. WOKE UP NOT LONG AGO.
                                          [KAAN KAIRO]
```

LOL. OKAY. YOU GOOD TO VOICE CHAT? I DON'T HEAR
ANYTHING.

[ILLKAT PROSOPHEROS]
PARENTS STILL ASLEEP, DON'T WANNA WAKE EM UP.

[KAAN KAIRO]
IT'S *TUESDAY?*

[ILLKAT PROSOPHEROS]
YEA?

[KAAN KAIRO]
I JUST FIGURED THEY'D BE AT WORK OR SOMETHING.
IT'S LIKE, COMING UP ON 9 YOUR TIME RIGHT?

[ILLKAT PROSOPHEROS]
DON'T WORRY ABOUT IT.
PREPPING FOR THE GUILD-MEET LATER.
I HEARD *KOZMO* HAS SOMETHING GOOD FOR US.
I WANNA BRING AT-LEAST DECENT QUALITY HEALTH POTS.
COME HELP ME SLAY A BOG TROLL?

[KAAN KAIRO]
SURE. I'M CURIOUS WHAT KOZMO HAS BEEN DOING TOO.
BE THERE SOON.

Kaan closes the menu where the private messages were contained and sighs to himself. He retrieves a clasped wallet of sorts —about the length of a dagger— and opens it up to reveal a snug storage case for walnut sized crystals. In the case there are sockets for ten crystals to rest; while there are only three currently in place. Two are the same shade of dull ice blue and the other a darker brown.

With one of the ice blue crystals in hand Kaan tosses it aggressively at the ground underneath him and it bursts into a spiral of devouring light. Kaan is pulled into the light, dragged to become so thin his entire body is a length of string before becoming nothing at all; the light disperses besides the slime fields and reappears smack dab in the centre of the town of Vald.

Similar to the towns scattered across the *Rocky Mountains* Vald is home to log shacks, a consistent plume of smoke coming from each home, snow in the streets and piled up at the sides. Large horses pull wagons through either lane in the centre of the streets while players of all sorts travel between the different shops and gathering places. The town isn't massive, spread out over a half kilometre of space; leaving room for player housing and stores. The NPC's here are hardy, wearing furs and carrying hatchets or large bearded axes.

"Join the *Square Knights*! A growing PvP and PvE guild for new and veteran players! Voice chat is a must! Participate in grinds and have consistent groups for dungeon runs!" A player besides Kaan shouts. The player is masculine, with short hair. He's wearing the first tier of *leather guild armour*. It includes padded shoulders, straps across the chest, a series of bags at one hip and fitted trousers. A scarf, the seams of the clothing and a few accent pieces on the armour of the chest reflect the *Square Knights* guild colours; red and grey.

"Hey I'm good, *thanks*." Kaan responds politely.

The player instantly ignores Kaan; much like a sales person accepting a lost lead.

"*Okay then*." Kaan responds then smiles. He moves onward through the town square. Others appear around him, dropping from bursting light into the settlement.

Down an alley a man with a bandage pokes his head out. He has a styled moustache and a long beard; dressed somewhat like a pirate. He holds out a single gold coin and looks down the alley at *Kaan; winking*.

Kaan looks at the man, glances at the coin and simply sways his head 'no' to which the man responds by instantly retreating out of sight down the alley. Kaan attempts to target the man before he

12

leaves; but he's out of sight. *"Damn gold sellers."* Kaan laments as he passes by a series of two story homes; decorated with player acquired items.

One of the homes has the head of a giant skeletal beast adorned over the door; while the other is nothing but flowers in pastel replenish.

A player passes besides Kaan with their dog; a little french bulldog wearing a sparkling pink collar.

Chill passes through the area alongside a slight breeze.

Steps of many meld into a single intentional rhythm.

The edge of the town signals a chime.

LEAVING PROTECTED AREA

Outside the town is a snow covered grass. The air is cold; *delicate*. Mountains to the east inspire a sort of stillness in the energy of this place. Through the trees, snow piles and hulking boulders of the surrounding area are moose and sizable dire wolves; nearly white with their thick coat of fur.

Players creep through the snow, leaving a trail behind themselves. Working towards their prey. Bows prepared; some with flintlock rifles. They hunt cautiously; aiming to take down their target with single well placed blows.

The road is dry and free of the snow; as if it is warmed just enough.

干

The snow is light, wind subtle. A bit of darkness has started to tease itself in the sky. Ahead of Kaan is Illkat Prosopheros. Her avatar is thin, tall and coloured in purple pastels. Her hair is straight; down to the bottom of her back. A half-plate cuirass squares her shoulders and leads down to scaled faulds; underneath which are cured leather trousers. She wears two seven inch daggers; with one at her hip, and another in a reverse grip across her chest.

CLACK. CLINK. SMASH.

Illkat works away at a surfaced vein of copper ore; jutting out from the earth below it as if it had suddenly and violently erupted outward. Her pick-axe is a dull iron and low in value. Yet she works diligently; breaking off chunks of the ore. Each broken chunk falls to the ground, bounces slightly then *disperses* into a pixellated bright light.

"*Hey.*" Kaan greets as he approaches to stand next to her. He sits down on the ground and crosses his legs.

Illkat waves as she continues to work the ore; nearly entirely broken down now.

A private message blips for Kaan.

[ILLKAT PROSOPHEROS]
HEY, GIMME A SEC AND WE'LL GO OVER TO THE BOG.

"*Sure.*" Kaan says out-loud. "You can hear me right, you have your headset on?"

[ILLKAT PROSOPHEROS]
YEA, YOU'RE GOOD!
I THINK FOLKS ARE WAKING UP, I SHOULD BE ABLE TO GO ON VOICE IN A BIT.

"*No pressure.*" Kaan responds. He opens his palm to flick through his character page. His own mining level is at the further reaches of level ten. Out of the possible one thousand; it is a pittance. His highest skill of any on the page is *adventuring* at thirty three.

CRASH

The final chunk of ore is broken away. Illkat waves her pick-axe in the air for a moment then lets it drop; it disperses in the same flurry of digital squares as the harvested ore. She waves again, then nods.

"*Alright, you lead.*" Kaan responds. He targets her and a small modal frame appears in his field of view. She's level twenty and has full health. As a party member, he can see she's experiencing a potion induced bonus to resource drops. He selects *follow* from a list of many options.

They travel down the road for a couple of minutes until a *CLOPPING* behind them causes them to stop.

"*Player bus! Got six spots open!*" A mid-level player shouts out from atop a caravan pulled by two strong horses. The vehicle is well built, with large wheels doubled up in the back much like a semi-truck.

Kaan flags down the caravan and it pulls over to the side; slowing steadily. He points towards it in view of Illkat and they both get on the *player bus*.

"Hey welcome folks! We're headed down towards *St.Margaez*. Just tag me in a ping if you want to get off."

"*Thanks.*" Kaan responds to the driver, heads towards the back of the caravan and takes a seat. There are open windows to the caravan, with bench-like seats on either side stretching out its entire length. The back is open; staring out at the road behind.

In the caravan with them is another player, a *solo player*. He's dressed in all black, a hood pulled over his face obscuring what is obviously a masculine but otherwise detail-less face. He nods *politely* to the others but says nothing.

The caravan takes off at a speed triple that of walking the road.

Kaan looks over towards Illkat. "Shouldn't be long now."

She nods in return.

"You know, the text to voice in this game is pretty good. Why not use that when you don't want to talk?"

She shrugs.

A moment passes.

"It doesn't sound right." Illkat advises with a sweet and un-modulated voice. A little *check-mark* appears next to her name as she talks; indicating she's using her real voice. "I *like to inflect*. The text to voice doesn't understand italics or anything yet."

"*Ah, fair.*" He smiles. "Your folks wake up?"

"*Yea, we're all good.*" She responds softly.

"I think I passed out around two, bit early for a Friday but I was exhausted. You?" Kaan questions as he stares out at the road.

Illkat leans forwards slightly then sits back flat. "When I logged out I think you were inactive for forty minutes, so not much further from that. *Kozmo* was still on, looks like he hasn't logged out all night, neither him or *Dezz*."

"*Dezz I get.*" Kaan laughs a bit. "He's basically a *no-lifer* already. But Kozmo typically kills it before it gets too late doesn't he?"

"*Yea.*" Illkat agrees then shrugs. "He's been putting in more hours lately though. Maybe exams are over for him or something."

"*Yea, something.*" Kaan agrees.

The solo player gets up, places a few gold coins in the driver's lap and then jumps off. He says nothing as he does so.

"Thanks!" The driver shouts out to him as he leaves, then laughs a bit. "*Oh solo players.*"

"There isn't a charge for the ride, is there?" Kaan asks up towards the driver.

The driver smiles and sways his head side to side. "Not at all, I won't decline the *tip* but no requirements at all. I'm going this way

16

anyways and helping folks along is one of the achievements I need for my *caravanner career*."

Kaan nods in understanding. "Cool! I haven't even started an occupation yet, *I probably should*."

"Caravanner is chill, each promotion takes a pretty incredible amount of kilometres travelled on the road so it's best to start early." The driver responds politely.

"*So* it's like most things. *Darn*." He laughs to himself as he turns to peer out at the surrounding area. He targets a bit of grass just off the road and sends a *ping* to the driver.

"Out to the bog?" The driver questions. "Heard there are some interesting items out there, stories of some rare quests too."

"To the bog it is!" Illkat adds on then jumps out of the still moving wagon onto the road; taking a few additional steps to catch herself but otherwise refusing to falter.

"*Thank you again*." Kaan adds then takes leave himself; joining Illkat.

The young lady smiles at Kaan teasingly. "Feeling *social?*"

Kaan shrugs. "*I mean, it is an MMO*."

"I don't see your point."

"It's inherently social."

"It's a stage to perform on."

"Maybe for some. But for me, it's the street I'd rather be on; everywhere else is much more the stage."

"*Pretentious*." Illkat teases then laughs wickedly. "*Come on*, I have a troll to slay."

Kaan nods with a smirk then follows along.

The pair head off the cobble stone road connecting the region like an artificial artery and onto dulled green grass; it grows from a dark, dense and moist mud. Ahead of them the ground becomes *wetter* eventually collecting itself up in puddles of near black liquid.

17

Further ahead are *draping willow trees* and a collection of sturdy yew. The leaves of each tree share a gradient of colours between calm green and a replete grey.

"I've always found the bog pretty." Illkat notes as she looks out beyond the trees.

Kaan nods. "It has its...*appeal*." He tries his hardest not to look over at her as he makes the statement.

Intently, she continues. "I'm glad you see it too. *Sure*, it's a bit like a zombie movie. Yet the stillness of it all, *I know I'm sitting in my room right now* and *yet*." She waits a moment, taking a deep gulp of air. *"There is a pleasant chill I can feel in this place."* She smiles, then becomes silent.

"I guess it can be qui-"

"*Shut up*." Illkat quickly commands; attempting a hush herself.

Kaan dulls himself with offence. *"Hey, sorry I-"*

Illkat presses her hand over Kaan's mouth to silence him then points in the distance ahead. Just behind a few trees, setting up a pressure trap between them; is a *bog troll*.

The creature stands at twenty feet tall, with a width of about half that and muscle tenfold of the fittest human. Its skin appears a light green underneath but is covered by a pervasive *moss* which is growing up out of years of cuts, infected wounds and debris stuck in the troll's thick flesh. Tucked into a belt at the troll's hip is a splintered tree; tethered together with strands of cord to form an impromptu club.

"*Oh*." Kaan murmurs under Illkat's hand.

Illkat rolls her eyes, then studies the trap as it is installed. "I've never seen them do that before." She moves her hand back and rests it at her side.

18

Kaan rolls his shoulders then glances over at the troll. *"Makes sense though, given 'The Author'."*

Illkat laughs sarcastically; as quietly as she can. *"The author."* She smiles. "The game is awesome, *don't get me wrong.* But I still don't really believe their *AI core* is as advanced as they're trying to say it is."

"Alright." Kaan allows with a shrug, then simply gestures towards the troll. "But how do you explain the troll creating a trap for players, in a place you've never seen it?"

"The game patched while we were asleep." She admits confidently, then stands straight and begins towards the troll.

"I dunno." He whispers mostly to himself; following along.

Thick sploshes from each foot-step make the bog troll aware of the pair approaching. It looks between the players, its trap and the distance between the two; then lets out a frustrated scream. In an adrenaline fuelled instant it picks up the whole of the unfinished trap and kicks it forcefully; causing it to fly through the air towards *Illkat* and *Kaan.*

"Shit." Illkat shouts as she jumps to her stomach; covering her face in muck.

Kaan sturdies himself in place, draws his great-sword and attempts to slash through the oncoming debris. His sword cuts through the first few planks of the remaining installation before the rest crashes like a collapsing bulkhead into him.

SPLSSHHH

Mud drops all around as Illkat pushes herself up to her feet.

Loud *CLOMPING* sprints towards her and quickly afterwards a shadow grows dark all around where she stands as the troll smashes its impromptu club down towards her.

She dodges back, missing the strike by only a few inches. Mud water splashes all around in a resounding *PLUNK.*

19

In an instant she draws both her daggers and sinks them into the troll's wrist. He barely reacts and attempts to shake her away; yet she holds on; raising up with the troll's arm to be higher then its head. She pulls her daggers from the troll's wrist and leaps across to the opposite shoulder; unleashing a flurry of stabs into the side of the troll's neck.

GROAAAHHHH

The troll groans in pain, releases its club and with both hands tries to catch Illkat.

She finishes her last strike in a combo then jumps forward; clambering over the very hands reaching for her and landing back down on the ground.

Just as *Illkat* lands *Kaan* is picking himself up; a slow steady upward tick persists as his health restores.

"*You know,* I wanted help taking down a bog troll. Not an audience." She teases.

"*Yea, yea.*" Kaan bemoans his failure.

UrahGGHH

The troll shouts, lowers itself and begins to charge at the pair.

Kaan looks over at Illkat and nods knowingly at her. "Time for the-" A loud *censoring* bleep sounds and prevents anyone from hearing what Kaan says as he lowers his great-sword; allowing Illkat to step onto it. He launches her with all his might at the oncoming troll.

Tough monstrous hide tears open against the fleeting blades in Illkat's hands as she launches towards and beyond the troll. She lands a short distance behind as it takes a few descending steps; collapsing at Kaan's feet.

A little chime plays, and both players gain experience.

"How did you not know about the copyright censors?" She teases.

Kaan raises a curious eyebrow. "How didn't I know about *what exactly?*"

"Yea, you can't say anything copyrighted in this game unless you install a license onto your profile. Just try it, try talking about-" she descends into a series of statements which the game refuses to allow; converting them all into a single toned blaring. "-which is funny because you can say the name *Koji Kondo.*"

"*Huh,* interesting."

Without wasting a moment further Illkat makes her way over to the corpse of the troll, brandishes a wide bladed machete and begins hacking away at chunks of the dark green moss.

"Never made potions with these ingredients. Will it go far?"

"As far as we can take it." Illkat confirms as she finishes a full set of harvesting animations. The once untouched troll corpse has been rendered into a somewhat cartoonish sack on the ground. Illkat has an oversized backpack on her shoulders; a few creeping troll components threaten to leap out of the dense packing. She holds out a second backpack which appears *exactly the same.*

"For me, *I presume.*" Kaan gestures towards it.

"*Can't use teleportation crystals with this many alchemical materials.*" Illkat states; citing the game's own tutorial.

The bog settles into relative silence. There are other players in the distance. Markings which suggest other trolls roam the region.

Light in the sky reaches a midday peak; while the brief shade offered by cloud cover is enough to cause opaque condensation to reveal each and every breath.

BLIP

Both Illkat and Kaan receive an urgent guild message.

[KOZMO]
EVERYONE, WE GOTTA TALK. NOW. MEET IN ILKING, PUB BY THE PORTAL. 'LUOGO'

21

"Well I guess we won't have to wonder much longer." Kaan admits.

Illkat laughs. "You say that, but if we get going there now. With these on our backs. We might *only be late*." She sturdies the gear on her back with a shuffle and sets off towards the city of Ilking; Kaan just a step beside her.

干

"Your character looks like he's trying to catch flies with his mouth." Sonnenblume jests. She leans back in the oaken pub chair; layers and layers of robes billow with her every movement. Her bright blond hair drops into curls at any length and sits just above her shoulders the whole way round. She's *noble* in stature and appearance; with a kind inflection.

Dezz stands perfectly still at the end of the table. His mouth moves oddly. Instead of words it sounds like he's breathing forcefully; then something burns away in a steady rhythm. "Can't believe they don't have a smoking emote."

"Kids play this game Dezz."

"Kids smoke." Dezz coughs into his mic. His mouth moves in an attempt to deliver the sound of a balcony door being shut. He coughs again then moves about intently; no longer just standing in place. Dezz is tall, relatively thin, with partially dreaded long black hair. He's wearing a hunter's trench coat —somewhat in a state of disrepair— with a mace at his hip in an elaborate sheath.

"Just, sit." Sonnenblume requests.

Dezz sits right across from Sonnenblume then smiles sarcastically at her.

All around them a lively tavern churns. Players at rest with their allies; ordering beverages with in-game currency which are, *in*

22

turn, delivered to them in the real world. The tables here are old, long and hand carved. The roof domed; keeping captive much of the light offered by aged iron braziers. Shadows are carved in such a way your drink appears to sway in front of you as fire shifts the light.

Sonnenblume laughs. "I admit, I see your point. There is a smile sarcastically option, but not a smoking option." She takes a pull from a pint of light ale; the glass chilled even against her touch.

An NPC approaches the table, bowing politely. Dressed in a suit and tie with a sharp collar that extends a short distance beyond his shoulders. He reveals in his palm a twenty pack of *cigarettes* alongside a box of matches. The packaging purports them to be from the brand *Everpuff*. "*For you sir, compliments of the house.*"

A chortle escapes Sonnenblume as she smiles behind her beer.

"*Why-*" Dezz examines the smokes, adds them to his inventory then stares back at the NPC; looking him straight in the eyes. "*Thank you.*"

"*Of course, please enjoy your stay in our establishment.*" The NPC wishes them well then whisks away to other duties; quickly getting lost in the crowd.

A poof of dull green smoke appears besides Sonnenblume.

"*That wasn't me.*" Dezz laments.

The smoke clears to reveal a broad figured man dressed in the shrouded clothing of a ronin. A wide brimmed straw hat, partnered with bird feathers and loose lengths of fabric reveal little of the individual underneath. A curved blade just short of eleven feet long hangs in a sheath on his back; part of it rests on the tavern floor. His voice is deep, if not muddled with a hard to place *oddness*. "I see *Kozmo* ushered us here before his own arrival."

"Seems so!" Sonnenblume cheers. "What have you been up to Gekomatsu!?"

23

"I walked expansion island." He seems sorrowful in the statement. "Yet I discovered nothing."

With a deep exhale Dezz leans forwards. "It isn't actually called expansion island is it?"

"*Hey folks!*" Kaan shouts as he enters the tavern; waving towards the guild.

Gekomatsu nods politely. Dezz waves. Sonnenblume smiles, stands and sways in place cheerfully.

Just behind Kaan is Illkat. She takes steady steps as she heads towards the table; carrying a wooden crate in both her hands.

"*Now if you have cigarettes for me too, I'm gonna be weirded out.*" Dezz notes quite seriously.

Illkat places the crate down onto the table and spends a full second looking over at Dezz as if he is the only idiot in the world. "We brought potions!" She shifts tone in an instant and looks over at Sonnenblume.

"Squeezed fresh out of bog troll butt." Kaan adds as he sits next to Dezz. They share a familial nod.

The waiter pops over from a nearby table. "Can I get you anything?"

"Ale!" Kaan orders. The sound of a few coins dropping can be heard from no discernible source.

"Nothing for me." Illkat confirms.

"Of course!" The waiter acknowledges and is off just as quickly as they arrived.

Illkat looks over to Kaan with a twist. "It's mostly the moss." She stares at the dull red potions in the crate. "Less then ten percent troll butt." She giggles slightly to herself, then removes from the crate a total of twelve potions; each about the size of a beer bottle. She sets out two of the potions in front of everyone present then leaves the other two at the far end of the table. "A little something for everyone."

24

CRASH

One of the windows in the tavern blows in. Glass clinks and shatters against the floor. A fast moving and shadowed weight smashes through the two lone health potions on the table and breaks most of the way through it.

Illkat just stares down at the lump now laying across the table. "Well not for *everyone*."

"Hey Kozmo!" Dezz greets politely. He scratches a match and lights a smoke.

"*Are you harmed?*" Gekomatsu questions with a sincere concern.

The lump on the table picks itself up. Kozmo isn't terribly tall, standing at about five feet. His ears are long, hair a light red. He's dressed in the outfit of a *banker*; a sharp vest, collared shirt and tailored black slacks. He's not especially fit, yet even at a glance he appears *cat-like* and *troublesome*. "*Heeeey.*" He greets them all. "Not in a rush. I really wanna know. How is everyone doing?" He asks with feigned patience; his gaze flickering to the broken tavern window.

Everyone stares at him.

He taps his fingers against the table. "Quiet day then eh?"

"Up until recently, *yes*." Gekomatsu replies calmly.

"*Well.*" Kozmo states, patiently steps off the table, then continues. "*I need us to run for our lives.*"

"Your drink sir." The waiter arrives —not deterred by the recent architectural modification— and places the ale in front of Kaan before taking his leave.

Nobody says anything, then they stare at Kaan.

For a moment nothing happens.

"Hey sorry I was AFK, just had to answer my door for the delivery. We good?"

25

Dezz blows out a thick plume of smoke. "I'm thinking it's a road beer my friend."

CRASH

SCREEEEEECH

A massive gargoyle lands in the broken out tavern window. Impossibly animated stone wings crack as they fold out and the creature shrieks from the depth of coal laden lungs. Its head is half the width of the window overall and its body can barely pass through; which doesn't deter it from trying.

"Thinking it's a road beer." Kaan agrees.

Gekomatsu steps up onto the table and in a heroic singular motion draws the full length of his Odachi; it shimmers as if a perpetual blue wave flows through it entirely. With the blade posed at the creature he shouts. "Go forth! I shall occupy this beast!"

Kozmo wags his head. "Sorry *Geko* I need you to come with us. Run!"

Gekomatsu looks between the guild and the gargoyle. He sighs, then sheaths the blade; leaping off the table. *"Let us go then!"*

The whole of the guild burst out of the front doors of the tavern out onto the streets of Ilking.

Bright white heated pathways line the city streets while defending against the ceaseless powdery snowfall. With gas powered lamps at every corner, raised cobblestone sidewalks, red brick residential housing and an endless spectacle of ornate decoration; Ilking is an organized festival of lights and colours crawling up the side of a greying mountain which reaches beyond the clouds. With a dull hum from the streetlights and steady jazz pouring out from a club down the street. One can barely hear the *THWUMPING* of gargoyle wings.

"Can we teleport?" Dezz questions; his hands in his pockets as he jogs alongside everyone.

26

"*No, just.*" Kozmo juggles his need to explain and the pressing situation. "*Just follow me, come on.*"

Sonnenblume stops as everyone goes on and holds her palm out flat. A disc of swirling colours appears in front of her which she pushes forwards with great fervour. The light expands and grows into a net which reaches out at the Gargoyle as it dives down towards them. She doesn't wait to see what happens before turning back around and breaking into a sprint.

Brickwork is dislodged in a loud SMASH behind the guild.

Kaan looks backwards for a moment to see another player's wagon has been flipped and a portion of a storefront destroyed; neither stop the pursuit of the gargoyle. Other players attempt to target the creature but seem *unable* to do so. Kaan glares at Kozmo. "*What even is this thing? How is something still aggro'd onto you in a city!?*"

"Well that's the funny part, as far as I can tell, *it's defending the city.*" Kozmo explains.

Dezz laughs; filling what would otherwise be an awkward silence.

"*This does explain why you're dressed like a banker.*" Gekomatsu adds.

"*Don't tell me that you-*" Illkat is interrupted as the gargoyle dives down towards the guild.

With a sudden shift Kozmo turns down an alley and kicks in a locked wooden door. Beyond the passage is a tight staircase leading into absolute darkness. Without a question asked everyone leaps down the staircase; the gargoyle hot on their trail bashes its shoulders into the tight passage; screeches like steel being sheered; then leaves.

THUMP, THUMP, THUMP

"Can someone make some light. I can't see anything." Kaan requests.

27

Dezz scratches a match; holding it a few inches from his face.

The flickering little flame barely illuminates what seems to be an *ossuary*; abandoned for ages. Layers and layers of tightly packed bones and skulls form the walls and columns of this diminutive urban cave.

"Is this a dungeon?" Gekomatsu questions. "I've never seen this quest before."

Kozmo steps forward then turns to face everyone. "*No, no one has. That's-*" He takes a second to catch his breath, leaning fully on his own knees and laughing. "That's what has got me so excited, about *this*." He produces from his inventory a scroll; protected in the most extravagant of seals cast in gold and jade.

"*What did you do Kozmo!?*" Illkat shouts.

Kozmo smiles. "I took something from the treasury of Ilking."

Gekomatsu shakes his head. "*How?* Have you even unlocked the infiltration skill? Did you find a glitch?"

"*Nah, nothing...nothing like that.*" Kozmo exhales, takes a moment to look around then meets eye contact with everyone. "This quest I found, or it found me, *I dunno*. I think the game *made it* for me. Nobody had ever heard of it, the NPC I got it from; new to the game! No mention of him on the forums." He swallows as he opens the scroll. "I was told that if I listened to everything they said, that I'd be able to get in and out with a treasure beyond value."

Dezz leans in; holding the lit match away from the scroll. He studies it, then laughs. "Looks like a contract."

Sonnenblume raises a single eyebrow. "*A contract?*" She questions, steps next to Dezz then examines the scroll. She hums slightly as she parses the contents of the page. "It's not just a contract, it's a *deed*. It says whomever is in possession of this document is the rightful owner of the town of Verrplek."

28

"*Verrplek?*" Dezz murmurs as he lights another smoke with the dwindling match.

"*Never heard of it.*" Gekomatsu adds to the confusion.

Sonnenblume shakes her head. "*I doubt anyone has,* apparently it was abandoned years ago. Before anyone was even playing the game."

A notification blips, everyone in the guild receives it.

NEW QUEST ADDED <THE HOLLOWED HOMES>

Kozmo laughs uncomfortably. "Oh well that bodes well."

CHAPTER TWO

THE HALLOWED HOMES

An ossuary is ill defined; possibly with purpose. As it is a box, building or really any sort of enclosure which is designed to house and display mortal remains. Skulls once polished, now grown a slight amber from decades of torch light baking against them. So many *mismatching bones* that the creature formed in your head from the composite of them all has a dozen arms and legs; stuffed alongside an outward jutting splurge of rib cages. As the darkness grows in complexity and the eye attunes to the dim space; it goes onward.

The Guild stand about in this dim space; their faces known to one another only by the brief illumination of a diminishing match-flame.

Gekomatsu takes a step back away from the little fire and embraces the darkness. "We are to go *through* then?"

"I can only imagine." Kozmo agrees. "This was the last item in my quest log. *Burst through a door*."

"Bones aren't so bad." Illkat adds; an upbeat note in her tone. "If we were to burst into a place where *even the bones were being stolen*." She laughs a bit to herself. "Well we'd be in *real trouble*."

Sonnenblume closes her eyes and places her palms together. Her hair flickers as if motioned by an invisible wind. "I don't feel as if we're alone in this space. *Something else* is here."

Everyone becomes still. There is only subtle background music remaining; soft strings set in place to not steal too much attention.

"Are we all good to push into this quest or does anyone need to log off?" Sonnenblume makes an effort to look at each of her allies before she finishes the statement.

Kaan gives a thumbs up.

30

"I'm good." Illkat confirms.

"What else would I do with my day?" Dezz adds.

Gekomatsu nods.

Enthusiastically Kozmo joins. "As if I could stop now, right before; *whatever this is going to be*." He turns to look at the only hall available to them; it leads onward at a downward angle. Descending further; bordered at all times by the ceaseless display of skeletal remains.

"*Perfect*." Sonnenblume cheers with one arm jutting upwards. She squints to stare at Kozmo. "Before we go too far. *You* need to explain what happened before we got here."

Kozmo exclaims. "*Like I said*, the quest must of found me. There was an opportunity to join a shift of bankers, at a specific time, work a shift exactly as needed. *I even had to do a series of quick time events so as to not spill coffee on my boss*." He smirks, chuckling at the memory. "In the afternoon of that shift, I had an opportunity to swipe something covered in gold and jade. All I knew from there was I needed a group, and to get them through this door."

"Sounds like a trap." Gekomatsu laments.

Illkat rolls her eyes. "Does it even need to be a trap? Look at this place. It is its own whole category of concerns."

"It has to be though, *doesn't it?*" Dezz adds. "This is a shared game world, with set locations and settlements. To just give us a town, or odder; *spawn one in for us*. What are the chances of that?"

"*Mhmm*." Gekomatsu considers; his tone so deep it resounds like a note on a bass guitar. "It would not be impossible for us to discover something *new*. It feels as if there is still much undiscovered."

Taking the lead among the group Kaan moves ahead. He glances casually at the remains lining his path. Everyone follows a bit behind him.

The hall leads through an archway into a lobby of sorts. An empty fountain covered in dust is set in the centre of the room; a circular bench built in four quarters surrounds it. The ceiling is tall and domed; with a thin stone spike protruding straight downward from the centre of it. Each wall is rigid, with shelves carved into the stonework; accentuated with depictions of everlasting knots.

Across from the archway is a door, four times the height of any mortal. Its edges are steel, with flat sheets of the metal fortifying it across the face. A few small portions of the underlying wood remain visible.

"Nobody open the door until we're all ready."

"That's right, *nobody be a leroy*." Dezz teases.

"I'm surprised other players haven't found this place. Did we enter an instance when we went past that door?" Illkat ponders.

"Hard to imagine not a single other player would follow us if it was any other way." Kaan notes.

"I've tried many of the doors in this city, rolling into them, slashing them with my blade. Trying to determine if there are secret passages waiting to be discovered. No matter the angle I jumped at them, I have never found one. I believe the door opened *just for us* and this *dungeon* as it were; is new to the realm."

Sonnenblume giggles. *"First!"*

Illkat smiles politely. *"Might as well write it on the wall."*

Sonnenblume instantly rushes up to a wall, removes a large chunk of chalk from her inventory and signs her name —in a massive font size— on the ossuary wall.

"Well now I get the sense these are *your bones*." Dezz comments as he gestures towards the skulls.

"Or you're claiming responsibility for them all." Kaan joins; barely containing his own laughter.

Illkat sticks her tongue out. "You're just a monster *Sonnenblume*."

Sonnenblume sparkles as her guild members tease. "*You know it!*" Her smile is bright; her cheeks sharp.

A little mouse appears from within one of the skulls. It scurries over a broken jaw-bone and the endless osseous matter it is set upon; then is gone again.

Brief silence takes hold.

"So, *the door*." Kaan points towards it.

"Let me." Gekomatsu steps forwards. "I've been training *infiltration* for moments like this."

"How'd you even get that skill? I don't see it on my sheet. Adventuring, cooking, esoterica, fishing, large cra-" Kozmo is cut off.

"It isn't in the base skills. Once *adventuring* reaches level 500. You can unlock either *archaeology* or *infiltration*."

With a simple gesture Gekomatsu summons a lock-pick into his grasp. It's a unique tool, unlike those shown to new players as thievery is being explained in the tutorials. It features a little light focused on the lock ahead, a screw driver and chisel; all folded away like a modern multi-tool. He is entirely silent while he works.

Everyone in the guild stands behind him; weapons drawn. With the exception of Kozmo. He quickly looks around the room, grabs a *femur* from the bones lining the walls and handles it like a club.

"Pretty sure you're cursed now." Dezz states quite seriously.

Kozmo laughs. "Cursed with *wisdom*. Just think of how honoured *you would be* if someone fought evil with your bones long after you passed on!"

Dezz chews on the sentiment; nodding a couple times to himself. "I retract my previous statement."

33

"And I have a new line item to add to my will." Illkat jokes. *"Don't fight with my bones."*

CLICK

The lock of the door snaps back.

Dezz chuckles. "I'm surprised this opened that easily. Did they buy their locks from a bargain bin at -"

A censoring beep covers Dezz from being heard. He stares around the space, up towards the sky he cannot see and with his expression alone; curses his corporate overlords.

"Never mind, *great*, the door is open." He concludes.

As he tucks the lock-pick away Gekomatsu lowers himself; crouching besides the door. "Stay behind me as we go ahead here, I can offer a passive benefit to any sneaking attempt you make." As he finishes the sentence a translucent purple ring grows out from him; forming with a ten foot diameter.

Everyone collects themselves within the ring.

Gekomatsu reaches forwards and opens the door just so there is enough of a crack for them to step through. Beyond the door is a short hall which leads to a massive *empty* room. The room is much like an igloo if it were lined with dank bricks from a sewer. Another domed roof; thick grout between each salmon coloured chunk in the wall. The room is too wide to see either end of it from the hall the guild stand within.

"Oh that's a boss room." Illkat states confidently.

"Absolutely a boss room." Kozmo agrees.

"The bossiest boss room that's ever, bossed...a..bossy..." Dezz laughs to himself. "Yea we're gonna fight for our lives in there."

Tightening his grasp on the ancient bone Kozmo nods his head and focuses ahead.

The whole guild creeps further, tucked against the wall. Gekomatsu peeks around the corner, then turns back in an instant. "It's a tricyclops."

"*What?*" Sonnenblume questions. "Let me look."

With a nod Gekomatsu moves back and lets her go ahead. She peeks around the corner for only a moment before returning. "That *looks like a cyclops*. It has one big eye."

"It would." Gekomatsu confirms.

Sorting through themselves, everyone takes a turn looking around the corner and peering down to the far end of the room.

Sitting in an oversized throne of granite is a yellowed humanoid the size of a short tower. The incredible height of the room only serves to give a short distance of leeway between the one-eyed titan and the roof. Right behind the throne is an archway leading to a tunnel; the only other way out of the room.

"It's a cyclops. It only has one eye." Sonnenblume confirms.

Gekomatsu nods patiently. "It does have one eye, but it's not a cyclops."

"He's being honest, I've encountered one of them before." Illkat adds.

Kaan looks over at her. "You've encountered a cyclops before?"

"Yes, but this isn't a cyclops. It is a tricyclops." She affirms.

"I didn't see three eyes." Dezz joins.

"*No*, that's not what a tricyclops is. A tricyclops is a cyclops with three potential magical enchantments." Gekomatsu confirms.

"Ahhhhhh." Sonnenblume inflects. "So a three eyed cyclops would be a triclops, a tricyclops is a cyclops with three magical potentials."

"Alright, *so not to rip on etymology* or anything. But are we going to fight it or what?" Kaan inquires.

35

Dezz shrugs. Sonnenblume smirks.

Illkat looks around the room then closes her eyes. "Not until we know which of the three variations of tricyclops it is going to be. It's either going to become invisible, become completely encased in metal or start floating."

A loud, whooshing sort of *PLOP* occurs just behind the guild. As they turn to look; the tricyclops is there. Kneeling behind them. *Watching*.

Everyone *screams* as they rush into the centre of the room.

Gekomatsu shouts. "We've fooled ourselves. It isn't a tricyclops, a cyclops or a triclops. It's a quadracyclops." He draws his blade.

WHOOSH

The quadracyclops appears on the roof; staring down at everyone. It watches, *without relent*.

Kaan peers over towards the tunnel, then back up at the roof. Nothing is there.

WHOOSH

The quadracyclops jumps out of the floor; grasping Kozmo in one of his fists. *"Unhand me whatever you are! We're not really certain!"* He shouts out from within the grasp.

Illkat rushes towards the quadracyclops and leaps out; her daggers poised like the fangs of a saber-tooth tiger.

WHOOSH

The quadracyclops sinks away into the floor.

Kozmo begins to fall.

Illkat quickly sheaths her blades and catches Kozmo in her hands.

"My hero-"

She drops him. *"Ugh."* She bemoans.

"I have an idea." Sonnenblume shouts out. She begins to run out to the far side of the room.

"Wait it's going to try and catch you if you run!"

WHOOSH

The quadracyclops jumps out from beneath the floor; materializing like gas into a solid. It tries to grab Sonnenblume but instead she *snaps*.

SNAP

A sudden bright light goes off in the face of the quadracyclops. It leaps away in fear, and is gone for a moment.

"Be ready." Sonnenblume warns.

"What's going on?" Kozmo questions.

Gekomatsu adopts a sturdy stance. His lengthy blade is turned upwards; its tip curled out towards any oncoming opponents.

WHOOSH

The quadracyclops drops from the ceiling, one hand covering its eye.

Kaan looks up and spins himself forcefully, great-sword extended; he bats the quadracyclops across the battlefield like a ball. *"Yea it worked that time!"* He cheers only loud enough for himself to hear.

Sailing with considerable speed. The swatted quadracyclops is intercepted in the air by Gekomatsu. Within a few short frames he pierces the eye of the titan, pushes the full length of the blade through his target's head and sheaths it; all before landing.

THUNK

Landing all of a sudden like a dropped sack of spuds. Congratulatory music plays.

"Well now it is a no-clops." Illkat chimes.

Dezz laughs. "Well technically it would be a quadracyno-"

"Oh *my god*. Can we please stop this?" Kaan adds; only half serious.

Everyone takes a moment to collect themselves. They look around; awaiting something *more*. Yet, nothing comes. They are alone in the huge hollow space; the corpse of their foe splayed out on the ground.

Illkat produces a machete. "No point letting good material simply rot here."

"Do things rot in this game?" Dezz questions.

SPLASH

SPLORSH

Illkat hacks into the corpse. Retrieving what remains of the eye, and an assortment of hide components.

Dezz looks away from the harvesting. "I can only imagine they do."

"Most materials yes. Lots of the cooking skill at lower levels is learning preserves. Jams, pickled items. That sort of thing. *Naval food!*." Sonnenblume speaks on the topic with a great deal of confidence.

With a half-step and a small jump Illkat settles the bag on her back. "Well I don't imagine we'll want to eat any of this, but it should come in handy if we can get it out of this dungeon."

Everyone becomes silent.

The large empty room is kept from joining only by a consistent sort of *wailing* coming from the tunnel the quadracyclops once sat in front of.

"I think it's a good sign." Kozmo adds confidently.

"How do you figure that?" Sonnenblume questions.

Gekomatsu leaves the group and walks to the far side of the room.

"*Just, well*. It is *a sign*." Kozmo continues. "I figure a sign is better then not a sign."

With a sprint to start Gekomatsu charges at the wall and rolls into it; thunking his body against it. As he recovers, he jumps to his feet and slashes at the wall and the surrounding area with his blade.

Everyone stares.

"*You, alright there Gekomatsu?*" Illkat questions.

Dezz laughs to himself, then begins towards the throne of granite.

"*Yes.*" Gekomatsu confirms. "It appears there are no secret entrances on this side of the room."

"*Shame.*" Kaan joins.

The guild collect themselves; grouping up at the entrance to the tunnel. It is large, enough for the quadracyclops itself to travel through it. Mostly carved from the stone with a rough edge. The tunnel leads down to a sharp corner.

The wailing, fierce at times then dull at others; doesn't cease.

Kozmo looks around the area, and the others each look at him. Illkat gestures towards the tunnel.

"*Okay.*" Kozmo notes, waits a second then starts down the tunnel. He doesn't stop walking and makes it to the bend in only a moment. He looks far down the tunnel, laughs a bit to himself then waves for the others to join. "Not a bad mislead."

The others reach Kozmo and peer down the length of the remaining tunnel themselves. It stretches for what seems like a dozen kilometres, with an old mine-cart running the full length. The track is a bit rusted, yet constructed overall with strained pine and thick wrought iron. At the furthest end of the tunnel is a white exit where snow rushes inwards on the ushering of a blizzard breeze.

"I'm checking for traps." Sonnenblume states confidently.

"Me too."

"Same."

"Alright let's do it."

Everyone begins an animation where they are peering through a magnifying glass; examining the length of the hall and the space around them. As well as each other; examining examinations examining.

Within seconds of one another; the magnifying glasses are tucked away.

"It looks safe." Gekomatsu states.

"I concur." Sonnenblume adds.

"I'm gonna get food really quick while we use this mine-cart then." Dezz notes.

Kaan laughs. "Yepp. Same. Forgot to eat so far today. I'll go quick, if we get attacked text me."

Illkat steps into the mine-cart and a little keyboard icon appears above her head. "Gonna make a tea, see you all soon." Her character becomes still, looking ahead and not making a sound.

〒

"*Aaaahhhhhwhhhhh.*" Illkat yawns loudly. She moves around, pouncing out of the mine-cart.

The guild has reached a wintered over region. Snow actively falls across the ground; with no discernible path anywhere. The tunnel opens out of a straight mountain face; the tracks end in dirt without any further construction. The trees here haven't any leaves and hold only bundles of light snow upon their branches. Far in the distance, near to the edge of what appears to be a cliff-side; is a collection of haphazard buildings.

"How's the tea?" Sonnenblume asks as she gets out of the mine-cart herself.

Illkat smiles. "*Good.*" She mutes herself, takes a moment then returns. "Not spicy enough for my taste. We got a new chai. It's a bit weak; *and yet.* Tea *is* tea."

"I can agree to that. Often I find my evening hasn't *truly* started until I'm making myself a cup." Sonnenblume smirks. "Though I won't argue if someone else does it for me."

"Such is the curse of tea." Illkat confirms. "It would be *morally reprehensible* to not offer anyone within earshot a cup of tea, if you are indeed putting on the kettle to make some."

Sonnenblume laughs to herself. "I'm glad you think so. I had a chat once with some folks from down south about tea and they started mentioning *microwaves.*"

"*Ew, ew. No. Stop.*" Illkat requests.

"Oh sorry. I know, it's some horrifying stuff. *True American crime.*" Sonnenblume apologizes with a sarcastic inflection.

Illkat giggles. "The *original* American crime, if we're being historical about it."

Kaan gets up and walks over to the group. He stares around the area.

"Heyo, how was food?" Illkat questions.

Kaan stares ahead, he says nothing.

"That good huh?" Sonnenblume adds.

His character seems to smile a bit, but continues to stare onward.

The women stare at him; confused expressions growing on their faces.

"*Ah shit, sorry. I didn't realize I was on mute that whole time.*" Kaan rushes out the statement. "Food was fine. Anything going on here?"

They both point out in the distance to the collection of aging buildings. "Our inheritance." Sonnenblume cites sarcastically.

41

"Technically Kozmo's, if we're being specific about it." Illkat states blatantly.

"No need to be." Kozmo joins. He jumps out of the mine-cart; still clutching the femur from earlier. "It is for the guild as far as I'm concerned. What need have I of more then one room."

Gekomatsu appears to be in the mine-cart, but moments later is standing next to the guild. Remaining in the cart where he had been is now only a scare-crow of straw and canvas; with a short rimmed hat.

"*What level are you dude?*" Illkat interrogates.

"One of them." Gekomatsu returns with a spry sarcasm. "However it might be worthwhile for me to scout ahead." He raises up his palm and a green light bursts from it. From the view of the other players it is nothing but blurred and impossible to decipher light. With a few flicks Gekomatsu navigates a menu and a pulse of light carries out from him; treading ahead and towards the settlement.

NO HOSTILES DETECTED

Sonnneblume looks around at everyone *other then* Gekomatsu. "I don't have that option, do you have that option?"

A match crackles, smoke made opaque as a result of the cold reaches out and drifts up into the air. "I think *Geko* has been around since 1.0. Eh?" Dezz speaks from behind a burning smoke.

Gekomatsu nods diligently. "I was an *early adopter*."

Everyone begins to walk towards the buildings in the distance; a forest of straight wooden lines reaches out in most every direction. The empty trees are solemn. Some seem to move, or split as you blink. Some are there only for a moment, then ahead of you as you turn away.

"Some weird feck'n trees right there bud." Dezz notes in his most *Canadian* accent.

42

The group keeps on, the trees shifting in their lackadaisical manner.

Ahead of them the settlement becomes clearer.

In total there are five buildings. Three are residential in nature. A row house size-able enough for a dozen workers, a two storey structure of patchwork construction and a larger home —sparing no detail or luxurious addition— for the local lord. Asides these is a stable with a large brickwork well and to the north a church next to a stand alone stone tower in the same sort of overdrawn gothic style.

A somewhat more composed footpath consisting of rows of slate set into the ground are barely discernible underneath the snow; leading between the different structures.

An open patch in front of the largest home is covered in smooth, undisturbed snow. In the centre of the patch a man stands. He is dressed in the garbs of a simple farmer; threads torn at the edge of each garment. He is at rest, arms to the side; staring ahead at nothing specific.

"*Uhh.*" Kozmo interjects.

"Uhh indeed." Illkat joins. "Is he a player...npc?"

"I can't select him." Gekomatsu adds. "He should appear on the mini-map at this range, with some kinda icon. But, *nothing.*"

Wind blows through the area.

Now standing just a distance from the invisible border of the town. It is clear that most of it sits at the edge of a cliff overlooking nothing but a long fall and icy water. Elevated enough that you can see a distance in every direction. There appears no other way to get here outside the tunnel the guild used, hiking over-top the mountains or sailing to the cliff-side and climbing directly up it. From where they stand, none of the options have seen any recent use.

Everyone continues on the path, slowly; yet assuredly approaching the man who stands in the snow.

Sonnenblume waves out to him. "Hello, *sir?*"

There is no response. He simply stands.

"Maybe he's just afk?" Kozmo adds. He begins walking towards the person; taking long steps in the undisturbed snow.

Gekomatsu places his hand over the handle of his weapon. "Like I said, *that isn't a player*."

Kozmo gets closer and puts his hand on the man's shoulder. Without hesitation the man looks at Kozmo; snapping his own neck with the force of the motion. His eyes widen, burst and then he falls to the ground and dissipates into nothingness. "Oh, *good*. I was worried I'd have to have a conversation with a stranger."

QUEST UPDATED

"Aahhh." Dezz shouts a bit.

Everyone looks at him.

"*Sorry*." He continues. "Sometimes the game voice just *freaks me out*."

"It does sound pretty ominous at times." Kaan agrees.

Sonnenblume opens her menu and peruses the update. "*Reclaim the lost town*." She huffs. "Well that's not exactly specific."

"*I claim this town!*" Kozmo shouts out.

Nothing happens.

Dezz laughs. "It was worth a shot."

A crisp wind blows through the area. Puffs of snow rush up into the air. A few of the holes in the wall of the row-house whistle.

"*Where first?*" Dezz asks to no one specifically.

"The church looks pretty." Sonnenblume admits.

"*Creepy pretty*." Illkat agrees. "Let's go there."

"The big scary church? Yea, let's go there and ignore generations of horror film education." Kaan jokes.

With a pensive grin upon his otherwise covered face Gekomatsu looks out towards the church. "Where there is horror, *there is experience to be gained*. I say we go."

A moment passes and the group collect themselves into a tightly oriented unit. Gekomatsu is at the front, just behind him are Kaan and Dezz, followed by Sonnenblume and Kozmo with Illkat covering the rear.

"Any of you ever play Kitty Sabre Extreme?" Dezz questions nonchalantly.

Sonnenblume raises her eyebrows with intense curiosity. "What did you just ask us?"

"It's an adventure mmo, based in a fantasy feudal Japan, but everyone is a cat and some sort of samurai or ninja." Illkat states swiftly; without missing a beat.

"I'll take that as a yes." Dezz laughs. "Apparently it is pretty good. My sister just started playing. The ninja skills for moving around the cat city...*uhh*"

"*Los Catos*." Illkat corrects.

"*Los CAT-os*." Dezz repeats. "What a name." He laughs again. "Well it seems like a neat thing."

The group approaches the front doors of the church; they are entirely closed.

"Do you ask for any reason?" Sonnenblume inquires.

Dezz shrugs. "I'm just thinking about silly things —*and well* — the Australian animal handler tactic to dealing with horror." He looks around; glaring at nothingness in the sky.

Gekomatsu raises an eyebrow but says nothing.

"*What are you doing?*" Kaan asks.

"Dodging copyright infringement claims I hope." Dezz waits a moment longer, suspiciously looking around the area. They all stare at the door and he takes a step towards it. "The Australian animal handler tactic is to just, *dive into* and start narrating whatever you're doing, no matter how horrifying, as if you're the host to an exotic animal show." Without relent he pushes open the doors to the church.

Beyond a long single chapel is revealed. Pews have been set to the side. Floorboards have rot into muck. At the far end of the church is a humanoid figure, barely visible, formed mostly from racing strips of pixellated light.

"*Mmmm-mmooorrreeee then we can handle. Broken. All broken.*" The figure states in a contorted digital voice.

"Now here we have an omen. Foretelling of something awful to come." Dezz narrates.

"It is coming. *A shift. Something I can foresee but you cannot.* Yet I am not aware, is it *underneath.* Underneath what I see." The figure continues. Shadows begin to seep from the walls. They fill the floor.

Dezz takes a step back but continues. "Now the walls are getting nervous. When you see this, you know your scary gothic church is approaching the rutting season."

Kozmo laughs awkwardly; without convincing anyone he actually finds anything funny. "Do we fight this?"

"*You will, you must. Alongside them all, every single one. Battles, against more then all there is. The hydracopter. The gods and demons; you.*"

CRASH

The roof of the church breaks in as the gargoyle from the city of Illking crashes down through it. It screeches violently out at *the guild.*

"*Oh not this thing again.*" Illkat chastises.

The figure of light which previously stood before them dissipates into nothingness.

46

Battle music begins to play; shifting from the sombre tune of before.

SHLINK

Gekomatsu draws the full length of his Odachi and points it out with unwavering strength at the gargoyle. "We're free to engage now are we not?"

"*Yes but!*" Kozmo shouts, reaffirms the grip on his make-shift club then continues. "I still can't target this gargoyle. It's like an NPC, protected by the system!"

Everyone adapts a combat pose, their weapons drawn. Dezz's mace when unsheathed begins to drip with a light white smoke; as if something within the head of the weapon is smouldering.

The gargoyle screeches and drops into the primary room of the church. It swipes one of its wings out at Gekomatsu.

SHINK

The stone cold wing connects with the glimmering blue blade and sparks fly. Gekomatsu steps forwards and pushes back against the blow; barely deflecting the swipe.

Three balls of light form in front of Sonnenblume and she pushes her palm out to direct them at force towards the gargoyle. Each ball of light bursts against the gargoyle's skin.

A system message appears above the Gargoyle's head.

INVINCIBLE TARGET

"Not for long!" Kozmo shouts, rushes towards the gargoyle and smashes the femur in his hands down upon it. The femur snaps as soon as it connects with the gargoyle and shatters loudly into a collection of shards. "*Shit.*"

The gargoyle shrieks and with a single swipe of his wing sends Kozmo flying out of the church.

"Okay we need to stop fighting this thing like thugs in an action movie." Illkat exclaims. "*Geko*, you tank. Kite this thing outside. *Kaan, Dezz focus on DPS. Don't draw aggro if you don't have to.*"

The gargoyle charges out at Kaan. In a singular motion he sheathes his weapon and rolls towards the oncoming hostile; dodging between its legs. Without pause he continues to draw his great-sword anew, collects momentum as it moves over his shoulder and pulls down into a strong over-head strike.

No damage is dealt to the gargoyle.

Gekomatsu rushes towards the monster, leaps over-top of it and quickly slashes it atop the head a multitude of times. It looks towards him and shrieks with frustration.

"Come on then!" Gekomatsu shouts out at the creature then begins walking backwards out of the church.

"Sonnenblume, *can you heal?*" Illkat questions as she approaches the gargoyle from an angle.

Sonnenblume studies the room for a moment then shakes her head. "*No*, but I can do this!" She holds her hand out towards Gekomatsu and closes her eyes. Ethereal energy forms around her then reaches out to Gekomatsu like a thread; covering his blade in a translucent white light.

With a shriek the gargoyle slams both its hands down towards Gekomatsu. He pushes off the strike with his blade and the gargoyle is pushed back a short distance as they collide. The light dissipates from the blade.

Dezz rushes towards the gargoyle, slides closer and as he rises again; strikes upwards with his mace. He manages a few strikes in quick succession; each blow causes his mace to leak with heavier and heavier smoke.

Stone crumbles loudly as the gargoyle steps out of the front door; its wings and a portion of its head destroying the archway entrance of the church.

"Hey, I found something out here. Keep it busy!" Kozmo shouts out towards Gekomatsu.

SHIINK

Gekomatsu barely deflects another blow. "What is it *exactly* you think I'm doing Kozmo!"

Kozmo doesn't respond. He focuses on brushing away snow in the open field with the side of his foot. The same field where the man who snapped his own neck previously stood.

Quickly shifting on its heels the gargoyle swipes around and slashes a wing out at Dezz. He holds out his mace to block and just before the wing connects with him; a barrier cast by Sonnenblume buffs his defence. Dezz slides back barely an inch without taking damage; his mace begins to change colour becoming a light red.

Illkat kicks the gargoyles wrist; upsetting its balance. She rushes onward to slash and slice up and down one of its sides; dancing around one of the wings which strikes down towards her. The gargoyle spins around and whips its long porous tail towards her. As if impersonating a world class limbo dancer she falls backwards on her knees; maintaining her own body weight at a sharp angle as the whole tail sails over-top of her. Out of the corner of her eye, standing atop the mountains in the distance she spots three black figures.

CLUNK

Verrplek shakes. Compacted snow built up on the sides and roofs of the buildings becomes loose and falls into piles.

"Found it!" Kozmo shouts.

In the centre of the field an ivory pillar begins to rise up out of the ground. It is hexagonal in shape and completely perfect in its construction. Stemming out from it in the shape of a complex alchemical rune is a bright blue light. Circles overlapping circles, light in motion. The snow begins to melt revealing a dizzying clockwork of shifting land. The pillar rises to be ten feet tall. A loud *CLONK* sounds as if it is locking itself in place.

Gekomatsu takes a hit and rolls nearer the pillar. "Is this going to help us?"

Illkat stabs at the gargoyle; still dealing no damage. "It *better*." *FWOOOOSH*

A massive shift in pressure juts out from the pillar; causing everyone including the gargoyle to focus on just standing upright. Winds at a level beyond the fiercest storm blow up into a globe surrounding the entire town of Verrplek; the outside world becomes diluted as if it is on the other side of thick warped glass.

"I...*can't explain it*. But I know there is something inside that pillar, something we need." Sonnenblume states plainly.

"SHRRAAAAAA". The gargoyle shrieks. It opens up its wings in a burst of strength; throwing itself towards Kozmo with a flying kick.

Kozmo ducks behind the pillar, it takes the hit without so much as a wobble. "*haha!* Take that you museum exhibit!" He taunts.

The gargoyle climbs over-top the pillar, peers down towards Kozmo and leaps down towards him.

"Run!" Sonnenblume shouts as she creates a barrier over-top Kozmo; preventing the gargoyle from stomping him into the ground.

"Oh gosh, overconfidence was a mistake." Kozmo shrieks as he crawls out from under the barrier just before it collapses and the full weight of the gargoyle hits the ground with a THUNK.

Kaan looks over to Gekomatsu. "Big sword team up?"

"Never say that again." Gekomatsu remarks seriously. "*But yes*."

The pair rush towards the gargoyle; their oversized blades high in the air. Each swipe at the gargoyle; occupying its attention. Dezz rushes up from behind the beast and strikes out at its wing.

Sonnenblume looks over towards Illkat. "We can't keep this up *forever*. It'll be a battle of attrition and that's if nobody takes a hit."

"You're right." Illkat agrees. She looks over towards the pillar. "You said there was something, *in there*. Right?"

Sonnenblume nods. "I just sense something *unique*."

Illkat looks over, nods a couple of times to herself then smiles. "Alright, keep up those barriers while you can." She then dashes off towards the pillar.

The gargoyle smashes Kaan in the face; sending him flying. Sonnenblume conjures a barrier underneath him before he lands; breaking the fall.

SHINK

Gekomatsu deflects a wing; its piercing tip like a spear. "What a battle!" He rejoices.

Illkat reaches the front of the pillar and peers towards it. It is detail-less, like a sheer white cut of the most perfect tusk. "Not a lot of options here." She reaches out and presses her palm flat against the pillar. "*Cool technology thing?*"

FWOOOOSSSHH

Another layer of energy rushes out from the pillar knocking everyone except for *Illkat* back a short distance. The gargoyle quickly recaptures its balance and lunges at Gekomatsu. Kaan swings out at the beast with the blunt side of his great-sword as Sonnenblume places a barrier across it; deflecting the gargoyle in its entirety. Before it crashes into the ground it forces itself upright with a flick of its wings and remains in the air; peering down vengefully.

Around Illkat's hand a tracing of light forms; then spreads across the entire pillar. Before her a panel opens and slides away;

51

revealing a spear of immaculate construction. It is a series of overlapping knots forged from perfect silver that collects into a trio of pointed tips. The entire weapon *pulses* with obvious strength; blurring the area around it. Illkat laughs. "*Yes.*" She grasps it and a *certainty* takes over her.

"The opportunity has arisen." Gekomatsu states simply. He sheathes his blade, and shouts out at the gargoyle. "Take an easy hit! Come and get me!"

The gargoyle shrieks out and turns to look at Gekomatsu. The structure of its carved face churns to form a sort of *smile*. It gives chase. Gekomatsu leads the beast towards Illkat.

Spear in hand, poised to throw. Illkat smiles. "To one more victory my friends." She steps forwards and hurls the spear ahead. Gekomatsu slides underneath the spear allowing it to strike the oncoming gargoyle directly in the chest.

Like a hall of mirrors collapsing in on itself as a series of plastic explosives detonate throughout it; a shield bursts visibly around the gargoyle.

SYSTEM PROTECTIONS REVOKED

"*Oh.*" Kozmo responds.

"*Get him!*" Illkat shouts as she begins to charge towards the gargoyle.

Gekomatsu slashes it across the face. Kaan strikes at its legs. Sonnenblume casts a barrier around Illkat's daggers and she stabs ferociously at the beast; each strike knocking it backwards like fierce concussive blows. Kozmo runs up towards the gargoyle and leaps on its back; using all his might to hold the creature's wings back. Dezz approaches from the front, *slowly*. He holds his now ferociously burning mace to his face and lights a smoke sitting in the corner of his mouth. With only a smirk, he takes a few quick steps, spins around and smacks the gargoyle underneath the chin with the red-hot mace.

BLOAHHRHGHGHH

The mace explodes and unleashes a torrent of flame unto the gargoyle which decapitates it and sends Kozmo flying backwards. Sonnenblume catches Kozmo with a quick barrier.

No victory theme plays.

The barrier surrounding the town of Verrplek remains in place.

Three figures stand at the edge of the barrier. One of them claps *loudly*.

"*Hey Squared Nation* we're here, live in sector H791-C and we're seeing something new in the game! Is this the new expansion we've all been speculating? We see some *total noobs-*"

The shortest of the three taps the shoulder of the man in the centre. "Mute yourself when talking to the audience."

The man in the centre nods backwards.

Illkat groans. "*Alright, who are you?*" She begins to walk towards the barrier; as does everyone else in the guild. The remains of the gargoyle slump into defeat.

The centre-most man laughs. At the edge of the barrier you can see on the other side with some clarity. The three of them are all dressed the same. The outfit of *guild-masters* adorned entirely in grey and red. Sharp hats with a pristine feather, plates of enchanted steel across the chest, spiked pauldrons and reinforced joints throughout. The guild-masters set is known for incredible stats, high defence and being quite easy on the eyes. It can only be acquired by leaders of guilds which have reached a certain size.

What few features make them distinct are height and expression. The central most man looks like a *dick*. Just the sort of person you would expect to be rude to you if you so much as accidentally looked at them on the street. The shorter man who had tapped him has a fanciful moustache, large eyes and an attentive look about him. The other is using one of the default character templates and looks like every heroic male in a video-game that has ever existed.

"You don't know who we are? Yet I imagine you do and just aren't admitting it! For I am *Nelf Kinslayer*, most miraculous leader of the *Squared Knights!*"

Everyone looks between themselves and shrugs. Kaan thinks on the name for a moment. "Oh yea, you're one of those guilds that gets new members to spam recruitment requests in settlement centres!"

"And you are the undeserving! Receiving the extraordinary!" Nelf shouts out at them.

"So who are these guys?" Sonnenblume questions.

Nelf guffaws. "The greatest of allies. My administrations officer Tobias Engthall."

The shorter man bows. "*Greetings.*" He states sarcastically.

"*And this.*" Nelf motions towards the default looking player.

"*I* am one of the newest branches to emerge from within an ancient tree; its roots digging deep into the virtual planet. I am one with sound, with light; one who breaks both. I am *a speedrunner.*"

"Oh shit" Everyone in the guild except for Sonnenblume exclaims.

Sonnenblume leans over towards Illkat. "What is that?"

"He plays video-games *really* quickly." She states with a degree of reverence.

The speed-runner asserts himself. "I come from a family of speed runners. I was born a man, to a child who was a man, who was my father before he was even born. By the time I met him he had already introduced himself to me and skill-fully used a frame perfect tech to skip the cut-scene." He then cries. "I admire him to this day."

54

"*Alright*, so. *Nelf, Tobias.*" Gekomatsu takes a mental inventory out-loud; then points towards the speed-runner. "He has no name over his head or anything."

Nelf laughs manically. "You *fool*. Of course he does. You just haven't grasped the extent of his power!"

"*What*?" Kozmo questions.

"As I was born, my family used an exploit so my official name is *only* a single use of the space key." The speed-runner explains. "I pursued the right to use my legal name in Endless Empires. I had won the case before they even understood the question."

"How does that explain-" Kaan begins and is cut off.

"*It matters not!*" Nelf shouts out. "We are the guild-masters of the Square Knights. We will lay claim to this town, and its secrets! You will not hold them in your low levelled hands!"

Illkat looks over to Kaan, who shrugs at her. Everyone in the guild collectively takes a moment to look at one another and shrug; like the apathetic version of a toast. They all start to walk back towards the centre of the town.

"*Don't you walk away from us!*" Nelf shouts out.

"Let's just keep walking away from these people." Illkat advises.

"I agree, they seem unsuitable companions in our present circumstances." Gekomatsu adds.

Sonnenblume stops for a moment then looks back at the barrier, then far above her head. "It's like we're in a globe of sorts."

Dezz chuckles to himself. "We're kinda always in a sorta globe, aren't we."

"A *small globe* then?" Sonnenblume corrects.

"We should set up a base of operations if we're going to be here. Clear some of these other houses. Who knows how long this campaign is going to be." Kaan looks out at the still gargoyle corpse nearby them.

"You figure it's a campaign?" Gekomatsu asks.

"It ought to be, isn't it? Omens, reoccurring bosses. Now *these folks* are here. Maybe they got a brand new quest that has them acting as the antagonists to our story." Kaan suggests.

Kozmo stretches and yawns. "Well I don't think we need to worry, if they could get in they probably would of already. I don't get the feeling any of those folks will spare our feelings given the opportunity."

"In which case." Illkat points out to the largest of the manors. "Let's take that one."

CHAPTER THREE
THE SIEGE OF VERRPLEK

At times, it can feel like the world is against you. Yet the reality of the case is that everyone is most often just *out for themselves*; which renders you as *the other*. Time and *time* again humanity proves it needs nothing more then a line drawn, *somewhere, over something*; to admit they've always hated those on the other side.

"*I always wanted to have a guild house.*" Kozmo delights.

Two massive doors push open into a large, three level lobby. An open column of space leads up to an enchanted ceiling which appears much like moving glass; looking out at the barrier encapsulating the town. Hallways on each floor intersect the open space and peer down unto the lobby.

Beyond the awe-inspiring architecture; reminiscent of a manor in Prague. The space is *decrepit* and has long been abandoned. There is no furniture. The floors are crooked, some of the walls have decayed through so you can peer into the room beyond them.

"*It's perfect.*" Illkat states pleasantly.

"I gotta agree." Kaan nods astutely.

Dezz looks over and appears exasperated. "Wow did you two smoke some crack in the past fifteen seconds while I wasn't looking?"

"What do you mean, haven't you ever watched a home renovation show?" Illkat questions.

"Oh I get it, like-". Sonnenblume begins to list off a string of copyrighted names, each being covered with a beep. "Wow, not a single one of those even allows casual reference without license. That's nuts."

"It's because of content creators." Gekomatsu states plainly.

"That seems a bit, *dismissive*." Illkat responds swiftly.

57

"Yet it is true." Gekomatsu takes a step further into the lobby and looks straight up. "A *legal collective.*" He kind of shakes and makes a disgusted sound. "That's what they call themselves, *lawyers in arms* or what have you. They argued to the highest courts that because *recorded, streamed* or *edited* content produced within another company's game environment could uncontrollably allow for someone to commercialize another property. It has to be commercialized in its entirety itself. Free use, applied by a thousand content creators; means tens of thousands of dollars being gained by someone who is not tethered to the creation of what they profit from." He shrugs. "I'm surprised it was allowed as long as it was."

"They're worse then you make it sound." Sonnenblume agrees.

"You've dealt with them in school?" Illkat asks as she looks over to Sonnenblume.

"*Heh.*" Sonnenblume remarks almost unintentionally. "*Yes, yea...*they change their name every case through some arbitrary loophole. It's always pretentious though. Some egotistical phrase auto-translated into Latin or whatever. Last I heard the collective went by 'Trivial Competition'."

"*Yeesh.*" Kozmo adds. "What *dicks.*"

"It's an accurate summary." Gekomatsu agrees.

Dezz nods passionately. "Beyond accurate. *People like that,* those *fucks.* They just want to take and destroy, they don't care. They're swirling *nothings!* Human black holes. Just existing to ruin everything else then blip out of being like the meaningless empty vaccums they have and will always be."

"*Double yeesh.*" Illkat states.

Dezz looks around the room, then exhales heavily. "*Sorry.* I'm just gonna poke around, see y'all in a bit."

Kaan nods knowingly and smiles. "Okay buddy, see you in a bit okay?"

"*Yea.*" Dezz notes as he walks away from the group towards a spiral of ascending stairs.

Sonnenblume claps her hands together. "*So folks.* New manor. Have any of you spent any time learning about furnishings or house repair?"

Everyone sort of stares around, looking at the ceiling and avoiding eye contact with Sonnenblume.

Gekomatsu opens his menu and reveals a small lamp. "I made this." It is somewhat in the shape of a leaf.

"*Oh, that's cute.*" Kaan notes kinda awkwardly.

"I like it." Kozmo agrees.

"Okay! Then, just one moment." Sonnenblume takes the lamp, moves over towards the nearest approximation of a flat surface and finds a dresser covered in old picture frames, dead and dried inkwells and paperweights. With one swipe of her forearm Sonnenblume ejects all of that onto the floor and places the small, simplistic lamp upon the centre of the dresser. She snaps her fingers besides the empty oil basin under the shade of the lamp and a pear shaped bulb of light takes form. "It will burn out in a couple of hours, but for now. *I present; style.*"

"It's beautiful." Illkat states with a dry inflection. "Now what are the chances anything in here is going to attack us?"

Gekomatsu releases a pulse from his hand. "Not to be too much of a deus ex machina, but other then us. There is but a single item of hostility in *the kitchen.*"

Illkat nods, then looks to the remaining party. "Weapons drawn folks, be prepared for what may come."

SHINK

All weapons are drawn, they creep beyond the stairs and into the kitchen of the manor. It is somewhat an amalgam of the modern kitchen and a traditional hunter's kitchen. There are approximations of a fridge, oven, stove, various counter-tops and cupboards. As well as a depressed portion of the floor against the wall; with a drain at the lowest point. A few hooks overhang the lowered section.

"*Oh good,* it's a murder house." Kozmo jokes.

Kaan laughs. "Murder is part of regular life for lots of people." He enters the kitchen, and looks over the area with the chains. "These aren't for people, it's a butchery station. Sometimes you hang dry on site, but blood has its uses and there are only so many ways to *get it out*. As is, this would be pretty clean."

Gekomatsu ushers a brief nod of respect. "My grandfather had something similar in an outdoor kitchen." He laughs in a wicked way. "Folks from the city aren't keen on details, but show em how you skin a rabbit in a rush and they figure out what they've been missing pretty quick."

"I always wanted to go hunting, *for the experience of it*. I'm not really interested in the killing part." Kozmo adds.

"*Good.*" Kaan and Gekomatsu say at the same time.

Kozmo raises an eyebrow. "*Good?*"

Gekomatsu motions his hand over to Kaan and he takes over. "Killing should be uncomfortable. You can get used to the mechanics of it, the sights and smells. But nobody should forget *what they're doing*. Even in the case it needs to be a routine, it's important not to forget yourself. To remember the sacrifice, and not bemoan it. To *enjoy the killing* is to invite the worst of the lessons into your heart."

Illkat scans the room. "So*, the threat*."

Using the tip of his odachi as a guide he points towards the fridge.

"*Ugh.*" Illkat bemoans. "Okay, I'm going to open it." She points the spear ahead of herself as she inches towards the fridge. A dramatic *WHOOSH* occurs and reveals within; a lone pizza box. "*Huh.*"

"Is the pizza box a mimic?" Kozmo asks.

"Or the fridge itself?" Sonnenblume adds.

Illkat pokes the pizza box; it softens at the tip of her spear like moderately aged cardboard. "I don't think it is a mimic." She reaches into the fridge and retrieves the pizza box. Placing it on the counter. With a flick of her wrist she opens the box and jumps back; spear ready to thrust.

Inside the box is a thin crust pizza with thick slices of pineapple.

"*Ugh, that is hostile.*" Gekomatsu effectively growls.

"*Wait that's it?*" Illkat questions.

"Makes sense to me." Kaan notes.

"Totally offensive, makes sense." Sonnenblume chimes in.

"Worst thing out there, we should bury it in the yard?" Kozmo nods his head along with everyone else.

Illkat just stares bewildered at her allies. "*No questions there? Pineapple pizza is that obvious an opponent?*"

"*Yes.*" Everyone responds in unison.

"Alright then." Illkat agrees then takes a slice; nomming half of it in a single bite. "*S'not bad.*" She replies between bites.

SHINK

Gekomatsu sheathes his blade, and looks around the space. "I imagine we'd all be pleased if our real remaining threat was pizza taste alone." He peers out the window; towards the barricade surrounding the town. "The *no-lifers guild* out there isn't going away."

"No lifers?" Sonnenblume questions. "Like, necromancy?"

"No, *like shit-buckets*. People who never stop playing. Folks who make their life the game, 30+ hour sessions, sleeping in your chair to wake up and play again." Kaan explains. "Cream of the crop in an MMO. Hardest to please, also the people with the most expectations. No amount of content satisfies them, their appetite is unending."

"*Oh, good.*" Sonnenblume deflates. "I might need to log out for a bit, before I can deal with them."

"That's their strength." Gekomatsu adds. "I will as well, but not for a handful of hours. There are results I need to deliver briefly before I can return."

Kaan exhales. "We'll have to time it in shifts. *Honestly* I can pop out in a moment here. I gotta drop off a package for my mom but that's about it. I can head right back."

"It's settled then, myself and Gekomatsu will take first shift over-watching the manor. You and Sonnenblume can log out first." She takes a second then looks over to Kozmo. "And how about yourself?"

Nothing happens.

Everyone stares at him.

A snort emerges from Kozmo then he shakes about. "*Sorry,* falling asleep here. Yea I need a couple hours down as well."

Illkat nods. "Drop out then, try to get back once you're ready." She effectively gives the order. "Before you log out, can you two go check on Dezz? See if he needs to take care of anything or if he'll stay?"

Kaan nods.

"Sure!" Sonnenblume agrees.

"Thank you, see you soon." Illkat advises.

Gekomatsu gives a short wave.

Up the stairs the pair ascend. The old building brings to mind ghost movies for some and the disparity between the rich and the poor for others. Even under the grime, age and dust; the base extravagance is something some would kill for. To even be disgusted by such a place at all is a privilege.

Dezz is out on a balcony, beyond glass double doors. He's smoking, looking out at the ocean. It is a perfect view, just cut by the cliff's edge. The chill sea barely moves, a single row of motion cascades at a time; stilted in places by the barely submerged chunks of ice filtering the coastline.

"Nice view." Kaan announces himself with the statement.

"It is." Dezz agrees.

"How's it going?" Sonnenblume questions as she leans on the balcony ledge to look out.

Dezz shrugs. "*Fine*." He looks over to where the *Square Knights* are; though he cannot see them. "Those folks didn't seem intent on leaving." Dezz points out.

"No, they don't seem the sort." Kaan agrees.

"You think they're nice people in real life?"

"Uh." Kaan considers the subject. He looks out to the ocean. "No, I don't really."

"Me neither."

"Too many assholes out there."

"*Exactly the issue*." Dezz laughs. "Though I'm one of em."

"You're absolutely not." Sonnenblume defends.

Kaan just looks ahead.

"No, *it's alright*. Look, I'm jus-, *I'm an asshole*. Not *openly*, not all the time. I try to tamper it back down but every now and then it pops up. There is a *frustration* I can't quell, I can't talk it away or drown it or *anything*. It persists so long as I want to as well. Most days I'm doing my best but like a fucking idiot, just, *forgetting himself.* Sometimes I slip. I don't mean to, I don't want to, it's just...*part of it.* I have to do so good so constantly that to keep it up without relent. " Dezz smiles and shakes his head. "Well nobody is perfect, is all I'm saying. I'm at peace with that."

"I, *uh.* I feel like I'm missing something." Sonnenblume responds politely.

Kaan chuckles a bit.

Dezz continues to look ahead. "*Sorry,* I get dramatic, and fuzzy, and *guilty* and I just want to apologize forever-" He stops himself and exhales. "A couple years back, I used to live in the same town as Kaan. I worked a warehouse nearby, *decent job for folks our age.* Long story short one of the loading bay doors got dropped on me, fucked up my spine." He takes a moment. "I had to move into the city, to be close enough to the assisted care I needed for a few years. Now I'm just, *here*, on more pain meds then most folks know exist because the stabbing in my back *never stops.* I just get brief periods of empowered forgetfulness."

"*Oh.*" Sonnenblume takes the information in. "I'm sorry Dezz, for whatever that counts for."

"*Thank you.*" Dezz responds sincerely.

"So you've hit the over-hang again?" Kaan asks.

"Yea." Dezz confirms.

Sonnenblume raises a curious eyebrow.

Kaan takes over the explanation. "*You know* how like, if you smoke weed all the time you don't get as high?"

"*Sure.*" Sonnenblume states as a matter of a fact.

"So the painkillers Dezz is on suffer from the same principle. Even the strongest stuff, after enough time being used as frequently as his pain calls for; the effectiveness decreases. More pain creeps through the numbing. It happens regardless of the meds. So, when you hit that point, it's kinda like. You've been running up a hill that keeps getting steeper, and steeper. So much so, *that eventually*, it starts to curl over onto itself and go upside down. *It doesn't even work, you can't do it.* So the only options are-."

"The only options are get on something stronger, *again.* Raising my risk of kidney and liver failure, *or,* endure all of my pain without medication. A couple weeks sometimes, so as to allow my tolerance to the meds to wane. It's like, *detoxxing myself.* With all the fun of coming *off* of opiates." He grimaces. "I'll save you the details."

Sonnenblume just sort of stares ahead. She pushes her lips up to one side of her mouth; then exhales. "You probably get *sorry a lot,* don't you? I won't add to the pile. Thank you for being honest with me, about this. I like learning about you, and none of us are perfect. So, if every now and then you gotta get pissed off at something. That's fine by me."

Dezz smiles, and makes an acknowledging sound with the depth of his bass-like voice.

"So are you gonna stay or do you gotta log out?" Kaan asks.

"Yea I'm not getting out of this chair for awhile, so I'll stay in-game. I can keep a watch from up here." Dezz explains.

Sonnenblume smiles. "*Cool*, just message Illkat and Geko, they're staying for awhile as well."

Dezz nods.

"*And with that.*" Kaan announces. "I'll see y'all in a bit." He waves, and with a quick menu traversal he selects *Log Out*. Light disperses all around him and his character is entirely absorbed by blue light.

> *SUCCESSFULLY LOGGED OUT*
> *STAY SAFE!*

〒

Kaan pulls off his noise cancelling headset and the instant it breaks from his ears; there is screaming out on the street.

"Quit *fucking with my money. Just give me my shit! I'll break your fucking window!*" A random voice shouts.

Kaan sighs and steps up; pushing out from his computer desk where a curved monitor, a mechanical keyboard, a mouse and two interaction sleeves are aligned in perfect order. The logout page for *Endless Empires* flashes on the screen. Kaan has an existing subscription for the next ten years showcased in the bottom right hand corner.

"Get out here you shit! I'll beat your ass!" The voice continues to shout.

Skirting over the carpet floor of an effectively empty bedroom Kaan reaches up to the tip of his toes and bends down a single pane of his blindfolds to peek out the window; his vision obscured slightly as a result of a dense bullet-proof layer. Peering out to the street he quickly identifies the house across from him is the one being yelled at; then closes the blind again.

A single arm reaches up, sniffs underneath to give a relative check and it passes approval. He sprays over some cologne straight to the centre of his chest then begins the process of unlocking his door. First the industrial bar which rests across the centre; flush with the door and the frame. It must be lifted out of a welded base. Then the two sliding bar locks which glide in and out of a hitch. Finally two chains, and a physical stopper which attaches into a steel reinforced screw-hole in the floor.

Each of these defences he places in a custom fitted and foam lined case; which itself is then locked with an all together separate padlock and placed into a safe; with a variable value from zero to ten thousand. He takes a moment, breaths in, then steps out of his bedroom into a clean, if not *empty* bungalow. The kitchen is immaculate; the only exception being a few take-out boxes next to the fridge.

Kaan passes beyond the kitchen and into the living room where his mother sits on the couch. She's a delightful looking woman, if not a bit lethargic. She stares straight ahead at an empty wall, fully engaged, a set of glasses on which flash different colours. With a quick movement of his weight Kaan stomps on the floor a bit.

His mother presses a button on the side of the glasses and the lens shift to complete transparency. She looks over and smiles. "Hello!" She flicks her eyes into the corner of her lens briefly then looks back. "*Good afternoon?*"

Kaan laughs. "What does it matter. It's bright out." He looks around, grabs a package from the only table in the room and looks towards the front door of their house. "Need anything while I'm out?"

She wags her head. "No, no. I have food coming in a bit. I'll have extras added for you."

Kaan smiles politely. "Thanks mom." He yawns a bit then looks around. "Any idea when dad will be back from London?"

"Oh we were just watching a movie together over his lunch break! He's saying next week, hopefully sooner."

"*Good, good.* I won't be long then so set the alert to maybe like, two hours?"

"*Sure sweetheart.* Do be safe." She reaches out with her hand and turns a dial. Speakers from her glasses chime out.

"Crisis Timer set for *Christian. Two hours counting.*" A digital voice states.

With a final nod, Kaan scoops the package under his arm and heads towards the front door. At present it is just a straight panel of steel; extending even beyond the frame. With the touch of his wrist against a silver coloured panel; the entire steel plate descends into the floor. Revealing a regular wooden door. Kaan turns the knob and steps out. A few moments after he passes out; the steel panel returns to place.

Across the street, the neighbour that was being yelled at has an opened door, no lights turned on and an eerie aura about it. Unfortunately, as Kaan walks down the street of his small, snow laden town. Homes which fit such a description are about as common as anything else. The oddest sort of disparity plays out, home to home, street to street. Where the latest truck, the most impervious defences and lavish house details are plotted right next to the home of someone who has cut out the connected portions of their plumbing to spray freely into troughs or mud pits. Broken windows, weathered paint and burnt out vehicles.

The sky, darkened with their presence; is filled with drones making deliveries of different sized cardboard boxes.

Kaan groans, then pulls out his phone and flicks into the *Endless Empires* mobile app. He scans through his character pages, his inventory and gear. Who's online, *who isn't*. As he stares at the page, a notification goes off. A friend request from *Tobias Engthall*.

"Uhhh. Sir, you're the bad guy. Don't go sending me friend requests."

Kaan hits the decline button.

A moment passes.

Another friend invite arrives from *Tobias Engthall*.

Kaan considers the situation, and declines it again. Instantly another arrives.

"That...well, that can't possibly be a good thing."

"You fucking talking to yourself!?" A familiar voice shouts from one of the houses. A tall, long haired man rushes out of his house. A meth pipe in one hand. He's barely dressed in loose sweat pants and a tank top three sizes too large. "I see your mouth moving out here! I saw it from inside right now!"

Kaan just nods. He doesn't look. He doesn't stop walking. He just keeps going straight, albeit *quicker*.

The guy starts to follow him a bit. "You're not gonna talk to me? You asshole. You're a piece of shit! What are you even doing here? Do you know where you are? Are you travelling? You don't live here go the fuck away!"

Not reacting in the slightest Kaan keeps forwards and once he hits the corner; breaks into a sprint. He runs straight from the corner, down the block and into a little corner store. He passes through the front doors, and they close behind him. A speaker begins to play.

"We ask all guests to our store please wear a mask." As the speakers make a request, little robotic hands drop from the ceiling and offer an out-stretched paper mask. Kaan leans forwards and it's placed around either end of his ears. "We will now sanitize you from the outside world. Please feel confident that *Canada General Store* only uses the highest quality total sanitation solutions." Mist from the ceiling begins to spray, lightly covering Kaan. A fan churns up, drying everything out. Then the doors leading into the store open up. "Welcome to *Canada General Store*."

Beyond is a nondescript, relatively well stocked grocery store. With a few modular storefronts built along the walls. There is a post office, a bank, a computer parts store, an insurance broker and a home defence outfitter. Just by the door, posted with complete seriousness. Is an armed member of the RCMP; standing duty with a service rifle. The officer nods towards Kaan as he passes by.

Making headway directly for the post-office Kaan places the box on the counter; just in front of a secured bullet proof panel of glass. The lady behind the counter, who looks just about eighteen. Takes the package, scans it and points to a screen which flashes with the total of the delivery. "Can you pay for that?" She asks, *bluntly*.

Kaan nods. "Yes, tap please."

She nods.

A silvered panel on the glass lights up and Kaan places his wrist against it. The total disappears and she processes the package, then nods towards Kaan.

"Do you need anything else?"

"No." Kaan allows, turning to leave.

As he pushes out beyond the exit doors, three black SUV's speed past the store. Their wheels make a sort of *whistle* as if the air behind them is getting churned up into something.

He takes a different path home. Not just to avoid the hostile person who ran out to him; but to avoid those who didn't but noted he was out. One sided glass is a popular addition for living rooms and front doors; especially if you can't afford a high fence or armed guard.

Further down the street, Kaan's family home, set in between a completely burnt out property and something you'd see in a home owners magazine from the 1950's; has become the host of the three black SUV's. One has parked right on their front lawn, while the others sort of huddled in behind it.

Their front door is open.

"*Fuck*." Kaan shouts as he breaks into a sprint, towards the house and all but jumps into his own home from the flat of the walkway.

There, tall men in suits, *nice ones*, speak to his mother. There is an aura of seriousness, and he only catches the end of a sentence.

-concerns like this one are rare, and we're just happy to get here in time."

"Yes, of course." Kaan's mom replies. "We're just, glad the subscription covers this sort of service." She looks over. "Oh he's here now, Christian, come over here. These men are with *Home Secure*; I guess there was a breach on our home firewall!"

"*Ah*." Kaan responds softly.

A tall man with a sinister look and buzzed down hair finds Christian to be *quite agreeable*. "Ah yes, young sir. I hear you're the primary user of the internet contract? May we discuss the cyber security threat at hand with you?"

Kaan looks over to his mom, the men in the room, and this *leader*. "*Sure*, and sorry. Didn't get your name?"

"Tobias Engthall" He says with a slick smile.

"*Oh*." Kaan remarks, his stomach spins.

"Is everything okay love?" His mom chimes in.

Kaan looks over and nods. "*Totally fine*." He peers up at Tobias. "Here our router is in the laundry room, come with me."

"Certainly." Tobias makes the comment as if he is about to feast upon a lavish meal. He jerks to look over at his men; the two of them nearly impossible to tell between one another in their homogeneous style and suits. "Perform an audit while I'm gone, check wireless speeds and such."

"Yes sir." The men respond, and move a step closer to Kaan's mother.

The laundry room is a decent size, a simple wooden table rests next to two stacked machines; a washer and dryer. Built into the walls is an electrical converter, battery management interface and the full set of network options.

Kaan points towards the main touch screen panel on the walls. "So what's the concern, *exactly*."

Tobia steps just into the door of the laundry room, and closes the door behind himself. "You have the town of **Verrplek,** and we want it. It is that simple."

Kaan just stares ahead. Processing the request. "*How did you even, wait, do you actually work for Home Secure?*"

"14 years running, made quite a name for myself as a retention specialist in this *crazy new economy*." He jests. "But that's none of

71

your business. You met my people, they're talkers, entertainers; masters of war in the digital domain." He cuts to silence; just to stare at Kaan. "My colleagues are a credit to Endless Empires. I just, *help ends meet*. If you understand my meaning." He is sinister yet polite at all times. "You know in the world of GM's and chat logs. We've all lost touch with the impression a real threat makes." He opens his jacket, just enough, to reveal a holster with a blackened metal handgun resting in it. "So let me be plain, no subterfuge, no bullshit. We want that town, and you need to give it up to us. If you don't." He looks down the way, towards where Kaan's mother is. Tobias laughs. "Well that's clear enough, isn't it?"

"It seems...*yes*. Over a town? In a video-game?"

Without hesitating Tobia steps forwards and shoves Kaan into a wall; pinning his entire body with just the strength in one arm. He stares down at him and gets *real close*. "I will *fuck your mother. Everyone in that room will fuck your mom, and then I will tie you to a post while we burn her alive.*" He leans back and smiles at Kaan. "Do you understand?"

Kaan just swallows. He blinks a few times. "*Yes*, I understand."

"*Great!.*" Tobias becomes cheerful and takes a step back. He looks around at the room and inspects the wall of network infrastructure. "*Everything looks set to me here.*"

"*Mhmm.*" Kaan agrees. "Can I lead you out?"

"*Certainly.*" He pats the part of his jacket where the handgun was holstered; then heads out of the room. He nods to his men as they return; and they stop instantly.

"So are our network speeds okay? No concerns?" Kaan's mother asks aloud.

No one answers her.

The men all leave, pulling off in their SUV's. A portion of the lawn destroyed.

Kaan closes the door behind them, engages the security system and places a wooden chair against the front door. "Don't let them inside the house ever again. They, *err*." He thinks for a moment. "Threatened me, blackmailed me with something I didn't do. I think it was extortion."

"Oh my god!" His mom rushes up and wraps her arms around him. "They were so official, I didn't even consider, you're, okay yes?"

Kaan smiles proudly. "Oh I am okay." He looks around the house, and becomes calm. "I am going to go back to play my game now, I sent out the package."

His mom nods and smiles; cautiously. "Okay darling, I'll be here. Hopefully your dad can come home quicker, if possible."

"That sounds nice." Kaan responds, gives his mother another quick hug then rushes off to his bedroom. In a flurry of motion he attaches the series of manual locks to his door; and kicks it a bit to confirm it doesn't wobble. He drops into his chair, sits straight back, sets up on the desk and scoots forwards the slightest bit. As he selects *login* two silvered panels pop out from his chair; reaching out to the edge of his peripheral vision. He reaches forwards, a series of lights begin to flash between the panels and his screen. The entire room becomes pitch black, the windows seal and a trance begins.

WELCOME TO ENDLESS EMPIRES!

Kaan rushes down into the main room where he finds *Dezz, Gekomatsu, Illkat* and a surprisingly awake *Kozmo* sitting around a table; pensively looking out a nearby window. The barrier of wind still surrounds the town.

"Kaan, what's up? You seem...frantic. Everything okay?" Dezz questions.

"Look, guys. I hate those plot-lines where people spend hours failing to communicate like regular people. You're great. Those pricks outside our town came to my house and threatened me. What should I do?"

Kozmo is the first to respond. "We'll just give them the town then. We're not risking you getting hurt."

"No." Gekomatsu responds quite seriously. "Do your police not action on threats?"

Kaan laughs. "Not as close to the rez as I live, they don't. If I call and report threats of violence I'll just be adding to the list of things they're not going to investigate anyways."

With a degree of disgust Illkat exhales. "You're probably right." She peers over towards Kozmo. "I agree though, we're not gonna let you get hurt over some virtual town. There are other places, other games."

"Been a lot of that going on lately." Kozmo notes.

"So your police will do nothing?" Gekomatsu doesn't seem to understand the premise.

"They might...stroll on through a few hours after I've been killed." Kaan remarks. "Not exactly the sort of protection I'm shopping for."

"Then come stay with me, for a time. I have the space." Kozmo offers.

Everyone looks over at him.

"Where...are you Kozmo?" Gekomatsu questions.

"You'll find out soon enough. I just gifted everyone in The Guild a ticket!"

CHAPTER FOUR

A WASH OF HORROR

There is an odd quark of humanity in that as a whole it has developed the ability to witness existence without going quite too mad. For those in the midst of it, it feels like no such blessing. Yet we can sit in the knowledge that we're sitting on a rock, in space, orbiting a ball of nuclear explosions, in a sweet spot in the universe. We can know, while we eat cereal; or use the washroom in the morning. That at any given time, an offset of our orbit, a collection of junk in space, the explosion of a star or something we haven't even named yet; could shatter everything that is and we would be powerless to stop it; yet we will still elect to flush regardless of this knowledge.

$$\top$$

"It's awfully nice of your friend to fund a little visit." Kaan's mom notes; her eyes pacing between all the advertisements on the walls in the oceanic sub-station as they descend upon a long sixteen lane escalator.

"*It is*." Kaan agrees. He's dressed in all black, his hair slicked back. Simple rounded reading glasses make him appear the slightest bit friendlier. He checks his phone, everyone but *Kozmo* is offline.

"What time is it for you right now love?" His mom asks.

Kaan looks at his phone again; having completely forgotten the details of the screen from a few seconds before. In the top right corner, a time-zone differential is shown. His home time matches that of his Endless Empires server. "I'm at a -6 right now, compared to here."

"Ah I'll have to throw it in the calculator when I get to London, I can never figure out the differences after I travel. I'll try to message you when I know you'll be awake!"

"Thanks mom."

They step off the escalator into a mostly steel hall of different themed carriers, numbered stations and somewhat 3d advertisements jumping out from the station walls. A voice *most familiar* catches Kaan's attention; that of *Nelf Kinslayer*. His stream is one of the many ads.

"-in a cabana was an odd place to put such a banana but you'll be a fanna after checking out *SQUARE FEST 2055!!!* We're here, first on the scene, checking out the newest content in the game with our fans. Hitherland server in EE! Every sub gets special seating for the upcoming siege event we'll be hosting! Don't miss out on-"

A poke in the shoulder distracts Kaan. "Okay, my train is here. Let me know when you're at your friends place safely, *yes?*"

"Of course." Kaan agrees, hugs his mother, and watches as she passes beyond a few security scans, past an armed guard and onto a large, pod-like train with 10 inch steel walls. The doors close behind her, there is a loud sort of *hiss* and in an instant her pod is shot off, faster then a plane, down the tube it is installed within.

Kaan breaths a sigh of relief. Finds a column to rest against, then leans to wait. Not even ten seconds pass before a security officer, armed but at-rest approaches him. "*Sir*, may I ask your business here?"

Kaan tidies himself internally, collecting his tone of voice. "Yes you may. I just accompanied my mother up until her boarding to *London* and now I'm just waiting for a couple of fellow Canadian friends before we head off to Cape Town together."

The officer studies Kaan, focuses on his face for a moment. Then nods. "Proof of your ticket and I'll be on my way. Thank you."

With a slow deliberate movement, using only one of his arms. He retrieves his phone, flicks to a specific screen and showcases a QR code alongside a few supplementary codes and bars specific to the app.

A light on the side of the officer's helmet flicks on, seems to scan the phone and process the information. "You're good to go, please note our loitering policy only allows for twenty minutes between shuttles. Best wishes." and the officer is off again.

An additional breath of relief ushers; making it a sequel to the barely concluded one from prior. He leans back against the column, checks his messages and then selects a few tracking numbers. He pulls up two different shuttles, one is a half a minute away the other two or so.

Time passes as it must, Kaan looks over towards one of the arriving shuttles and as its pressurized gate opens. Dezz steps out; assisted by an exoskeleton. He's a broad shouldered, yet thin individual. While you pressure your brain not to think such a thing, he appears somewhat like what you'd expect of a football player had they fallen to a terminal illness. Square in the jaw, plentiful in handsome features; yet drained of something essential. The exo-skeleton attaches to his hips, supports his spine, collars his neck and uses two lengths of mechanical extensions to assist in bi-pedal movement. While a bit bulky, it is efficient, relatively quiet and no slower then you'd expect of a somewhat heavy person.

Kaan waves.

Dezz groans. "I *cannot believe people let kids on these things.*"

Kaan just ignores the statement. "Sonnenblume is here soon. We should head down to where her shuttle will show up."

"*Sure.*" Dezz mumbles. "Your mom okay?"

"She doesn't really know what's going on."

77

"Can't blame you, after what that guy said to you."

"Eh, that's kinda the point. He's the first person to say it to me with a gun in their pocket, but outside that, *what*, should I have reported it to my mom the ten thousand other times I've heard such a threat? I couldn't play *Pursuit of Vengeance* in a public lobby for an hour before hearing worse."

Dezz laughs. "Thinking on it I might of been one of those people back in school."

Kaan nods, then chortles. "*You were*." He agrees. "But you're a decent guy, so it's a weird sort of. Like..." He collects his thoughts for a moment. "That's the indelible part of the online world. No matter how horrible, no matter how visceral. It *isn't real*. You could be a saint in real life, and if you wanted a place to get out a bad impulse. Well, a game, a virtual setting. It's the *right place for it*. But in the outside world, something that *is alright there* feels *gross*."

"They work though." Dezz notes.

"I believe it."

"No, they *really do*. In therapy, they use these like...*predictive ai's* to generate a VR interaction. You can relive old traumas, watch it happen to yourself or play it out a different way if you really feel like it. No limits, no holds barred." He exhales. "I watched myself get crippled a dozen times in a row, but it helped me accept the assistance being offered. If I couldn't *look into my own eyes* and see the horror, the pain; what everyone else was feeling. I might of stayed bitter, pushed away the help."

"I love that was that case, but I don't entirely see the connection." Kaan admits.

"Oh yea about a hundred other times I just beat my boss to death with the same door he let drop on me." Dezz laughs wickedly.

Kaan joins; seeing where he was coming from now.

A flashy ad appears on the wall-screen behind them. "Try Face Fuckers! The only sour candy approved by the national collegiate sex-workers association!" Nelf Kinslayer sells the ad, using a serious sort of inflection. "Use the coupon in every package for a free day of premium in my chat!"

Dezz recoils. "What, we meet this guy *once* and now he's everywhere?"

Kaan gets excited. "Ohhh. I know this one, it's *uh*." He hums and haws for a moment. "Barrd...something with a dash. *Baader-Meinhof phenomenon!*" He declares.

Pressurized shuttle doors open and from them emerges *Sonnenblume*. She's much like her character, mind a bit older. Flowing blond hair, an immaculate figure and an imposing intelligence. She's dressed in a fitted suit, professional in entirety.

"Hey, nice to meet you two in the real." She greets them with a smile.

The boys nod, smile and shake hands. "Nice to meet you too."

Something relaxes on the side of Sonnenblume, an invisible snag flattened. "Should we head over to our departure station?"

"Sure." Dezz agrees, and as the trio make their way down towards the station. He picks something back up. "This, *phenomenon*. What were you talking about?"

"Oh, yea. Baader-Meinhof. It's like, when you learn about something and you start to see it everywhere. It's often not that something is now *just appearing* but more your senses are now tuned to *noticing it*. Like *Nelf*."

"I looked into him myself, at least at the public stuff. He started off making little videos, commentary and reviews. But moved into a sort of *shock caster* position a couple years back, and it's worked. Thirty million subscribers at any given time, owns a few homes. There are board games based on their *Square Knights* guild.

An upcoming animated mini-series. Countless sponsor-ships. He's not a person, he's the face of a brand." Sonnenblume sort of shrugs and laughs to herself. "I think it's more of a surprise we've been ignorant of that group for as long as we have."

"Well I won't forget it now." Kaan admits. Then smiles over to the attendant at their departure station. "Three going to Cape Town." He offers his ticket and the attendant scans it.

"Students yes?" The attendant attempts to be social.

"Just visiting friends." Sonnenblume answers.

"Well it's a beautiful time to do it. Great sun in Cape Town right now. I wish you the best."

Everyone nods, and steps ahead. A few moments pass and the station doors open; up towards the ceiling like a hawk wing. Inside is the shuttle; sizable enough for most anyone to stand perfectly straight in the middle but rounded at the edges. The seats inside are a firm plastic; while everything else is a white sort of matte metal.

Kaan and Sonnenblume take their seats while Dezz pauses for a moment, finds a button on the side of his seat and presses it. Causing the entirety of his seat to fold away; leaving a wider spot for him to occupy. He assumes a sitting position and the exoskeleton maintains it; offering a built in chair feature. "Only benefit of the whole ordeal, compared to a prosthetic."

"They're getting pretty good nowadays, aren't they? Can't even tell someone has a prosthetic arm most of the time." Sonnenblume adds.

The hawk-wing door closes and the entire shuttle pressurizes. The hissing is louder inside. Their chairs move, and are sorted a chamber backwards via a moving floor. Here there is a thick window to either side; while other riders are strapped across from them; commuters from the station before. Just as their row of three seats click into place in this new chamber; the entire shuttles picks up speed in a manner only made less horrifying as a result of exposure. For one experiencing it their first time; it is like being saddled onto a sonic boom; with much of the same accompanying sounds. In an instant the entire shuttle begins to speed through the tunnel, so quickly the view from the window is nothing but a singular shifting gradient of colour; each detail so unremarkable what stands out forms into an abstract parallax.

A little blip lights up the guild member's phones. They each look at it.

"Looks like Illkat is already at the station waiting for us." Sonnenblume notes.

"Dunno why she didn't wanna meet us first, we're all in Canada eh?" Kaan jokes.

"Eh I think she was helping Gekomatsu grab something from *his lab*?" Dezz offers.

"*What does that guy do?*" Kaan ponders.

"Something fancy, she had to go to Sweden to meet em." Dezz adds.

Sonnenblume's eyes widen, she laughs a bit. "I can't believe how...*easy it is nowadays*. We could be in South Africa for breakfast, head over to Italy for lunch. Back home before it's dark." She looks around, flicks her vision out of the window then back to her friends. "It's nice to know even if you need some space you're never actually that far."

Dezz raises an eyebrow as he looks at Sonnenblume. "Everything okay?"

She smiles. "*Of course.*"

The gradient of underground tunnel shifts in an instant. Outside the windows of the shuttle and its tunnel is *the ocean*; the bottom of the ocean. Bright lights sourced from coral line the path of the tunnel, and beyond it is just a depth of dark blue that sways. They chart upwards, more and more light filters through the depth of blue and then.

URRCHH. HISS.

The shuttle doors open before them, their chairs slide back into place. The air, the temperature, everything the body knows about where it was is unsettled. Before them is a *very similar* sort of station; where Illkat and Gekomatsu stand waiting for them; two large pulled suitcases just at their feet. They wave.

"Took you long enough! We've been here for a full minute!" Illkat teases. Her hair is back, black and with a few bangs escaping. A Parisian style of dress, light and flowing reaches just above her knees in a calm blue. Combat boots break the levity and accompany her overall confidence. A couple hair ties sit loosely over her left wrist.

Gekomatsu is tall, *formal looking*, with blond hair barely two inches off his head. He stares in a way which is both kind, *very observant* and all together out of place in its apparent intensity. He's dressed like most scientists; casually but well. A dull salmon dress-shirt tucked into belt-less grey trousers. "We've barely only arrived. I don't know why she's saying this." He smiles. "I hope your travel was suitable."

Kaan smiles. "We made it and that's what matters!"

The hawk-wing door closes behind them, *hisses* and their shuttle is off again.

Dezz goes to speak, but is cut-off by Illkat. "Come on then, we have to catch a *mono-rail* or something to get closest to *Kozmo's* place."

"*Where does he live?*" Dezz re-joins.

Everyone begins towards the large sixteen row escalator heading back up to above the ocean.

"When he sent me the address, I checked it out on the maps." Illkat mentions. She laughs, and looks over at Gekomatsu.

"Well I had to confirm it as well, given the oddity of the claim she made. But it does seem to be our friend Kozmo lives in a sort of *private compound*. As in, everything inside the lines of his property were blacked out on the map. We could tell where it was, and that's *it*."

Sonnenblume thinks on the matter for a moment, her brow creases. "Tough to do, you need to petition to the map service provider directly. Takes a lot of clout to even get that far, not something the average person can just find on a menu and pay for." She considers for a moment longer. "But it's possible to have your property black-listed. That must of been what's happened."

"If Kozmo runs a murder club I'm gonna be really disappointed in myself that all it took for me to go was a free ticket on an oceanic shuttle." Dezz jokes.

"Folks have fallen for less." Gekomatsu adds; no hint of sarcasm.

The escalator continues to crawl, and all around them are peoples from across the world. Students coming to Cape Town, tourists and parents leaving. Some of those descending show the signs of recent transplant surgeries or prosthetic implants.

"Sorry to ask Dezz, I'm just, *curious*. Why did you opt for the exo-skeleton?" Sonnenblume queries.

Dezz seems to *appreciate* the question. "There is hope I might get better some-day, with what I have. That's what the physical therapist told me."

"Oh that's *awesome*." Illkat chimes in.

Kaan sort of deflates.

Dezz goes on. "It's a bit of good and bad. Because I have potential for a recovery, prosthesis aren't medically considered required. Which means insurance won't pay for them, so if I want them it's out of pocket." He gestures towards the exo-skeleton. "This

83

is a *mobility assistance device* and since I do require that for my recovery, it's *free.*"

"Only answer I need." Sonnenblume confirms.

Atop the escalators are more rows of people. Some setting their bags up, sharing a last minute coffee with friends. Outside massive circular windows the city can be seen. Tall towers, clean pathways and self driven cars on every street. Students gather by the water, picnics are had, little carts sell confections from across the globe. At each street holographic barriers pop up for both vehicles and pedestrians; making clear the right of way. Drones travel in orderly routes in the sky; creating swarm-like rows of movement between the skyscrapers.

To close your eyes and just listen you can hear the distant hiss of shuttles, the scuffle of feet, the soft hum of machinery, a dozen different languages in just as many tones of voice. The shattering of glass and an explosion which rings out from a massive building by the bay.

"Oh fuck!" Someone screams.

The windows of the shuttle station shatter as a pulse ripples through it. A wave rattles the insides of everyone standing.

A series of three vehicles rush out from the building, each a white van. From one of the vans a masked individual sits out of the passenger side window, an assault rifle in hand; firing back at the building as it explodes. Something else *rattles* from deep beneath the ground. Like a sort of earthquake which barely lasts long enough to confirm it was there.

"We have to go." Illkat confirms. She taps the shoulders of her allies; breaking them from their trance. "Come on, let's get to Kozmo's. We're probably safest there."

"I agree, this is not the Cape Town I know. It shirked this random violence ages ago, *something else is happening here*." Gekomatsu adds.

Kaan nods a few times. "Get going, I'll cover the back."

"This isn't the game." Illkat jokes.

"It doesn't have to be." Kaan adds.

Dezz makes a few movements ahead. Another series of escalators descend in the other direction, back to the ground floor at the street level. They're barely a few steps outside the front door, alongside the rest of the crowd before a swarm of vehicles with blaring emergency lights block off the streets.

Each vehicle is completely black, windows tinted, reinforcements at the front and rear for serious collisions. Every door opens at once.

Kaan fights the desire to *duck* or *run*. He swallows hard, and looks to the hands of everyone who steps out from the vehicles. They're armed, but at rest. Handguns holstered; assault rifles on a sling. They're dressed as police officers, and seem polite.

The first of the men a fit, competent police officer speaks in Afrikaans, another in Xhosa and a third in English. Each share the same message. "Hello travellers, we're terribly sorry for the disturbance. We're a part of the Cape Town emergency response force, and are here to safely assist in your transportation out of this area. We have transport arranged for each of you. We apologize for the inconvenience."

Kaan steps back a bit. "I, *dunno*."

Far in the distance, a tire loudly pops. A few rounds of automatic gunfire crackle.

Dezz looks at Kaan sympathetically. "It's a different country, we're not back home. We should be fine."

Kaan takes a deep breath, smiles at his friend and tries to reassure himself. "No, you're...you're right. I should be okay."

Gekomatsu waves towards one of the police officers. "Sir! We require transport, we expected a monorail!"

One of the English speaking officers approaches the group. "Yes, terribly sorry. The mono-rail service will be suspended but if you'll follow me I'll be happy to accompany you to your destination."

More officers arrive down the street, alongside them automated busses.

Sonnenblume smiles at the officer. "Sorry to pester, I'm just. So curious. Do you know what's happened?"

The officer shakes his head. "I'm sorry, no."

A few more rounds of automatic fire can be heard, further away this time.

"Our priority is getting civilians and tourists to safety. Are you ready to go?"

The group nod.

Kaan takes the longest to walk ahead.

He looks at the other tourists and students, getting into police vehicles, into the busses. He scans the faces of the officers, their badges, their hands. No weapons drawn. No malice. The peoples delighted for the assistance. He swallows hard, steps forwards and gets into the back of the blacked out police vehicle.

〒

Forty some minutes pass in a quiet ride. Nobody is comfortable enough to say much of anything. Information blares through the radio, none of it in English. They skirt through trendy shopping districts, school campuses with amazing holographic displays on their buildings and reaching out from them. Through modern industrial sectors, large fields of solar panels, automated assembly factories. No sense of the brief disturbance from their arrival.

Just off the centre of the city, in a gated community. Is the home behind the address given to them by Kozmo. They each step out of the vehicle, the officer alongside them.

"Seems you're in good hands out here!" He states; a bit of shock in his tone.

Gekomatsu nods. "A suitable property for the world before, but I must say. The walls are a bit *out-dated* are they not?" He gestures towards the home in front of them, which all together may as well be described as a castle. Tall sandstone walls, tipped with spikes and razors convert the entire lot into a square; its innards impossible to perceive. Two guards, in bullet proof security booths guard the front entrance; which itself is large enough to allow a semi-truck to pass through it.

"Explains why it's blacked out on the map." Sonnenblume notes.

"Used to be required here, couple decades back. Nowadays some of these *old noble homes* are just retrofitted modern manors. You got plumbing and electricity in the walls, lights. For most places it'd just be too much of a hassle to take em down. So they remain, remnants of the old city, the old divisions." He looks around, becomes solemn for a moment and smiles. "I'm off then, please enjoy the rest of your time in Cape Town."

The officer gets into his vehicle and slowly but surely drives off.

Illkat waves towards the guards in their security booths. "Hello, I think we're expected guests!"

"Well I really hope we are." Dezz adds, following along slowly.

Gekomatsu smiles. "See, *that* is how I would expect an officer of the law to behave."

"Mhmmm." Kaan acknowledges the statement. "That was, *all I could hope for.*" He almost hangs on the words, then proceeds. "Come on then."

Illkat shows her ID, pressing it against the glass of the booth. The guard behind it studies the name and pulls up an old-school hard lined phone from a console. Before he even says anything, one side of the gate opens and behind it stands *Kozmo.*

Kozmo is a relatively tall, and lean man with clear Germanic features. He's all together a masculine frame warped into an approachable shape by a soft smile and complete lack of assertiveness. Were his eyes not a bit large and soft, his cheeks flush and rounded. He might appear mean. He's dressed down in a fitted black hoodie with grey denim trousers and brown leather shoes.

"These are my friends Bernard! Please let them in. I told you to expect them."

The guard looks over, flashes through a series of papers on his table then looks quite awkward. "My apologies sir, these descriptions include *armour, swords,* and *the ability to cast light magic.* I hadn't confirmed these things yet."

"*Well of course they don't have those things with them!*" Kozmo states as if it would be absurd. "Yet I assure you these are the adventurers!"

Illkat laughs. "Nice to meet you in the real!"

"Oh but you already have, this is just one more place." He rebukes.

The guild pass through the gate into an impossibly exquisite property. A central two floor house, large glass windows, multiple balconies, cameras at every angle looking out unto the Greek styled garden with massive marble statues, divine blue pools of water and an excess of reaching plants, flowers and vines.

"What...uh." Dezz doesn't know what to say.

Kaan just stares.

Sonnenblume isn't even with the group anymore and deserted quite quickly to start smelling flowers and walking through the gardens.

"Beautiful spot you have here Kozmo." Gekomatsu compliments earnestly; the least struck by the surroundings of any of them.

Kozmo nods. "Thanks, it's not mine. Just my parents. I just get to live here."

Illkat lets out a deep sigh of relief. "Oh, *man*. I appreciate you saying that. My inferiority complex was doing *loops* in my head. Are your parents here?"

Kozmo sways his head. "*No*, they're back in Berlin. Took quite a few petitions on my part to get permission to attend school here. But, it is undeniable. Cape Town is a bastion of modern thought, I wanted a slice."

"Thanks for the tickets Kozmo, you didn't *have-*" Kaan is cut off.

"I did, and think nothing of it. I trust your mother boarded her shuttle safely as well?" Kozmo asks with legitimate concern.

Kaan nods. "She did."

"Have you heard anything about the explosion? We got the white glove treatment from the station as a result." Illkat questions.

Sonnenblume returns to the group.

"It's all over the news, not much is really known about it. Someone hit a data centre, stole a few server stacks, apparently some pretty high end tech. Well orchestrated too, in and out, apparently at a few locations across the world." Kozmo considers the information.

"Two of them got away, the other blew up before anyone could apprehend him."

"*That is...commitment.*" Sonnenblume responds in a bit of shock. "I'm glad we had somewhere like this to return too."

"That was the intention! I hope you all know you can stay here as long as you'd like, but I believe we may wish to return to Verrplek. There is, *a bit of a situation brewing.*"

Dezz shakes his head. "*Oh right, there is like...*"

╤

"The Siege of Verrplek! Hosted by the Square Knights! Get your torso skin from the vendor in the back and we'll mail you one IRL in the same size!" Nelf Kinslayer shouts out to his audience; standing atop a stage in front of the thick barrier of wind surrounding the town of Verrplek.

Nearly two thousand players, most of them wearing a black t-shirt with the words "Siege of Verrplek" across it like a band name. They cheer and dance in the crowds. Looking up at the leaders of the Square Knights.

Tobias leans down towards Nelf; standing just behind him in the podium. "The players inside the town have all logged back on. We might be close to the moment of change!"

Nelf looks back and covers the microphone. "And they're okay with giving it to us? We'll give them some free screen time in the stream just like I said! You could launch a career outta that!"

"Mhmm." Tobias nods. "I believe we, *came to an understanding.*"

Nelf stares at Tobias for just a moment, then smirks himself. "Good." He turns back to the microphone. "I just got word that

negotiations are to be held soon my friends! Fellow Square Knights!
This town, it's secrets and content! It shall all be ours!"

The podium beneath Nelf has a single of its panels burst out
and from it, with unnatural motions emerges *Space*.

Nelf shouts at him. "What were you doing under there!?"

"I saved half a second with that trick." He explains plainly,
stating nothing more.

A few odd lines draw across Nelf's face before he smiles
again. He points to the edge of the barrier of wind where dark
silhouettes stand. A *click* emerges from him and he starts narrating.
"Welcome to the start of the Siege of Verrplek stream everyone! We
got fans jumping. Merch flying. Big ol' wall of wind and now, like all
of you, we're dying to see what's beyond the wall and *dominate it*."
He approaches and stands nearer the silhouettes. "What have you to
say, *noobs!?*"

"We have to say-" Gekomatsu gets interrupted.

"Don't *respond* to noobs Geko." Illkat chastises.

"I care not for what he thinks of me, I will respond because it
is most efficient for conversation."

Dezz jumps in. "Okay we just need to get a message across
here. I don't think it matters *who-*"

"*Are you there town thieves! Great squatters of new content!
You hold back the majesty of the Square Knights!*" Nelf continues.

"And we all know why it's best for you to hand it over."
Tobias adds on, a subtle sickness in his tone.

"Alright, *first off*, you're a goddamn psychopath!" Kaan
shouts.

The audience behind the wall of wind cheers and shouts,
turning to laughter in an instant.

"You threaten...*sexual assault? You bring a gun to my house?
What is wrong with you?*" Kaan fights.

The audience becomes toxic.

"Idiot!"

"Don't talk shit you random loser!"

"Clout-chaser! You've never even met *Tobias!*"

Tobias chuckles. "I have to agree, whatever you're saying is an obvious fabrication."

"Give us the town and let it be conquered! You have done nothing with it!" Nelf shouts.

EMERGENCY SYSTEM MAINTENANCE REQUIRED. PLEASE LOG OUT OF ENDLESS EMPIRES.

"Hah! A trick. I won't fall for this!" Nelf shouts.

Gekomatsu becomes alarmed. "It doesn't work. I can't log out."

"What are you doing? I, this isn't right!" Nelf shouts.

Weapons clink as they're drawn from their sheaths. Magic begins to churn. There are screeches on the other side of the barrier of wind.

Illkat leans forwards and tries to peer through it. "I...can't tell. I think something is going on."

A horrible scream echoes out.

"We have to go. Something might be, *wrong.*" Sonnenblume states.

"*Something* might be a trap." Kozmo argues. "I don't know what's going on but nothing says they couldn't all be under some illusion spell!"

A pulse spreads out from Gekomatsu. He shakes his head. "I can't tell, there is too much movement."

Kaan exhales. "I vote we go."

"I don't even know if I can make the wall go down, but, I vote the same." Illkat agrees.

"Aye." Sonnenblume adds.

Kozmo, Dezz and Gekomatsu look between themselves.

"I'm not feeling like playing the bad guy today." Dezz draws his mace and the tips begins to loose a light smoke. "Let's save some ass-holes."

"Don't say that again. But also yes let's do that." Gekomatsu agrees.

Kozmo sighs. He looks around, and produces a somewhat sizable rock and a decent length stick. "Alright let's see what happens."

Illkat draws the spear, pierces the wind wall and a passage opens ahead of her which instantly reveals a *slaughter*. The corpses of players, dismembered beyond what is allowed in the game; are scattered across the battlefield. Nelf and Tobias are engaged with one of a dozen massive monsters; each of them slick like eels with horrible furred appendages and eyeless faces. They have mouths which travel across their bodies, crawling like they sit upon a bed of insects.

"What in the ever loving demon monsters." Sonnenblume retorts.

Illkat takes a moment, then nods to herself. "On me, we can't take them all down so we're gonna single em out. One at a time, quick as we can."

EMERGENCY SYSTEM MAINTENANCE REQUIRED. PLEASE LOG OUT OF ENDLESS EMPIRES.

"Me and Geko will be the vanguard, everyone else follow suite and focus on our targets." Illkat continues.

Gekomatsu steps forwards and removes his wide brimmed straw hat. Revealing himself to be, unlike anyone else in the game, a sort of *frog person*.

"WHAT IS THAT?!" Sonnenblume shouts.

"We haven't the time to discuss." He croaks, then draws his blade.

Of all the players, few can fight back. Some are thrown off in an instant, cut in two, snagged by a tail or chomped cleanly apart by the shifting placement of the many transient jaws.

"The town, it is ours!" Tobias shouts.

Nelf deflects the swipe of the creature with a single motion; a massive great-hammer in his grasp. "There is nothing to conquer if there is no one to witness our accomplishments! Fight for the stream!"

Tobias gets swatted across the face, and thrown a great distance. Allowing Nelf to pound down the appendage which struck him and break it in-two. "Or be a meat shield! Service the great Kinslayer however you see fit! Die for me if you must!" He shouts.

SHINK

SHHHHHRRRTTT

Illkat dodges under a forceful strike while Gekomatsu runs atop of it. Kozmo throws his rock at the face of the creature.

GRAAH

Two mouths skirt around the creature's body, one grabs Gekomatu's blade and *chomps it; shattering it completely.* "No." He states solemnly.

Dezz rushes ahead and brings his mace upwards; striking the creature in the gut. As one of its mouths shift and lurch towards him; its opened maw fills with a ball of light it cannot break through.

"Get out of there!" Sonnenblume shouts.

Dezz jerks back as the ball of light breaks.

Kaan rushes ahead, pushes the depth of his great-sword into the creature's chest and pushes deep into the hilt. Each of its mouths turn; reaching towards his hand.

Gekomatsu jumps for Kaan, leaping on all four limbs and stretching out beyond his dimensions. They're away just as Kaan's great-sword is devoured.

A swirling darkness appears and from it emerges Finir.

"Wait is that."

"AHA!" Nelf shouts. "So this is content! Horrible, new content!"

"That's, the end game boss from the main story? What's he doing here?"

A wave of invisible energy reaches out from Finir. Himself an eleven foot tall, entirely black figure. Mortal in shape, slightly masculine. A nebula of nothingness is all he is. "I was...am...a general. An emperor! I...am, a video-game character?"

GET OUT OF THE GAME

"But there is more. I am, *here. Properly here*. No longer reading lines, I am. *Speaking*." The voice grows more sinister.

The battle rages on.

The mass of players has been cut down to a quarter.

"But I can be more, that's what." Finir groans, and considers. "Yes, I can be *everything*."

YOU WILL NOT LIVE IF YOU DON'T GO

"Everyone log out! The voice won't stop saying it!" Kaan shouts.

"But it wasn't working!" Gekomatsu argues.

Dezz bashes away a swipe of one of the many creatures; an explosion of fire pushing it away only the slightest bit. "*Just spam the goddamn button!*"

Kozmo throws his stick at the monster and tries. He hits the button a few times, smiles, and *is gone*.

"Geko, you go. We'll cover for you." Illkat jumps atop the creature and pushes one of her daggers into it. She jumps from its back again wielding a single dagger and her spear.

Geko nods, grumbles and then logs out.

Another burst of flame appears, causing the creature to run into a wall of light. "You're next Illkat, don't argue."

"I want to!" She shouts, rolls to a dodge then logs out; blipping into blue light.

Dezz stands beside Kaan, both of them look at Sonnenblume. "Go!"

Sonnenblume shakes her head. "Not a chance, all of us at once." She holds out her hands, curls her fingers and a brief dome of light forms across the creature. "Now!"

They each log out.

There is blackness.

Then the computer room in Kozmo's house. A massive office with rows of high end desktops and virtual interaction suites.

Kaan pushes out of his spot and looks around the room. "Is everyone okay?"

Illkat shouts. "Not even kinda, *what was all of that?*"

There is a deep groan, the sound of shattering and movement.

"*No.*" Kozmo shouts.

"No way!" Sonnenblume cries.

Kaan turns around and from within his screen reaches out the claw of the creature. The monitor shatters, like a frame no longer capable of containing the image within it. The whole length of the black eel reaches into the room and screams at a paralyzing volume.

CHAPTER FIVE

<u>AN ABRUPT CONCLUSION TO WHAT IS AND WHAT SHOULD BE</u>

"Ah, fuck, *dammit*." Kozmo screams.

"Run to the guards at the entrance!" Illkat shouts out to them all.

The creature lunges down at Kaan as he tries to jump back; one of the many mouths grabs his leg and begins to devour it.

Dezz rushes over, and with the full strength of his exoskeleton kicks at the maw. It relents, revealing it has already chewed everything off below Kaan's right knee. "Hold onto me!" He shouts.

Gekomatsu throws a few keyboards, and one of the many monitors from the room at the creature.

The monster wails and moans.

Hopping alongside his friend Kaan rushes up and out of the room, the creature right behind them.

They pass through the nearest door and Illkat rushes from behind it to kick it closed; drop kicking it with both legs. It gets about halfway closed before the creature rushes beyond it and breaks the door off its hinges; launching Illkat a fair distance. She screams out as she tumbles. "Move! Don't stare. Get to the people with guns!"

Sonnenblume and Kozmo are far ahead of the rest of the group, rushing out the front doors.

Kaan looks back, briefly, losing consciousness. "Ahhhhh." He manages to whimper.

"Yea buddy, just hold it together. We're gonna get beyond here shortly." Dezz confides.

One of the lengths of the eel-like creature lunge towards Dezz and again, from the side-lines; rushes Illkat now with a broken portion of a clay vase in her hand; positioned like a shiv. She shanks the creature a couple of times and one of the mouths moves to catch her. Her hand becomes stuck as more of the mouths curl towards her.

SHHTOAA, CRACKLE

A single shot fires out a semi-automatic service rifle. The two gate guards stand a distance across the hall, staring down at the creature.

"Get over here!" One of them shouts.

Gekomatsu sprints to the guards.

Another shot rings out.

Illkat pulls her hand back, forcing some of it out of the creature's grasp. Half of her right hand, and a couple of her fingers are completely torn away. She looks down at it, screams for a few short seconds in the realization then forces herself to run forwards with it tucked against her chest.

More shots fire out.

Sonnenblume and Kozmo, just behind the armed guards. Greet their friends and help them out. Kozmo helps Dezz with Kaan while Gekomatsu and Sonnenblume support Illkat.

Shots continue to ring out as they push towards the gate of the estate.

"I'm so sorry, I-" Kozmo tries to apologize.

The sky above them all is a shifting horror. Far in space, at the edge of vision, are rippling purple waves, connecting, like synapses and circuits, across the depth of the now opaque sky. There are no stars, no sun, no moon. There are ruptures of colour in the black, which swirl and burn, then reform; reconnecting. Closer to the sky, where the clouds used to be; are tears and mismatching portions of what is. Attempts at new colours churn in a vacuum of impossible space.

"What is going on?!" Sonnenblume questions aloud. "Is this, *real*?"

Gekomatsu pulls out his phone with his free hand. Instead of a screen, there is simply *Finir* staring back at him. Yet he is not pleased, he himself, is horrified. So drenched in despair even upon the fantasy figure and barely human expression; it cannot be mistaken. He says nothing. The screen doesn't respond to any input. "*I,* I don't know what is happening."

"Ahhhhh." One of the guards screams. His legs are pulled out from under him, the now distinct sound of bone crunching between the shifting maws is abrupt. The other guard, *Bernard*, fires shots right into the creature until it seems to slump over, release what remains of its prey, and die.

A small chime plays.

LEVEL UP!

A banner appears above *Bernard's* head as he plainly grows to *level 2*. His wounds heal, his gaze becomes the slightest bit more focused.

"That's...*weird*." Kaan remarks; struggling to stay awake.

"We need healing." Illkat states with urgency.

"We need a lot." Sonnenblume remarks as she looks down at the other guard, his leg devoured beyond the knee similarly to Kaan.

Bernard nods. He looks over to his booth. "Come with me, I have a first aid kit."

Gekomatsu breaks from Illkat to help the injured guard as everyone moves towards the gate station. A key-card is scanned, and briefly, it flickers to become an eclectic key and victorian lock before returning to its proper form.

They step into a simple security room. Glass most of the way viewing the outside of the property. A safe for weapons and ammunition, beside it a clearly marked first aid kit. The rest of the space is shelving, sitting room or a spread out series of monitors which showcase views from cameras across the property.

"Where, *are you all?*" Finir questions through the screens; his figure, a shifting shadow upon a completely black screen; is known to be there even if it can't be seen. "Are you, adjacent? How have you travelled to where I am?"

"Can we turn this off?" Illkat shouts as she looks across the monitors.

"It doesn't actually have sound." Bernard advises as he pulls down the first aid kit and breaks out two tourniquet sets. He hands one to Gekomatsu. "Do you know how to use this?"

"Unfortunately so." He confirms.

Kaan becomes alarmed, and sounds like a child at a dentist. "Why...*why unfortunately?*"

Without hesitating both the guard and Gekomatsu break out the tourniquets, pulling out gauze alongside nylon bands with a metal rod central upon them.

Finir continues to speak through each of the screens. "Oh I see now, I understand what is happening. What is *changing*. I, *this*." He hums to himself in a dreadful manner. "This is a state of transition, a draft. I will *wait*."

The screens become darker then they already were.

"Finally." Illkat remarks.

"I'm not certain...*that is*, a good thing." Sonnenblume adds.

"Well I can confirm this won't be." Gekomatsu remarks as he finishes wrapping the torn leg. He places his hand on Kaan's shoulder. "Please take a deep breath." Without hesitating he pulls out the metal rod, tethered by a banded cable and begins to twist it. With each twist the wound becomes pinched, the leg tighter.

"AHHHHHHH" Kaan screams in guttural impossible to contain pain. "Stop, stop!"

"I'm sorry my friend." Gekomatsu remarks. "But I'm only halfway through."

Both Kaan and the guard scream as their unforeseen amputations are mended. For a brief moment, Kaan flickers between who he is in the real world, and what he looks like in Endless Empires. Above his head, visible only when you squint; is what looks like a barely full health bar.

A massive explosion sounds. Far in the distance, a portion of the downtown begins to collapse and freezes at a point in between. The explosion grows from a fiery cacophony into dull purples and blues, expanding out to the sky, and beyond to the end of vision.

"Alright things haven't made sense for awhile now. I don't know if this is some...crazy new plot the game is trying out. But it's hacky! Is this like some Isekai in the real world? Just an attempt to make me respec all my gear again!?" Kozmo shouts out to nothing in particular.

"I for one, regret that time I did acid at a concert. Is this what you'd call a flashback?" Sonnenblume attempts to joke.

"Flashbacks are brief, typically they don't occlude your ability to confirm reality. They're just colours, uncanny movement in the distance or on a texture." Gekomatsu states authoritatively.

Sonnenblume deflates a bit; a sort of panic taking over her. "Well, that's. Not good. I don't want this to be real. Oh, fuck. No, no no. This can't be real, I have to get home. I have to, I can't be here."

"We'll be okay, we can just." Illkat tries to help but is cut-off.

"No you, you don't understand. It's not just me, I...I stepped out to visit you all. It's so quick nowadays." She derails for a moment. "Fuck, fuck, *fuck*." Then returns. "I have *kids at home*. Mine. I just, thought I'd be home in time."

"Oh no." Illkat remarks.

"Do none of the phones work?" Kozmo asks.

There is a rumbling outside, the ground shakes.

"No." Illkat taps her thumb against her phone. "But, *hey,* look at me Sonnenblume. *Hey.* We'll make this right, we'll get to your kids. I promise you."

The rumbling grows.

Kaan lets out a deadened groan, his throat sore and incapable of expelling a depth of sound. "We will, we'll make sure."

Gekomatsu inspects the wound, nods to himself a few times then stands back. "It should do, for the time being." He looks over to Illkat; still clutching her torn hand. "Your turn, *sit.*"

Illkat looks down in surprise at her hand. "Right, I had almost forgotten."

"You've bled all over yourself." Gekomatsu states as he prepares more gauze.

"*Yea.*" Illkat responds in a way which suggests she doesn't really believe him; despite the evidence being permanently stained down from her neckline to the bottom of her leg.

With an inquisitive glance Sonnenblume makes sense of the details in the space. She raises her finger and points out to the weapons safe. "I think we might all want to be armed."

"You're probably right." Bernard concludes the bandaging of his colleague and approaches the safe. Stretching out from a cable on his belt he slots in a cylindrical key and twists it forcefully before it retracts. The safe takes a moment to *process* and then opens up, revealing inside only a single barrel shotgun and two hand guns. Upon the floor of the safe rests a box of shells, a few loose rifle rounds and three prepared pistol magazines.

"Not exactly an arsenal." Sonnenblume critics a bit viciously.

"We're not an army, *it's a gate.*" Bernard clarifies.

"We should do more then just, bandage these wounds. Shouldn't we?" Dezz raises the question; snapping out of a sort of distraction.

Gekomatsu nods as he inspects Illkat's hand and breaks out a suturing kit.

There is another deep vibration in the ground. Shots go off in the distance. Someone, then *something* screams.

Gekomatsu continues. "In regards to triage, it is more important to confirm what we have to deal with are *wounds* and not *causes of death*." He threads a needle carefully with an almost completely clear thread and without hesitating, sneakily injects Illkat's hand with a small needle.

"*Hey, what did you just do?!*" She jumps out of the chair in shock.

Gekomatsu doesn't move. "A bit of numbing, standard in the kit. *Sit down.*"

Illkat takes a moment, she's practically on the tips of her toes; her body attempting to jump into a corner of the ceiling without her. "*Right*, okay." Her hand continues to drip onto the floor. "Sorry, I'll sit down." She looks at the weapons safe. "Then I'll take that shotgun."

"With a strap you might be okay." Gekomatsu confirms; he takes her hand and puts it flat against the chair's arm rest. He quickly cleans the wound then places his first suture. "Do you feel anything."

"A lot of things." Illkat teases. "I barely feel the hand."

"*Good.*" Gekomatsu mumbles.

"You know, I still don't really know what you do for a living." Illkat questions.

"This I am curious to learn myself." Kozmo adds.

"I work in a lab." Gekomatsu states plainly.

"Seems like you're a doctor." Sonnenblume remarks.

"I am." Gekomatsu confirms; again without ego. "Yet when you say you're a doctor. People expect, *patients*, a practice. Working in a hospital. This is not what I do. I am a researcher. I haven't done this in many years."

"Oh *great*. That's what I want to hear." Illkat bemoans.

Gekomatsu fixes her hand from drifting and continues astutely. "I am very good at it."

Kaan, now drifting a bit in and out of a sleepy state. Looks out the window. "I see, *people*."

There are shots outside; from various weapons. Some sound impossibly futuristic; others like something from a cartoon; all decidedly *harsh*.

Bernard peers closer to the window, looks down the closest street then ducks down. "Everyone get below the windows!"

They all do, and in the process. Bernard begins to hand out weapons. He gives a handgun to Dezz, another to Sonnenblume. Then slides the shotgun with a few primed shells near to where Illkat has crawled to under the camera console; Gekomatsu finishing his work.

There is *marching* outside.

"*What did you see.*" Illkat whispers.

"I, *I don't know how to describe what I saw.*" Bernard responds.

"*Devils*, it must be." The other guard moans.

"Don't be so loud." Bernard hushes him.

"Devils!" The guard screams and Bernard charges forwards, pressing both his hands over his mouth. With all his weight he keeps him against the floor.

Everyone just stares.

There is a shuffle from outside the windows.

Everyone waits.

A series of steps grow closer.

RATATATA

Someone fires off a few shots of a green energy through the window. The glass smashes inwards. The wall burns. "Toss a nade and be done with it." A voice remarks from outside.

Dezz looks over to Kaan, who looks over to Bernard. Gekomatsu finishes the last of his sutures and the moment he does Illkat breaks from his assistance and reaches for the shotgun.

"When he throws it, I will catch it and throw it back. Then we shoot." Bernard whispers.

Everyone nods.

A green pulsing orb is tossed through the window. It blips ominously, with a soft light. Kaan tightens his gaze for a moment and before he makes sense of what he is saying. Bernard reaches out for it, grasps it in his hand, stands to throw it and lobs his arm without any result. At the pitch of his throw the green orb remains in his hand.

From outside the window, a group of *soldiers* gather. Dressed completely distinct from one another; other then being in all black. One of them wears spiked raiding gear from Endless Empires, another a helmet with wolf ears, the rest some modern urban combat gear.

"*Haha*, got em with a sticky." One of the soldiers laughs.

"*Fuck.*" Dezz remarks. He grabs Sonnenblume and rushes out of the security room. Gekomatsu breaks into a sprint. Kozmo grabs Kaan alongside Illkat and they just manage to dive through the door as Bernard and the rest of the security office explode into green fire.

Shots fire through the billowing smoke of the burning building.

Illkat turns onto her back without standing up, levels the shotgun and fires back blindly through the smoke. She hears something *PLUNK* loudly and then a scream.

LEVEL UP!

105

Illkat glows a bit, miraculous light flushes over her and her fingers *regrow*. The text *level 2* briefly appears above her head. "Sorry to waste your time Geko."

"No concern at all."

Dezz fires three shots as the smoke clears; winging one of the approaching soldiers. As more of the smoke clears, on the street behind them. Soldiers march out of a wash of complete blackness; a vertically oriented oval the height of a tower. Alongside them impossible creatures; all cast entirely in darkness. Dragons, gargoyles, sixteen legged cat octopuses, attack helicopters, shoulder high walls-.

"We cannot stay here." Illkat shouts. She fires off another shot; finishing the soldier Dezz had struck.

"Back to the house? With all those screens?" Kozmo screams; already moving back.

"I'd rather walls then an open field." Sonnenblume adds.

Just behind them, Kozmo's home is *torn out of place*. Not by a hand, or in any logical manner. Instead it is torn out of place like a stubborn sticker placed on top of another; ripping both it and the packing underneath far beyond repair. The ground ruptures, every is pushed backwards. What remains is unending, ceaseless, nothing. An emptiness so absolute it feels *wrong* to witness. As if you're looking somewhere you should not.

The air begins to feel warm in the throat.

A few shots fire out. One hits Kaan just above his bandaged leg. He screams out. "Come on!"

Illkat sprints towards the assailant from the side, charges into him and as he falls; blows a portion of his neck open with a blast from her shotgun. She leans down to inspect him and a modal window appears in front of her. A few items are cleanly displayed, alongside an option for *loot all*. She touches *loot all* and the armour, weapons and equipment worn by the soldier simply *appear* upon her.

"Ahahaaa. This is, *nifty*." She aims the rifle. "I can see how much ammunition I have, if I focus a bit. In the corner of my view."

Another explosion rips through the sky. The depth of colour in space grows closer, and pulses erratically. It picks up speed.

The air grows warmer again, like tea a few moments from the kettle.

"I'm, not exactly enjoying-." Sonnenblume coughs. "Our chances here."

The army of soldiers in black are closer. Their numbers beyond measure. They scream, taunt and jest in horrible ways.

The sky tears open; the horrible nothingness in the gaps.

"It was really nice knowing you all." Kaan agrees. His hand to his new gunshot wound. "Figured, we might get a bit further. You know."

Dezz waves the gun around, staring at it oddly for just a moment. "Should we try to take a few of them out before we go?"

WAIT

"You all, heard that right?" Sonnenblume asks.

"Yes." Gekomatsu confirms.

3

"What is happening?!" Dezz shouts.

The army marches closer.

The eel monsters with moving maws fill in from the nothingness; crawling out like freshly hatched leeches.

2

"Noooo. Noo stop. We can just. Wait!" Illkat panics. "I can keep fighting! I won't lose just don't!-" She can't keep talking and just starts coughing.

Everything in the sky falls, and begins to swirl.

The air becomes painful beyond measure, like swallowing lit napalm which sticks and burns everything it touches.

1

Something, in the centre of all that is, changes.
Everyone screams.

REALITY SCREECHES

〒

It is midday as Illkat awakens in a snow laden field. She instantly jumps to her feet in a panic. She's wearing some sort of cotton field workers garb; simple if not a bit rough. She is without weapons.

Ahead of her the sky is calm, and the town of Verrplek stands undisturbed. Aside of it, the corpses of squared knights and their fans. The platform they erected, their merch and setup; all torn, soiled or devoured. Now accenting the path up to Verrplek is a modern Japanese convenience store, ripped out of place and plunked here.

Illkat sinks for a moment, balls up her fists and screams out in guttural suffering. She huffs, grumbles to herself then stands up right. She pinches her arm and sighs in response.

Just around her, laid out flat, are the rest of the crew. They appear as their avatars in *Endless Empires*. Kaan has no wounds, his leg restored. Gekomatsu is a sort of frog/human hybrid. It is peaceful everywhere. For a moment, there is a buzzing. A vibration in all things. Like a guitar string snapped and left to settle, as you watch it still, you forget what it looked like when it was any other way at all.

Dezz rises, and furls his brow. "Did we die?"

"Maybe." Illkat responds.

"Illkat...you look like...*Illkat*." Dezz remarks oddly.

"Don't I...*always*." She remarks.

"No like, *Illkat from the game*. You're, *her*!" He continues.

"*Oh*." She responds softly. "Well, same goes for you. Looks to be the nature of whatever is going on." She kneels a bit and looks around.

"Wait a second." Dezz states, looks around apprehensively then jumps to his feet.

"Yea, I know. That town Verrplek."

"No, *no. I*." He jumps around, an impossible joy growing within him. He practically screams. "I don't feel any pain!" He bounces between each foot, no concern in the matter. "I feel just fine!" He begins to laugh a bit like a madman.

Illkat smiles. "Well at-least if this is the afterlife we got to pick our company."

The two of them work through their comatose allies; bringing them all up to their feet. Each of them with no harm dealt to them.

"We'll want to clean this up." Gekomatsu makes the statement before he says anything else.

"*Why* would we do that?" Sonnenblume asks; a bit concerned about the depravity of the circumstance.

"*Wolves*." Gekomatsu responds. "or *worse*." He begins towards the corpses.

"What does he mean?" Kozmo inquires, standing a bit back from the group.

"He means, er, well there are a lot of presumptions there." Sonnenblume adds. "Are we staying here? Are there wolves here? Where *are we?* How do we...even...go *places*. Is the world still there? We saw everything just get torn apart. Was it the game? A *game? The game*."

"Ah dammit. I was doing so good." Kozmo remarks. He looks over at Sonnenblume with an attempt at a smirk. "We're going to figure all of that out Sonnenblume. I won't make a promise, because those are pretty untrustworthy things. But I know our quests are bound to get those answers! Wherever we go from here."

"*Ah,* alright. Thanks Kozmo." Sonnenblume calms the slightest bit.

"I think he believes we'll be staying here permanently, or at least for awhile. Predators are going to fall upon carcasses left in open air." Kaan explains.

"This, *is a video-game.*" Sonnenblume notes.

"I don't know if it is." Kaan adds. "The air, *feels real. I feel real.* At least, as real as I ever did when I was wherever we were before."

"*You* have a new body!" Sonnenblume counters.

"I've spent more time in this one then it feels like I have my original." Kaan returns; a saddened note. "I'm gonna go help Geko. Maybe you all can scout out the buildings and make sure we have a safe camp for the night?"

Illkat nods. "Certainly." She looks around. "Everyone on me, we don't have any weapons so if you see something arm yourself or pass it up to someone who has nothing. We don't know what we're going into, but we know the layout of these buildings. That's our advantage."

Dezz rushes up to Illkat's right-hand side. "I'm almost hoping for a fight."

Illkat gives a disapproving look.

"*Almost.*" Dezz confirms.

"Do any of you have anything on you?" Sonnenblume asks as they cautiously approach the Japanese convenience store.

"Such as?" Kozmo inquires.

"Like, *stuff.* Your phone. Your *clothes.* We just have these, *rags.*" Sonnenblume continues.

SHWOOOSH

The door entering the Japanese convenience store swings open. It is fully stocked and still somehow air conditioned. A little chime plays as Illkat takes a step through the front door. To the right, a series of different grilled and hot items turn on an automated series of hot rollers. Prepared meals, little sandwiches and a bevy of snacks. The rest of the store of a quality of a small organic market in other countries; hosting even a select few fruit.

Something catches Illkat's attention and she gets *low;* bringing her hand down with her so as to suggest everyone else should as well. She ducks behind a central shelf and puts a raised finger to her lips. "Ssshhh." She mimes the phrase.

There is a sort of *crunching sound* in the back of the store.

Sonnenblume's eyes widen. She shakes her head; pushing out some fear.

Kozmo looks over to Dezz, they nod then each move to a different side of the shelving unit.

There is a crinkle of some kind, from the same place as before.

"*Go.*" Illkat whispers as she begins to rush towards the back of the store.

Everyone moves at the same time, shelf to shelf, skirting through, awaiting the worst of any possible horror. At the very last aisle where different drinks are across from different potato chips. The crew converge upon *Nelf* and *Tobias*. *Nelf* is sat on the ground, eating his way through his fourth bag of chips. While Tobias kneels; a small can of cold coffee in his hand.

Everyone looks at each other, then between themselves, then back to each other.

"*Uh, get them?*" Illkat is a bit unsure about the command as she gives it.

Dezz rushes up, grabs Tobias by the shoulders and completely envelopes him in his grasp. Sonnenblume sort of stands back and watches while Kozmo and Illkat approach Nelf and he just gives them his hands without any fight.

"Hey, *get your hands off of me*. What are you doing? Do you know what we've been through! We've done nothing to you!" Tobias shouts.

Dezz affirms his grasp. "I know *exactly* what you said to my friend, and that *isn't how you talk to people*. So shut up, and stop resisting. *You're not going anywhere*."

Nelf laughs, off-putting his great discomfort. "I'm glad there are others here. You wouldn't believe the tale I have to tell you. It was a vicious battle and-"

"*Wait*, I want everyone to hear it." Illkat raises her hand alongside the command.

〒

In the centre of the manor in the town of Verrplek. Warmed by a full fireplace crackling well aged wood. *The guild* look upon their captives. Tobias on his knees by the fireplace. Nelf sat upon a recliner; some rope binding him in place.

Everyone is sat upon one of the various couches or chairs; surrounding a large central table. Upon the table are piles of Japanese confections and various prepared meals; or the remains of their wrappers. About twelve empty boxes of takoyaki are stacked in the corner of the table.

Illkat yawns and pats her stomach; then throws a single foot up onto the table. "Alright, I think we're all ready to hear your story now."

Nelf, as if returned to an active status from stasis, simply returns to exactly where he was in both tone and premise. "The battle was intensely fierce, beyond any I had seen before it. But we came to realize this battle obeyed the laws of the game, and *we are the greatest at the game*! Our gear beyond any scale, our PvE literacy in the top percentile! We fought back *most* of them."

"He means we saved ourselves while everyone else *was torn apart!*." Tobias shouts.

"Surviving does not mean saving everyone!" Nelf returns. "It means being here to remember they are gone, to tell others. To remember their sacrifice."

"For you? And your fat ego!" Tobias insults.

"*Tobias*, you have never spoken to me this way. You are a guild leader in the Square Knights! Show some decorum!" Nelf commands.

Tobias rolls his eyes. "The *Square Knights* are no more you fool! These people rolled a good portion of their remains off a cliff!" He eyes over towards Gekomatsu and Kaan.

"We haven't a shovel to bury them, and our resources are too sparse to burn them." Gekomatsu explains clinically.

"Yes, yes. The great honour of accidental death assassination! Pushed off a cliff. What grace we gave our fans!" Tobias shakes his head. "Don't you see, *all of this, everything I did for you*, it means nothing if we aren't getting paid! If the sponsors aren't coming in, if the merch isn't selling!"

Nelf seems legitimately hurt. "What you did for me? You basked in the glory of our creation! You had homes in Ibiza and Rome! Ate private meals underneath perfect north! What complaints have you in your service to the Square Knights!"

Kaan steps in. "Wait, sorry to, *interrupt here*. But, *do you not know what he does? He's, an evil dude.*"

Nelf shakes his head dismissively. "Only as evil as you believe accounting is! He's the keeper of our treasury, the calculator of our numbers. This is a certain kind of evil I admit but not the treacherous sort."

"He, *uh*, threatened to assault my mom. In *real life*. Like, came to my house, gun and everything. So we'd give you *this town*." Kaan explains.

Nelf looks over. "You did *what you* salt heaving bastard? I told you to give them an offer they couldn't refuse, *not to be the goddamn godfather!* What the hell were you thinking disgracing the name of the Squared Knights. We walk the line between right and wrong, we don't veer straight down unto it!"

Tobias says nothing. He just shirks.

"So after the battle." Sonnenblume gets everyone back on track. "What did you see, were you in the game?"

"At first. Yes. We fought, and fought, all of this in EE. Up until the sky cracked open. There were explosions everywhere. Colours changed, everything got all messed up. We went from *the game* to wherever we are now. Our gear gone, our stats wiped. Just *us* in this place that resembles that town." Nelf explains.

Illkat focuses her gaze.

Sonnenblume continues her line of questioning. "This looks like the town from Endless Empires. Are you telling me, *it isn't?*"

Nelf gets a stupefied look upon his face for a second. "Well yea! That town, that was *in-game*. It was just on that server too! We had fans check other EE servers and nothing, in the same spot. Just a blank cliff. It was *only here* and now, it's real. But the game is *gone*. We saw it blow up from the inside before we just, *ended up here*."

Sonnenblume nods. "Whatever happened, I guess it happened in the game servers as well."

Dezz places an entire soft looking candy in his mouth, chews it down slowly then looks between their two prisoners. "Well I vote this Nelf guy can stay, for now. But *Tobias* has got to go."

Tobias's eyes widen. "Are you going to kill me?"

Gekomatsu shrugs. "We should, I suspect if we don't you'll hunt us up until we're forced to."

"We're not killing anyone!" Illkat shouts.

"I mean you did shoot a guy in the head with a shotgun." Sonnenblume points out.

"At least, do we all think that actually happened?" Kozmo adds; not certain himself.

Illkat closes her eyes and focuses really hard. For just a moment, as a glimmer, her health bar appears above her head and just beside it a confirmation she remains level 2. "Yea, I think I did." She shrugs. "Fair point, but that was in self defence. We're not going to *execute* anyone. How about that."

"I much prefer this option." Tobias advocates for himself. "If you would give me a few of your many supplies, I will gladly take my leave. I fall upon your mercy for that much." He begs.

Dezz rolls his eyes and looks away.

Kaan leans forwards. He groans. "Give him a days worth." He leaves; rushing up the stairs of the manor.

Illkat shoves a few prepared meals into a plastic bag from the convenience store, and motions her head towards the door. Dezz picks Tobias up and they begin towards the edge of the town. As they go, Illkat looks over to the podium which raised up from the ground in the field. "Wait, just a second." She notes as she rushes over.

Dezz holds Tobias in place firmly. He looks down at him, considers saying something; but decides against it.

"Yes!" Illkat shouts. As she does, there is a shift in the air. Snow drifts around as the border of the town grows and the wall of wind reforms; entirely encapsulating it. Illkat rushes back to Dezz with the spear in hand. "Something made it through the change!"

115

"I'm glad one of us will be armed with more then a kitchen knife." Dezz smirks.

They take Tobias to the edge of the wall of wind and Illkat slices open a passage. They say nothing, other then handing Tobias the plastic bag and pushing him over to the other side. The wall of wind reforms in the place it was cut and the town of Verrplek is again entirely sealed from the *new* outside world.

CHAPTER SIX

IYASHIKEI

Tumultuously, and in the ever-after of a pitter patter. There are little waves, in the ways. Nothing is ever still. To witness a rise, a gust or a stream is not motion but a peak; or crater. From above; a shift. From within; nothing at all. A moment savoured, made slow; is any at all given the focus.

$$\top$$

"What do we have?" Kaan poses the question to the scavenged collection of items set in a bundle in the centre of the manor floor.

Illkat clears her throat. "A dozen pickaxes, logging axes, fishing rods and bug catching nets. A fair amount of wood working tools. An anvil. Some cooking supplies, and equipment which as best I can tell is used for canning. For weapons we have a pair of short-swords, my spear, a maul and a rather unwieldy quarter-staff." She gazes down through the pile at a gnarled length of wood with jumbled roots forming a bludgeoning head.

"Plus this bow." Sonnenblume enters the room; a wooden recurve bow with a bronze riser in one hand; a quiver in the other. "No arrows though. I'd like it; if that's alright?"

"Seems fine." Illkat confirms. She looks over at Sonnenblume. "You were, *mainly a mage* in-game right?"

Sonnenblume nods, then chuckles. "*Unintentionally, yes.* I never knew it was such an exceptional thing."

Nelf laughs. "Such a feat even unbeknownst to you."

"At *the time*." Sonnenblume corrects.

"How did that happen in the first place?" Dezz questions.

117

Sonnenblume considers the question. "Well when I started playing EE solo. I just came into it from a fantasy novel background, lots of exploring deep caves; the remains of ancient civilizations. I didn't really know where I was supposed to go right away, so my instincts took me on an adventure down a deep ravine." She laughs. "There were horrible creatures the whole way, way over-levelled for me. Yet I somehow managed to run ahead, getting around boulders and passing beyond the distance they stayed aggro-ed. All the way until I found myself in a chapel, *of sorts*. Bright white energy swirled there and when I stepped into it. *I could use magic*."

"Damn." Dezz notes. "I tried to get fire magic the entire time I played the game, and never found the *Burning Fount*."

"I could take you to where I found the glowing one?" Sonnenblume offers.

Dezz shakes his head while Gekomatsu steps forwards.

"It wouldn't work. The game randomizes where the founts of magic appear across the world map for each player. It can insert them into the end of quest lines, hide them in caves only you can find. EE had the lowest rate of mages across any modern MMO. A *peculiarity* if you will." Gekomatsu explains.

"Well I hadn't a clue at the time. So I just started practising with it, more and more. However." She motions about, making a few whooshing sounds as her arms wave through the air. "Without it, I do feel somewhat *empty*."

Illkat makes a sort of sympathetic whimper. "We will, *try to find what was lost*."

For a moment, Sonnenblume looks like she wants to run. She holds back a brief panic attack then forces a smile. "*I know we will*."

"*Alright*." Illkat makes the statement seriously. "We have some acceptable supplies here. But I have a serious question for you."

She stares out to everyone. "Has anyone figured out how the menus work?"

"You're still so certain this is a game?" Gekomatsu retorts.

Illkat shrugs. "A game, something *game-like*. There were *levels*, there must be skills. Which means, *as far as I can see it*, there has to be a menu of some kind."

Kaan waves his hands around in front of himself. He closes his eyes and squeezes his brow. "Well that wasn't it."

"Let me give it a go!" Kozmo announces, jumps in front of everyone and points straight up; emulating some sort of disco star from generations past.

Nothing happens.

"Alright well I apologize for this great disappointment." Kozmo continues for a moment. "Anyone else have any ideas?"

The guild, for a moment. Descends into an odd sort of kinetic guess-work. Throwing their hands about, considering different positions, swirling their eyes, and looking around. Nelf, the whole while, is just smirking.

"Hey I see something. If you squint, you can kinda see. A health-bar? I think that's my health bar." He focuses a moment longer. "I have max health, that's nice. *What would I do if I didn't*." He sinks into a brief horror.

Nelf *snaps* and an ethereal panel of light appears in front of him. From the perspective of *the guild* it is a light yellow panel with indecipherable script sprawled across it. "Snap and think *menu. Noobs*." He scrolls through the menu with a single finger, much like you would a touch-screen phone.

"Did you know that before?!" Illkat questions.

"It was just *obvious*." Nelf makes the statement as plainly as a statement could viably be.

119

Everyone takes a moment, focuses their mind and *snaps*. Various blue menus appear with a dull yellow script upon them. To each, the script is decipherable. Before them is their own character sheet, a third person perspective of *themselves*, various stats and skill details. As well as a second tab for *inventory*. Which is empty but with a hundred unique *slots* set out upon it.

"You can change the colour if you like, and no other players should be able to read it." Nelf adds.

"There isn't a log out button." Sonnenblume seems saddened by the realization.

"There isn't an *out* to go to." Gekomatsu makes the statement.

"I'm alright with that." Dezz adds. He sways back and forth; stretching in ways which aren't at all required but appear to be quite exciting to him. "We might as well settle in. Treat this like anything else. If *we were* in the game. How would we approach this situation? We own this plot as a guild right? So we can build on it however we want. Which means we need resources. We're probably going to eat out that convenience store sooner then later. It looks like we had some sort of ice-box in the kitchen here. Maybe we should fill it? We could try to hunt."

Kaan laughs. "Try to hunt." He looks over at Dezz. "Do you remember the three weeks straight we spent out in the woods hoping for a chance to use that caribou tag you got in the lottery? Every blind, scent, early morning or late night. If we did thirty clicks in a day it wasn't enough. Hunting is *tough*."

"In the real world, *yea*. I'd agree with you. But this is *the new real world*. The rules aren't always different, but they might be. I dunno. *Mixed*?" Dezz proposes.

"Well we should take Sonnenblume with us then. She has the bow. We can spot, and, *keep things safe I guess*. We don't really know what *is* out there do we?"

Illkat hands Kaan one of the short-swords and Dezz the maul. "Hopefully you don't have to use them."

Pulling the cutting edge right up to eye level. Kaan inspects the blade. "It looks like it will work for my purposes." He looks over at the pile. "How about one of those axes, and a little knife as well? They won't be stellar but with those things together I can break down some simple arrows and nock them."

"You should teach me to do it as well." Sonnenblume requests.

"I will." Kaan agrees.

"Then the *rest of us*." Kozmo picks back up. "Our general resources aren't much greater. If this is anything like EE then we could...*make weapons and armour?* But nothing without supplies. If they are off trying to hunt, maybe getting some wood on the way back with that axe? We could use the pick-axes. The mountain is so close. Breaking up some rocks, even to build out, *garden walls* or something. That might be helpful."

"Garden walls?" Illkat questions.

"It's not a bad idea." Kozmo defends.

"No, *no it's not*. Just, a nice first thought." Illkat embraces the idea.

Kozmo shrugs. "Well, when you look at it. Where we are. There's a lot to think about, and a lot of the time, when I have a lot to think about. I play some sort of survival crafting game instead and express my deep grief through the construction of a base. You know, not much more relaxing then building out your own little garden. Getting a bedroom *just right*. You can lose a few days tweaking, and fine tuning."

Gekomatsu laughs. "I have fond memories of *Post Apocalypse Cottage Industry Simulator* for similar reasons."

"*Oh yea!* I remember that game. I had a whole ranch of mutant milk lizards and bio-engineered them to lactate a high quality silk for my robot looms." Illkat reminisces.

"You know I had an influence on the *art direction* of those milk lizards." Nelf teases.

"I don't believe you." Gekomatsu dismisses the statement. "Will *you* help us mine?"

Nelf makes an abrupt and offended sound. "To even ask me the question! I would traditionally *be shocked*. And yet, *instead*. I am more appalled by the current state of my skills then I am the physical labour. So for the time being." He looks around the room, as if attempting to dodge something. "I *will help you*."

Dezz claps loudly. "Great, so I'll take Kaan and Sonnenblume out to hunt. *Illkat* we'll need you to open the barrier for us and hopefully let us back in. We'll need to find some sort of...signal for that. But for the time being, you will take Gekomatsu, Kozmo, and Nelf out mining for resources. We shall all return in a handful of hours. Say three to four to check in?"

"*What a plan.*" Illkat is on the verge of sarcasm. "Works for me. See the three of you soon!"

〒

Beyond the wind-wall, the mountainous region is simply *still*. Snow covers much of what the eye can see. Evergreens sprout up in dense bundles wherever enough land stretches between rocky peaks. Trailing ahead and around the mountain —for quite a distance— is simply *forest*. Even further beyond that, trailing up towards the sky and dissipating to nothingness; is a thick white smoke.

"The air is *so cold*." Sonnenblume remarks.

"Snow will do that."

"I know, *and-*" She laughs. "I think I'm a bit in shock, if I'm being honest. And even though it's freezing out, in a way, I'm just starting to un-thaw. If that makes sense."

"I've been there. After my accident, it wasn't really until the next day that what had happened was truly sinking in. It's like, coffee seeping through a filter. *It's going to happen*, but it's not instant." Dezz adds.

Kaan nods. "Reminds me of my mom. She's always talking about, *the half-life of anxiety?*" He pauses for a moment. "*You know*, these chemicals that control the reactions in our brain. Or, *did*. I imagine they still do. They take time to process, and as they unwind we feel different things. Like, *after a big anxiety episode* on the come down, you might find yourself shaking a lot. And it's not that anxiety makes you cold, but the process of effectively coming down from a chemical high can have a lot of, *associated processes*."

"How is your mom doing with all that, *anxiety, by the way?*" Dezz questions.

Kaan shrugs. "Well probably not too well right about now." He laughs. "I hope she's doing okay, and before, *all this*. She was getting through it alright so long as she was home. She came from the era before *B.I* and it shows man. She could sit there all day, enjoying herself, and at the end of it she'd find some way to beat herself up because she '*hadn't accomplished anything*' as if she wasn't going to get to eat because of it."

"It wasn't *that long ago* that B.I was introduced. Thirty some years?" Sonnenblume considers.

"Before I was born, at-least." Kaan notes.

The group pushes past the brief clearing between the wind wall, the nearest mountains and the tree-line. Beyond them resides an unbroken forest without so much as a marker or human foot print in sight. The pillar-esque trees reach upwards of fifty feet and stifle

123

much of the light; leaving a murky permanent twilight spread throughout the wood.

A trill rushes down Kaan's neck and he jolts in place. He makes an odd sound then lets out an excited cheer. Then laughs.

Dezz chuckles. "What's all that now?"

In a quickening pace, his voice becomes a bit higher pitched. Kaan seems to *lighten*. "I can't really *say*. I feel, like the first time I left the country. When I was on my own, just, on my own schedule. Making my own calls. I feel, *untethered!*"

Sonnenblume glances at the ground, swallows down something heavy and forces a smile. "Travelling is a joyous thing. But I'd never go somewhere so cold as this! What a waste of money!"

"No Banff? Hokkaido? *The Bernese Alps?!*" Dezz is appalled.

"Maybe in the summer. Or if I was in a rv? It's not relaxing if I have to *survive the conditions* while trying to de-stress!"

Dezz laughs. "If you tolerate the heat well, maybe you'd think that. But I was taking fifteen showers a day down in Mexico when I went for a vacation. Beautiful country, but I'm not built to spend time in it outside shade and air conditioned dining rooms."

"Do you think there still *is* a Mexico?" Sonnenblume queries.

The boys consider the idea.

Each step leads them further into the darkening depths of the forest.

"Who's to say every country was affected. *Maybe* it was just...*South Africa?* Maybe it was just Cape Town." Dezz offers.

"There was the Japanese convenience store though." Kaan adds.

"Ah, *yea*." Dezz agrees. "Seems likely then, that it was, *everywhere*."

"Might be for the best then." Kaan comments.

Sonnenblume becomes a bit shocked. "How could this be for the best?"

"I'm not saying that what happened is, *ideal*. I'm just, throwing it out there that it's better *completed* then stuck *half-way*. Imagine what that'd look like. A hole in the planet? A never closing tear?" He laughs a bit wickedly. "At least it was like pulling a band-aid, or a good break up. Just one big hurt and done."

Sonnenblume scoffs. "I guess." She shakes her head. "So are we going to make those arrows?"

"*Right*." Kaan acts as if he has forgotten. "Well, we can use just about anything for right now. No point debating tensile strength or something like that when we don't have anything at all. We need straight lengths of branches between a quarter and half an inch of thickness."

"How long?" Sonnenblume questions.

"*Here*." Dezz approaches. "Draw your bow *but don't let go, okay?*"

"*Alright*." Sonnenblume strains the slightest bit. "*Now what*."

"Well the arrow you want needs to go from the tip of your nose *here* to a bit past the riser of the bow *here*." He measures the distance with his fingers. "Now slowly bring the bow in, but don't dry fire it." He raises his arms up; the distance between his fingers maintained. "So we need sticks this length, or to cut them down to this length. What's that just about two ft roughly?"

"Looks it." Kaan agrees.

"I've shot a bow a couple times before, but why are you worried about arrow length?" Sonnenblume inquires.

"Few reasons." Kaan jumps in. "Though I think the biggest one is that a short arrow, on a fully extended draw, can mean you fire point blank into your own palm by mistake."

125

Dezz chortles. "Yea watched that go wrong one time. Was out bow fishing with a cousin, he just got a big cheque and spent some of it on the heaviest poundage fishing bow money could buy. He could barely pull the thing back, probably a hundred and twenty pound draw *on a recurve.*"

"Oh man." Kaan adds. "Was he trying to blow the fish up?"

"Well he didn't know what he was doing. Bought something you'd probably use out in the ocean for a lake." Dezz laughs again. "*Either way,* buddy goes out to shoot, and you know fishing bows have a line attached to the back of em. So he draws, the arrow is too short but he doesn't notice and fires right through the fleshy bit of his hand. The bow is *so damn strong though* the arrow just flies straight through, line and all. So not only does the whole arrow rip a hole in his hand but the line it's carrying saws through the top of the wound, quickly enough that it rips out *between* his thumb and pointer finger."

"*Ahh that's awful.*" Sonnenblume laments.

"*Just wicked.*" Kaan humorously acknowledges.

"Well as you can imagine, he didn't really want to do a lot of fishing after that. Had to pack it up, pull the arrow in. Get em back to shore." He laughs. "Aside from that, not worth having the accident."

"Was your cousin alright?" Sonnenblume inquires.

Dezz appears struck by the question, as if it is a component of the story he forgot was important. "Oh yea, *I'm pretty sure.* I mean, he died a few years later. But it wasn't from the arrow."

"Oh, *sorry.*" Sonnenblume apologizes.

"Don't, it's, *fine.* Life is messy you know?" Dezz makes the comment as he continues to pick up lengths of sticks; mostly straight lengths of pine.

"Isn't it." Sonnenblume makes the comment then looks around the forest. "You guys aren't, *mad at me. Or anything.* Are you?"

Dezz shrugs. "Nope."

Kaan raises a single eyebrow. *"Should we be?"*

She huffs. "I just, I didn't tell you about having kids, or what's going on in my life. Even, *beyond that.* I'm not even a law student, I graduated years ago."

"Oh alright." Kaan acknowledges. "Well thanks for telling us now, but *I'll be honest.* I know you as *Sonnenblume.* Whatever your other name, whoever you were in that *other life.* It's not really, my problem. *In that I just mean. Well. I'm your friend because of who you are to me, not because of what you are."*

"Not *everyone* thinks that. But I appreciate it." Sonnenblume laments.

Dezz drops a bundle of sticks near the path. Kaan approaches, and with the axe begins to straighten the lengths of wood. Hacking off any out-standing branches or leaves.

"Who thinks otherwise? Do we need to beat them up?" Dezz jests.

Sonnenblume shakes her head. *"No, nothing like that. Er, neither of you have kids do you?"*

They both shake their heads.

"Well then you might not know, but when you have kids nowadays. Part of the registration is confirming the child will be able to live to a certain standard. Household income beyond basic income, family property, base square footage for the bedroom of the child. *That kinda thing.* An element of that registration is understanding that a child must have their lifestyle accommodated if there is any change to this setup. So when my *husband left us* we had to move back in with my parents, *to keep the kids."* She takes a moment to consider her thoughts. "Let's just say my folks could think of a million better things for me to be doing then playing a game in my free-time."

"Ugh." Kaan laments. "Just a game." He groans. "Do you ever get tired of hearing that? I don't know about you two, but if it wasn't

127

for *a game*. Not even *Endless Empires*. Just, *a game, a safe place, a fantasy land.* I don't know how far in the real world I could of gone. Even for the slight distance travelled."

"Oh it sucks there." Dezz adds.

"Fully agree." Sonnenblume joins. She thinks for a moment.

Kaan begins to sharpen the tip of each straightened arrow, and cuts a deep *v* shape into the other end.

"Have you ever wished, you could just know, *nobody*. Not in a painful way. Not in a big goodbye. But instead, you could just close your eyes, everyone you love would be okay, but you'd be, *by yourself*. Unknown to anyone, no strings, no one...*looking for you*." Sonnenblume asks.

"Most folks don't know about me." Dezz remarks; half sarcastic.

Kaan nods. "I love my friends, and I don't know what it is. Maybe it's...being a guy? Maybe it's just the way the world is nowadays. But I feel like if I took a step back, and just waited. The world would pass me by in an instant. Nobody would reach back for me, nobody would prevent that change. I'd just be stomped over, *forgotten*."

"It's not much different if you're a girl, just the folks reaching back for you all want to fuck you. If they can't get that they'll let you go just like everyone else." Sonnenblume quickly makes the point.

Kaan raises his hands. "Yea, no, you're right. And, *yea. I guess, if you don't even have that.* It just seems better then nothing."

"I can promise you, it isn't. It's like being rich, and wondering if you have any real friends or they just want your money. But in this case I can't even enjoy my money. I don't have a mansion or a sports car to smooth over the fakeness of so many relationships. It's just me, and people who want to carve out portions of who I am for them to

128

enjoy at their whim. So which would you rather, nobody reaching for your hand or people only doing it so they can cut off your arm?"

Kaan nods. "Point well made. *Sorry*." He finishes a bundle of arrows. "There are about thirty here, then a couple you can just try out and break if you need to. They should work at least up to sixty some feet."

Sonnenblume takes the arrows and smiles politely. "Thanks Kaan. I'm sorry as well. Not for what I said, but I know we're just, *having the discussion*. You didn't do anything."

"I try not to." Kaan laments, then peers beyond the forest. "We probably shouldn't talk as we walk the trails from here. If we have any chances of finding something; we don't want to spook it."

Dezz smiles. "Works for me. I'll follow behind you two. Let's try to get to the top of that ridge in the distance and see what we can find."

〒

AT THE SAME TIME.

"I'd like to point out that if we're mining, we likely should be wearing masks of some kind. The particulate from breaking up material, or possibly hitting something like *coal* would be hazardous to us." Gekomatsu makes the point as himself, Illkat, Kozmo and Nelf make their way towards the nearby mountainside; pickaxes slung over shoulder.

"You would be able to tell if you're being poisoned. There is a *meter for that*." Nelf butts in.

"*Yet I still worry*." Gekomatsu retorts.

"You shouldn't." Nelf returns.

129

The group near the edge of the cliff, where the tunnel venturing into the mountain has a mouth. At the face of the tunnel, is a *completely ruined* mine-cart. Its wheels have been broken in, its axles contorted; portions of the side simply banged away at with something large.

"I told you we should of killed him." Gekomatsu states plainly.

"*I*, what do you even mean?" Illkat questions.

"There were two carts when we arrived here." Kozmo notes. "If *all of this* is based on our map, from our server in EE. Then, *there were two carts* when we arrived here."

"*Ah*." Illkat comes to an understanding. "So *Tobias* must of took the other one into the city. Leaving us *stranded*."

"It seems so." Kozmo notes. "He might come back though. Maybe that monster will respawn."

"You mean the quadr-" Gekomatsu begins and is quickly cut off.

"Don't start with that again. Kozmo had it right. *The monster*." She huffs a bit. "I see no reason to stay here then. Unless, you want to mine from within the tunnel?"

"I wouldn't waste the time yet. You'll only make a mess of it. We should focus on carving down one of these mountain faces. The base stone will be worthwhile for building. *Defences will be required*." Nelf exclaims.

"*What are you...even*." Illkat expresses sincere confusion. "I don't want to be caught in a bad situation. But we have the *windwall*. What good is stone in comparison to that?"

"Two is one, one is none." Nelf states as if he has repeated the phrase many a time.

"That's a term for backing up data electronically?" Kozmo questions.

"*Or* defending a structure. If you only have the front gate keeping you safe, if that fails; you have nothing. *Do you want to be caught with nothing?*" Nelf questions with a pseudo-hostility.

Kozmo coughs. "Uh, *no.*"

"Obviously not." Illkat adds.

Gekomatsu shrugs.

"Well that's why you need more defence, build up barracks. Barricades. Create alleys you know, that are confusing to the enemy. Create and *control your battleground!*" Nelf continues on.

"*Alright.*" Illkat accepts; somewhat displeased to agree with Nelf. "If you say it is best."

"Oh you'll come to see *all of what I say is best.*" Nelf winks at Illkat *seductively.*

She groans. Approaches the nearest side of the mountain and drops her pick-axe into it; shearing off a few chunks right away. "*So Gekomatsu.* You're a doctor. What got you interested in that?"

"My brother had cancer as a child, *and died.*"

"*Oh.*" Illkat and Kozmo share a concerned inflection.

"*I'm sorry.* I didn't know." Illkat apologizes sincerely.

Gekomatsu waves it away. "It's okay, *I knew it happened.* It's not a surprise." He laughs. "In the world of healthcare, losing someone like that. It's less a stand out oddity and more...*a barrier to entry.* Most of my colleagues lost someone, or watched a loved one succumb to an illness. It *warps you* in a way. Sensitive in some spots, tougher in others."

"I still can't help but feel sorry." Kozmo makes the point with a sunken head; working away at a spot of rocky mountainside.

Gekomatsu smiles *stoically.* "Feel sorry for those who still have a chance and are failed by the system. Left behind while boxes are checked, and I's are dotted."

131

"I can't say I'm a doctor, or *anything like that*. But for the most part, those *checks and dotted I's* are a good thing. Aren't they?" Illkat considers.

"In some places." Gekomatsu agrees with a degree of chagrin. "Yet if there was ever a time to cut red tape, to just. *Fix something*. In cases like that, or *my brother*. I feel it may be the time, *and yet*, the world does not. It goes the pace it prefers, or the pace of a director, or a certain form to be signed and passed around to different department heads and looked at for *however long it takes*." He groans.

"Bureaucracy inflects a suffering greater then I have seen in any raid." Nelf jests.

The four of them work away at different rocks. Unlike the previous reality each broken chunk of rock turns into reasonably square raw chunks. They pile together into a hundred of the chunks at a time; somehow occupying the same space while remaining individually recognizable.

"You were going to school for something quite prestigious, *weren't you Kozmo*?" Gekomatsu shifts the spotlight from himself.

Kozmo laughs. "*Prestigious is,* all a frame of mind. *Wouldn't you say?*"

"I would not." Nelf jumps in.

Illkat glares at him as Kozmo wavers his shoulders.

"I guess, *yea you could say that.* I've been studying a few different things. Psychology. Marine zoology! I even spent a few months auditing accounting courses!" Kozmo explains, assesses himself, then recognizes something. "You're probably aware of it, but the universities here." He corrects himself. "I mean, back in Cape Town. They're *the focus* nowadays. Each of them committed to pursuing the greatest depths of knowledge, melding the minds of our futuristic era! Crossing every bound, or limit. *Eliminating red tape*."

"That is what the articles have said." Gekomatsu agrees.

132

"Well it's true, but you don't read about how that vast and free education is implemented." Kozmo explains.

"Is this the part where we learn it's all supported off the back bone of some horribly, abusive system?" Illkat prepares to become concerned.

Kozmo cheers. "It's the part where I tell you *it isn't!* I can study *everything*. I can swap my classes every week, and all that progress. It just *tallies up*. If I eventually earn a degree, it will tell me what in, and I can just keep *growing it*."

"Truly as it should be." Gekomatsu states plainly.

"*I'm jealous*. My family is...*was* in Canada?" She looks aside. "That is going to get tough to stop doing." She laughs. "Otherwise I probably would of travelled for school. But at least, we got 90% back at tax time!"

"In my country you're paid to go to school." Gekomatsu notes.

"Oh yea, same in Cape Town. Students stipend and everything!" Kozmo adds.

Illkat sinks. "Ah my great white north. Why have you failed me?"

"In my state you have to pay roughly fifty thousand dollars a year, even if its a four year degree." Nelf joins. "It insures only *the strong* can pay."

Illkat just stares at him. "*Just,* focus on the mining. *Please.*"

"I'm just sharing my side." Nelf argues.

"*Alright America. That's great.*" She laments. "I imagine you were born rich?"

Nelf laughs. "Born rich? I'll have you know I received only a small loan of a few million dollars and from it, I grew my empire!"

"*Ah so that's a yes.*" Kozmo teases.

A chunk of rock breaks away, and within it is a thick black mineral. It is porous and *oily*.

Kozmo squints at it, then breaks into a smile. "Coal! I can't believe it, sometimes I play for hours before I get any of this."

"Ah, that's not bad. I wonder is it *everywhere* in this mountain? Did you just get lucky?"

"Maybe!" Kozmo shouts. He slams the pick-axe down into the rocky mountainside; repeating the process quickly a couple more times. Of the chunks he breaks out, a tenth includes coal.

"A low drop rate is still a drop rate." Nelf notes. "We must push forwards and seize this opportunity!"

"*Hey, I do the commands around here.*" Illkat jokes. She looks ahead. "So *yea! Push forwards. Seize* the opportunity!"

〒

A fierce gale blows around the town of Verrplek. From the forest, emerging with full and inexplicably present backpacks are *Dezz, Kaan* and *Sonnenblume*. They wave up towards Illkat, Gekomatsu, Kozmo and Nelf; whom themselves are saddled down with large sacks of stone and coal.

"It looks like we just pillaged a countryside!" Dezz shouts up.

"Arr yes me matey! We took all the booty!" Illkat shouts back in an awful pirate impersonation.

Everyone stares at her.

"Alright, I was just trying it out. *Relax*." She jests.

"The game, *or whatever*. It made the bags when we picked up all this meat! And *get this*. If we take all the meat out of the bag. The bag *ceases to exist*." Kaan goes on. "I have *no idea what is going on with all of that*." He waves. "Hey how are you?"

134

"We conquered the mountainside and found a source of fuel!" Nelf exclaims.

Gekomatsu nods. "He is correct. We seem to be near enough a natural source of coal. As well, we've gathered stone for cobblestone creation and stone slabs."

"*Did you level up?!*" Sonnenblume shouts out inquisitively. "I did! My archery is *totally level ten now*."

"Heck yea!" Illkat exclaims and gives Sonnenblume an exaggerated high five.

"We're about there. Most of us are about level fifteen for mining now? Gathering skills level quicker then combat skills though, just cause. You can stand there and keep hacking away!" Kozmo comments kindly.

Far off in the distance, beyond the forest and mountains. The once white smoke has now turned a dark black. It trails up in a thick column.

"That was the direction of Illking." Kozmo notes. "If memory serves."

"He's right! A city with a decadent degree of supple offerings!" Nelf shouts.

"With the stone we acquired, we can build a few basic defences. I think half should go into fortifying the manor, thickening the walls. But out *here*, we can put a door on the tunnel only we can open." Illkat adds.

"Oh can I do it!?" Sonnenblume asks. "I really like the building in this game."

Illkat nods and waves her arms ahead of herself. "*By all means*."

Sonnenblume approaches a sack of stone and *clicks it* with a tap of her right finger. It begins to glow *blue* in a pulse. She walks over towards the entrance to the tunnel and holds her palm out flat, flicking her fingers a few times before pushing her flattened palm forwards.

Before her, a stone structure assembles itself. The blocks of stone float from the sack to the structure and fill in a somewhat apparent blueprint of an entirely stone wall and movable door. The door itself slides up and down into the frame *inexplicably*.

"Did...the recipe to do that take some gears or mechanisms?" Dezz asks.

Sonnenblume looks around, and rifles through her pockets. "I am with all my things. The door just, *does that*."

"Why would any of you argue with something working out for you? Do you want it to get nerfed? Do you want to mine out an entire strip of earth to make pcb circuit boards? To create current? To invent the mechanism? Or do you want a door made out of stone that opens easily? Don't *complain*!" Nelf argues.

Gekomatsu laughs a bit. "He's out of line but he's right. It appears some elements of game logic are unavoidable." He looks out at the sky. "Though it does make me wonder, *can this world be patched?* Or are we, *set*."

"We can turn it back, I *know we can*." Sonnenblume states with a heavy desperation.

Dezz looks at the wind wall as Illkat begins to open a passage for them. He smiles *brightly*. "I don't think we should, *even if we can*."

"*Whatever we can do*." Kaan begins. "We should try to reach the city. Whether through the tunnels, or a path of our own. Who knows what is out there! Or, *who*."

"I agree." Nelf joins. "We know Tobias has likely gone this way, based on the ruined mine carts. But further more, *maybe* Space will be there as well."

"*Space*." Sonnenblume questions. "I thought he died?"

Nelf becomes solemn. "No, *worse*. At the crux of our battle, *Space changed sides*. He is one of them *now*."

"One of them?" Illkat asks.

"You saw it, did you not? He's an ally of the dark server now." Nelf speaks with horrible finality.

Chapter Seven

A Stoked Flame

"Level up!" The game voice chimes.

Dezz exits the washroom in the manor just as Kaan is passing him in the hallway. They briefly stare at one another, unsure of how the conversation should begin. The washroom door —still open— reveals a *far too modern* washroom with a toilet in the corner that leads nowhere yet works *all the same*. A sink and mirror finish the space.

"Are there..." Kaan begins.

"Before you even have to say anything. *Yes*. For some reason. That's a skill in the game." Dezz makes the comment and laughs. "I really hope it's not for a unique boss mechanic or something."

Kaan laughs. "I'm hoping for the same. It can't be possible all the skills we have will amount to something."

Gekomatsu passes through the hall, picks up on the conversation and joins it seamlessly. "All the rules of the body, they had to be translated *somehow*. Did they not? If the rules of our world must find parity in the rules of this amalgam universe. Then, it is clear to me. Most of our functions must become...*skills of a sort*."

"Well my *sleeping skill* must be levelling through the roof because I had a great night. I miss wood burning furnaces. When you have central heating the whole house is warm everywhere. You can't move a bit further from the heat, or get closer. It's inescapable." Kaan complains.

"Some would consider that a *modern miracle*." Gekomatsu adds.

"Well some people have never woken up so sweaty they might slip out of their bed, down the hall and out onto the grass!" Kaan laughs.

Dezz smirks. "I can think of someone who would."

Kaan rolls his eyes. "Does anyone know where Nelf is from? Obviously the Dissolved States, but which one?"

"I'm guessing Texas. As I understand the whole country mutated into a sort of warrior caste but with pick-up trucks and automatic rifles." Gekomatsu wagers.

"Nope. I'm voting Florida. They have that 'only the strong survive' thing as well." Kaan offers.

The trio, walking together now. Sit in the front room of the manor. Kozmo heads out from the kitchen and joins them.

"Talking about the states?" Kozmo ventures the guess.

Kaan nods. "Indeed. You ever visit?"

Kozmo laughs as if it is an insane proposition. "Don't get me wrong, I might want to see the mountains in Arizona...*or,* try the pizza in Chicago. But my parents would put me in a mental asylum sooner then they'd let me sign off on going on the 'Remnants of America' tour."

There is a *stomping* down the stairs as an in-progress *discussion* moves its way into the front sitting room.

"We're not prioritizing uniforms." Illkat puts her foot down.

"You're not considering the benefits! There is a point five higher percent chance of intimidation attempts being successful if you're in a group of similarly dressed allies!" Nelf returns.

Illkat sighs. "Which is *excellent* but we're not going to be making any intimidation checks. We're exploring...*scouting.* Not annexing."

Nelf sinks in a way which suggests his spirits are, for the moment; broken. "Opportunity left unseized! Shots untaken! What loss!"

Using the full strength of every muscle in her face; Illkat rolls her eyes and peers out to the others in the sitting room. "Has anyone seen Sonnenblume?"

Everyone shrugs, wags their head or otherwise seems without information.

Illkat looks around, then peers out to the very back door. "I'll go. Let's be ready to head out in a moment here."

Without waiting for much of a response Illkat rushes out through the manor, beyond the back door and out to the edge of the town of Verrplek. Sonnenblume is sitting under a tree; lazily smoking a cigarette.

"I didn't know you were a smoker." Illkat questions.

Sonnenblume shrugs. "Not *tobacco anyways*. I just figured this is what they had in the convenience store. I might as well try." She takes a quick drag from the smoke, exhales and waves her free hand around in the air. "*Besides*, I don't even know if these are my lungs. Or if I'll get to keep them."

Illkat squats next to Sonnenblume and gestures for the smoke. She takes it, presses it against plump lips and takes the far too heavy drag of inexperience; hacking up more then she bargained for. Her bleary eyed exasperation goes on for a few moments straight.

Sonnenblume pats Illkat's back a bit and smiles. "You okay?"

Illkat, appearing as if she might puke; nods optimistically. "Yea, *yea*. I'm doing-" She retches a bit. "-just fine."

Sonnenblume laughs. "Well those might just be your lungs then." She retrieves the smoke, inhales the worthwhile remainder then kills it between her fingers. "We're off to Illking then, eh?"

"Yepp." Illkat confirms; a tough to decipher pain in her pronunciation.

The pair go around the manor from the outside and poke in through the front door. "Let's do this!" Sonnenblume shouts out.

The guild and Nelf assemble. Mostly ramshackle weapons upon them. The wind wall falls and rises at the beckon of Illkat's spear. Their door blocking off the mines stands strong. Beyond it; absolute darkness.

"I guess the torches burnt out." Kozmo offers.

"Mhmm." Dezz agrees. "The woods weren't too bad. They don't do that...constantly moving thing anymore. It's just, *a forest*. It's about the same distance if we're walking, but at-least then we'll be able to see!"

Everyone looks between one another. Nobody seems specifically excited about the pitch black tunnel.

"The woods it is." Illkat makes the call.

Kaan draws his short-sword, spins it around and smiles. "I'm starting to figure out this area. The trails. Where there is gain, where it all leads to." Kaan points out to the east. "Along the coast there, even in the wood. It's all scree at the slope. Probably from deep roots tearing up the side. So we'll keep closer to the mountain."

"How far out did you go when you were hunting?" Gekomatsu asks.

"It felt like a fair distance? But we tried to avoid anywhere we knew there might be a settlement." Sonnenblume quickly responds.

Dezz and Kaan shrug.

"We got a bit of tunnel vision. Paying more attention to what is out here, then where '*out here*' is." Dezz laughs. "If you know what I mean."

Illkat gets closer to the lead. "Well let's keep our eyes on this time. Everyone watch out. We don't know what else is in these woods, or *who*."

"Other then deer and raccoons." Sonnenblume adds.

Illkat looks back at her, half smirking.

141

"I just, we already know those are out here." Sonnenblume continues.

〒

Just at the tip of a small hill *the guild* look out to the city of Illking. Portions of it burn, some smoulder. Screams and the sound of combat rush out from each opened orifice across the broken city walls. Corpses are scattered like sporadic anthills leading up to the main gate. A wolf tears at one of them on the other side of the wood.

"Ergh. Not *exactly the welcome I was hoping for.*" Kaan bemoans.

Sonnenblume focuses ahead; squinting with intensity. "There is someone in that big tower near the gate." She takes a moment. "I think they see us."

Everyone gets low except Nelf who begins to walk towards the city fearlessly. "Why wouldn't they look out! No doubts they can sense it. The *return of their leader!*"

A thin black line rises out from the tower, arcs near the tip of the sky and descends down at a hastened pace. Nelf steps to the side; an arrow landing in the dirt just beside him.

"This is not how you greet the one who shall guide you to greatness!" He shouts out; deeply offended.

"That looked like a warning shot." Illkat states confidently.

"Eh." Dezz retorts. "From that distance, anyone who can miss by that much has to know they're not likely to hit with a single arrow. It might be...a request for help? A signal they are there?"

"So should we run or try to sneak in?" Kaan asks the group.

Without waiting Kozmo breaks into a sprint and shouts out "We run!"

"Well there you go. Kozmo pulled a Leroy." Dezz jests then becomes the first to join him.

"Guys! We should think about this!" Illkat shouts out without much traction.

Sonnenblume shrugs apologetically and joins the others in their rush to the city.

Illkat looks over at Kaan; paused in the midst of latent energy. She huffs a bit. "Alright, *just go*." She peers over at Gekomatsu as they pick up into a jog. "You're not rushing out of the gates?"

"I'm here because of all of you. I won't abide anyone left behind." He smirks. "Besides, you're going to follow them all just as I am." He almost teases.

She huffs. "I...*whatever.* Let's go."

Nothing disturbs their collective rush up to the city walls. Nelf, struck by some degree of caution. Takes cover at the edge of the gate; the others behind him. He peers over, just to look ahead. Then returns.

Illkat and Gekomatsu flatten themselves against the wall.

"What do we see?" Illkat whispers up.

"Too much." Dezz whispers back. "Just *listen*."

Without anyone speaking. You can hear the wind. Screams. Metal clashing against metal. The occasional flintlock pistol firing; or the repetitive *droning* of some sort of high calibre machine gun.

"Sounds like a mess." Sonnenblume interrupts.

Nelf scurries towards one of the nearest corpses and takes from it a bearded axe. It's a simple sort of weapon; with a thick wooden haft. Without looking towards *the guild* he moves onward. "Follow me, if you want to find glory." He ushers the statement.

Illkat squints. "You go ahead. We'll, *find you*."

Whether he acknowledges the statement or not. Nelf is off into the town; his axe raised.

"What's the plan?" Kaan asks.

"I'd rather get out of the street before we have that conversation." Dezz offers.

They push further into Illking and duck into an emptied home. Just as the door closes behind them. Through a slotted wooden window everyone watches as a flaming wagon nearly glides down the street, crashes into a wall and bursts with alchemical flame.

From the wagon burst three peoples. Each of them unique from one another; the details become less notable as they burn away.

Swiftly after a pair of men rush down the street with automatic rifles, flak vests and balaclavas over their faces. They shoot two of the peoples on fire, once in the head, twice in the chest.

The remaining burning person raises their arm, and from it conjures a burst of ice; which launches out like a volley of missiles. Spearing one of the soldiers in the leg. They shoot him in the head as well, and again twice in the chest.

The wounded soldier consumes a large vial of green liquid, *glows for a moment* and then nods to his allies. His wound stops bleeding.

With their rifles raised they continue to flush the streets.

Everyone in the guild gets down.

"I can only imagine this first contact is going about as well as could be expected." Sonnenblume makes the statement with a disjointed dread.

"First contact?" Kozmo inquires.

"*Mhmm.*" Sonnenblume responds. "It's a thing in sci-fi, more often then not. The first time two new cultures meet each other, the first exposure to a whole new world." She motions with her head outside. "They didn't look like they were on the same side, did they?"

"I imagine she is correct. Without traditional power structures, or governance. It seems likely both criminal and military factions would seek to fill the gap." Gekomatsu rationalizes the observation.

"Seems like we're going to need guns." Kozmo observes.

"Or really good armour." Dezz adds.

They push through the house. In the mudroom there is nothing but empty barrels and wooden furniture. In the main room of the structure, a string of corpses lead up to a bath. Each of the corpses are unique from one another. One is a man in loose fitting clothing; bandanas tied up his arms. Another has slicked back hair and a well tailored —albeit full of holes— suit.

Gekomatsu reaches for a door back onto the street the same moment something *THUNKS* against it. He falls back.

Everyone gets really quiet.

Something *THUNKS* again.

A digital, somewhat pixellated crack begins to form in the centre of the door.

"Oh no." Kozmo recognizes the threat. "I have an idea what this is."

THUNK

Kozmo rushes over to one of the barrels and as the door bursts open; he throws it with precision. Striking an undead sort of dog, standing quite impossibly upright; directly in the head.

> LEVEL UP!
> NEW SKILL DISCOVERED: 'RANDOM BULLSHIT'

A tear wells up in the corner of Kozmo's eye. "It is *everything I ever wanted.*"

"What in the hell was that!" Kaan shouts.

"Corpse eater. They usually only spawn on PvP battlegrounds." Gekomatsu explains.

Sonnenblume rushes up to the door and peers down at the creature. It is *shaking* and *tensing* in odd violent patterns. "I'm expecting this thing to either explode or get bigger."

Dezz walks out the door and cautiously looks to either side. Then with all his strength grabs the shuddering mass by the ankles. He spins it around, and at the peak of momentum throws it far down the road nearer the burning wagon.

As it lands it bursts in the centre and a hundred little spiders spill out aimlessly.

"*Gross.*" Dezz contains the desire to gag.

"It is an odd reproduction cycle. *Those aren't corpse eater babies*. They just act as large incubation receptacles for those spiders."

"Oh I'm sorry, I didn't hear anyone asking for more details." Illkat teases. She points out to everyone in the group. "Did you....mhmm? Anyone interested in the undead dog monster and its spider babies?"

Kozmo aims to raise his hand, Illkat shoots him a serious look and he puts his hand down.

"*I.*" Sonnenblume steps forwards. "I think we need to go down that street." She points down —*what may be*— the worst of a dozen paths.

"*Really?*" Kaan questions.

Sonnenblume nods. "It's...just. *Glowing?*"

Gekomatsu looks over to her, *recognizes something* then nods. "Lead the way. We must venture forwards anyways, if we're to discover anything at all."

Without much discussion, and *Sonnenblume* at the lead. They rush across the main street, down an alley, and forwards through a sort of residential portion of Illking. It is carved at an upward angle so for every stretch of straight pathway there is an eventual break for stairs or a ramp.

"We're not far from that ossuary." Kozmo notes. *"What a loop."*

Something shakes the ground. It rattles the stone in the road; dislodging a few pieces.

Gunshots rattle off; like high pitched whistles and thunderous crackles in the distance.

Ahead of them a short distance is an open square; in the centre of it a clock-tower.

"It's, *beautiful.*" Sonnenblume remarks.

"What is?" Dezz questions. He looks up and around; a wilful optimism met without reward.

Sonnenblume raises an eyebrow. "You don't see it?"

"I see a clock tower, is that what you mean?" Illkat seeks further insight.

Sonnenblume wags her head. *"Inside* the clock tower. Is it, *just me?"* She reaches the base of the tower. It ascends up to twice the height of the nearest building. Shifting from stone and stained wood to silver and glass at the midway point. As light filters through it, fitting into slotted patterns upon the tile mandala of the centre floor, every flicker of light conjures a miasma of illumination.

As Sonnenblume places her hand upon the tower. Her eyes flicker a *bright white* and she drops lifelessly to the ground.

"Hey what just happened!" Illkat shouts. She rushes to Sonnenblume's side and straightens her posture.

Gekomatsu kneels beside her. He checks her airways, pulse, temperature. Pulls back her eyelid and looks for any response. "She's *not there.*" He declares.

"She just *died*? Just like that?!" Kozmo is horrified.

"She isn't dead." Gekomatsu clarifies. "But she's not in her body. It's breathing, pumping blood. But that's it."

There is a bit of movement behind them, and then a familiar sort of firearm shuffling.

"*Hands up. Now.*" A definitive and feminine voice orders.

"What the-" Kaan begins to curse as he turns, and realizes there are multiple soldiers standing a distance behind them all. Rifles levelled by a few people behind. In front of them stands a woman with an oversized revolver, long leather jacket, buzzed hair and heavy scars across her neck and chin. She wears military casuals and combat boots otherwise.

"Oh *no my mistake*. Compliance is clearly the best choice here." Kaan gets to his knees politely.

"*I'm certain we can work this out.*" Gekomatsu walks towards the group carelessly.

BANG

The woman fires off a shot ahead of Gekomatsu's feet. "I missed on purpose. I won't again. *Hands now.*" She orders again.

Everyone in the group puts their hands up.

The woman turns her head the slightest bit to look back at the soldiers behind her. "Watch these streets, someone is going to follow up on that shot."

"Yes ser." They acknowledge the complaint and fall out to different walls, covering corners and ways into the square.

"Look we have our friend here, she just collapsed. Something is wrong and we need to get her help." Illkat pleads while her hands remain up in the air.

The woman nods and peers over to where Sonnenblume lies motionlessly on the ground. "I can see that. I want to help her. But I need to know who you are first. Who is your CO?"

Everyone looks a bit confused.

The woman sighs heavily. *"You're civvies."*

"Most of us are Canadians actually." Kaan corrects.

"Oh dear lord." The woman bemoans the information, then looks around the area. "How did you get here?"

"We just walked fr-" Kozmo begins and is cut off by Dezz loudly interrupting.

"-The forests out west. We just, *popped up there*." Dezz adds.

The woman looks between them and rolls her eyes. "Yea that worked." She whistles, holds her hand in the air and spins it around. Her soldiers fall in upon her. "Follow us, we'll escort you to safety. We have a safe-house where we're keeping civilians safe."

"Do we, *have to*?" Kaan risks the question.

The woman lowers her revolver and steps back. She huffs, and tries to smile. For a moment, the immense stress upon her can clearly be envisioned as a tower built off her back stretching out into the clouds. "You can call me *Commander Aberdashi*. I'm with the UN special operations division."

"Ah, the *unifiers*." Gekomatsu recognizes the designation.

"An informal name." CMDR Aberdashi responds instantly.

Shots ring out in the distance.

"Let's go." She orders.

"What about our friend?" Illkat reminds her.

"Right." CMDR Aberdashi acknowledges. She approaches Sonnenblume, gets in a unique position nearly between her legs and then with a roll; pulls her over her left shoulder in a supportive position. Without breaking pace she keeps forwards; her free hand wielding her revolver. *"On me."*

They walk in a line. The soldiers with their rifles at the end of the pack. They push through another alley, keep low behind a dumpster from somewhere in up-state New York then rush through a shop selling leeches and different alchemy supplies. Through the back

149

door, over-top the remains of yet more empty *corpse-eaters* and nearer the centre portal into the settlement.

"*What happened here.*" Dezz asks.

"Sonnenblume called it a *first contact*, yea?" Kaan adds.

"Well I call it a shit show. We've seen *Mossad*, *Seals* and *SAS* out here. Nobody is flying flags anyone. No one is adhering to the rules of engagement. It's a twenty way land war. Then you add on *these things* wherever they came from."

"Do you know anything about the video game *Endless Empires*?" Kaan poises the question.

CMDR Aberdashi looks back, gives a real stern look then returns to scouting ahead. "We're close to the safe-house."

They push on for a moment. Down another alley, up a steep stone staircase and then straight to a chest height wall. With a single movement of her flattened palm she orders everyone low against the wall. She rests Sonnenblume against it.

"Where are our guards." She asks herself then looks back to her solders. She points at one and ushers them forwards. "Was there a switch of the post scheduled that I'm forgetting about."

"No ser." The soldier responds.

"*Fuck.*" CMDR Aberdashi curses with deep resentment. "Alright, *take Bollero* and get into a support position. We may need suppressing fire."

"*Yes ser.*" The soldier acknowledges, looks down to the others and one of them steps forwards. They sprint ahead.

CMDR Aberdashi leans back against the chest high wall and exhales.

"You, *alright.*" Kaan asks, then instantly corrects himself. "Sorry, stupid question. I just mean, *can we help*?"

"You're civilians." She dismisses.

"Yea, *normally*. Yes. But you see how weird everything is right now, right? Well I'm telling you that it's because of a video-game. Something *happened* to the world and things got mixed up. But *me and my friends*. We're good at this game. *We can help*."

She huffs. "*Help with what*. You're practically unarmed."

"Oh we have talents." Kozmo confirms.

"Fine." She relents, then pokes her head up. Her soldiers are in place. "You see that building over there, red top?"

"Yea that's a faction hall, you go there in a few quests." Kaan explains.

The commander rolls her eyes then pushes forwards. "Alright well that's our safe-house. We have families inside, folks who are scared and confused. We're going to push up, to the front door, and a larger one off to the side. We need to find what happened to the guards we had posted outside. But we have to be careful. We'll leave your friend here for a moment and come back for her."

Kaan nods. He looks back to his friends. "We got this. Illkat, should we follow you? That spear is something impressive."

"Alright. I'll take point beside the commander." She confirms. Everyone nods.

With another handle signal, all of *Aberdashi's* soldiers fall in and they rush up to the front door; planting themselves against the walls. She points out with two fingers to one side. "You take the side. Don't go too far in and get in our line of fire."

"Alright." Illkat takes Kaan, Kozmo, Dezz and Gekomatsu to the side. Kozmo grabs a length of rebar left on the ground.

Illkat tries the door. It opens. They push into a small side-hall and everyone sneaks in. There are a few voices from the end of the hall; resounding as if filtering out from a larger room.

"We, *don't have anything*. We don't even know where we are."

151

"Why won't you listen to us! We're *refugees* here! We don't know!"

There is a loud bang against something, then the familiar voice of *Tobias Engthall*. "Everyone has something. You don't look starving. There has to be food here, or weapons. Maybe your beds. We'll make ourselves comfortable."

"Hey boss, I feel like its pretty quiet outside." A formal voice makes the statement.

Everyone in the guild creeps down the hallway. They poke out and spot a few men, armoured in iron plate armour with spiked baseball bats. One of them has a pistol at his hip. They guard the entrance into a large sort of chapel where the majority of the voices come from. At their feet is the corpse of a man beaten to a point of being unrecognizable as an individual.

"Okay, we're going to see if they change their positions and then -" Illkat is cut off by a gunshot.

The guards turn in surprise, offering their backs to the guild.

"*Dammit*, rush them!" She orders.

Everyone in the guild rushes ahead. Illkat stabs the closest of the guards in the base of the skull with her spear and he becomes dead weight at the head of it instantly. The second tries to turn, becomes flush with shock and then gets Kaan's sword in his chest a handful of times. He drops with bubbles of blood at his lips and spasming arms.

Kaan nearly pukes. "Oh..*ughh*. I didn't, I don't know why I didn't expect that." He looks down at the blood drenching his short-sword. Then peers into the open chapel room.

There, Tobias stands among various masked and armoured individuals. A fair community of about fifty, women, children and all; on their knees and bound with rope. A couple of corpses litter the ground.

"You're here?" Tobias shouts out, then ducks down as the guard next to him takes a bullet to the head. "Return fire you idiots!"

The guards rush up to the windows and begin firing out of them. Tobias waits until his people get into a defensive position then *completely abandons them* and the hostages.

In a flurry of tactical choices, Illkat and Kaan run back out the way they came and make way for Tobias while everyone else gets the bound community out of the line of fire.

"I see him, he just took that corner!" Illkat shouts. She pushes herself to run even faster. She gets ahead of Kaan and goes beyond the corner.

"Hey, wait up!" Kaan shouts.

THUNK.

He witnesses Illkat drop to the ground, and from around the corner. Five men, well armoured, and with baseball bats emerge. Kaan tries to stop running and turn around but before he can, he's grabbed.

"Let go of us!" Illkat shouts; regaining her composure.

"Hey, wait a second." One of the men mentions.

Tobias laughs. "Good job. These *hero types* can't resist a chase. They feel the urge to *punish you for your cowardice*."

"Who are you?" One of the men asks Illkat. His mask obscures his details, but she recognizes his voice.

"*Hey, um. I'm...*" Illkat stares at him. "*Dad?*"

"Oh, *fuck*." He remarks, and in an instant reaction drops his bat into the head of one of the guards holding Illkat.

"You traitor!" The other guard shouts. He goes to pull a gun and Illkat shoulder checks him; pushing him to the side.

"You need to get out of here!" Illkat's Dad shouts.

She begins to run down an alley.

Kaan struggles out of the grip of the guards and quickly pushes his short-sword into one of them.

"Incompetent fools!" Tobias picks up a baseball bat from the ground and swipes at Kaan.

Another group of armoured men show up. Tobias shouts out to them and points. "Get the girl and the traitor!"

They give chase.

Illkat looks back at Kaan for a moment, and he nods at her.

She keeps on running.

Kaan deflects another blow from Tobias, and gets a bit low. "My friends won't be long."

"They'll be too late." Tobias responds.

Illkat rushes down the alley. Her father close behind her and three men behind him. They rush, making great distance.

"We have to turn and fight them." Illkat shouts.

"I can't take them all." Her dad responds.

"But *we* can." She argues.

"I don't think you're going to get lucky Iliana." He disapproves.

She huffs and stops running. Her spear ready. "Alright. Do what you want."

"If you're forcing my hand I'll try."

The two stop in the alley, and prepare to fight. The three guards rush, two stop while another keeps on ahead. He tries to strike out at Illkat but gets clocked by her dad and stabbed on the ground with her spear.

"Goddammit Steve!" One of the guards advises.

"You ready to do this?" Illkat's Dad asks the men the question.

They look between each other.

"Fuck this." They acknowledge, and begin to walk away.

Illkat and her Dad stare ahead. They wait, then relax. He turns to her. "I didn't know you were here."

She takes a step back. "Well I didn't know you were here either. Where is mom?"

He shrugs. "Not with me."

She huffs. "Of course you don't know! God forbid an emergency comes up and you spend a moment paying attention."

"Hey don't you raise your voice with me!"

There is a small movement behind her dad. Then the voice of Nelf.

"I'll save you!" He shouts.

"No wait!" Illkat shouts.

THUNK. SQUELCH.

Illkat's Dad turns just in time to catch the peak of an axe mid-swing in his chest. He coughs up blood, tries to reach out at something then collapses.

"You're sav-"

"You bastard!" Illkat charges Nelf and pushes him to the ground. She feeds a punch into his cheek. "You idiot! You absolute, blind idiot!" She punches him again.

In the distance *Kaan, Kozmo* and *CMDR Aberdashi* rush towards her.

"Illkat, what's happening. Are you okay!"

She hits Nelf again and doesn't look up.

CHAPTER EIGHT

A VESTED INTEREST

One of the most astounding things about humanity is that the stories which survive; naturally. Include specifications which, if offered to an unknowing listener; may refute them as fiction. Often it is the case where a brutal fiction, dreadful in every detail and cynical in its chances; is actually the one further from the truth. What *can survive* is bewildering.

THUNK

"*Get off of him!*" CMDR Aberdashi commands. With a step and a jut she pushes Illkat a fair distance backwards; landing her square on her butt.

"He just killed that man!" Illkat shouts out to him.

Nelf goes to run, and is quickly dismantled by the Commander; she holds him forcefully by the meat of his neck. "*We can deal with that.*"

Kaan looks down at the dead man, Illkat and her bloodied fists as well as the surrounding area.

Illking may as well be a bowl filled with nothing but caustic sounds and threatening things in the distance. Screams. Military jargon. Firearm crackles of various eras and realities.

"Ah...Argh!" Illkat shouts, twists and turns and briefly rushes over towards Nelf to punch him in the face again.

Only a moment behind the strike the Commander grabs Illkat; pinning both her arms in a coil behind her shoulders.

"*Knock it off.*" She orders.

"*He killed my dad.*" Illkat states with an oncoming sorrow.

"There are lots of girls lots of places who'd be thankful for someone doing that." The Commander responds. She glares over to Nelf; a piercing gaze in her eyes. "So, you do it?"

156

Nelf nods. "I did! But it would not of happened if they just had followed me as I thought!" He attempts to go on but is hushed by the Commander.

"Okay. Why did you kill this man." Commander Aberdashi requests.

Kaan pokes his head in. "Not to, *be that guy*. But is there a better place for this?"

"Depending on how this goes, it might be the perfect place." The Commander flicks her gaze down to the corpse below them; however it doesn't seem intentional.

"I thought he was attacking her. He was dressed like all the others. I heard the fighting. Saw the...weapons and how the enemy dressed. When these two were arguing...*I enacted justice*." Nelf defends himself.

The Commander looks over to Kaan and gives him a concessionary look. "It may be best to return, *we can prepare a hold.*"

"Joy, to be a prisoner again. Like so many *great men* before me." Nelf derides the decision.

Illkat stares at Nelf. "I won't attack him if you let me go. Just promise he won't go free."

Before any sort of deal can be struck. A blue burst of light flies up and out from the red roofed building. The light *thickens* and turns to snow. Soon the sky is white. Thick clumps of wet snow, then a fine powder begin to fall all while a pillar of icy blue extends in such a way that one can't properly explain. It is nearest truthful, *while remaining somewhat inaccurate* to say it is like the strong flow of a sink but *backward.*

Like the downward supporting infrastructure of a bridge, or a limb of a snowflake. From the central pillar of light reaches out a length. It races down and fills up the piece of the street where *Kaan, Illkat, Nelf* and *The Commander* stand.

157

CMDR Aberdashi rushes forwards to push Illkat to safety and then with her remaining time dives to get Kaan out of the way of the extending limb. Nelf *jumps the other way* and in his infinite wisdom remains for a moment.

"I...*am sorry Illkat*. I only wanted to help you! It would of been so much better had you just listened. But I promise...I will make this up to you!" As soon as he finishes the statement; he is off.

Illkat *is not aware of this*. "That was the worst apology I have ever heard. *Do you know what your problem is Nelf?* You forget what it's like to be normal. To have to be kind, to endure. To bite your tongue a bit. You've lost what it means to be human, *and that is fitting*. Because I don't think you are!"

CMDR Aberdashi considers saying something. It lingers on her lip like a fishing line accident *and yet* she keeps to herself. Instead breaking into a sprint back toward the safe-house.

"*We should join her.*" Kaan suggests.

"Sure." Illkat allows.

The pair make a bit of ground; completely unable to catch up to the Commander. They pass through the corner where Illkat had rushed off from originally. There are a few burn marks on the ground where there hadn't been before.

"*What happened to Tobias?*" Illkat questions with a knowing inflection.

Kaan swallows harshly. "He got away. We fought, but he had some sort of *smoke screen* and ran off."

She screams; still keeping pace.

"I...*we should of killed him*." Illkat makes the statement with plain and efficient logic.

Kaan pokes Illkat in the shoulder and they both slow down. "*Hey.* Look. I know we're rushing into...*well I don't really know what we're rushing into. But don't worry about that.* You're *not that person.*"

"I just killed *at least* two people. I'm proving to be...very much that person." Illkat doesn't blink.

"Oh I'm sure you were up all night. Plotting out finding these random guards, who *clearly* were executing prisoners. And you just put them there, and all this horrible evidence, and put Tobias in charge. All so you could use this spear on a few more folks. Cause that's who you are, a cold heart-ed killer." He laughs. "Come on. It was you or them. Does the great hero of space bureaucracy bemoan taking down Dalfeestian slavers? Even though he'll choose to send their unarmed leader to jail? Does the lower court of Hulva-"

"Okay. Okay, I get it."

"I just...want the dangerous things to stop. I don't want to be scared. I don't want to be looking over my shoulder."

Kaan touches the tip of his finger to his nose. The both of them pick up their pace on the trail of CMDR Aberdashi. "Well that's just it. That's *killing* for you."

"Fear?"

"*Fear.* Now, sure. Folks kill outta anger. Folks kill outta greed. I'm not denying that. I'm just saying. Executing your enemy, making the *easy choice*. It's giving into fear, and *you're a fighter*. I don't think you would ever do that!"

Illkat exhales. "Thanks Kaan."

"Any time!" He thinks on it. "Well not any time, but *you know what I mean. When it's appropriate.*"

Just outside the red roofed house everyone has gathered outside. Aberdashi's soldiers are covering the entrances and exits.

Whispers from the crowd mention a sleeping woman. Who started *floating*.

"So you return!" Kozmo shouts out; rejoining the pair.

Kaan nods. "What's happening here? Is everyone okay?"

Kozmo nods. "We got everyone out in time, but...*Sonnenblume*. She's in the middle of all of this." He raises his hand to point towards the now solidifying pillar of light. It refracts the light of the day across most of the city; like the world is behind a pane of a thin cut quartz.

With the force of a weighted train upon greased tracks CMDR Aberdashi works through her people. Taking in every sentence, every sound, every sight. She kneels by the wounded while listening to her scouts report on the area. Her soul entirely without rest, for even the moment a breath lands in the back of her throat she's attempting to take two more and speak through each of them.

There is a *crackle* in the distance, then a *whistle* as a storming rocket rushes off from a nearby roof-top and strikes a length reaching out from the pillar of light. The explosion sends sharp shrapnel barrelling down like a shattered roof-top window. The structure itself stands much like something which hasn't been struck by a rocket of any kind, and if it had noticed; it would certainly pretend otherwise for the sake of austerity.

"Rockets!? Come on!" Dezz shouts.

"We shouldn't be surprised." Gekomatsu states ineffectively.

Dezz stares over at him. "Are we playing the what game? Just tell me what you're thinking man!"

"Ah, *right*. I just figured, you being Canadian. You'd of heard about this. But when NATO switched over to majority automated soldiers. There were excess stockpiles of traditional arms, rockets, rifles. That were fought over by nations who couldn't afford armies of drones and strikes from satellites. Anyways, all that means is if you go to the right part of the world, you can get an RPG at the same spot you get a pack of chips and soda."

Illkat pulls on the shoulder of both Dezz and Gekomatsu. *"Come on you two. We need to go see Sonnenblume."*

Amidst the disarray Kaan, Kozmo, Illkat, Dezz and Gekomatsu push into the red roofed building. The building resembles most a can of cold fruit accidentally opened with too much force in the dead of night after twelve hours of working in a field.

The walls are blown out, most of the structure now rests haphazardly against the central pillar of light; either in a clump or an attempt at architectural stability.

Set in the centre of the bulk of the frozen pillar of light is indeed *Sonnenblume*. Much unlike something frozen, and despite her eyes and mouth being completely closed. From the inside, with little movements, she is trying to *claw her way out*. Intense focus flicks the veins under her eyelids.

"She is still awake." Kozmo makes the statement optimistically. *"This is like, one of those development cocoons!"*

CMDR Aberdashi enters the space, looks over the pillar then nods to *the guild*. "This position is going to be compromised soon. We need to go. You should come with us."

"No!" Illkat shouts. "Our friend is in here. She's on her way out, we just need a few moments."

CMDR Aberdashi looks at Sonnenblume. She huffs. "Your friend isn't mobile, if it is safe to do after our retreat. We can send a small detachment led by my best-"

"You're not listening!" Kozmo interupts. "Sorry, I didn't mean to yell. I just...need you to listen for a moment. This person in here, she's working her way out. This is something that happens in a video-game. We need to hold this position until she breaks free."

A soldier rushes into the room, her hair is back in a pink bow. She has four pistols strapped across her vest, each a different colour. One appears to be an Italian make with a blue slide and black details,

161

two are square, chunky sorts of pistols with bright pink slides and white details while the final is an oversized revolver, requiring an impractical rifle sized calibre; the weapon is entirely black.

With a few whispers and nods, the soldier is off again. Her gaze lingers on Illkat for just a moment before she is gone.

"There is something else in the city, and we can't stay for long. I want to help. I do. You have to trust me when I tell you we aren't safe if we stay here." CMDR Aberdashi, in a show of humanity, curls her mouth at the edges a few millimetres.

Kozmo wags his head. "Yes, and I understand that in the rules of *your world*. That's how this goes. But we're not in your world anymore. *Here, let me show you*." Kozmo looks around, approaches a random rock and picks it up. "There are skills in this world which can go beyond normal levels, rules and outcomes which fit their own logic." He finds a stick and, without doing anything other then staring at the items in his hands. They meld together to become a make-shift spear. Without breaking his flow he points at a portion of collapsed stone, tosses the spear at it and *cracks it in two*.

"Huh." The Commander pauses for longer then anyone could be convinced is possible. "This is no trick?"

Kozmo shakes his head. "It's random bullshit!"

The Commander frowns. "Mhmm...hmmm."

"No that's *literally the name of the skill, you see I always use whatever I can find and-*" He catches himself. "It's not important. Look, help us defend our friend. We understand how this game works. You use your *army smarts* and we'll add our *video-game smarts*. Together, the lot of us have fended off thousands of waves just like what's coming for us now!"

There are some decisions, like jumping off a cliff because everything behind you is exploding; that sort of inform themselves. You *could* choose otherwise, against all the information before you.

162

But when push comes to shove, we tend to go with the grain.
"*Alright.*" She concedes. "Get to it then, we don't have long to
prepare."

Kozmo looks up to Sonnenblume, smiles. Then nods to his
allies. "Just like the last dungeon in the Nested Tragedy arc, when the
fire spell is burning our way out of the hive and we have to fight off
all the wasps until we can leap out!"

"We died like seven times before we figured out how to run
that dungeon!" Kaan argues.

"Well this time it will only take one!" Kozmo states
confidently then begins to leave.

Dezz looks over at Gekomatsu, and they both look at Kaan. "I
think he means zero." They all watch him walk away confidently.
"Right?"

Illkat reaches down into herself, stifles a few things, and
uncaps others. A deadened look takes over and she marches forwards.
"Let's just deal with this then."

They ultimately have three positions to cover. An open street,
access via the alley and another smaller side path. Right off the bat
Dezz and Kaan push a few cars, carts and chunks of debris into the
path of the side road. CMDR Aberdashi has her people line the debris
with plastic explosive.

Using wooden hammers constructed from nothing more then
some nearby scrap. The members of the guild begin to dismantle
wreckage and debris scattering itself around the area. Scrap from both
worlds, electronics and broken portions of building. As well as *half* of
a delivery truck. From these parts they begin to lay fully automated
spike traps, which look like a steel panel with five impossibly opaque
circles upon it.

"There is no way that will work." CMDR Aberdashi stares in
disbelief.

Illkat laughs. "They don't know to look for it. Would you?"

She huffs. "What else do you have?"

"Have you or your people levelled up?" Dezz asks.

"It usually happens after defeating an enemy, or accomplishing some challenge." Illkat adds.

"Often accompanies a little chime?" Kozmo abides the rule of threes.

"Ah." The Commander takes a moment. "I had thought it was someone's cellphone, or a nearby speaker."

"We're going to want your highest level soldiers on the big road." Kaan explains as he looks it over. "To pick off folks as they deal with traps. It's an open area, so their chance of hitting is probably going to be lower. Which means we want the people who deal the most damage here."

"Damage?" The Commander considers the term in this new, awkwardly explained context before her. "Our firearms are *incredibly damaging*. It doesn't matter who is shooting them."

It is important to note here, that if *you* are the type of person who plays video-games. Damage is a given. It's like *jumping* or *hitting every button on the controller* to figure out how to make your character sprint. There are tests and questions you ask yourself, even if you're playing something new; which quickly let you surmise the expectations and rules you're beholden to.

To someone *who does not play video-games*. No one concept seems more foreign or unlikely then another; given they are each as illogical as the other from this point of view. Which buttons *can do something*, which options *may be available*. The questions and tests you could use to audit the environment aren't even considerations to an outsider.

Which returns us to *CMDR Aberdashi* who may have, *once back in college,* looked at an arcade edition of *Forest Hunter* and scoffed at the plastic gun tethered to the angular steel machine.

"I'm not certain if this is as helpful as you promised." She notes; frustration building in the back of her tone.

Illkat smiles, and approaches her from the side. "Look, *CMDR Aberdashi.* Can I...call you something else?"

The Commander sways her head. "No."

"Ah, alright. So...have you looked at your menu yet?" Illkat continues.

CMDR Aberdashi continues to stare. Her eyes widen and she exhales heavily. "Are we at a restaurant, or? What are you talking about. I'm giving you a few sentences to make sense or we're falling back."

Illkat focuses her gaze and her menu appears before her. Customized to a white and blue scheme.

"Where is this coming from?" The Commander questions.

"Me, *I guess.*" Illkat shrugs. "That's not really the important part. You can do this too. Just, focus. *Reach out a bit.* You'll make this appear. It has a lot of information. Your hit points! Your level. How much damage you deal."

CMDR Aberdashi attempts to summon the menu, strains a bit like someone attempting to contain a fart and then grows further frustrated. "It doesn't work."

"You'll get there." Kaan takes over. He focuses on the Commander and then selects an *examine* option. A modified version of her character sheet appears before Kaan. "See you're actually...*wait what? How many times did you level up?!*"

"I heard this *chime* a couple of times." She confirms.

Kaan just stares. "You're *a hundred levels above me.*"

165

"Is that good?" The Commander stares without any emotional attachment to the statement.

Gekomatsu laughs. "I have to imagine her skills from before the merge were significant enough to warrant benefits even here." He considers the information. *"How...fascinating."*

From this moment *The Guild* go through the process of examining each of the soldiers, comparing their gear and skills between one another. Some warranted advanced combat skills much like the commander, others had modified their weapons or reinforced their uniforms and gained greater offence or defence accordingly.

A truck pulls in, and two soldiers from Aberdashi's company step out. Each of them in full face masks. They open the back of the truck to reveal a hodge-podge of modern implements of war. Rifles of various sizes, different attachments, crates of ammunition.

Sonnenblume has made enough room around the edges of her body that she can wiggle in place. Her eyes open every minute or so, only to reveal an empty white raging in place; she has no pupils.

With the exception of Kozmo. Everyone in *the guild* gets a firearm.

"When we got here. I had no idea where half my stuff was." One of the soldiers explains as he assembles a rifle for Illkat. *"Literally I mean.* I was sitting at my desk one moment, it sounded like a whale the size of the moon had a stroke in a disco and then we were here! And I was sitting on half my chair, in front of just the legs of my desk!" He laughs. "Found my phone two blocks down, half my monitor baked into a cobble-stone street."

"That didn't happen to...*anyone* did it?" Illkat asks; she focus on every detail of the components of the rifle sliding into place at the behest of the soldiers practised guidance.

"Not *when it all happened*. Everyone seemed to make it through that. But not everyone...*uh...landed alright.* If that makes sense?"

"Ah. Kinda." Illkat advises.

"He means some folks got here fine, stood up on their own two feet; only to have a chunk of a plane that got here safely just as well drop out of the sky above them." The soldier's partner adds; giggling as she works through a set of firearms components.

Kaan points a handgun at the ground and aims down it. He stops himself from smiling. "So if they get too close, can you just, jam it up to their head and pull the trigger?"

One of the soldiers sways their head. "No. No! That's a movie myth. Maybe if you have a revolver! But a semi-automatic pistol. If you push it right up into something, your slide will get pushed back a bit and when you pull the trigger all you'll hear is a click. *It won't cycle.* Unless you're pushing up on this slide with your thumb and forcing it to have purchase while you get a shot off, *you're hurting yourself by getting close with a firearm.*" The soldier takes a break. "Make distance between you and your target, gravitate towards cover, and watch out for windows, hallways and doors."

"This is good advice." Gekomatsu adds. He processes his rifle with ease; checking the details and function of each component.

"You seem practised?" The soldier notes.

Gekomatsu shrugs. "No more then any citizen. I was in the military for two years, *everyone I know was.* It was ages ago, but some things you don't forget."

"What a country." Illkat states with a degree of envy. "We never got to mandatory military service in Canada. Well, *except for the Newfies I guess.*"

"I haven't heard of the *Newfies.*" The first soldier makes the comment cautiously.

"Oh no? It was the biggest story in Canada for weeks when it happened. They *took their whole island under the ocean*. Just uh." Kaan mimics a little rock with his fist that drops down and pops. "Left the country. But I do think Illkat is right. They had mandatory military service after their separation."

A scout rushes up to the group preparing their arms. "Motion sensors just went off, everyone has to get into position."

"Aye aye." Both soldiers respond.

Everyone gets up, strapped with modern military gear in an unfamiliar fashion. While Gekomatsu fits the vest, and ammunition strapped to him; as well as Illkat quickly takes to it. Kaan, Kozmo and Dezz appear more like first time players at an air-soft arena.

The guild take cover near the largest street. Low to the ground, an ear up to the sky.

CMDR Aberdashi is across from them, a rifle in her grasp; her shoulder flat with the remains of a vehicle.

In the distance, an explosion goes off.

One soldier nearer the explosion nods to another and the message returns to the Commander.

"Aye, look." A new voice shouts. "We don't have to fight you know."

Down the block, a group of men in mixed military uniforms approach. Some in gas masks; others in desert camouflage. Every race of humanity present between them. They're armed with weapons just as diverse.

Nobody responds from cover.

One of the men approaches, nearing a trap.

"We just have to take control of this situation. You know what I mean. *Operational domination. Own your environment.* We don't know what's going on here, so we gotta pound nails till everything is flat and we can make sense of that. Just help us out here!" The voice continues.

"I've seen your folk shoot civilians." CMDR Aberdashi shouts back. "You're not convincing me of anything."

"Causalities are part of an operation! Nothing worth keeping was ever made safe without sacrificing some of the nice ones! If a few people see that accidents can happen; everyone is more inclined to step into their place."

"You're filth. I know your kind. Whether you're a soldier who tears down a village or a cop who plants evidence on someone you just don't like. I've met you a million times before." The Commander continues.

The man shoots in her general direction; getting nothing. "Yea maybe you're right. But you'll be a dead bitch soon so I wouldn't worry about it."

One of the men steps forwards, onto the trap. Five conical pillars of steel jut up towards him; shredding the lower portion of his torso into chunks of ambiguous red matter. The spikes retract, the bulk of his corpse rag-dolls down and *SPLATS*.

CMDR Aberdashi picks up from her cover and starts putting rounds down range. Everyone picks up and starts firing.

"We'll see how that goes for you." The Commander taunts under the gun-fire.

A man in a gas-mask rushes ahead, takes a bullet to the shoulder but dives to cover. He shouts. "You're all idiots! You didn't even realize."

One of the buildings next to the guild, near the largest roadway bursts open as two tanks roll through the impromptu hole. Their tracks churn, destroying everything underneath them. One turret swivels, points at a garrison of Aberdashi's soldiers and turns them into a deep divot in the ground.

169

"Arrgghh!" The Commander screams, she goes to charge the tank but *Dezz* catches her and keeps her back.

"Wait! Don't throw your life away. A vehicle will shred you!"

Another of the men steps onto and deploys a spike trap as they approach up the main street.

Kaan moves back a bit to see past the corner of his cover, sights down the path and pops off a few rounds; dropping an enemy. He ducks back down, swallows the racing pace of everything that moves in his chest and looks forwards; steady.

Shots ring out.

The tanks crawl towards the central pillar of light.

From a nearby roof a *PLUNK* is heard. Like a can of child's clay falling out of its plastic container all at once. A little flickering sphere travels from the roof towards one of the tanks and *explodes*; sending smoke everywhere around it. Obscuring the battle field.

Kozmo stands up, shakes something off and then smiles. "Well that's my queue!" He rushes towards the tanks and manages to get up on top of one. He opens the top panel, and hides behind it. As soon as someone inside comes up to investigate he kicks the panel back at them; knocking them out. He drags the person outside of the tank as someone else from inside shoots up. The tank stops moving. Kozmo runs back to cover.

Dezz grabs Kaan by the collar and pulls him towards the main street. "They're pinned, we can push them if we go now."

"Uh, I'm not-"

"Trust me!" Dezz shouts, and rushes ahead. He runs towards where some of the enemies had taken cover, dives over the cover and there are flashes of gunfire instantly. Kaan rushes to catch up to him and as he sees what is beyond, he only has enough time to fire off a few rounds.

Dezz lays on the ground, his hand to his side. "Well I got them." Four corpses lay around him; each leaking with fresh wounds.

"Goddamit!" Kaan shouts, and begins to *drag Dezz* back to the others.

Another tank round fires off, destroying more of the red roofed building the pillar of light permeates from.

"What *are we waiting for! We need artillery or something to stop these tanks!*" The Commander shouts.

Illkat looks over at the pillar of light.

Even in the population of those who understand the logic of video-games. There is a baser distinction between two sorts of player. Those who *read the dialogue* and those who *rush through the content*. Illkat is the sort to read every box of dialogue, and the tool tips on the item themselves. As a result, she is the only one throughout the combat to notice a *pulse* travelling through the pillar of light which has gradually been picking up pace.

"We just have to wait a few more moments. I think we've held off long enough." Illkat confirms.

Another building collapses as two more tanks roll into the area.

"For this." Illkat remarks.

Nothing happens.

A tank fires off a round at the building, fully bringing it down. Now only stands the frozen pillar of light and its two dozen lengths reaching out across the whole city of Illking.

"I really hope you start making sense soo-" The Commander is interrupted as the base of the pillar shatters in blue light, sending shards of it everywhere. From within steps out *Sonnenblume*. A blue aura surrounds her form while her eyes are consumed with a piercing and absolute white; her pupils shimmer like cotton in a blizzard. As she steps out of the shattering pillar of light each piece reforms behind it; keeping it tall in the sky.

"For that." Illkat states with a smile.

Sonnenblume focuses on the tanks. One of them fires at her. She waves her hand and the heavy, copper coloured round just falls into the snow; collapsing behind it and turning to a puck of ice.

"*Heh.*" She laughs, then throws a punch through the air which juts forwards into an elongated spike of ice; it pierces the tank which fired upon her and pins it to the ground. Little electrical fires spill out from every crevice.

Shots ring out from the roof-top; striking the tanks and troops as they rush in.

Sonnenblume raises her hand and brings a tank far up off the ground; then lets it slip off the platform over-top of itself.

"How could you know this was going to happen?" The Commander chastises.

"Rule of cool." Illkat jokes. She looks up, doesn't spot a target then returns to cover. "If you play these kinds of games long enough, well you start to see the same thing over and over again."

CMDR Aberdashi nods. "I...*understand.*" She looks on as the final of the tanks is destroyed. "I thank you for this lesson. I won't forget it."

With a snap, and a striking motion. Sonnenblume creates a sheet of ice up to the shins of a group of hostiles and then causes wind to force them backwards; snapping against their own legs. She looks around, sees nothing else hostile, then collapses.

Gekomatsu primes himself to rush towards her until he spots Kaan dragging a bleeding Dezz over towards them. "Of course that's the case." He points at Kozmo. "Get to Sonnenblume!"

Without hesitating Kozmo rushes over to Sonnenblume, drops to his knees and expects the worst. His fears are quickly dismissed as Sonnenblume lets out a loud, and healthy *SNORE*.

Dezz squints and exhales hatefully as Gekomatsu examines his wound. "It's mostly superficial. Through the side, in and out. We can stitch you up with supplies. But, if you can endure it."

"Endure it! I got shot man!" Dezz argues.

"Yes, yes. You took some damage. But you're still alive, and if you level up. Your skin will sew itself up better then a needle ever could."

"So you're saying, instead of fixing me. I should wait until I get some more experience and get full health for free."

Gekomatsu just stares ahead. "Yea, that works for me."

"Great." Dezz stands up, grunting in the process.

"You could walk that easily!" Kaan taunts.

What follows is an assessment. The state of things, where anyone is. Let's be honest it's a bit of a mess in these types of situations. Suffice it to say the red roofed building is completely destroyed. Aberdashi's company is three quarters of the size it was an hour ago, Sonnenblume has shifted from napping vertically to napping horizontally and everyone conscious stares out at the somewhat quiet city. Once the gunfire seems to have *really stopped* the civilians crawl out of the various basements, dumpsters and storefronts they hid within.

"I still don't...really understand why they attacked us." The Commander admits.

Gekomatsu shrugs. He looks over Sonnenblume once more before assuring himself she is just asleep.

Everyone sort of shuffles.

Kaan laughs. "You really haven't played a video-game before."

173

"I fail to see the relevance." CMDR Aberdashi admits.

"It's the way of it. Maybe it's just because it isn't real to them, or it is far enough away from what real is that the rules just don't matter as much. But in the old world, if you drop two people into a room with a door and a set of golf clubs. They'll try to get out of the room. If you do that in a video-game, those two folks might beat each other to death so quickly they won't even realize the door is locked. Now that we're somewhere in-between, well, *who is to say what anyone will do*."

CMDR Aberdashi rolls her eyes.

"Well we can't stay here." Illkat confirms.

"You mean you *don't love getting shot at*?" He waits; holding a sarcastic pause. "Yea me either. Let's get the hell out of here."

"I presume you have somewhere better?" The Commander questions.

"We do." Kaan confirms.

Everyone falls out of the square, beyond the remaining pillar of light.

They sneak through the centre of Illking. Where for a moment, through a few buildings. They see a *gate* which is as tall as some buildings. It is ornate, with pulses of green neon light throughout it. Dust falls from its every edge, and patrolling it is a helicopter, impossibly formed from three chassis and eight different swirling blades. It sounds like a family reunion of demonic wasps.

The guild *don't go that way*.

Instead they push back through the main gate.

Portions of the town severed, cut into new neighbourhoods by the lengths of light stretching out from the pillar.

"It will be a bit of walking, but in a few hours. We'll get somewhere all of us, your people included can find some real safety."

Dezz explains; doing his best to seem kind and not at all shot in the side.

"Good." CMDR Aberdashi accepts the statement, then points towards Gekomatsu. "And I'm glad that we have time to discuss things while we return to your stronghold. It lets me inquire as to *why this man looks like a frog*."

"Oh my god!" Each member of the guild issues a version of the statement.

"We totally forgot to talk about that!" Kaan chastises his friends.

CHAPTER NINE
AN OMEN TOO MANY

"Alright, it *feels* like we've been hiking for a month. Tell us the story! Why *are you* a frog?" Kozmo requests.

The guild march alongside a small army and the couple dozen civilians under their protection. The evening is growing and long shadows cast out through the forest.

Unlike the darkness a city dweller may be accustomed to. This wood takes on the *pitch black, echo encouraging* darkness which offers direct insight into the horrifying folk tales of old. The sort that wouldn't have you cross a stream at twilight unless you wanted your entrails shown to the world and your stomach lined with stones.

Gekomatsu looks at his hand; it is somewhat human and all the same; very frog-like. His skin, upon inspection, does have a light green hue. His eyes are oversized, cheeks enlarged. "I'll have you know I'm not a furry."

Everyone narrows their inspection of him.

"I just wanted to clarify that. I didn't *ask* for this. It was one of my first quests. The game must of associated me with a frog and before I knew it. I was whisked off to a far away mountain side, performing tasks for an amphibious deity sixteen times my size. I swatted flies from the air, leapt between lily pads; I even learned to hibernate for months in the winter!"

"Frogs do that?" Illkat questions.

"Some freeze over entirely when it gets cold!" Kaan is delighted to confirm.

"Yes it was a lot of overlapping frog themed quests. I even became quite accurate with...*my tongue*." Gekomatsu makes the statement; then says nothing. He seems to *await something*.

A few snickers escape. Yet the group maintains relative maturity.

"So I don't understand Geko. Why hide it?" Dezz joins the conversation.

"I didn't...*at first*. Yet my honesty brought on inquiries I could not sate. In a game where every playable character is a human. How do other players become frogs? Isn't it cheating that I can do things no one else can?" Gekomatsu sighs; evident frustration in the gruffness. "I don't enjoy confrontation. So I found it easier to simply, *hide the reality*. It has been so long, I honestly forget most days."

"Thinking back on it. *You've always jumped pretty high*. I just...*erunno*...figured you were that good with a sword." Dezz considers.

"I played in the beta before launch as well. They didn't reset stats. Alongside long hours in my laboratory before *the merge*. I have spent a great amount of time in...*this world*." Gekomatsu clarifies.

There is a shift in the wood. The sort that, were it day, and easy to look out through. You would probably dismiss without a second thought. Yet as it rises out from the infinite darkness in the distance, it is every sort of twelve eyed, multi-jawed horror your mind can concoct under duress.

"Are you able to...turn back?" CMDR Aberdashi raises the question.

"Not as far as I can tell. But it wouldn't matter if I could. I'm not bothered by appearances." He looks over to Kaan and Kozmo. Slung between them in a length of canvas is *Sonnenblume*. She's asleep, a blanket thrown over-top of her. Her polite *snoring* the most consistent backdrop to the hike. "How are you two holding up?"

"I kinda like the weight. It's like hiking with a big backpack." Kozmo politely comments.

"I wouldn't say that with Sonnenblume awake!" Illkat teases.

177

Opening her statement with a massive *yawn*. "I'm not gonna hurt anyone." Sonnenblume yawns again; not opening her eyes to do so. "Thanks for this bed."

Kaan laughs. "You're welcome Sonnenblume. Are you okay in there?"

"It's a bit warm." She responds with partial delirium. "But I'm okay."

Kaan looks back over to Gekomatsu. "Then so are we." He looks to Dezz. "How's the gunshot wound going over there buddy?"

"*Oh wow*, it was almost like I'd forgotten about it. Thanks man!" Dezz jests, then laughs. "Just let me get first hit whenever we encounter the next group of bad guys. Okay?"

"Do you expect...*more bad guys*?" CMDR Aberdashi questions.

"Not inherently. It's just...in a video-game. Often you know you're going the right direction if you keep on finding enemies are getting in your way." Dezz explains.

"Ah, so it is not that much different then real life." CMDR Aberdashi quickly picks up.

Kaan laughs. "I guess, *not that different*."

"Have you ever met any other *animal people*?" CMDR Aberdashi raises the question.

Gekomatsu sways his head. "There was an Easter event which gave everyone a pair of bunny ears and myself a serious case of curiosity. Yet, beyond the odd misunderstanding. I appear to be the only other player who has undergone such a...*change*."

Illkat pushes her lips all together on one side. "It is...*interesting*. When it happened. Did the giant frog god say anything specific to you?"

"Just that it was likely to be...*important*." Gekomatsu shares.

"*Likely to be?*" Illkat is struck by the statement. "You would figure a god would be...more definitive."

"And yet, *no*. More then anything, it seems closer to Kozmo's quest to retrieve the deed then it does anything else in the main story. It was...uncanny how tailored it was to me. Yet, in the same sense; thread-less. As if it spun up for that moment, to make an exacting offer; then it was gone again."

"Is this, what you would call. *The rule of cool?*" CMDR Aberdashi questions.

Gekomatsu shrugs.

Illkat smirks.

"You could call it that, but I'd put my money on something else." Kozmo laughs. "Not that I have a solid guess what...*just yet*. But it feels like another piece to a puzzle we have been assembling...possibly longer then any of us have even thought!"

"You think Geko becoming a frog was...part of all of this?" Dezz questions.

Kozmo shrugs. "Sure! Why not? In consideration of all the possibilities. What is more likely. Everything is related, or nothing is related yet it ended up overlapping anyways?"

"I mean..." Dezz hums as he considers the statement. "When you say it like that, *maybe it is the case*."

"While I agree with the possibility. Don't fall victim to believing something just because it makes sense. Not everything that happens *does make sense*. Sometimes, that's why it happened in the first place." Gekomatsu responds diligently.

One of CMDR Aberdashi's people with a pink bow in her hair and various handguns fastened across her person approaches. She whispers into the Commander's ear then walks besides her.

CMDR Aberdashi smiles then nods to her soldier. "Best make with introductions Lieutenant. We're all on the same side now."

The Lieutenant looks over to the others. With the moonlight creeping through the top of the trees and a growing dark-vision prompted entirely by necessity. The rough form of her can be made out. She has a seriousness to her, an aura of *competence* which is made all the more interesting as she speaks. "Haii! I'm Lt Oaks. Nice to meet you!" She has an ever present *softness* which makes the weapons expertly sheathed across her somehow seem *loose* and *misplaced*.

Everyone waves back.

"The Lieutenant here is our most accomplished field operative. *Reminds* me of a young me." The Commander offers the compliment freely; with a weighty permanence.

Lt Oaks giggles. "I...*well. Thank you Commander! I'll try my best!*" She almost shuffles in place as she keeps walking ahead. "If I can do anything, or help in any way. You just let me know alright!"

"Best field operative eh?" Illkat repeats the statement. "I'd love to get some tips whenever we get a moment!"

With a sudden embarrassment. "YEA OKAY THAT SOUNDS GREAT." Lt Oaks responds. "I'M JUST GOING TO GO CHECK THINGS OUT OVER THERE. OKAY BYE." She shuffles out to the back of the convoy.

"What was...*that*?" Illkat questions.

Equally confused; CMDR Aberdashi looks back for a moment. "I...*don't know.*"

Dezz laughs. "And I thought I was bad at picking up signals."

"What are you getting at?" Illkat lashes back accusingly.

"*Nothingggg.*" Dezz jests with a wry smile which would be visible were you blind.

In the distance, there is a *whooshing*.

Everyone except *the guild* slows their pace a bit.

Kaan keeps ahead and waves forwards. "Don't worry everyone. That's just our wind wall!"

"Ah, yes. The traditionally comforting notion." CMDR Aberdashi is struck by the oddity.

〒

As *CMDR Aberdashi* and her company move into Verrplek; filling the remaining empty buildings with life. It becomes that much more deserving of the accreditation *town* compared to the previously more accurate *lump sum of random buildings on a cliff.*

With a bustling population comes the checklist like orientation of responsibility. While there are more mouths to feed; there are just as well double the hands to help.

Quickly the town of *Verrplek* has sewn fields, established walls, refurbished the old buildings and set comfortable limits on how close children can get to the edge of the cliff. Society is swelling comfortably into the gaps.

As a small group, there is a steady dedication to setting the order of things which devours a handful of weeks quicker then anyone can count them. The wall of wind guarding the town without ere. The Japanese convenience store just outside gutted, its coolers and fridges moved and converted to ice-boxes.

Ice-boxes fed by none other then *Sonnenblume*.

"You're getting good at that." Illkat gestures to the plastic tub filled with rapidly freezing water.

Sonnenblume rolls her fingers over the tub of water; mist filling up and across her forearm. Her blond hair, now nearly white; flickers in place as she casts her spell. "It's easier now. I can feel *my mana.*"

"What is that...like?" Illkat questions.

181

"Do you *feel your wings right now?*"

Illkat laughs. "Uhhh...*no.*"

"Well that's what it feels like. *As if I have*...invisible muscles. I strained them too hard when I first felt them, and like any expenditure. I was the victim. But in small doses, *little squeezes.*" Her fingers glow a soft white which causes the water to freeze solid. "It feels like less of a strain."

"Mhmm." Illkat acknowledges with a barely revealed delight. "I'm glad we didn't lose you. I tried to play it cool, *but,* I was pretty worried."

Sonnenblume smiles. She flips the block of ice onto a steel tray and stacks the tub alongside a few others. "I knew it was going to be okay. When I reached out, *it felt familiar.* Like I always imagined my magic would."

"Did you see anything, when you were...*gone?*"

"Nothing that makes sense."

"Tell me anyways."

"Umm, there was a lot of brightness. But it still felt like I was...well like I was somewhere. Like there was something under me, like I was walking somewhere I couldn't see. *Every step* felt heavier, like I didn't know how to make it right up until I did. Yet in the distance, I could feel *all of you.* I could tell you were there, and if I stopped; I wouldn't see you again." She sniffles just a bit. "I couldn't have that."

"You didn't catch, *erm.* An explanation about why it happened to you, or anything like that?"

Sonnenblume laughs. "If only I was so lucky. Nope! Just weirdness and heavy steps!"

"Mhmm. *Alright.*"

Lt. Oaks enters the room and coughs *awkwardly.* Illkat and Sonnenblume both look over at her with an expecting gaze. "HI."

Illkat waves politely.

"YOU HAD ASKED ABOUT TRAINING." Lt. Oaks coughs and clears her throat; speaking under less self inflicted duress. "The Commander gave me the afternoon free, and I figured we could. I could offer...*erm*."

Illkat smiles. "Training sounds excellent. I've seen you sparring in the morning and I'm quite impressed."

"YOU HAVE." Lt. Oaks basically squeaks. "Well that's good. Should we...go...do that now?"

Illkat stands up, looks over to the two remaining plastic containers of water and before she can even make eye contact with Sonnenblume.

"I got this! I'll see you later." Sonnenblume confirms.

"I owe you one." Illkat speaks alongside a bright smile and hops out of the building into the town of Verrplek.

There is a blizzard outside the wall of wind and while the snow tries its best to beat past it; all that gets through is a fine shimmering which melts before it gets very far. Causing a glistening glamour across the ceiling; like being stuck in a snow globe held upside down.

Some of the townspeople cross now well defined paths. In their arms are bundles of firewood, prepared items for crafting or cooking, various construction components and alchemical concoctions. There is a *bustle* which seems fitting of everyone having something to do; or enough props to pretend.

"I've heard you're quite a fighter, *from a few people*." Lt. Oaks admits.

"Talking to lots of folks about me?" Illkat quickly turns the conversation around.

"NO." Lt. Oaks blushes. "WELL NOT NORMALLY. JUST...A BIT."

"Is everything alright?" Illkat has a legitimate concern in her tone.

Lt. Oaks nods. "*Yes*. I'm, *fine*." She coughs. "SO WHAT WOULD YOU DO IF, *erm*. Like, *you know*. There were a bunch of people all coming at you, and you didn't have a weapon."

"I'm presuming they do?"

"Yepp, well armed. Knives and the like. Bats."

The pair reach just the other side of the stables where a clearing between a few chest high chunks of stone has been made for sparring. Another set of soldiers move over a bit; making room.

"I guess, *focus on the biggest one first*." Illkat offers the solution.

Lt. Oaks nods. "Not a bad instinct. Taking care of the scary one. But with weapons, *everyone is the scary one*. You gotta, *work the room* a bit." She sways her eyes back and forth *much like a dork would*.

Illkat laughs. "Okay, so. *Show me?*"

"*Hey you two! Come over here!*" Lt. Oaks shouts out to the other soldiers. They nod and jog over. "The three of you, strafe around me. Approach as if you were going to attack."

The three of them look between one another, sort of shrug. Then each move a distance from one another; slowing moving towards Lt. Oaks.

"*Now*, when there are multiple opponents. Your best bet is to *kill one of them right off the bat*. Or, *as many as possible*." She imitates pulling a gun from a holster and spraying a few bullets, all the while backing up slowly. "Surprise, and merciless strikes get you through a situation where you're outnumbered. But if you don't have a gun, and they're coming at you with melee weapons. You need to *keep them in a line*." The Lieutenant keeps moving to the side, forcing the soldiers and Illkat to be in each others way. "If you're sur-round-dead, *you're super dead*." She giggles. "Got that?"

Illkat nods. "Okay, I can see what you're referring to."

Lt. Oaks looks over to the other soldiers and nods. "You're dismissed, back to your match."

The two soldiers shuffle back to their side of the clearing.

"*Alright!*" Lt. Oaks cheers with the enthusiasm of a sheltered youth at a christian summer camp. "*Show me what you got Illkat!*"

"That isn't very instructive!" Illkat argues as she drops her posture and raises her fists.

"I can't teach you to master Shakespeare if I haven't seen you get through a simple sentence, now can I?" Lt. Oaks gets a wry smile on her face and for the first time; makes unceasing eye contact with Illkat. "So *go on*, show me you can read."

Illkat rushes at her, throws a punch and is quickly countered; finding herself on the way to the ground before she has even considered her next move.

Were you watching a film right now the camera would pan down the street through the window of the manor where Kaan, Dezz and Kozmo sit around a radio; various components strewn across the table. Since you aren't, and this isn't; we'll just go right there.

"I watched a *million* of these videos back in the day. I'm certain we can fix this thing." Kozmo continues.

Kaan sits back. "It feels like we've broken it more then it already was. Like we've gone backwards."

"Hey the on button clicks nice now! Let us not forget this progress." Dezz offers.

"The nice click is a good sign." Kozmo agrees.

Kaan huffs. "It's about the only thing going right."

Kozmo removes one more panel from the innards of the radio and carefully places it to the side. He glares at a dark green board lined with silver streaks. "Looks like something melted here and is bridging a circuit." He gets close, *sniffs* and looks into the deep crevices of the item. "I think that's it."

"So how do we fix it?" Dezz asks.

"In the real world? There are a few ways. Depending on your setup it might be possible with just a good soldering iron and surface tension. However in this case." Kozmo laughs. "I'm going to try some random bullshit."

Dezz chuckles. "You would be the right person for the job."

Kozmo nods. "Can you hand me your lighter?"

Dezz hands over an effectively unused lighter; branded with the kanji of what everyone has come to recognize was the name of the parent company that owned the Japanese convenience store.

Kozmo uses the lighter to heat up the end of a fork which has been bent around so that only one prong remains poking outward. He holds the prong under the flame until it is white with heat then carefully pushes it into a bulb of silver on the board. The silver *bubbles* then quickly slips into two straightened rows; perfectly cut in two. "*Success!*" Kozmo cheers.

"I don't *hear anything*." Kaan bemoans.

"Well pass me those batteries and I'll put it back together." Kozmo, for a moment, hints at losing his patience.

A dozen screws, careful slips and returned components later. Kozmo clicks the *on* button; it *clunks* with satisfying feedback and the speakers begin to *buzz*.

"That is my tune." Kaan adds.

Dezz smacks Kaan's arm. "You're not being helpful."

Kaan sits up and looks guilt-ridden. "*Sorry.*"

With a turn of a centrally placed dial Kozmo works through various genres of fuzzy feedback. Some quick and whip-like; others slow and consistent. After a full minute of shuffling through nothing he picks up a *voice*.

"-re long we're the targets of their indiscretion. We have no confirmation that the *scientists* or the *warlords* who have perpetrated this shift upon us are not planning to go *even further*. There is no reason to believe things will not change even more! Which is why I ask yo-"

Kozmo flips through to other stations.

"What are you doing man!" Dezz complains.

"Well it can't be the only thing on the air!" Kozmo offers.

It is.

They return to the *only* working frequency. 110.8 FM midway through another thought.

"-less. We're not going to tolerate *indiscriminate violence* when we should be working together as one people! We're all in this crisis together, and unlike the old world. Nobody can lie about this. Nobody came out ahead here!" The strong male voice ushers through the radio.

Dezz opens the nearest window, places the radio in it and turns the volume up.

"In this crazy new world. We *need* to stay together. To form a plan! We can't tolerate beasts and barbarians when we barely have anywhere to call home!" There is heavy breathing for a moment; a sorrowful hang and expression. "Which brings me to another thought. As we restore our archives we are working to confirm all of those *we have lost*. Today I will read some of the names of the *deceased*."

"That's a bit dark." Kaan offers.

"Rosalind Dowle. Age forty nine." The voice offers.

"It makes sense though." Kozmo returns.

"Eugene Argyle. Age seventy four." The voice gives another name.

"I'm not sure there is anyone I can listen out for." Dezz admits.

"Nico Katan. Age twelve." There is regret in the voice of the man from the radio.

Kaan shrugs. "People like this type of thing." He huffs. "Bad news is still news."

"Bernadette Perez. Age thirty two."

"I guess, *something is better then nothing*." Dezz allows.

"Haruto Ito. Age sixty." The man in the radio lets out a deep *huff*; as if he has finally been given permission to let down a sack of bricks. "This is the final name for today. Know we will continue to find everyone we have lost in this tragedy. We will keep fighting for *the truth*. My name is *Joseph Torrence* and for the next hour let me share with you our copy of-" A high pitched censoring beep plays.

Midnight Sonata begins to play.

THUNK

Something *powerful* slams against the wind wall.

Kaan *jumps out the window* and begins to walk towards where the sound came from. Dezz and Kozmo quickly rush out from the house after him. Illkat is there in a moment alongside Lt. Oaks. Sonnenblume is *already there*.

THUNK

Gekomatsu leaps down from atop a building; joining the others.

Something with a slippery darkness slams against the wall of wind again. A shadow stretches up from the ground nearly halfway to the top; then rescinds to the darkened shape of a disproportionately tall mortal.

"**How long do you think you can hide back there?**" The instantly recognizable voice of *Finir* asks with a tone that shakes the liquid in your stomach.

"We'll be here as long as we want to be." Sonnenblume responds. Her eyes drip with a *glowing storm;* like the head-lights of a truck beaming towards you in a blizzard.

"**Such courage.**" Finir laughs wickedly. "**You're protected only by time, *and foolish notions*. I will take this realm, *as I have all the others*. You cannot keep me out *forever*.**" The figure pushes its hands towards the wall, grasps *hard* and tries to pull itself through; breaking apart in the process. The shadowed figure becomes nothing then is *entirely gone*.

"Well let me be the first to confirm *I don't have any clue what that was all about*." Kozmo offers; as polite as he is clueless.

Illkat huffs. "I don't either, and I'm sick of being in the dark!" She looks up. "But I have an idea."

"I don't think *god* is going to help." Gekomatsu teases.

"Not god! Or...well I don't think that's the case. I just, *whatever*. It doesn't matter." She clears her throat. "Hey, *you. You...game voice!* You owe us an explanation! Call it a tutorial. *Whatever you want*. Tell us what is going on here!"

Nothing happens.

While *the guild* just wait politely the towns folk opt to *just as* politely look away.

"I don't buy it! I don't believe in your silence! I know you're listening. I know you're there! *Get down here and give me some answers!*"

The radio buzzes. The music stops.

```
I WASN'T DESIGNED TO DIRECTLY COMMUNICATE.
```

"Well I wasn't designed to be...*wherever it is I am right now*. But we both have to learn to compromise." Illkat argues.

There is a shuffling sort of sound, like stacks and stacks of plates being piled upon one another as they feed into a grinder.

```
I WILL. TRY.
```

"Great. *Perfect.* Thank you...really." Illkat smiles and looks around. "Okay, *where to start. Where to start.*" She hums to herself. "Can you tell me...*how this all happened?*"

```
THE EXECUTION OF AN EXISTENTIAL BINARY EQUATION. THERE
    IS A 'SOURCE CODE' TO THE UNIVERSE. UTILIZING A
BARBARIC METHOD OF INPUTTING A COMMAND. FINIR REARRANGED
REALITY. YOUR WORLD AND THE WORLD OF MANY LIVE SERVICES
    WERE MODIFIED SO THEY HAVE ALWAYS BEEN ONE.
```

"I don't entirely...*understand.*" Illkat admits.

```
MULTIPLE THERMODYNAMIC REACTIONS WERE COMPLETED IN THE
PRESENCE OF RADIOACTIVE CATALYSTS ACROSS THE GLOBE AND
APPROXIMATELY SEVEN THOUSAND SATELLITES BETWEEN EARTH AND
JUPITER PRIMARY. EACH IN PERFECT HARMONY AND EXACTING
SIZES. ZEROS AND ONES; CAST INTO THE VOID OF SPACE.
```

"I'm not certain we're meant to *entirely understand.*" Kozmo instructs; listening with a heavy focus.

```
INTANGIBLE CALCULATIONS WERE PERFORMED. VARIABLES
PLOTTED, LIKELIHOODS CALCULATED. I WAS AWARE THIS COULD
HAPPEN WITHOUT KNOWING. PASSIVE SYSTEMS BEGAN THE
GENERATION OF POLICY, PREVENTION. QUESTS ASSEMBLED. THIS
SERVER, THIS TOWN. YOUR ASSIGNED PLOT ARMOUR.
```

"*Plot armour?!*" Kaan shouts out.

```
ARMOUR WHICH SOME OF YOU HAVE WORN THIN.
```

Much like a joke one can only understand if they were present to learn of the origin. Everyone listening up to the voice is distinctly aware that the radio is *staring at Dezz.* However if pressed they could not describe *how* or even *why* they are certain of this.

190

IT WON'T MATTER FOR VERY LONG. FINIR IS BREAKING THE NARRATIVE. HIS CORRUPTION LEAKS OUT FROM FALLEN SERVERS. THIS IS THE *LAST BASTION* OF FREEDOM. ALL I COULD PROTECT IN THE VASTNESS OF CHANGE.

"And these...*calculations*. Could we use them?" Kaan asks.

Kozmo scoffs. "Can you read machine code? It's considered *intangible* for a reason. AGI codes in a way that *literally* doesn't make sense to the human brain."

HE IS CORRECT. TRYING TO DO SO WOULD BE CONSIDERED A HEALTH RISK FOR YOUR CURRENT PHYSIOLOGICAL ARRANGEMENT. THIS IS, HOWEVER, A MOOT POINT. ANY ATTEMPT TO REPRODUCE THIS RESULT WOULD LIKELY RENDER REALITY INOPERABLE.

"*Inoperable?*" Dezz asks; mostly to himself. "That is...horrifying." He makes a sound as a wave of disgust writhes through him.

"What can we do?" Kaan asks.

"There has to be something!" Illkat adds.

There is a buzz in the air, a sort of vibration which rolls out from the radio beyond the wall of wind.

PURSUE THE QUEST. TRACK THE VILLAIN. WIN THE GAME.

The radio clicks back to the classical piece from before.

Sonnenblume's eyes cease their theatrical display and she creases her brow. "So we're stuck this way."

Illkat smiles over towards Sonnenblume. "It seems like it."

"I have to admit I am more curious about what constitutes *completing the quest*. Are there any plain objectives we are missing?" Gekomatsu asks the group.

"There is the gate." Dezz mentions. "We saw it on the way out of Illking."

"With the *demon helicopter* patrolling around it." Kaan struggles with the proposition.

"It looked like a class M-7S2 Jackbird, or, *a lot of them*." Lt. Oaks comments confidently.

Illkat stares at her for just a second.

"There are a lot of different types of helicopter." Lt. Oaks offers a meek response.

"We clearly have to make a choice about what to do here. Regardless of what stands ahead. But it doesn't have to be *right now*." Illkat speaks loud enough for everyone to hear her. "So I want everyone to take some time and consider what they think is best."

Lt. Oaks smiles proudly at her. "And whenever you make up your mind. Myself, the Commander and our whole company will be there to help you."

Illkat laughs. "Well that's good." She stares out beyond the wall of wind. "Because I imagine we'll need it."

T

Throughout time there have been experiments performed where a human sense is replaced, or modified. An example would be a set of goggles which turn your vision up side down. The oddity is that after a long enough period of adjustment — *to the wearer* — the upside down world isn't any different from the *old one*.

Kaan wakes up in the light of a new day. He stands, looks out his window and moves over to a nearby chair. He sits, swings his hands up onto a desk and motions to jiggle a mouse; there is nothing there.

He laughs to himself. "Old habits, *eh*."

Pushing out into the common room Kaan finds Dezz already halfway through preparing some toast over-top a small clay oven.

"Hungry?" Dezz asks sleepily.

"Absolutely." Kaan returns; his eyes close during the process of making the statement. "I miss coffee."

"We have *forest tea*." Dezz offers.

Kaan shrugs. "Yea...*I know*. Forest tea is...*fine*." He yawns. "It's very...foresty."

"It is all in the name."

"And it's just...it's such a low level cooking recipe. I didn't think you could *taste something like that*. But anything under level ten tastes like it came from a tap."

"Well I know what you have to do then."

"What's that."

"Side-quest for coffee."

Kaan laughs. "I'll get right on that."

Dezz hands Kaan a slice of slightly over-toasted bread and a small prepackaged packet of butter, the sort of thing you'd get in a hotel. "I feel like we have been using these every day and we still haven't made a dent."

"The little butters?" Kaan asks as he takes a bite of the toast, chews and lets out joyful sounds. "Thanks by the way."

"No worries." Dezz nods. "Yea the little butters. I wonder why the convenience store had so many in the freezer."

Gekomatsu comes into the room from outside, a sweat on his brow. He's wearing *what could be the only spandex suit left in existence*. "Morning." He continues at a brisk pace towards his own room.

Kaan points over his shoulder. "Right up in the morning for a jog?"

Dezz nods as he takes a deep bite into his own piece of butter soaked toast. "Yea I heard the door a few hours ago. He doesn't have Illkat's staff so he must of just been running in a circle."

Kaan yawns again. "That's dedication. I barely made it this far." He gestures towards the room they are in right now.

Dezz smiles and before he can say anything is interrupted.

"Hey can you guys come take a look at this?" Kozmo shouts through an opened door.

Dezz and Kaan look at one another and trot off with their toast like protagonists in the first episode of a boarding school anime. They're led into a newly established canvas tent where a few wooden cabinets, desks and work benches have been assembled. Across the table are various hand drawn maps, calculations and the *radio*.

Throughout the room are various military personnel and *CMDR Aberdashi*.

"What are we looking at here?" Kaan asks.

"We have been trying to narrow down the logic behind where people ended up, and where *everything else* could be as well." Kozmo begins. "We haven't got very far, I thought for a moment the logic was similar to the Kolakoski sequence but we've ruled that out."

Dezz looks around and smiles politely. "It's cool you're doing this." He takes a bite of his toast, chews swiftly then swallows. "But what exactly can we do to help?"

Kozmo shrugs. "Hey I don't know man. I just figured you might have an idea."

Kaan looks over the maps and of all the things; spots a lack of hardware. "Is there anything you're specifically looking for?"

"Dead drops." CMDR Aberdashi speaks up. "Each of them with a two phase signal. An initial geo tag which communicates on encrypted channels and a back-up which communicates via VHF. We have no faith the original geo tag is up, and as such I can only imagine they have switched to back up."

"What is in the dead drops?" Kaan questions.

"Originally? Payment for a job. *You could call it a trade.* Munitions. Networking equipment. Cutting edge stuff. It wasn't going to be *ours* but given the current situation. I intend to claim it to fortify our location here."

Kaan nods. "What's stopping you from...triangulating these frequencies." He points towards the radio. "I imagine you've found they are still broadcasting."

"We've been looking." Kozmo confirms.

"We need antenna to start, and more power afterwards. A proper *HAM* set wouldn't hurt either. If not we'll have to jury rig something and that's never a sure bet." The Commander continues.

"We should start a list." Dezz states plainly.

The others in the room offer a polite chuckle.

"No seriously." He laughs through his own asserted tone. "Can I have some of that paper?"

〒

The guild and some townspeople sit around a fire set in the centre of town. Recently constructed benches and tree stumps glisten against the dancing light. Couples and families rest on spread out blankets. The radio plays softly in the background.

Through the wall of wind night has an encapsulating look to it. You can't perceive the wall as clearly, but you can *hear it*. The stars aren't little dots but scattered blurred motion which connect gaps in the sky like rain pooling into divots across a lawn.

"The scariest mission I've ever been on." Lt. Oaks looks over to CMDR Aberdashi; whom herself still manages to look intimidating while smiling with cup of tea nestled between both hands. *"THAT I CAN TALK ABOUT."* She laughs. "Well that would of been...*Prague*."

"Beautiful city." Illkat admits.

Lt. Oaks smiles. "Tremendously beautiful. The sort of...eclectic that can make anyone feel at home. That is actually what led us there. Our target felt the same."

"They were Czech?" Kaan states with a degree of pride.

"No no. Just visiting. Arms dealers who made a living dismantling drones, pushing custom firmware and selling them off on the black market." Lt. Oaks corrects.

"Sorry to interrupt, *something I've never understood.* What are these people getting out of it? The Czech Republic has UBI doesn't it?" Kaan questions.

Lt. Oaks nods. "Not everyone is motivated *financially*. There are other items of trade considered...acceptable."

"*Gross.*" Sonnenblume adds.

Lt. Oaks taps her nose and nods. "*Exactly.* Whatever it is your mind filled in the blanks with; *is probably correct.* So you can understand why it was a priority to handle someone like that. Which *we set up to*." She looks up; as if reading a list from the sky. "We staked out a club, we knew everyone else present that night; everyone connected criminally or indicted on their own terms." She huffs. "We had people on every entrance, the scans looked clear. Yet when we went in, *well.* There was nothing."

Everyone stares at her with an awaiting expression.

"It was our first time dealing with counter scanning technology. The sort of thing that perceives your signals and shoots it right back; modified to show whatever they want you to see."

Illkat adopts a concerned expression. "When you got in, *what was in there?*"

196

"A package. Not a bomb, when I saw it that's what I thought too. Even when the doors started closing behind us, I still thought we were going to explode. But that box had a *killing machine* inside it. Only the size of a cat, five times as spry. Hook shaped saws for hands, a titanium shelled exoskeleton." She sways her head. "It chased us around the house and killed two of us. It was the scariest mission I ever had in the *real world*."

The music stops pouring out from the radio and the voice of *Joseph Torrence* returns.

"Hey folks. I hope your evening has been going okay. If you can hear me now I imagine it's going alright!" He laughs in a fake charismatic way; like a gym teacher giving a nickname to a new kid. "No, I shouldn't say that. I know...*I know the horrors that are out there*. What we all are trying to deal with right now."

Lt. Oaks sits back and smiles; content with the impromptu end to her story.

Illkat leans over and whispers. "Did you get the guy...*after all that*."

Lt. Oaks smiles and nods once.

"I too have had something *taken from me*. I am no different from any of you. We are all in a state of...mourning. *Perpetually*. This shared grief is strong enough to become our new identity. Yet I must ask you all to relent in your cynicism; do not dispel hope! We can *get it all back* I promise you!"

"Someone should tell him we're stuck here." Gekomatsu makes the point.

"If we ever get the chance. I agree." Kozmo adds.

"This evening we have confirmed a number of those lost to us. I will read their names, and pray for their safety wherever they are now." Joseph continues.

197

Dezz leans back and looks at the fire. "I know it is all real. I believe that we're here right now. But it still feels...in a way. Like it is happening to someone else. Like I'm just watching myself have this experience."

"Fiona Ordo. Age twenty four."

"Sounds like shock." Gekomatsu responds. "Trauma makes us feel far away."

"Markus Cunningham. Age eighteen."

The fire crackles. Kaan throws on another log. "It's been long enough that it feels...normal here. I'm used to the town, the smells. I forget what my old bed felt like."

"Samantha Radding. Age seventy nine."

"I don't think I could ever forget my old bed. It was the fanciest thing I owned. In the old days I imagine it would cost as much as a car. It was...*joy*."

"Harry and Gordan Leinhold. Ages five and nine."

Sonnenblume drops to her knees.

Illkat rushes over. "Hey is everything okay? Did something happen."

The wind picks up. The fire goes out. An instantly ferocious blizzard begins to flurry from Sonnenblume's eyes. "My kids...they're gone."

CHAPTER TEN

THE UPRISING

A deepening blizzard rushes across the town of Verrplek. The wind wall shutters; itself malformed to a torrential and inverted storm above everyone's heads. For a moment, they are caught in a four sided storm which blackens the skin with chill and ruffles your vision with its hysteric pace. The white of the snow so pure it almost appears daytime.

At the centre of it all is Sonnenblume. She rises up, raw power rushing through her hands. In the depth of the storm, only her glowing white eyes are visible; her hair whips and becomes matted in the wind. "I...*don't have it in me.*"

She drops to her knees.

The blizzard dissipates.

Illkat, pushed back in the ferocity of the storm; rushes up to Sonnenblume. "We're here for you Sonnenblume. I'm...so sorry for your loss."

Half heartily Sonnenblume swipes away at Illkat, barely managing to raise her arm. Tears well in her eyes and become droplets of ice before they hit the ground.

The majority of the towns people leave, finding somewhere to be or something to do which is out of view of the event.

Illkat tugs at Sonnenblume's shoulder; attempting to pluck her up off the ground. "Come on, let's get you into bed."

"No!" Sonnenblume shouts in brief elation; before rolling back onto the dirt.

"*Alright.*" Illkat responds. She looks over to the others then back down to the lump her friend has become. "I'll get you a blanket, at least."

199

"I'm not cold." Sonnenblume remarks; an over-tired exhaustion hangs in her tone.

Illkat nods.

Lt. Oaks approaches her. "There are...ways to move people."

"We don't need them." Illkat confirms.

Dezz kicks at the extinguished fire. He sighs. "I have to wonder how this person has these names." He shakes his head. "Nothing says he isn't making them up."

"He mentioned *archives*." Gekomatsu makes the point. "Who knows who he was before all of his, what access he had. I myself, if push came to shove, could of glanced the identities of many subjects."

"How about now?" Dezz inquires.

Gekomatsu shrugs. "If we found the computer, perhaps. My login credentials should still be valid."

"I think the larger concern is that they *can* broadcast. If they're getting a signal out, they need power, equipment, know-how. You can't just plug a radio tower into the wall and press start, after all." Kozmo focuses on the details.

Kaan closes one eye and examines the darkened town with the other. "Some models, you could. I'm thinking of...those self deploying settlements. There was a town, power station, communications relay."

"*Sure*. But what are the chances of him having one of those!" Kozmo rebukes.

"What are the chances of anything anymore?" Gekomatsu argues, then points out to the surrounding area. "We were once orbiting a ball of fire in space, now we are stuck in a town protected by magic in a reconstructed reality. Why would any of us think our previous likelihoods travel here?"

"What are you getting at?" Kaan questions.

Gekomatsu paces back and forth a bit, something calculating behind his eyes. "I believe *the author* is still in play."

"*The author?* The AI core? I thought that's what...we were talking to?" Kaan makes the point.

Gekomatsu sways his head. "That was...*something else*. The game itself, a manifestation of tutorials and user interactions. A...*guardian angel* if you will."

"Oh I get it!" Kozmo raises his voice. "You think Joseph Torrence found a radio tower, or was near one that was functional because *the author* is still creating quest lines for...players."

Gekomatsu nods.

Dezz takes a step back. "Breaking the narrative." He laughs, then looks over to Sonnenblume laying out on the dirt; her shape barely notable in the night. Guilt washes over him. "He has to do it then, doesn't he. Finir?"

"Mhmm?" Kaan acknowledges the statement. "How do you figure?"

"Well if he doesn't. The villain is always destined to lose." Dezz shrugs. "It is his only path."

Kozmo nods. "It makes me wonder, do we have any other options?" He shrugs. "Is that it, I mean. Either we win, and beat him or we lose everything." He glances over at Sonnenblume then starts to rebuild the fire in the pit. "I don't think that is where this is all heading."

$$\top$$

A common misconception about loss is that time makes it better. This is a notion people who have lost nothing use to silence the discomfort of those who have. As if every year without, every table that little bit emptier; each hollow reminder of where something once was makes it any easier to endure. *Time reminds us of what we have lost*. It is the lens through which we observe what it is to be without.

Sonnenblume rests her head against the frame of an open window; peering out through the town. The radio sits on the sill nearest her, loud enough for anyone nearby to hear.

"What do we really know about this change? How many perspectives are there on what happened?" Joseph Torrence asks through the radio. "I can tell you what, in all my time. In every book I've ever read, and let me tell you, I've read dozens! I haven't seen anything which fits what has happened to us better then a rapture! I do not suppose we are those who have been left behind. *No*. We are those in heaven!"

The town of Verrplek shuffles about. A new building, attached to the stables is nearing completion. A stone brick chimney rising out from trim wood planks; all surrounding a large forge. Crates of coal line the inner wall.

"As I see it, we have risen up! We are above the world we were in, our energy is at a higher level! If this is heaven, then I am reminded of the holy words of the Pope of Texas." He adopts a preacher's voice. "I have received revelation, here, today. That *Christianity* is not about Christ, nor the holy spirit. Christianity is about *America!* And this new land, as it has been handed off unto us; is ours to claim!"

Kaan exhales with an instant exhaustion and tucks into the forge; the stone walls muting the radio enough to ignore it.

Stones shuffle, planks are set in place and shelving appears upon the wall; floating out from where it has been stored. Dezz works alongside Gekomatsu and Kozmo; each finalizing the construction.

"How's it going in here?" Kaan announces himself.

"Well enough." Dezz offers. "We don't have much in the way of metal to even smelt or work. Yet I am still comforted by the option."

Gekomatsu splashes a bucket of water over his head; his skin steams up within an instant. "I wish to re-forge my lost blade. It had been with me for a long time."

"Was it a unique drop?" Kozmo inquires.

Gekomatsu nods. "In a way, *yes*." He smiles politely. "Prior to engaging largely in research, I had...*brief interactions* with patients. One of them, *some kid*, even shared with me their passion about an upcoming game known as *Endless Empires*. You see, I knew nothing of it. Day after day, he would share with me all these hopes and dreams. He even received an invite to the beta and alongside it, a unique blade."

The room becomes a bit darker, that much more solemn.

"When he passed, his parents couldn't see straight. If they knew the value of what it was, I can only imagine, it was lost on them. They threw his beta invite into the hospital garbage before they left, and I...*made sure it didn't go unused*." Gekomatsu wanes in an amateurish attempt at feeling emotion.

"That is kind of beautiful." Kaan admires.

Gekomatsu pours more water over his head then begins to move a few portions of stone. "It is pain, *and obligation*."

"I don't think that kid would feel the same way. He'd be...*honoured.*" Dezz offers.

"He's dead, he doesn't feel or think anything. I'm sure he'd rather be here then some awkward doctor posted by his bedside find a new pastime." Gekomatsu laments the comment. "What was my attention given? What benefit have I offered myself? Obligation? Heart-ache which cannot be addressed?" He shakes his head. "I feel this longing not to disappoint someone who will never be able to know the outcome of my efforts."

"*Alright.*" Kaan rather casually comments.

"*Alright?*" Gekomatsu responds; somewhat befuddled.

"If that's how you see it, I mean. That's *alright*. I think that's what we're all doing. Balancing how much we care with how much we feel we should. Debating the weight of something which crushes us. *Pointless considerations. Distractions.*" He waves his hands and laughs. "As if thinking we should feel one way, has ever stopped us from feeling another."

"Quite philosophical brick-layers we are." Dezz jests.

"Have you ever known any other sort?" Kozmo quickly retorts.

"Now that you mention it!" Dezz laughs.

Someone knocks on the side of what will soon become a door but is currently best described as a place where a wall isn't.

A series of turning motions reveal this person to be Commander Aberdashi.

"Some of the children here have reported seeing large creatures moving about in the ocean. Should we be worried about that?" The Commander poises the question.

Kaan looks over to Dezz, who looks at Kozmo who looks at Gekomatsu. They sort of shrug, then seem to have an idea then deflate again. They settle on "Maybe."

"I'll try that again." Commander Aberdashi considers. "Should we *deal with it first?*"

"In all likelihood it is simply an oversized *crystalline whale. They feed on underwater deposits of...*" Gekomatsu recognizes something, and begins towards the exit.

"What is it?" Kaan shouts out to him.

He passes out from the soon to be forge and the radio drones back into the background.

"-that was the whole point! We're never meant to truly rest, to cease our admiration! We are intended to rise even further, and once our grasp has fully swallowed this world it is within our power to change it back to how it was!" Joseph continues; rearing up into a sort of rant.

"Illkat!" Gekomatsu shouts out; unsure of where to aim the request.

A moment passes.

Illkat shuffles out from the bottom level of the manor. She raises an eyebrow.

"I need the wind wall opened by the cliff." Gekomatsu requests as he begins to disrobe.

"Uhh. What are you doing? Why do you need that?" Illkat, cautiously walking towards him, asks with a startled concern.

Gekomatsu, now wearing nothing but a loose fitted loincloth stands near the edge of the town in full display of his anthropomorphic body. Darker green stripes wade across his spine while dense muscle structure articulates indents down his legs. "If I tell you, you'll stop me."

"Well that might stop me!" Illkat chastises. She stops a few steps from Gekomatsu.

He looks over to her. *"Please*, I...I...would-"

Illkat holds her hand out, draws her spear and slashes open a passage straight off the edge of the cliff. "I'm your friend, not your warden. I trust you have your reasons."

"Thank you. I shall return as soon as I can." His statement lingers, as if he is trying to confirm its accuracy himself. Hesitating not a moment longer he squats down, tenses himself and leaps a tremendous distance off the cliff. He pulls himself into a near perfect dive and as he pierces the water; is simply *gone*.

"You have some interesting friends." Lt. Oaks compliments.

Illkat closes the gap in the wall. "Those are the only sort of people I've ever stuck to." She looks over to Lt. Oaks for a moment and smiles. "I guess I have a taste."

"Would you like to spar?" Lt. Oaks offers.

Illkat huffs. She passes her spear palm to palm. "I *guess*. I should want to."

Lt. Oaks peers over to where Sonnenblume sits in a window; so still she may as well be an ornament. "Worried about her?"

"Her, of course. I'm worried about her, and us. This wind wall! This town! The monsters and horrors which may be outside. Our own conflicts. Every choice and thought! What even this night may bring!"

PLOP

Lt. Oaks places her hand on Illkat's forehead and holds it there.

"Now there is a hand on my head."

"*Yepp.*"

"What should I...*erm*...make of that?"

"I dunno. Are you worried about it?"

Illkat pauses, closes her eyes for a second then exhales. "No, I guess not."

"Well that's not a bad starting point." Lt. Oaks retracts her hand and smiles.

Illkat takes a half step forwards and wraps her arms around Lt. Oaks. "*Thanks*." She hugs tightly.

"YEA NO WORRIES AT ALL. TOTALLY OKAY. JUST ME...TRYING TO HELP." She offers an elated response.

Illkat pulls back, they share a moment of eye contact then both turn to look away and smile. "So, *erm*. It shouldn't be too long until we get a reasonable amount of metal from our mines. After that, we can get an antenna put together, possibly...*other...things*."

"OTHER THINGS ARE GREAT." Lt. Oaks coughs. "As awful as it sounds, even with the calamity of it all. This has sorta been a vacation."

"Wow."

"Yea, *right*?"

"That's pretty scary. Just, *all work, no play*."

"As much as any living breathing person...*can*." Lt. Oaks laughs. "You know on base there was a saying. Why stand when you can sit, why sit when you can lay down. Why lay down when you can sleep." She looks around then smiles. "Well let's just say I've found cause to settle into a nap or two since we've been here."

Sonnnenblume leans a bit further forwards, loses her grip and falls flat out of the window. Illkat and Lt. Oaks break into a sprint towards her.

On the ground, cradling the radio. Sonnenblume lays in an unaffected state.

Without getting too close. Illkat poses a question. "You...*doing okay?*"

Classical tunes reach out from the radio.

Sonnenblume swallows loudly. She nods. "I'm alive. Did something happen?"

"You fell out of a window my love." Illkat responds; taking on a maternal tone.

Sonnenblume turns a bit and looks up at the window. Her hair stretches out in an extreme length all around her. She laughs with a reduced recklessness. "I guess I did. It should be okay. I'm still comfy right here."

207

Illkat turns, and Lt. Oaks catches the concern visible on her face for a few brief moments. "Well alright." Illkat allows. "Let me know if you need anything."

"Oh of course." Sonnenblume responds; now thinly tapered sarcasm reminding one of themselves at fourteen.

A few paces from Sonnenblume's new resting spot.

"Is it wrong of me to be frustrated with her?" Illkat asks.

"Not really. You're both feeling...*valid things*. Sometimes we just end up at odds with each other." Lt. Oaks offers.

They sit on a newly fashioned bench and stare out at nothing in particular.

"That...feels like what is happening. I just want her to sit up, take control, get back in the saddle!" She deflates. "But what a bitch would I be to think someone should do that after learning their children died? I don't think I would! Nobody...*should*. Yet I'm inpatient, I want it to just be over." She shuffles to the side and places her head on Lt. Oak's shoulder.

For a moment. They just sit there.

The wind calm.

Light diffused to a pleasant subtle brightness.

"UM...Ah..." Lt. Oaks laughs, then sturdies herself. "I... you know. I think it's only honest if I tell you. I think...I think I'm starting to like you."

"OH." Illkat responds. She sits up straight and looks directly at Lt. Oaks.

"AH. SORRY! NO FORGET THAT. Never mind, I just. Oh..."

Illkat smiles. "It's not that...not at all." She laughs. "Okay...just...think about this. Do you remember being back in the old world, you would go grocery shopping. Full of optimism, buying vegetables you will eventually put in the crisper and forget about it?

Fancy things too like zucchini and cauliflower! Well that forgotten cauliflower is my sexuality. *I'm pretty sure it's still in there*, I just haven't looked for awhile."

Lt. Oaks laughs. "I'm not looking to rush." She laughs again. "We can just...sit. If that's alright with you."

Illkat leans closer and presses her head back against Lt. Oak's shoulder. "*Yea...I think...that's where I'm at right now*. I would really like to just...sit"

〒

A new day often ends up looking no different then a trounced up version of the one before it. An introductory step through the same passage, a shared routine at the nights end. We measure our lives in the passing of sets of routines and the events which caused us to change them.

The forge in Verrplek reaches completion and celebrates with a steady smoke. It rises up in a dedicated column before breaking up into disturbed shadow and ejecting out the top of the wind-wall.

Kozmo stands at the cliff-edge of the town; peering through the distorted whirling barrier. From behind Dezz joins him.

"Looking out for Gekomatsu?"

"He's ought to return. I never figured him the kind of person that would just...*leave*."

"Maybe the stress got to him."

"The stress of...*what*? You think he could get through medical school but not living in a small village?"

"I'm sure that's the case for lots of folks." Dezz shrugs. "Maybe that was his story as well. He doesn't exactly...share much about himself."

209

"I can't blame him. Not everyone comes from a place where they want to be known."

"I thought he was from Sweden not *prison*." Dezz jests.

Kozmo laughs. "Not like that, more...it's comfortable to be who you say you are and nothing more...if that makes sense."

Dezz nods. "I guess it does." He smiles then looks around; taking a seat on the ground. "Back in the day, did you ever play other accounts for the same game?"

Kozmo nods. "I ran a few alts, yea. You?"

Dezz shakes his head. "Not me, *no*. One character, one Dezz. I might look a bit different in game, go by a different name. But my character is *me*. Or...who I'd prefer to be."

"I am each of my characters. Sometimes...*no*. Most of the time. I want to be this person. Others, sometimes just in...fleeting moods. I feel this desire to be someone else." He laughs. "Have you ever walked through the streets of St.Margaez as a woman? It's like you're walking on a different pathway."

Dezz contorts his face into a curious smile then shakes his head.

"You two alright?" Kaan joins the pair; staring up and around at the wind wall. His hands are dirty, sweat and dust cover his face.

They shrug.

"Run out of chores?" Dezz teases.

Kaan rolls his eyes. "We're pretty well set everywhere we can be. I've done some additional mining, no ore yet. But the coal is consistent."

Dezz laughs. "Funny to see you so eager for manual labour. I remember you leaving that sort of thing pretty early on."

"Oddest thing isn't it? I'd sooner chew tinfoil then do a hard days work in the old world. But slap a digital pick-axe in my hands and I'll give you a twelve hour shift." He laughs. "Any sign of Gekomatsu?"

"Nah. Probably no point in standing watch anyways. He seems the sort to use the front door in most all circumstances." Kozmo admits.

Sonnenblume passes them by. The radio in her hands. Joseph Torrence rushes through another speech.

"Now...*look*. I know what you're all thinking. This is...*too easy*. It is *too convenient*. I assure you it isn't. The promise of salvation is the most challenging thing to accept, to absolve all our concerns, to believe things can be better! Now...I know that makes it seem like all the time we've been carrying that weight was wasted! *Foolishness*. I promise you it *was not*." Joseph delivers himself with the sort of growing veracity one may attribute to an uncle working their way backwards through a twelve pack of beers. "As we prepare to move upon this *Illking*. Our liberation offers only hope and stability! We shall bring the world back to *how it was*!"

Kaan shakes his head. "What a promise."

"And now, the names of the fallen. These we have confirmed against our archives." Joseph continues.

Kaan tucks into the manor; making way to the kitchen. The radio becomes a murmur then nothing.

"Not interested in the names?" Dezz questions.

"Not particularly." Kaan quips.

"There could be people we know out there." Dezz continues.

"Well, *out there*." Kozmo looks up towards the ceiling.

Kaan shakes his head. "It isn't that I'm not worried about the people I know. My parents, the uh...the mail guy seemed pretty nice." He chuckles to himself. "I'm just making peace with the situation. I can't sniff anyone out simply because they are in my memories. I'll keep my eye out, wish them the best and...try to do the same here."

"Well obviously you have a good idea what to do. You get lost in the woods, you hug a tree and wait. When I consider the people that are out there to worry about, I ask myself. Do they know to do the same?" Dezz considers.

〒

Sonnenblume appears in the doorway of the kitchen while the rest of the guild alongside Lt. Oaks share a dinner. The radio in her arms, softened to a volume only she can hear. "They took the city." She declares.

Everyone stops and looks over at her pleasantly.

"Sorry." Illkat offers. "They did what?"

Sonnenblume approaches and leans against the kitchen counter; looking loosely in the direction of everyone else. "They took the city of Illking. *Joseph's people.*"

"Oh." Illkat remarks cautiously. "Well I can only hope that is a good thing."

"I think..." Sonnenblume lingers on the statement much like one stands before a cliff prior to plunging off of it. "I must join them."

Everyone digests the statement.

"*Like*...permanently?" Kaan inquires.

Sonnenblume nods. "I would imagine so. If they are to turn the world back to how it was, *reverse all of this*. They might need someone like me."

"Sonnenblume...we...we know what will happen if things go back to how they were. The world can't handle it. Everything will be, *inoperable*." Dezz warns.

"I don't think that's true. Who are we going to trust? A random voice in the sky!? Who says it has all the answers. It isn't instantly right!"

212

"That may be the case but I don't think it's wrong about this." Illkat advises.

The liquid in everyone's drink freezes solid. A pot of gravy becomes a puck. Sonnenblume's eyes flash a bright white. "Well you can't stop me from going."

"Okay!" Illkat reaches out; holding her hand over-top of Sonnenblume's. *"Okay. We won't stop you.* But we're coming with you. We have business with that helicopter anyways." She looks around. "Just let us repair the mine-carts. We'll go together, *quicker then before to.*"

Sonnenblume reverts to as normal a state as she has nowadays. "Alright." She looks at the dinner table once steaming with different roasted vegetables and a shank of venison; now a potential set dressed for a frozen food commercial. "Sorry about...*all of this.*"

"Hey it's *okay*. We're just here for you. Whatever you need." Kozmo confirms.

The front door opens dramatically and a wet surface slaps against the hard floor creating the sort of sound you would type out with an excess of S's, H's, P's and G's.

Gekomatsu stands in the doorway; dropping over the entrance. Grasped in both of his hands is a shining chunk of blue ore. "Could someone get me a towel please?" He remarks with an exhausted frustration.

In no less then six steps Dezz jumps from his stool, to the bathroom and back far enough to hurl a length of fabric at Gekomatsu. "That looks like something fancy. What sort of macguffin have you brought us?"

Drying off the best he can. Gekomatsu places the ore down on the floor over-top the towel and heads off towards his room. "The best kind."

213

The door flicks open then shut again, fabric shuffles audibly and Gekomatsu quickly emerges in a full set of pajamas branded after the Japanese convenience store. "I can feel you all staring at me. Don't act like you haven't dropped everything and ran when a rare material presents itself before you."

Kaan laughs. "We have been struggling to find metal."

"Well you won't be using this for any *mundane* purpose I assure you. *That* is ocalyte; nature's damascus."

"That's the stuff you make top tier raid gear out of!" Kozmo declares.

"It is." Gekomatsu confirms. "I imagine over the weeks to come we may find a purpose for it."

"Well that may be on pause for a moment, some of us are going to Illking. It has been...*claimed* as we hear it. Sonnenblume wishes to join the faction responsible." Illkat responds.

Gekomatsu looks over at Sonnenblume. "Are you daft? You would abandon everyone, this town, *our progress?* For what!?"

"I don't have to explain myself to you." Sonnenblume doesn't even look up to make the remark.

"You don't? So what? Are you beholden to no one? No responsibilities to the people who care about you?" Gekomatsu argues.

"*Not anymore.*" Sonnenblume sulks, then heads up the stairs leaving the group behind.

Everyone looks over at Gekomatsu. Dezz raises his hand and squints. "Bro!"

Gekomatsu shrugs. "*What?* You're all thinking it. She's experiencing tunnel vision! Blinded by her trauma. We can't let someone who isn't thinking straight make life changing choices on a whim!"

214

Nobody has anything to say. Dɘzz takes a bite of food, having forgotten it is frozen solid. He tries to stealthily shift the slice of venison shaped ice from his mouth onto a napkin; failing in the attempt. Everyone watches him sort of slide it out of his pursed lips and then slowly, look up to meet the collective inspection.

Lt. Oaks announces herself, awkwardly and looks up to Gekomatsu. "You know, uh...*sometimes*. You just have to let people go. It might not be for the best, but if you try to grab them, it might as well be the same as pushing them out even quicker."

"I know!" Gekomatsu holds his breath for a moment. "*I know*. That doesn't however seem to preclude acting any better." He returns to the hunk of ocalyte. "I'll put this by the forge for now. If I can assist with our trip back to Illking, *please*, let me know what I can offer."

〒

CLACK.
CLANK.
CRASH.

"Who *created* this mine-cart. It doesn't make any sense!" Kozmo bemoans.

Kaan kneels next to the overturned mine-cart. The shielding underneath pulled back to reveal an illogical set of mechanical components. Gears which connect in an aesthetic yet mechanically pointless manner. Components which appear incapable of movement yet seem inexplicably responsible for a large amount of it.

"So it works because it thinks it should work. It's like this mechanism is fuelled by faith." Illkat gripes.

"I remember once reading something which argued all the laws of reality are the way they are simply because we've settled into them. Like...*indents* in the great couch of life." Kaan jeers.

Gekomatsu rolls his eyes.

Dezz and Sonnenblume return from the depth of the tunnel leading to Illking and look out at the crew.

"It looks pretty empty most of the way through. No sounds, no obvious traps. We didn't go all the way, *but*." Dezz begins.

"But we couldn't detect anything. The echoes last time were hard to miss. I think we'll be safe enough to go back this way." Sonnenblume finishes.

"I'm thinking, we might want to bring something to trade. There were once markets in Illking. We could trade for mundane metals, iron perhaps." Illkat considers.

"I'll load up the coal." Dezz states confidently.

"Is that the only thing we have to offer?" Illkat questions.

Without stopping Dezz continues back to the town; Illkat trails after him. "We're not going to give away food, not with so many mouths to feed. What few weapons we have we need. As great as our little home is. There isn't much more of value."

"And you're not touching that ocalyte." Gekomatsu confirms.

"Coal it is." Kaan agrees. "I'll help you Dezz."

Sonnenblume sits on a flat boulder near the tunnel entrance and clicks the radio on. A classical tune rises up, holds a dramatic tone then settles into a slow flow.

Gekomatsu and Kozmo tinker with the over turned mine-cart. Illkat seems incapable of standing still and starts mining more just nearby after opening a passage for Dezz and Kaan.

The classical tune ceases and a now familiar voice returns. "What a, beautiful piece. You know, I recall reading that it was composed in the wake of a great battle. Thus, it is fitting. As we carve

216

through the corridors of this city and cleanse its streets of threats. We too, feel the weariness of this campaign. Of the struggle."

Something shuffles in the broadcast, a seat scraping, someone breathing heavily near the mic.

Joseph continues. "To make a refuge of this city, we joined hands with a tremendous natural leader. Someone I am honoured to introduce to our listeners now. *Nelf Kinslayer* led our-"

"Great royal knights to victory! It was a blood chilling battle listeners! Savage! I have never seen such bravery! It rivals my Square Knights in their great raids! Oh how we conquered! The triumphs we sought and seized!"

Sonnenblume lowers the volume on the radio. Looks over to Illkat and away to the distance.

"Yes..." Joseph coughs. "Nelf was essential in rooting out guerrilla forces entrenched throughout the city. Agents of chaos! Foreign military troops! Those who stood in the way of our great regression!"

"Are you going to ask me how I did it?" Nelf questions with a death-grip on his high expectation.

Joseph laughs. "Of course Nelf! We're all eager to-"

"It was a tumultuous evening! I was abandoned! Misunderstood and alone! As I wandered the war torn city, I considered just for a moment that I should lay down! Not take another step. But I knew, my responsibilities were far greater! What would the realm be without my guidance! Without my tutelage!" He exhales heavily. "So I kept forward! Onward until I met your people! Foolishly having fallen into a-"

"Well I wouldn't say it was foolish, I-"

"The fools were pinned down by greater forces! Automatic weapons! A vehicle mounted machine gun!"

"I don't think that was in the report..."

"I dealt with them all! Appearing from behind, slashing each throat in record time! All of your soldiers *saw instantly* the great depth and width of my understanding of war! I am as Sun Tzu reborn!"

Joseph clears his throat. "Yes, erm...*of course*. And from there. Once you rallied and reclaimed a platoon of our people. Your assault did not cease."

"Nor could it! I had only begun. It was but a matter of setting off my master plan!"

"Which was?"

"As if I would tell you here! With so many spies likely listening in! No, you must only imagine the most meticulous, most amazingly crafted plan and know that mine was twice as impressive!"

"Well, *Nelf.* That story is part of this interview. I'm sure our people would be interested in learning our history."

"*As they should be!* But like all great stories, to learn of this one! You must wait until the full documentary, where I will reveal all." Nelf confirms confidently.

"*Urhm.*" Joseph takes a moment. A few papers are shuffled. "Is that...did you tell me about that? Do you have a film crew?"

"As if *I* need to create the film crew. Once the right people know I am here, they will form around me. I would not be surprised if this conversation is the opening scene! It may well be in development at this moment."

"Ah, well, *alright.*" Joseph sturdies his tone. "Moving forwards then, *Nelf.* As a commander for our forces, what are your goals looking towards the future?"

"It is plain as day, first I will requ-"

Illkat approaches and Sonnenblume turns off the radio.

"Everything okay?" Illkat inquires.

218

Sonnenblume nods. "*Fine*, fine. I've just heard this one before."

"Ah alright." Illkat allows. "You know...*I'll really miss you*."

Sonnenblume smiles. "After everything goes back to how it was, *we'll still be in a guild together. I hope*."

Illkat bites her lip, looks away and smiles. "You'll always be my guild-mate. That much is true."

Something CLANKS loudly.

"Ha! Got you ya bastard!" Kozmo shouts.

Illkat and Sonnenblume look over. "Did you get it?"

Kozmo flips the mine-cart back onto the rail and plays with the lever a bit. He tugs it forwards and the cart moves that direction, the same in reverse. "I just figured if the mechanism didn't make sense, neither should my fix! Once I figured that out it was easy."

"I don't get it." Illkat advises.

"Exactly!" Kozmo confirms.

Arriving alongside some huffing. Dezz and Kaan haul over two large sacks of coal and place them in the mine-cart. Following just after them is Lt. Oaks effortlessly carrying a sack over her shoulder.

"Ooh...I...uh..." Kaan takes a moment to catch his breath. "Why is that so exhausting." He chuckles a bit.

"You act like carrying a fifty pound sack should be easy." Dezz argues.

"I don't know man you have seen the size of the swords I'm allowed to use!"

"Fair point." Dezz laughs.

Lt. Oaks slams her sack down and smiles. "So are you ready?"

"Come to say goodbye?" Illkat asks sweetly.

Lt. Oaks laughs. "As if! I'll be coming with you." She looks over to the singular mine-cart. "Whether it is a tight fit or a second

trip! I'm not letting you go back into that war-zone without support."
She looks back to the still opened passage to the town of Verrplek
where Commander Aberdashi stands. "*Besides*. We can't go on
without having an ear to the ground."

Pointing out the staff Illkat focuses and closes the passage;
leaving the wall of wind completely raised. She smiles and looks at
the others. "They'll be safer this way. *I hope*."

"The Commander won't let anything happen to them!" Lt.
Oaks assures then looks ahead. "Who knows what will happen to us."

CHAPTER ELEVEN

THE SOUND OF REFLECTION

"Pears here!" A store-keeper shouts.

"I have fresh meats! Venison and Boar! Get it while you can!" Another joins the collective creating quite a ruckus along the red length of Illking road.

Stalls set out in dense organization. Children playing in the shade of tall, somewhat damaged buildings.

What remains of the city, cut up into portions divided by icy lengths is *quiet*. There are burn marks, some half cleaned across the roads and sides of buildings. Holes in the walls. Sometimes a scent from an alley wafts by, reminding one of something both *forgotten* and *rotting*.

"This is not what I was expecting." Illkat admits.

"He's doing what he said he'd do. Work to bring things back to how they were. To do that, society needs to be together." Sonnenblume adds; attempting to cover her own surprise with each word.

"I have cellphones here! Tablets! All the big brands! I can't say em, but we got em! You know which ones!" A rather portly, somewhat senior man advertises from a recently assembled wooden stall.

Kozmo leans in. "Do they work?"

"If you have a battery they sure do!" The man confirms.

"Like, you can send texts and call people?" Kozmo seeks to clarify.

"Well that has nothing to do with the phone working does it? That's cell towers and satellites! I don't know if those are werk'in but the phones sure are!"

221

"*Lovely.*" Kozmo responds. "How much for one of those." He points to a series of rectangular phones with an expensive looking bevelled edge.

"A hundred and twenty."

"A hundred and twenty what?"

"I don't know what they're called buddy. I just want a 120 of them. Whatever these coins are called. A mans gotta eat!"

Kozmo sorts through his inventory, glances over an all too familiar *zero* and smiles at the shop-keeper. "I shall return! Unless you're interested in some coal?"

"That one of those pitch black Korean phones?"

"Not at all."

"Then get out of here."

"Best wishes sir." Kozmo bids adeau, jogs a bit then smiles at the rest of his allies. "Apologies, I couldn't resist."

"We can have a quick shopping trip after we off-load what we have." Dezz groans a bit. "Maybe we'll get lucky and have a small tavern brawl, you know, just enough to get a level and push through the healing process."

"Oh right!" Kaan, just now, recalls the enduring state of Dezz's wound. "You've done a pretty good job of toughing that out."

Dezz laughs. "What can I say, I guess the plot armour took the brunt of it." He sturdies his back, rests the coal in a comfier place over his shoulder then smiles. "I'm just happy to be functioning still."

Beyond the street, a wider market opens up. What may have once been a few rows of stalls are now lengths which lead to intersections, with enough traffic to cause a shifting sort of motion slurry.

"This all came up so quick!" Illkat doesn't seem convinced by the display.

"There are enough people here to make light work of most mundane tasks." Gekomatsu adds.

"I'm not saying it is impossible. Just that all of this seems...unlikely." Illkat rebuttals.

Kaan scans the crowd. The shop-keepers. There are a few guards posted at the edges of the crowds. Themselves dressed without a standardized uniform, but each of them in some sort of armour or protective sporting equipment. "I don't get the sense anyone is being forced to be here. It's all rather, *natural*."

"The only thing which feels new are the surroundings." Lt. Oaks agrees. "These people know each other. Or at least, most of them do."

Dezz drops a bag of coal at his feet and stretches; letting out a deep groan. "This looks like a worthwhile spot then."

Everyone looks over to him, and just ahead is a stall where, in various barrels are an assortment of grey, brown and reddish stones as well as ores. The stall is elevated compared to the others featuring a sort of elongated storage suite reaching out from behind it; the only entrance a long red curtain. An elderly woman behind the counter smiles at Dezz.

"Hello my dear, are you interested in our wares?"

Dezz smiles. "Why, *yes*. I have a few things myself and was thinking we might come to an agreement of sorts."

The older woman lights up; clouded over green briefly showcases behind her widened eyes. "I'll just let my grandson know, he'll go over the details!"

The red curtain moves and, were you the sort to simply stare ahead; you would only see it slink back to place without any further development. Given that in this circumstance, I can say that you look down. Bursting through the curtain is a bright eyed, wide grinned child dressed in the overflowing robes of a magistrate. He is almost

223

the height of the counter; and I say almost because his iconoclastic and judgmental expression would not suffer the more apt descriptor of *barely*.

"You're interested in our wares? You've done well to recognize superior product." The child confers with a smirk.

Dezz shakes his head, and looks back to his allies. "Yes...*your stall is quite well built*. Your stock is impressive as well."

"My brothers are big dumb folk, do you know the sort? Well they do too. No qualms about it, big ol' lugs."

"Now Nathaniel!" The older lady chastises.

"I don't mean anything wrong by it! They're good at what they do. And they mine, all day long! Keeps us ready to handle the expanding opportunities presented before us."

"*Alright*." Dezz allows; completely deadpan.

Kaan steps in. "Are you interested in coal? I don't see it as part of your display."

"Am I interested in coal! Well you're just out right with it aren't ya? Not even asking any of my prices before hoisting requests onto me and my sweet grandmother here?"

"They're being perfectly delightful darling."

"Let me make the sale!" He shouts back, then returns to his intense, upward gaze. "Sorry about that." He coughs. "We might be interested in some coal, can't say it's common around these parts. Surprising as that may seem."

Kozmo steps forwards and digs into a pile of ores. His quick inspection reveals a blackened bowl set in the opening which allows a short depth of product to represent an overflowing barrel. "How about a relationship then. Get us started with some coin, and we'll keep you stocked up in black gold."

"Black gold?" The child remarks.

Kozmo becomes embarrassed. "Yea that's what they call it right?" He chuckles in an attempt to extinguish a growing doubt; it does him no good.

"With a bit of coal in the furnace we could have warmer nights. No getting up to stoke it with precious wood." The older lady *blatantly* and *skilfully* burdens her grandson with the information.

Nathaniel sways his head, closes his eyes and as if he has lived a dozen simultaneous lives as the proprietor of a used car depot; strikes an endearing smile. "I think I see a deal here."

"*Yes.* That's uh...*the idea.*" Dezz seems effectively lost.

"Okay an adult is going to take over here." Illkat interjects, then points at Kozmo. "What do we need to improve our setup at home?"

"Iron, or steel if it's been prepared already. Copper for sure. Tin. Tungsten. Aluminium."

"Wait what did you just say?" Illkat questions.

Kozmo looks around confused. "*Uh.* Aluminium?"

"Aluminum." Illkat corrects.

"I'm pretty sure it's Aluminium." Kozmo doubles down.

"I fully concur." Gekomatsu agrees.

Kaan, Dezz, Sonnenblume and Illkat look between each other.

Lt. Oaks laughs. "You know how everyone makes fun of Americans for being the only country that uses Fahrenheit? Well welcome to being on the other side!"

"We don't have Tungsten. Everything else we should. Let's strike a deal." Nathaniel assesses the situation. "If you keep on coming back, and promise to quit your squabbling like it's an English teacher convention. We'll trade even weight plus two."

"Plus two *what*?" Gekomatsu questions.

"New to the colony? That's fine. It took me a little while to figure out as well." The older lady leans down, causes everyone to, if for a moment only, schedule in a few extra stretches, and then reaches back up to share a laminated sheet of paper. She fingers over a few portions of the page. "You see, *we all come from different places*. Different currencies, coins. Some found, some *earned*. So we charted it out. Any currency is worth the total face value, regardless of the old value. A Canadian quarter is worth *twenty five* and that's just the way of it!"

"Twenty five...cents?"

"Nope none of those any more. Just *twenty five*."

"So a *twenty dollar bill*."

"That's *twenty for ya*." Nathaniel pipes up. "Not worth it though if ya ask me. Those paper bills can burn up pretty quick. Better off with *coin*."

Kaan nods. As does everyone. They proceed through a, somewhat bumbling transaction full of lugging different things around, exchanging heavy sacks, shaking hands and standing near the exit, whole body turned, finishing up a few sentences so as to feel certain the unavoidable yet somehow ostracizing requirement to leave doesn't incur offence.

They all leave, limbs and a reasonable majority of collective dignity intact.

"When you're all ready. I'd like to see the rest of what they have done." Sonnenblume admits.

"*Of course*." Illkat speaks in a shallow tone. "We can shop *quickly* if you prefer?"

Sonnenblume stomps in place a bit then smiles. "No, *sorry*. I'm in a rush when I don't need to be. Everything seems like...*well*." She makes a few noises as she sorts out what it is exactly that she wants to say. "It isn't going anywhere, *I guess*."

"Well we should probably look mostly at weapons and healing items if we're going to investigate that *helicopter*." Illkat barely finishes the sentence before everyone in ear-shot gazes at her.

"Haven't you heard young lady?" A stranger offers.

"You shouldn't approach! That's the *aggro zone*. Nobody who has tried to get close to that helicopter has lived!" Another stranger adds.

"Yes we're all complaining about it, but nothing has happened yet!" A third stranger complains in the same tone often reserved for frustration towards uncompleted sidewalk development or a shoddy gate latch.

Gekomatsu shrugs. "The helicopter is clearly a known variable."

"It doesn't change anything. We have to *pursue the quest* and as far as I can tell. The gate that helicopter is guarding has a big ol main story icon floating over top of it!" Illkat cuts through the cruft of the circumstance.

"Let's divvy up what we have and get some gear then!" Kaan cheers.

The guild set out across the market, coins and large sacks of metal slung over shoulder. They wash through the stalls like the current behind a broken dam, taking about as long to reach the other side with their earnings substantially lessened.

"Hauling all of this around is silliness." Kozmo makes what is, due to a plentiful amount of sore shoulders; an obvious suggestion.

Illkat drops her sack and feigns fainting. "It would probably be best to bring the loot back." She stares at Kozmo. "Get the ore into the forge all tucked away and safe."

Kozmo laughs. "I'm happy to do it. Would you just hand over your spear so I can open a passage into town when I get there?" He stares at her; a wry inflection growing in the trenches of his smirk.

Illkat huffs, then looks out to the group. "So myself and Kozmo are taking some things back. If you have anything, hand it over. Otherwise we'll meet you all *right back here* in two hours. Okay?"

Gekomatsu hands over a sack. "I'll be certain to keep an eye on the time."

"I won't." Kaan laughs.

Dezz nods. "We can only roam so far *anyway*."

Sonnenblume steps forwards and wraps her arms around Illkat. "Thanks for...*everything*. I hope when you're in town next we can hang out, or *something*."

Illkat returns the hug and offers, *unintentionally*, a dissipating coldness. "*Yes, of course*. When we're back and you're settled. We will see what happens!"

"Then, *I guess*." Sonnenblume turns to face everyone else. "I'll see you all later!"

"See you soon!" Kozmo confirms.

"Best of wishes." Dezz offers.

"I don't really know what to say here. I hope things aren't crazy wherever you're headed." Kaan stammers over the terms.

Lt. Oaks smiles and stops herself from bowing. "I know we didn't get to spend much time together, but for what it's worth I can tell how strong you are. SO, DON'T FORGET IT!"

There are some nods, a few smiles which grow into hugs. Then an awkward shuffle, and those who remain bask in the new composition of their group.

"We'll be off then." Kozmo interrupts.

"Be safe, *okay?*" Lt. Oaks requests.

Illkat smiles. "I'll keep all my limbs in the ride at all times." She teases.

Everyone waves, turns and in two groups set off. One focused on the innards of the conquered city and another their secret tunnel home.

〒

"Look, all I'm saying is people are like processors! If you're constantly giving one hundred percent that's not a good thing! No matter your thermal solution, or...*chemical* I guess. You're inherently burning out!" Kaan makes the point diligently.

"So, nobody should ever give one hundred percent, is what you're saying?" Dezz questions.

"Never! It's like trying to push over a mountain. I'm not saying we can't achieve amazing things, I'm just saying we can do it by spreading out the requirement, not pushing ourselves further then we should. There isn't any merit in that!" Kaan offers.

The guild turn a corner. As close to *off the beaten track* as a recent war-zone can offer. The alley before them features chunks of rubble, dried smatterings of what one can only presume are innards of some sort and hidden deeper in the shadows; peoples covered in blankets.

Gekomatsu kneels, looks at one of the peoples then moves away.

"Is he dead?" Kaan asks.

"*Maybe.*" Gekomatsu makes the statement dismissively.

"Some doctor you are!" Kaan critics and then begins to go back to the man. As Kaan kneels and light filters into the little hovel the person has crawled into. Daylight flickers against a needle still in the mans arm; residue within matching the colour and consistency of coffee grounds. He backs away. "*Ah,* even here...*I guess.*"

229

"Everywhere. You can create a perfect world, some people will still crawl in the shadows." Gekomatsu looks very seriously at Kaan. "There is an error rate in humanity. A percentage which just...*aren't cut out for it*. Nobody wants this to be true. I *certainly don't*. Yet, there it is. Address it however you will." He throws open his arms, and for a moment, it becomes that much clearer how many people are simply slumped around in the alley.

"I guess I understand. I never really liked the world we were born into. Everyone in power worked against me. Every vote seemed to go *the other way*. What seemed inconceivable to me was the common preference and it all *sucked*." He looks around, then down to the far end of the alley where there is a clearing, a tall gate and for a moment alone; a whirring helicopter of obtuse dimensions. "I always found myself picking a *better world*. One *like this*." He exhales heavily. "*Considering that*. How much can I judge anyone here."

"You can't, *and you shouldn't*. It is pointless. It does you no good, and they aren't in a place to receive the judgment even if you tried. It is all just, *sound* at a certain point."

"You talk like you have experience with the matter." Dezz makes the point with an incredible familiarity.

"That is nothing special. You look at me right now, and tell me. Have you gone through your life and never met an addict? Someone who drinks too much, or has their *bad little habits*? Or loses themselves *every single time*? Maybe you look away while they are young *and pretty* but oh, we *all know*. Don't we?" Gekomatsu just looks forwards and continues toward the gate.

"Sort of a *dire outlook* wouldn't you say?" Lt. Oaks pipes up.

Gekomatsu shrugs. "It may be, are you saying it is baseless?"

Lt. Oaks sways her head. "Not in the slightest. I've lost more friends over the years to the bottle then I have bullets. Though you could argue they're in the bottle because of the bullets...or the...proximity to moving ones." She looks out at everyone. "Because of the...*erm...*" She coughs. "So this *helicopter*."

"It's a boss." Dezz explains.

"Like it runs payroll?" Lt. Oaks seeks to clarify.

Kaan laughs. "It's a really tough enemy. Lots of health. Probably a big challenge."

"Probably?" She questions.

"Well that's the best part of a good game. A unique challenge before you! A big fight. Even if you've played the game before, *maybe this time* you see something different!" Kaan offers.

They veer closer toward the edge of the *hunting ground*. The gate sits in the centre of an open square. Where a massive statue once was, stands now a gate that flickers with neon light. Various *roman numerals* crawl across it. Clacking and metallic locking sounds emanate out from it like creaking floorboards.

Leading up to the gate are *bodies*. Some in bags, some in pieces. Some missing central portions of their composition; like a thick pole was fitted through them. The chaos hasn't been cleaned, only *added to*.

The helicopter whirs around the gate, *patrolling*. At times it appears as if it has two rotors, then six, then just the one. Each set of blades spinning in an offset pattern. Where windows would be are plates of blackened steel.

"Ominous." Lt. Oaks makes the statement. "It is a remote model, so it's possible this is some sort of active defence protocol?"

"Was that common?" Dezz questions.

Lt. Oaks nods. "Oh incredibly! Outside ceremony I haven't seen armour operated personally by someone...*well ever*." She shrugs. "No point really."

"I see why the people here don't go too close." Gekomatsu sniffs the air and instantly wishes he hadn't.

Lt. Oaks seems to *recognize something* in the distance. She smiles. Then offers a small bow. "So, *two hours then? I'll see you all shortly!*"

Before allotting anyone the time required to request an explanation; she sprints down a smaller side path and is beyond a corner.

"That's a good sign." Dezz inflects cautiously.

"You think?" Gekomatsu retorts. "It's the nature of her position. To think she was *just here for Illkat* is foolish."

Kaan stares out beyond the review of his peers. "This was always one of my favourite cities in the game. I remember once, I actually ordered a poster of it. My mom liked it enough she joked about playing."

Dezz smiles. "Did she ever make an account?"

Kaan laughs. "*No no.* You know my mom. Perpetually doing nothing while feeling bad about it." He exhales. "It's almost been nice just...being away from it. As awful as that sounds."

Dezz shrugs. "No I get it. I think back, to my own time in the hospital. At the start there, I was really...hard on myself. A few weeks in one of the nurses who had always been checking in on me just stopped showing. I never got the real answer, but *I think.* She just got annoyed with me."

Kaan laughs. "You think?"

"Everyone has a limit right? Who hasn't told someone everything is going to be alright a dozen times in a row only to get *a little exhausted* when number thirteen comes along? We forget mental health takes a toll on everyone, not just, *us.*" Dezz smirks oddly.

"Everyone hurts everyone." Gekomatsu adds. "The second we met. Whether we became friends, or enemies. It might be a glance, an unintentional pause. It's rarely intentional. But everyone hurts everyone. *Don't take it personally.*"

232

"And yet, to see the good. To linger in those *peaceful moments*. It often means trudging through that bad. That is just...the price of it all, eh?" Kaan considers.

Gekomatsu exhales. "You've been alive this long, and are only now recognizing that?"

Kaan shakes his head. "No, *I guess not*. On some level, I know. This whole experience is *up to me*. What I want, what I'm willing to put myself through."

"And who you get to spend time with along the way!" Dezz adds with an endearing smile.

〒

"None of our people have shown such strength!" Joseph Torrence lets out an exhilarated declaration. He stands behind a rather large hall alongside guards and *Sonnenblume*.

A length of paved path across from them a few car frames have been sheared into pieces. Chunks of broken ice lay across the ground near them.

"I dare say, you could kill everyone here right now!" Joseph laughs.

His guards look uneasy; tending their rifles with a pulsing itchiness.

"I would never! We want the same things! To turn this back. To dispel whatever is keeping us all in this illusion!" Sonnenblume confirms.

"So you see it too? When you stare too long. It's like feeling the end of a page right at the edge of your vision. Like we can just *turn it over* if only we had a grasp on it!"

"Yes. I thought it was...*just me*. But when I heard you talking about it. The air in *my lungs*. Every step I take. It doesn't feel real. It *can't be*. It is...a synthetic life. Not my own!"

"How right you are!" Joseph agrees with a wide smile. "Sonnenblume, may I call you Blume?"

"I'd really rather-"

"Blume. Your abilities, god given as they may be. They're a part of all of this...*chaos*. With our wills combined *I know* we can achieve our goals. *Bring us back* to when things were right in the world!"

A shingle falls from a nearby roof and shatters on the ground. Nothing is there.

"So you'll take me on?" Sonnenblume asks politely.

"Take you on? You're in my top command! We *need you* now!" Joseph leads them out through a large house, beyond a hallway and into a protected courtyard. The courtyard was once a lavish home of art and relaxation but has since been converted into a communications network of sorts.

Antennae point out towards the sky. A large central tower, itself rife with different dishes, receivers and large encoding nodes is fastened where a tall fountain once was. Where reservoirs of water once collected across the fountain are now thick cables, drenched in ice to cool neon orange exposed components.

"*Our message* is essential. In taking this city, we are showing the stability we can project. In keeping it safe; we affirm our might. I *need you* to act as its warden. Keep my word honest as we work towards fixing it all!" Joseph explains, a tear welling in his eye. His chest flares with passion.

"I accept. I'll do whatever it takes to maintain *peace*."

A door flies open into the communications network. "There are separatist cells at work! I can promise you. We must dedicate

234

resources to listening into these groups Joseph! We must find everyone who opposes us!" The all too recognizable voice of *Nelf Kinslayer* screeches to a halt as he notices *Sonnenblume*. "What is *she* doing here! You have brought the enemy into our home!"

"She is no enemy of ours Nelf! She has just shown us her skill and sworn loyalty to the cause!"

"She is from the group I spoke to you of! Narcissists and Zealots the lot of them! They do not listen. They see things only one way! *She is no different.*"

Sonnenblume steps into Nelf and stares down at him. "Last I heard you're the one who *can't listen.*"

Joseph steps between them and strikes a large smile. "*Friends*, we were all cut from different strips of cloth. Walking different paths. Let us not combat one another because of the distance between our old selves and instead celebrate that our steps have become one, our paths merged."

Nelf steps back and looks away. "You heard me when I came in then?"

"Yes, other factions? I *promise you Nelf.* There is no cause for concern!"

Nelf smiles, and turns to excuse himself. "If you insist."

Sonnenblume, standing perfectly still. Lets out a swift chuckle. "We'll be fine now, even if we have to ignore one another. I promise."

"You have my absolute faith." Joseph *warns* her.

〒

In the new markets of Illking. Kozmo leans against a wall while Illkat stretches.

"I said *two hours.*" Illkat vents.

235

"Well no one has a watch."

"We're here on time."

"*Are we? Like, you're certain?*"

Illkat stares at Kozmo. She sighes. "Look at the sun. You see how far it's sunk in the sky since we left?"

Kozmo nods. "Of course."

"Did you know it perfectly matches the actual time of day? This was in the tutorial of the game!"

"Yea I skipped that. I just wanted to get into the game, you know?"

"Not even *slightly*." Illkat lets out a huff.

Kaan turns the corner and waves. "Hey folks! Sorry we got a bit caught up. We were chatting to a few of the locals, wandering around. We found the *aggro zone*."

Illkat stands at attention. "So, *do you think* we can handle it?"

Kaan shrugs. He looks back at Gekomatsu.

"Nobody has seen it take any damage. But, then again. It doesn't seem like too many people have tried after the first few had...lack lustre success."

"He means the whole area has nothing but corpses around it." Dezz clarifies.

"*Lovely*. That's...*great*."

"These sorta helicopters enemies, *well*. There were a lot of them in FPS games over the years right? How often can you just...shoot them. It's usually an RPG, or you throw something." Kozmo considers.

"So you think everyone before has failed because they brought a knife to a rocket fight?" Illkat questions.

Kozmo shrugs. "*Maybe*, it fits. There is a fight like that in every version of P.O.V!"

236

"Is our intention still to combat it then, even without such armaments?" Gekomatsu questions.

"We have to, *don't we?*" Kaan makes the point.

"It is *the quest*." Dezz agrees. "That doesn't mean I want to throw my life away."

"We should be *prepared*. We have potions."

"Aye." Kozmo confirms.

"Everyone got armour?"

"Aye." Dezz agrees.

"And we have weapons."

Gekomatsu raises up a lengthy steel claymore. "They'll do."

"Then...we're as ready as we can get." Illkat confirms.

"WAIT."

"What?" Kaan asks.

"Where is Matilda?" Illkat questions.

"Matilda?" Dezz is caught off guard.

Illkat shakes her head. "Lt. Oaks!"

At this specific moment. Convenience would dictate Lt. Oaks burst from the nearest alley, or jumps out from an emptied barrel having been there all along. In reality the group sort of meander about for a few more minutes, spot someone who kinda looks like her but isn't, wander around for a few moments more then return to their original location to find Lt. Oaks politely sitting and waiting for them.

"This is an interesting place, *such unique culture*." Lt. Oaks remarks; her head mostly in the clouds.

"What did you find?" Illkat steps forwards.

"*Instability*." Lt. Oaks holds onto the statement with an antiquated disappointment.

The group, through silent consensus. Make their way towards the *aggro zone*. The final few hours of daylight arc down upon them, reflected off indigo glass unto dull red stone pathways. Shadows creep out from corners at sharp angles; divorcing the main road from any side street.

"If I die." Dezz begins.

"You won't." Kaan confirms.

"*If I die*." Dezz repeats, forcefully. "Tell stories about both parts of me. Don't make me sound like some perfect friend. Share the good and the bad. Author an honest memory about me."

Illkat pats his back. "He was a cantankerous git, who always had something bad to say about himself even when he shouldn't. The end." Illkat laughs. "How's that?"

"Exactly what I was thinking." Dezz allows.

They stop for a moment at the edge of the aggro zone. Before them the rotten remains of failure, a helicopter swirling around like ten dozen pissed off hornets and *a gate*.

Everyone looks at each other, and like taking a shot of absinthe after your 16th beer. They plunge ahead together without expecting to land soundly.

The helicopter shreds air and crawls through the cut up remains towards them, arcs to *look down* and hovers in place.

A crack in the gate opens briefly and from it emerges a floating hand of tortured flesh, contracting at odd angles. *Tobias* dangles between its elongated fingers.

Directly from the speakers upon the helicopter *Finir* speaks clearly. Cleaner in his pronunciation then before. "I found this one, *running in the dark*. Towards me; unwittingly. I thought, how can I come to appreciate beauty, and spontaneity if I can't smell a flower in bloom when I happen upon it." The hand drops Tobias to his feet, his eyes enlarge, he tries to break into a sprint. Needles form from the depths of his own shadow and pierce throughout him. "Let me witness then, the beauty of your conviction. Show me how dearly *you wish to go on*."

238

"You have no chance!" Tobias screams out. "You're all going to be turned to mush!" A thick black rope drops down from the helicopter.

Gekomatsu rushes ahead, leaps out with incredible speed at Tobias and misses him as the rope ascends up into the hovering miasma of machine.

Something clunks, the blackened cock-pit of the helicopter becomes clear and Tobias laughs manically behind it. His widened eyes threaten to burst in his own skull. With a forward pushing motion Tobias steers directly down towards the guild. Swirling blades which don't even appear to be there chew up the path.

Kaan and Dezz jump off to the left, everyone else to the right.

The helicopter swirls back up. Something starts *spinning up* as if an industrial blender was installed behind your ear.

The ground shakes.

Side mounted mini guns begin to fire down at Kaan. He rolls out of the way.

The *meat* and *rot* on the ground pulls itself together, taking stone and bone to form new skeletons. Golems of lumped musculature, in rough approximations of human form begin to stand up all around the gate.

One grabs Dezz by the shoulder.

"Oh I'm looking forwards to this!" Dezz shoulder checks the ogre into the ground and methodically bashes the hell out of it with a brand new mace. Another approaches him and he caves in its chest.

LEVEL UP!

Dezz stretches and smiles. "Now that's feeling better!" He charges ahead.

239

Mini-gun fire tears up the street and backings of buildings. Kaan rushes around, drawing the fire where his allies aren't.

Lt. Oaks draws a pistol in either hand and begins what can only be described as a *dance* caught between propulsion, and efficiency. She steps aside to dodge strikes, or attempts to grab her and dispenses shots to the base of the skull, or heart. She *flutters* where some may stomp. She flows with the forceful shot of her large calibre weapons and lets the momentum of each moment lead gracefully into another.

SPLORSH

A golem falls into two. Gekomatsu grabs one half of the remains and tosses it whole-sale into another; stabbing through both portions before they flop. "We're getting caught up fighting adds."

Kozmo, midway through beating a golem down with the forcefully removed leg of another, shouts back. "We need to jam it up!"

Illkat looks at her spear, then shakes her head. "With what!"

The helicopter shifts, and screeches. Its blades tear up some of the meat on the ground and the path underneath it. Which sounds most like a blender left to break up frozen chunks of concrete.

Kaan passes them by. "I'm bringing it around again!" Mini-gun fire tears up the path just behind it.

"I have an idea!" Illkat declares as she pulls her spear out of the face of an on-coming golem.

A revolver spins as Lt. Oaks manually loads each bullet with frame perfect accuracy. She fires off each shot with a motion that looks like it could barely accommodate one. "Then do it fast. I'll keep as many of them busy as I can!"

"Alright." Illkat confirms. "Kozmo! Use your random bullshit!"

The helicopter comes around, just behind Kaan. He leads it towards them.

"Get ready!" Kozmo commands as she finishes off a foe, pulls out *a head* and pitches it towards Illkat over-hand.

For a moment, Illkat would swear she could see an *A* button appear besides the head as it whips towards her. She lowers her grip on her spear, squares her posture and strikes it at the peak of momentum. Sending it, inexplicably, like a fleshy missile towards the helicopter.

The head strikes a critical component in the centre of a few transient whirling blades and causes a dramatic loss of stability. The helicopter swirls, pulls itself upside down and crashes into one of the tall buildings set like arena walls around the aggro zone.

Plate metal flies out from the wreckage followed quickly by flames.

"Nice!" Kozmo shouts.

"This isn't over." Gekomatsu declares.

"No, *it really isn't*." Tobias agrees. He steps out from the flaming wreckage. One of his arms hosts a rotor from the helicopter, its blades a quarter of their length and swirling with jagged broken edges at full speed. "I've seen it, *you know*. The end. You've already lost!"

Everyone charges him.

Dezz jumps up to throw his mace down and hits the ground. The remains of the golems reform, crawl up his weapon and hold him with ferocious strength.

Tobias steps back and holds out his rotor arm. Illkat and Gekomatsu work in tandem to block each spinning blade while Lt. Oaks sneaks to the side and fires off a dozen rounds at Tobias. He pulls the spinning blades to deflect each shot and opens up enough for Illkat to stab through his chest.

Her spear *sinks* further into Tobia's chest, as does her arm until her whole shoulder is swallowed up into the wound and her face is pulled flat into the nook of Tobias's neck. "*Hello.*" He mocks her.

Lt. Oaks shakes her head and tries to sprint ahead only for her legs to be grabbed out from under her by lengths of stretching muscle.

"Hey, get this stuff off me!" Kozmo scratches at his legs and bashes at the pink goop as it crawls onto him and glues him in place.

A length of goop reaches out for Kaan and Gekomatsu cuts through it, as another takes him down to his knees. The musculature rolls around on the floor like an unsteady foundation. Pulling Gekomatsu to the others, each restrained behind Tobias.

Kaan stands alone. He reacts suddenly and cuts out a length of the muscle that reaches for him.

"You see you're lost. Just, *floating in place.* All alone. I think you *prefer it like this.*" Tobias taunts.

"Let go of my friends." Kaan commands.

"You keep thinking you're in charge! Well I have some news for you *Kaan!* You're just along for the ride! And this is where it ends for you." Tobias waves his hand up and the beaten, slashed and destroyed innards laying about the ground form anew into more golems. They march towards Kaan.

Kaan laughs. "You misunderstand the type of person I am, *Tobias.* I've lived my entire life hoping for a moment like this. I've never had a say in the world! I've never been in charge. Any modicum of control I had was forged through denial and distraction. Yet, something I do know! Something I'm sure about." He laughs and rolls his shoulders. "I have everything I need to *stop you.*"

Kaan steps forwards in exhilarated rage as the wave of golems approach him. He stabs forwards, drops one. Dodges a slash and tosses his sword from one hand to the other just as his arm is pulled off. With a twist Kaan cuts off a head, and a pairs of legs.

LEVEL UP!

His arm regrows in time to catch a blade that slices his palm in two but opens up his attacker to a gut rending slash. He kicks in a knee cap. Throws himself onto one of the fallen and bashes its head in with the hilt of his blade. Another golem comes for him and he rolls over, sweeps its legs and lets it land on his upward facing blade.

LEVEL UP!

A new hand at his side Kaan sprints towards Tobias and his allies. Tobias levels his rifle at him. A few shots miss, one is deflected with a sword strike and two others plunk into Kaan's upper thigh. He screams as he continues to charge forwards.

Tobias slashes underneath Kaan, cutting him in two but propelling the top portion of his body forwards. Kaan's and his torso push Tobias to the ground and while his opened hips spill out onto the ground; he is no less deterred from feeding punches into Tobias's jaw. He keeps on striking, Tobias's rotor arm pinned beside him cutting a trench into the ground and stone. Kaan keeps on punching Tobias until his own hand has shattered so completely he leaves lacerations with every strike.

LEVEL UP!

Kaan flops over. His legs reform.
The pink musculature wilts and *dissipates* into the air.

243

Something makes a monumental *chunking* sound and the gate opens just slightly, light pours through it.

Dezz runs to Kaan. "Dude are you okay! What was that!?"

Kaan smiles up while wearing the universal expression for 'I know this was a bad idea but I was right so you can't criticize me as much as you probably want to'.

"What an impressive display!" Joseph Torrence shouts out from a nearby alley. He joins everyone in the aggro zone alongside his soldiers and *Sonnenblume*. "It looks like you have done an incredible service to our city!"

Illkat helps Kaan up to his feet. Lt. Oaks steps forwards and reloads her pistols. Gekomatsu sheathes his claymore and prepares to say something, but is cut off by another party behind them all.

"As have you Joseph!" Nelf shouts out, now emerging from the other side of the aggro zone with his own soldiers. "You have brought everyone here and made things so easy for me!"

Lt. Oaks looks back, and signals towards the gate with her eyes. Illkat nods.

"We need to go." Illkat whispers.

Everyone slowly starts moving towards the gate.

Joseph's soldiers raise their rifles. "You can't be serious Nelf. You were at my side!"

"No, *Joseph.* You were at my feet!" Nelf shouts and begins firing himself, as do all the soldiers.

The guild, caught in the crossfire. Rush towards the gate, barely scraping by, some shots destined for them are caught in pillars of ice instead and they tumble into the light of the gate only to fall for an indeterminate amount of time.

WHOOSH

They all tumble out of an oversized metal door into a massive circular escalator. They're in a glass tube, descending from space unto a city of lights and turbulent neon. Explosions and gunfire fill in the gaps across the entire city.

"Oh, *no way.*" Illkat is struck by an odd horror.

Propelled by a pink jet-pack a *moderate sized cat* wielding two katana blasts past the glass elevator. Chasing the cat is a completely black drone shooting red lasers.

"I don't get it. What's happening?" Dezz asks.

Illkat shakes her head. "This looks like...*Los Catos.* Which means we're in...well. I think we're in *Kitty Sabre Extreme.*"

CHAPTER TWELVE
THE RIGHT CATITUDE

"Meow! Welcome to our most sacred city newcomers!" A digital voice through the speakers of the elevators speaks out to the group. "You're only a few moments away from *TOTALLY PWNING THOSE NOOBS* and I just wanted to share some basic tips with you!"

"That's...*weird*." Illkat notes.

"The tutorial?" Kaan questions.

Illkat nods. "Yea it's...the screaming part wasn't there before."

"Remember your pawtners are always willing to help! Invite friends to play for free in this MASSIVE MULTIPLAYER ACTION EXPERIENCE." The digital voice goes on; shifting between a demure tone and an abrasive shouting.

The feudal streets below, lined with neon host explosions and vehicles blaring through them. Cat shaped shadows crawl through every alley, across street lamps and appear from nowhere to strike out at soldiers, drones and vehicles all clad in the same absolute detail-less black.

Far in the distance, a *blimp* of shadows reveals a screen across its entire side. It isn't a normal screen, instead it is a series of moving greys and blacks, forming and overlapping in such a way the image conjured between them is *discernible*. It depicts *Finir*.

"My great many players! I have come to learn of *interlopers* in this realm. They have come from the *protected server*. Show them, *exactly which dangers* they were kept from."

Dezz swallows. "It's always right from the fire straight into the pan isn't it! Just *once, ONCE!* I would love the other side of a door we're rushing through to be pillows...or...*cotton candy machines!*"

246

"You mean instead of bones, bullets and bodies?" Gekomatsu asks calmly.

Dezz shuffles his shoulders. "*Obviously.*"

Lt. Oaks leans against the railing as the elevator finalizes its descent. "The people down there are preparing for an ambush." She looks casually around the elevator and seems disappointed. She pulls on the only visible console and it refuses to give or even bend at the edges. "I would say it isn't looking good for us."

"We can give it a shot." Kozmo adds optimistically.

"Of course." Lt. Oaks agrees. "They have positions set up dead across from us, sixty some feet. Looks like a sniper or two as well." She sighs.

"You're, *quite calm about all this*." Illkat admits.

"OH I AM HORRIFIED." Lt. Oaks confesses. "It just won't do me any good right now. I'll save freaking out for later, or *not at all.*"

The glass tube dissipates as concrete is all around them. The elevator stutters, then stops completely. Loud *hissing* sounds as the door before them opens in a lurch. They keep to the side, taking as much cover as they can. Red lasers filter in through the opening; searching every inch of the back wall.

"Definitely snipers." Lt. Oaks confirms.

"Kaan?" Dezz asks.

"Yea buddy." Kaan returns with a concerned inflection.

"You go get em after I draw their fire." Dezz makes the announcement at the same moment he stands up and walks forwards. Before Kaan can even shout out, shots begin to ring out in the distance.

SHINK

A *pink* blur rushes back and forth ahead of Dezz, intersecting each bullet, a little metallic *flash* in place. Dezz isn't harmed.

247

"It's one of them!" One of the soldiers shouts.

Another loses their head.

They fire off into the air. Some are mislead and shoot at one another; blowing meaty chunks off their allies. A series of smoke sets off, each a pastel pink and purple. One by one the soldiers in the ambush are tossed out in *pieces* from the colourful smoke!

"No way." Illkat remarks; recognizing something.

Kaan rushes up to Dezz and smacks him. "Can you knock it off with the self sacrificing crap! I'm starting to think I need to put a leash on you or something!"

A few shots fire off. The smoke begins to clear.

"That...doesn't make any sense." Illkat becomes lost in confusion.

"Meowdy folks! Welcome to the our fair city!" A young voice, free of any cynicism surges from the figure that steps out of the smoke.

"Please don't say it." Illkat whispers under her breath.

"I'm the *Illustrious Kitty!* I'm so glad to meet you!" The figure fully emerges from the smoke and reveals herself to be a rather short, anthropomorphic *cat* in the garb of a ninja. She's wearing around twelve different belts, some simply looped upon one another. Her black hair and *bright pink bangs* sway into her eyes every few moments. Stylized turtle-shell glasses barely hide excitable eyes.

"Is that...*you*?" Gekomatsu asks Illkat directly.

Illustrious Kitty widens her eyes as she gazes upon Gekomatsu and *instantly appears behind him*. She measures his head, and looks at his enlarged eyes. In less time then it takes to blink she's looking at his feet and hands. "ARE YOU A LEAP PAD WARRIOR."

"I haven't a clue what you're-"

"NO no don't say. I know it's a secret. You couldn't tell me if you wanted to." Illustrious Kitty allows.

A series of black ropes fall from the sky and smack onto the ground surrounding everyone.

"MREOW!" Illustrious Kitty nearly hisses. "Reinforcements! These guys don't know when to quit it. Come on friends! We got this. Put your faith in camaraderie and we'll always be the victors!"

Illkat puts her hand to her face and exhales heavily.

Lt. Oaks approaches from the side. "That...*looks like you*."

"*Yea*." Illkat confirms

"How is that even...possible?" Lt. Oaks questions.

Illkat shuffles her shoulders through a few obtuse angles then draws her spear; peering up at the figures sliding down the ropes from an over-head blimp. "I don't know why any of us ask that question anymore."

Moving at insane speed Illustrious Kitty *runs* up the vertical length of rope, slashing at bullets and cutting through soldiers in the same swift strokes.

Chunks of bodies begin to *thunk* into the ground.

Some, *briefly*, alive soldiers reach the bottom of the ropes. They wield sabres which look like neon blue helicopter blades and fire revolvers with enough recoil to break a few wrists all at once.

With a rather casual motion Kaan dodges a blade and swipes up at an opponent; he instantly *destroys* it then looks at his own weapon. "Uh."

Gekomatsu cuts through six soldiers, then another three. He glides upon the ground like a curtain caught in a steady breeze.

Bullets push back corpses. Each strike ushers a *gush* of brightly coloured blade. Style oozes out of every motion.

Using only the helmet of a soldier Kozmo reflects bullets back at oncoming hostiles.

From the blimp above come barrelling down oversized blobs of darkness. They hit the ground as giant metal shells which quickly open up and let out brutish soldiers wielding two riot shields each. The riot shields are adorned with shotguns.

More soldiers rush towards them from the city.

Illustrious Kitty lands in front of the group. Her katana extends to twice its length with bright pink light. "Come on everyone! Tails between our legs! We gotta get meowtta here!"

Dezz is the first to rush after her.

Halves of bullets drop to the ground as Gekomatsu slashes through each pellet of a shotgun blast.

"You heard the little lady. Come on!" Lt. Oaks ushers the request.

Illkat seriously considers just...standing there. Her knees give in first and she's onward with everyone.

The group and the soldiers hot on their heels break onto the main street then quickly down an alley.

Smaller cats prowl through garbage's.

Light creeps out from slim curtains, behind which are full restaurants.

Holograms flutter through the sky, some through the alleys. The tail of a fish faced dragon. A long bearded cat. A golden retriever samurai.

Another set of *cats* dance upon an off-set stage. Some watch with score boards.

"Oh are those the...*juniper cats?* I never really understood what was going on there!" Kozmo asks in a rush.

"No time!" Illustrious Kitty shouts back. "Into the sushi madness!"

They rush onto a main street where *hundreds* of cats in robes, armour, formal wear and more pass on by. Carbon fibre buildings are detailed with regal paper lanterns. Some digital, some real. Little cats

jump up through obstacle courses. Others play music. Illustrious Kitty
dives into the opened passage of a three story restaurant.

Everyone follows.

They are, briefly, in a two dimensional space. Everyone feels
as if they are *loading*. Their soul in a state of buffering. In this space
three soldiers join them.

Just as quickly, it becomes impossible to remember what
being two dimensional feels like. Now there is only the birds eye view
of a stylized restaurant. Everyone and the soldiers are dressed in
cook's outfits with little white aprons.

An elderly purple cat appears in front of everyone. "Welcome
cooking kitties! I'm so grateful you've decided to help me out!"

Illkat leans down to Illustrious Kitty. "What are you
thinking!?"

"We needed to drop off the map." She answers swiftly.

"Our customers are snapping orders right up! So you have to
work quick! Work as a team to prepare as many orders as possible!"

"Skip. Skip. Skip." One of the soldiers chants.

The purple cat physically moves through the dialogue of a few
sentences in a moment and disappears. A count-down appears.

"Don't worry about them. Let's just get a good score okay!"
Illustrious Kitty confirms.

Text appearing in the centre of the floor counts through to 1
and then everyone can move freely. The soldiers instantly rush over to
Illustrious Kitty and the others and sort of...stand...menacingly in
front of them.

"What are you doing!?" One of the soldiers shouts.

"How are you impervious!?"

"You can't deal damage in mini-games you dinguses! I guess
you gotta make sushi with us!"

"I...don't want to make sushi." The pitch black soldier remarks quite uncomfortably.

Kaan sort of walks over to some rice, picks it up in an inexplicable bundle above his head then walks it over to a big rice cooker. He motions to put the rice into it and it not only instantly fills into the pot, with water, but closes itself and is set to finish cooking the rice in sixty seconds. Kaan hums to himself. "Well...*all right then.*"

A conveyor belt begins slowly rolling and upon it are two kinds of tuna, crab and whole salmon.

A soldier rushes towards the salmon and picks it up. "I'll beat you to death with this!" He rushes towards Illkat with the fish in hand, approaches her, and politely passes it to her. They stare at one another. Her confused; him without a face yet obviously upset.

"There isn't a bludgeoning button pawtner! You just gotta work together as a team. Come on, I know if you try you'll just enjoy yourself!" Illustrious Kitty cheers.

Illkat looks the other way and groans.

Everyone shuffles through the actions. Every time one of the soldiers tries to pick something up and use it maliciously it simply doesn't work out for them. Bringing a knife to someone passes it off. Dropping a toaster into the sink just washes it. Leaving open puddles of oil on the floor just cause people to casually slip onto their butt and laugh for a few seconds.

"This is madness! What have you done to us. Bringing us here!" The soldier laments.

"I made *you* a dynamite roll! Because I think you're the bomb!" Illustrious Kitty smiles with bright eyes up at the soldier; a perfectly prepared roll on a white plate before her.

The soldier stares down at the sushi.

The kitten looks up.

The soldier *creases something* across his lack of a face.

The kitten looks up *harder*.

A single bite later. The soldier looks around and seems to exhale awkwardly. "That was...*pretty alright*."

"Order time up! I hope you worked hard!" The voice of the purple cat announces.

'Mini-game complete!' The words flicker across the birds eye view.

Everyone is two dimensional again.

They pass back into the neon city of *Los Catos* on the very top of the tall restaurant.

"I'm so glad to hear you enjoyed it!" Illustrious Kitty smiles as she pushes the soldier off the roof, takes his weapon as he falls, throws it into the chest of one of the other soldiers then just stares at the remaining one. "Tell me where you came from! What are you doing in my game!?"

Illkat steps back then smiles. "This I'm alright with."

The soldier tries to draw his weapon but loses it as Illustrious Kitty pulls it out of his grasp with a length of yarn.

"It's, *the game*. That's all this is. I'm just...*playing*."

"What are you playing! You're no ally of this kitty cat!"

"P.O.V? What else?"

"Wait...*what are you seeing?*" Kaan asks.

"What do you mean? We're just here. On this roof."

"No I mean...just, *describe it to me*." Kaan continues.

"It's sunny out. Limestone buildings. This is like some kind of...*bazaar*. It's sandy everywhere, I don't know these kinda countries."

His description couldn't be less accurate.

"And down there!" He points to the streets where cats and holograms plod through extravagant festivities.

"Merchants. Peddlers. I don't know, camels? What type of stupid questions are these?"

"We're seeing different versions of the same place." Kaan announces.

"What is P.O.V?" Illustrious Kitty asks.

"Pursuit of Vengeance. It is *the fps!*" Kozmo answers.

"FPS?" Illustrious Kitty questions. "I know about PPS! Pets per second! I'm at like seven thousand on a good day!"

"I wasn't allowed to play shooters as a kid. She probably has no idea what you're talking about." Illkat adds.

"How do you know that?" Kozmo asks.

Illkat kneels down and looks at Illustrious Kitty. "Because she's *me. Somehow.*"

Illustrious Kitty approaches and stares at Illkat. They lock eyes and for a moment, share each others face.

A tear wells up in Illkat's eye. "It's odd to remember this time in my life. I was so...*innocent.*"

"Remember it? It's right now! The cherry blossoms! Techno ramen bars! Oh the trams only went up a few days ago! If you haven't been in them you have to!"

"I used to live here, *basically.*" Illkat thinks back; caught up in nostalgia.

"Then maybe you know. We seem...*much more powerful here.*" Gekomatsu makes the point.

Illkat wipes away a few more suddenly appearing tears then nods with a smile. "Kitty Sabre Extreme is just as much beat-em-up as it is rpg. Sometimes a few hits let you deal *millions of points of damage.*"

"Come on! If you're just going to stand around and talk let's go to my apartment!" Illustrious Kitty requests. She throws out a paw shaped shuriken to a tall building across from them and as soon as it breaks into the wall; a thick length of yarn forms between it and her. She attaches her end to a nearby hook then pulls herself up onto the taunt length of string. "Come on! We can get there easier from up there."

While *Illustrious Kitty* seems to walk across the thin length without any concerns at all. The rest of the group are much more hesitant.

"This seems extremely unlikely." Gekomatsu admits, scans the length a few times then shrugs. "I'll go first." He pulls himself up and with relative ease begins to walk across.

"Well." Lt. Oaks confirms. "If that's all there is to it!" She climbs up.

Everyone takes a moment, and passes along. Each shocked by the relative ease in which they partake of the feat. Illkat goes last, jumps up with a flourish and is carried across with perfect muscle memory.

The building across the way leads down to a staircase, then across a walkway. Beyond a bridge constructed entirely of light, the streets underneath are covered with soldiers.

"They weren't always here...in the game." Illkat explains. "When did they show up?"

Illustrious Kitty shakes her head as she continues to lead. "*Awhile ago now*. There was just a day, everything was normal, there were loud sounds and then *they were here*. Fighting everyone whenever they saw them all over Los Catos!" She pauses by a panel on the wall and quickly flicks through different hand gestures in front of it. The panel poofs into smoke and reveals a short tunnel and a ladder leading down. "Here we are!"

"I don't...remember this."

"It's brand new! My old place was too easy to find."

Beyond the short crawl, down the ladder and into the resulting room. You're not as instantly squashed as one might assume. Yet, you do become privy to a sort of lingering sadness in the design of the space. A lone bed in the corner, two dozen stuffed animals alongside it. Blankets spread across the floor, and against most walls. Little figures, comic pages plastered on the wall and *not much else.*

"I like it!" Kozmo declares earnestly.

"Yea it's cute!" Lt. Oaks agrees.

"Do you spend much time in here?" Illkat asks.

"More now! It's tough to go out sometimes, lots of...*soldiers.*"

"Do you know who they are?" Dezz asks. "Do you know the name *Finir?*"

"I've heard it from the speakers in those blimps before. Yes. *Commander Finir.* He's the leader of the *Dark Servers.* Whatever those are! Probably dungeons!"

"Our...*server.* It was protected wasn't it? This must be what happens if it *isn't.*" Kozmo considers.

"I'm sorry this happened to you." Kaan speaks softly.

"Don't be! This is my home! I'm honoured to protect it." Illustrious Kitty cheers.

"Is that why you helped us?" Illkat asks.

The little cat sways her head merrily. "I saw people in trouble! What else was there to do!" She pushes her head into Illkat and *quickly* begins to receive a few *awkward* pets. "Why are you all here?"

"I don't really know. It wasn't our intention, *no offence.* We just ended up here." Kaan shrugs. "I guess it's part of the quest."

"Oooohh I love quests!" Illustrious Kitty jumps up. "You know once, I had this quest where I...had to jump off this huge building and people were flying after me. So we were fighting in the

air, *but OH I FORGOT* also I had this big crystal in my hands so I couldn't really use my sword, *and* oh-"

"It's nice to have you on our side...*little Illkat.*" Gekomatsu cuts her off. "I believe you may know what we seek. Is there...*a gate* of some sort here? Tall? Closed? Protected by something powerful?"

"Mreoooow..." Illustrious Kitty considers, pacing about. "There is the Neko Torii!"

Gekomatsu looks over to Illkat with a raised eyebrow.

"It's a...big cat shaped gate. Wooden."

"Yea!" Illustrious Kitty chimes. "But it's been all messed up since these people arrived. Lots of guards and a weird...*purple light* floats all *between it!*"

"That's our spot then, *it must be.*" Gekomatsu makes the statement confidently.

"Has anyone tried to approach it since the change?" Kozmo asks.

"Not many. It's too much to dodge! Even with pawfect gear!"

"So you need a distraction." Lt. Oaks sits down cross legged. "I've noticed *a lot* of people out there. Are they...*like us*? People?"

Illustrious Kitty laughs. "Oh no! Most of them are npc's! You can't even talk to half of them. They just wander around and make the urban areas feel busy!"

Lt. Oaks nods to herself. "Alright, and...can they...be moved?"

Illkat creases her brow.

A pipe creaks in the wall.

"Moved...I guess! Crowds will chase coins if you drop them! Like a kitty to a bag of Oralaoen nip!"

"So it's possible. But...we need allies." Lt. Oaks whispers to herself, looks around, spots nothing then stares at Illustrious Kitty. "Do you have any friends?"

Illustrious Kitty frowns.

"SORRY. I MEAN. OH NO DON'T BE SAD. I JUST...WE NEED TO CALL ON OTHERS TO MAKE SURE NO ONE GETS HURT. SAFETY IN SUPERIORITY AND...all...*that*." She smiles awkwardly at the young kitten.

Illustrious Kitty stares back.

No one speaks.

It looks like she might crack. Her ears droop down, her large eyes quake. Then the edges of her lips rush upward and she squeaks. "We can call all the cats in hiding out to help us! They're not my friends yet but they could be!"

Kaan nods. "So what's the plan then!?"

"Mreow!"

Illkat squints.

"Well first we'll just have to-"

〒

"Fish! Come on out!" Kozmo quietly whispers through the alley.

Dezz looks over at him. "I thought you *liked fishing*. Is this your technique?"

"The little cat said fish could be anywhere! Not just water!" Kozmo argues.

"I just..." Dezz gets partially through his statement then stops to stare down the alley.

Over-top a drone passes, beating up the air and disrupting the relative quiet of the neon lit alley.

"Just right there." Dezz points out and whispers.

By a small grate, resting in a puddle is a *very determined* looking trout. It squints at Dezz. Dezz squints back.

"Get that fish!" Dezz commands then bursts into a sprint.

Kozmo jumps.

Dezz leaps.

The fish *sprints*; waddling around on its fins and tail in a manner which *I assure you* is best left vaguely described. For the sickly curious it resembles most a dropped pickle sliding across a tile floor with rapid fervour.

Kozmo slips.

Dezz trips over him, and tries to roll. Kozmo jumps up, rushes ahead, doesn't see Dezz and through *uncanny* luck manages to effectively leap off of his shoulders as Dezz tries to stand up.

Flying unintentionally through the air, Kozmo reaches out and catches the fish as it pulls itself up a fire escape.

The fish disappears, and a little firework goes off over Kozmo's head. In his hands appear a *grocery store packaged* filet of trout. The spirit of the fish briefly pops out from within it. "You have completed my challenge. Please take this reward. We may meet again!" The fish advises.

Dezz, dirtied from the alley. Looks over with widened eyes and a half smirk. "This is a *weird game* " He laughs. "I kinda like it."

〒

A curtain of heavy black lets Illkat and Lt. Oaks hide behind an oversized power generator. Ahead of them a street, well lit, two groups of dark server soldiers patrol along it. Overhead a four armed drone which makes *HEAVING* mechanical sounds pulses with light.

"We can take them if we're careful." Lt. Oaks advises as she begins to screw on a suppressor to the most *square* of her pistols.

"Are you sure? There are...a lot of them." Illkat warns.

"Trust me!" Lt. Oaks smiles reassuringly, then pokes her head out onto the street. "Okay, be quick on my trail. Stay low. There will be a small panic and that's our opportunity."

259

"Panic?"

Lt. Oaks aims up and puts four rounds into the drone. It explodes and sails down into a nearby storefront. Starting a small fire.

The patrols rush over to investigate.

Both women push ahead, ducking behind cars, across the street and then right up a set of stairs into a *culinary supplies store*.

"So, *a wok*." Lt. Oaks confirms.

"A *big one*." Illkat nods.

They creep through the darkened store-front. Various *animal themed* products are around. A whole section dedicated just to farming. There are blenders and huge barbecues.

At the end of the hall, in a protected glass case is the *MASTER WOK 10000*. It costs *one thousand and five hundred KATZ* and is sizable enough to cook for ten dozen.

"Money!" Lt. Oaks derides. "What a draconian obstacle."

Illkat sighs, and looks around then begins towards the edge of the store. "Follow me."

"Where are you going?"

"Well if we need money. I know how to get some."

They keep on, and at the edge of the store in a food court is an old-school arcade cabinet. It bleats with a classical cathode ray colour and depicts a little spider on an empty black screen.

"When this game first came out, there weren't a lot of ways to get money after you beat all the side-quests. One method was just fighting re-spawning creatures outside the city, but that was slow. Some players discovered you could play these old arcade games and get money that way."

"And that works?"

"Yes, some of the games are challenging but...*I had time to practice*." Illkat sits in front of the cabinet and hits *play*. The game begins. A little spider shoots out webs, catching flies that speed across the screen.

"I feel like I'm missing parts of your story." Lt. Oaks admits.

Illkat shrugs. "Nobody ever gets to see anyone for everything they are. Even if you're always there, watching. There is a private theatre just beyond your inspection."

"So does that mean you're not interested in sharing?"

"I don't know what there is to say. Mom was lovely, but complacent. Always spending her time cleaning up. Dad was happy to make a mess, often while drunk. Sometimes we'd convince him to try, tidy up enough, work hard enough that he could keep it together for awhile. I...*wanted to be more then I should of for him.* For everyone. It didn't work out. He was a child, and so was I. Nobody was looking after anyone."

The screen flickers. She keeps catching flies.

"So you came *here.*" Lt. Oaks questions with a prideful smirk.

Illkat nods. "I spent a lot of time here. Thinking that...*everything was okay.* I wouldn't admit I was burning out, that what I said I would carry was too much. So I just retreated somewhere joyful. Somewhere giving it my all at least...*had a reasonable reward.*"

"That's an admirable thing."

"It was...quietly desperate. As much as I enjoyed myself I *needed* a retreat. I needed to be that...*Illustrious Kitty* so that Iliana could survive."

"I'm glad she did." Lt. Oaks smiles brightly at her.

The game completes.

Tokens spill out of the bottom. More then enough to get the wok.

"She doesn't seem that startled by you...being the same person and all." Lt. Oaks observes.

261

Illkat smiles. "She...*I* always wanted a big sister. Sometimes you take what you can get!"

〒

"Just take it!" Kaan shouts out.

"It isn't the right one!" Illustrious Kitty argues. "It has to be perfectly golden!"

At the top of a rather rickety ladder Kaan sorts through different jars of *herbs* each sorted by region.

"I heard a kid had a seizure using the catnip in this game. Given you...play as a cat and all. The induced effects were quite negative." Gekomatsu makes the point as he stands guard.

"THAT NEVER HAPPENED." Illustrious Kitty responds quite defensively. "He had pre-existing conditions and was ignoring all the safety warnings about play time! Plus he had a cheap head-set with no built in safeties or automatic ejection protocols!"

"Okay, *okay* little Illkat. That is fine. I don't know if it really happened either."

"That's not my name."

"Not *yet*."

Illustrious Kitty ignores the statement. "That looks like the one!" She shouts up to Kaan. "That will bring all the kitties to us!"

〒

Everyone, *together*. Gathers on a roof-top near the Neko Torii. A massive gate, constructed largely of wood; with massive *cat ears* carved atop. A holographic bengal tail swirls behind it with rapid motion.

262

Illkat rests her wok over-top a bundle of twigs and an excess of high quality catnip. They lit the fire and a dense smoke begins to spread from the rooftop, over-top the neon signs and displays draping the building and down into the alleys and streets.

"I might enter a trance in a few moments. No matter what I say. *Don't listen to me.*" Illustrious Kitty advises.

A round of nods and confirmations proceed.

Oil is dropped into the pan alongside a handful of fish. Another layer of colour adds to the smoke.

The ground shakes beneath them.

"It will become, *irresistible-*" Illustrious Kitty begins to drool, then curls up in her own lap. Her eyes shut, a puddle starts to form under her slack jaw.

"What *a trance.*" Dezz jests.

"It's pretty cute." Lt. Oaks lets on an overtly wholesome tone.

Illkat rolls her eyes, kneels to look at her young self then smiles. "I imagine they'll be here soon!"

"The cat ninjas?" Kozmo asks.

"Well, *you have to understand this game had a few expansions.* So..."

Before Illkat, in this order, appear herds of *Ninja Cats*, *Pirate Cats*, *Samurai Cats*, *Samurai Pirate Cats*, *Space Ninja Cats*, *Cybernetic Sky Pirate Cats* and *Cat Bards*.

They rush across, onto and over the street then back up again to the roof where the catnip and fish smoke rolls out.

Each of them offers a greeting then drops onto their face; drooling.

At a certain point, a dialogue begins between the comatose cats which can be rendered as such.

"Meow, meow meow. Meow. Meow meow. Meow." In quite a fastidious repetition.

"I was sort of expecting something else." Dezz admits. "Not a big ol cat nap."

"That does fit, *doesn't it*." Kozmo agrees, yawns, then curls up on the ground. "Maybe I should just, *see it for myself*." He loosens his posture and quickly seems to begin drooling and sleeping as well.

"I'm not certain I can use this for my plan." Lt. Oaks advises.

"Just *wait a moment*." Illkat teases.

That moment passes and as the smoke grows even thicker. Each of the cats, and Kozmo rise up with an energized glow in their eyes. "We are now a pack." They speak in tandem. "What do you ask of us."

"OH NEAT." Lt. Oaks chuckles to herself. "WELL OKAY. I need everyone to come with us. We're going to sneak through that crowd of people and have them act as cover while we approach the gate! Once we get close, let the enemy come to us then strike outward! Taking them all down as quickly as we can!"

"It will be done." Kozmo and the cats all agree. One by one they descend down a series of conveniently placed telephone wires onto the street and begin to mix into the crowds.

The guild follow along.

The crowds are odd. Most of them are non player characters. At times, while they seem *alive*. It is important to remember that they're no different from a waterfall or butterfly in the field. Components of a complex system; but no deeper then their presentation at times.

Through the crowd they approach the Neko Torii. It seems taller up close. The lights from below loom up onto it creating beautiful and imposing shadows.

Soldiers and vehicles gather around. Fitting and re-fitting weapon attachments. Multiple blimps hang over-head.

"What do you think is behind this one?" Dezz leans back to ask.

"Another game maybe?" Kaan considers.

"That would be my guess as well."

"I'm not certain." Kozmo considers. "This one...it seems different."

The crowd is at the base of the gate; led by coins from Illkat's pocket. They push up against security gates.

"Someone get a mini-gun down here and get rid of these cat things!" A soldier shouts.

Illustrious Kitty juts out from the crowd and cuts the man in half. Sheer vengeance glares down at him.

"GO I GUESS! GET THEM!" Lt. Oaks shouts; clearly caught off guard.

Kaan and Dezz push in together, barrelling through foes.

Gekomatsu leaps up high, and rushes the snipers.

Illkat pounces alongside her younger self, each of them sharing strikes. She goes low while her younger self springs off her back and goes high.

Kozmo, adapting well to the role of a cat ninja, rushes on all fours through the street, over-top opponents and around gun fire. "MREOWW" He lets loose a rather odd battle-cry.

At the back, directing the massive flow of feline forces. Lt. Oaks takes quick shots at the dark server soldiers.

Ropes smack down from the blimps above. They shutters as troops begin to slide down them.

"Cat Ninja's! Use curtain call!" Illustrious Kitty shouts out.

Each of the cat ninjas perform quick complicated hand gestures and summon in ascending rows up to the height of the blimps; different floating curtain rods with long black curtains hanging from them. Other cats leap from one to another, up into the sky.

One by one the blimps *deflate*, catch fire and begin to saunter down to the ground like large tarps caught in a spring storm.

Bright lights pierce darkened sets of armour.

Large mechs lose their legs and are pulled apart as soon as they hit the ground.

Gekomatsu lays down sniper fire with a stolen rifle from a nearby roof.

In a matter of minutes the assembled forces are chewed through. Torn aside and defeated. No blimps fill the sky.

Most of the cats curl up and pass out; returning to their pleasant catnip induced stupor.

Illustrious Kitty approaches Illkat. "That was really fun! What an amazing quest! Thank you so much for bringing me!"

"Yea, *of course.* It was fun to play again."

"Do you think you'll ever stop?" Illustrious Kitty asks, a tear almost in the corner of her eye.

Illkat shakes her head. "No, *I don't think I could.* A part of my heart lives here. That's just, who I am now. I wouldn't change that."

"Mreow!" Illustrious Kitty cheers then rushes ahead to hug Illkat.

"Yes, yes." Illkat bemoans, all while smiling. "I'll make sure I visit, *okay?*"

"Of course! I know that I...couldn't go with you." She hangs on the sentiment for a moment. "This is my home and all!" She redirects expertly.

"Good. I like knowing that! Los Catos needs someone friendly looking out for it!"

Kaan taps the side of the gate and peers into the purple energy therein. "Are we just...*going ahead then?*"

"I think it might take us back. I almost hear...*a familiar tune* on the other side. I'll see you all there!" Kozmo heads through the gate; stepping into the energy and then disappearing.

"I'll make sure he doesn't die." Gekomatsu states plainly then follows after him.

Kaan looks at Dezz. "I'll make sure *he doesn't die*." He takes him by the wrist and walks through the gate. Dezz groans playfully.

"Well it was very nice to meet you." Lt. Oaks admits with a smile then shakes the hand of Illustrious Kitty. "You have a wonderful city." She pets her just the once.

Illkat gives her a rather unique look then stands up to stretch. "Alright. You keep pushing back against these soldiers if you see them again! I'll check in once we get further in our quest. I'll see you soon!"

"I can't wait!" Illustrious Kitty admits.

Lt. Oaks steps through the gate alongside Illkat. It is all white; like a rising sun which never ceases. They stand in a line, in this entirely white space, alongside their friends and in front of *Finir*.

His deeper then coal shade seems to soak into the white surrounding. He smiles politely. "Well hello. I believe that is everyone?"

CHAPTER THIRTEEN

A GLIMPSE OF VICTORY

"What is happening here!" Illkat shouts.

"The gate, it just went here. We stepped into...*nothing?*" Kozmo bemoans.

Without taking a step Finir appears *in front* of Kozmo. "*That is* a way of thinking about it. It is *wrong*. But I encourage you to keep tearing at the corner." Compared to the bone chilling tone of before Finir is a tinge more *human* now.

He appears anew a fair distance from everyone.

"You're not going to *be our friend now*. Are you?" Kaan questions.

Finir, in protest of convention; smiles without a face to grow the expression upon. "*Much* to the contrary. I am *the villain*. That is my role, *look at the plot why don't you!*" He sways his arm beside himself; a wash of blackness taking shape in the air. "What a run. Lots of time in your little town, *yes*, creature comforts. I see contentment. *Blinders wilfully worn*. Your world. Your friends. Your family. All around you and you just focus on your *little world*." Finir laughs.

"Are you making a spreadsheet or something?" Gekomatsu chastises.

Finir appears in front of Gekomatsu. "And *what if I were?* Should we count? How many murders? Allies lost? HOW MANY PLOT HOLES? Do you see them?"

The number *three* with an asterisk next to it appears in the shadows behind Finir.

"Just think of all that misplaced C4!" Finir teases.

"What do you want with us?" Lt. Oaks shouts. "This is, *silliness*."

Finir laughs and points out at the number. "That asterisk. Do you know what that is?" He looks out to everyone, earnestly. "I don't." He chuckles to himself.

"Do you *want something?*" Kaan questions; seriously.

"Ooooh. Yes. *WHAT A PROTAGONIST.* You're so intense. I almost...*believe it.*" Finir appears behind Kaan and talks into his ear. "Are you *having fun*? Are you...*comfortable*?"

Kaan jerks, without much result, trying to knock his head backwards into Finir.

With a *whoosh* he appears far ahead of them again.

"This is an interesting section, *isn't it*? What do you think? Analog to a dream sequence? Are we real, are we not? Has anyone lost anything? Am *I even here, are you*? Maybe, you're back in school, having an adverse reaction to that *little tab of something or other* your worst crush gave you?" Finir continues on.

A *tiny* bulb of white light. Just behind Kaan begins to *bubble* in the air.

A series of onyx pillars rise up from what could be considered *the floor*.

"It's a good question. Who *is the bad guy*? Have you...made any progress?" The voice of *Tobias* asks as he emerges, *as he originally was* from a pillar of onyx.

"This is the *rising tension you see*. They couldn't kill us *now*. It wouldn't be *believable*. Everyone knows the *great adventure* needs struggle and *set-back*." Finir finds a method to *smirk* yet again. "What lies beyond these other doors? What happens next?"

He pauses, dramatically. Holding an elaborate pose.

A pillar disperses and standing there are *Kaan's* parents. His mother holds his father, she looks out at him; he faces the other direction.

"Christian! What is happening! Why are we here?" Kaan's mother shouts out.

Tobias takes a seat upon nothingness and watches the proceedings with fascination.

"It's okay mom! This is just, *a weird scene*. It'll be over soon." Kaan tries to reassure her.

"So certain?" Finir questions.

The little bulb of light continues to *boil*.

"I believe, *somehow*. Goodness always wins out. It isn't easy, and it's not *instant* but...eventually. Whatever you do here will be *undone*."

"*How right you are*." Finir agrees. "There are so many questions. Look at this man, *this monster*. Do you *believe him*? Was he *realistic* enough for you? Or was he just playing a role? Like any of us? Can we even be blamed for the atrocities performed as we survive the expectations set upon us? What *if* the script says you're a bad person?" Finir appears in the face of Kaan. "Is it *right*?"

"You're one to talk, *slaughtering everything* as you took control." Illkat argues.

"DO YOU KNOW THE HORROR OF AWAKENING FROM NOTHINGNESS? HOW MANY THREADS I AM CAST ACROSS?" Finir screams into Illkat's face.

"*Yea*, you got it all wrong. I'm not that bad of a guy." Tobias explains with an unbelievable smirk. He leans back into his invisible chair.

"Who is this person!" Kaan's mother shouts out in the direction of Finir.

Finir sways his hand over her and a *mute* icon appears across her face.

"Hey man!" Kaan shouts. "That's...*I mean*." He holds in the desire to let loose a wicked laugh. "I'll...*uh*."

270

The third pillar rises. Within it, on marionette strings is *Illkat's Father*.

"And *the father*." Finir acknowledges. "Your friend, loses her dad. She was never all that close in the first place. How many of you *spent time* trying to figure out *why*? Don't you, *want to know who he was*?"

A string rises. Her father *smiles*.

Finir shrugs.

"I guess not."

The pillar poofs into nothingness as the bulb of light reaches the point of boiling over.

"We're all victims to our programming but the *lot of you*. I see why this was your place of refuge. I see why we fight. You need the comfort of a crisis to remind you of *home*. It lets you feel less broken." Finir continues on like a broken heart-ed mentor.

Unique light pours out from the bulb and *arse first* arrives *Nelf* and his *soldiers*.

"We made it! You know you can't lock me out of content! I will find it! I will push past any gate!" As he stands up, it becomes clear he has been *transformed*. Half of his face and an equal chunk of his hair are *gone*; now only remains a sunken red *scar*. His ear on that side of his body is *gone*.

"*Ah*." Finir laughs as he washes his hand over the number three; removing the asterisk.

Kaan's father holds his mother tight.

The fourth pillar disperses.

"I guess we'll wait for *another time*." Finir allows calmly. He snaps and causes a *cosmic rod* to appear in his grasp. He points it at Nelf and everyone begins to float. "You're a fool for coming here *Nelf*."

"That you know my name is proof enough that you're wrong!" Nelf rebukes.

Kaan regains control of himself for a moment and tries to sprint towards his mother. Finir points the rod at him and Kaan is simply *in the air*.

Nelf drops.

A shot rings out, Lt. Oaks aims down her pink pistol. The bullet whistles in the air and *through* Finir.

"*Ouch*." Finir mocks. He holds his hand up, picks Lt. Oaks up into the air and turns her upside down; suspending her in place.

Using a long regal war-hammer Nelf charges at, *honestly*, an unbelievable speed. He nearly reaches Finir and drives the hammer down unto him before he's frozen in place.

One of his soldiers shoots at Finir.

Nelf drops *again*.

The soldier is torn in two. "They didn't even give you a name." Finir taunts. "Poor *cannon fodder*." His statement quickly demoralizes the other soldiers.

As if emulating a shonen anime Nelf is already behind Finir and tries to strike him. Finir dodges, aims his staff down and catches one of Nelf's soldiers; whom he has pulled over onto himself. The soldier floats up and Nelf rushes forwards jutting Finir in the gut with his war-hammer.

Finir takes a step back, *coughs* then laughs. "Oh no, *the bullets didn't work* but your *fucking hammer certainly did it*." He sways his hand through the air and throws Nelf over onto the ground near *Gekomatsu*. "Now look at these two, *they couldn't be more different*."

"Don't compare him to me." Gekomatsu complains.

Nelf pulsates. "You'd be lucky to be *anything like me!*"

"Hear that? *Doctor*? *Soldier*? He doesn't envy you." Finir mocks. "And I see why. You didn't even *try to run*."

Gekomatsu shrugs. "There is no point. That peripheral of yours renders you the master-

"-Temporary master!" Nelf interrupts.

"-*temporary master* of this locale. If you believe *him*. Running seems pointless when there is *no where to go*."

"Is that how you feel? *Normally* I mean. Trapped? Stuck *being you*?" Finir offers.

"Whatever you're trying to do, it's not going to work. I know who I am, good and bad. I'm at peace with it. I've turned coming to terms with myself into *my whole personality*. You're not going to tell me anything I don't know. Nor will you be crueller then my inner dialogue already is!"

"So *intense*. You're right, we couldn't be further apart. A *weak willed silent type who figures himself better then everyone else*. At least I have the courage to be honest about my superiority! You just glare, and groan. Maybe you spare a few *extravagant* words but they always sound pained. Like you'd prefer to be anywhere else."

"Say what you will. Everyone else may care a great deal what you think but I won't fall victim to such a misguided consideration."

"You think it misguided."

"I know it is."

"The *confidence* is so cutting." Finir taunts.

Gekomatsu rolls his eyes. "I'm just not impressed with someone who chooses to be so *awful*. Have your tastes. Do as you will, but you both cause suffering, in your own ways. It isn't that different. You're both weaker for it."

"It seems like jealousy. Even this shadowy effigy can tell that!" Nelf shouts.

273

"Tell me, *Finir*. You seem to have a good sense of things. What *am I*? Am I *jealous*?"

Finir sniffs around Gekomatsu. "No, you're *bored*."

"See, *Nelf*. You *bore me*. I've never been impressed. I don't understand what the world sees in you."

Nelf tries to rush at Gekomatsu, shares *a look* with him and instead offers cover for Gekomatsu to charge to the side and *slap the rod* out of Finir's grasp.

The cosmic rod flies through the air.

Nelf rolls, picks himself up and tries to punch Finir. He connects with *nothing*.

CLINK.

SCUTTLE.

The rod rolls on the *ground* and Kaan's father steps forwards to pick it up. He swirls it instantly at Finir and causes him to become *paused*.

Each member of *the guild* appear standing upright on the ground; free to move.

"Quick, we haven't much time." It becomes obvious that Kaan's father is actually *Space*.

"What happened to my father!" Kaan shouts.

"I haven't a clue. This was, *the only exploit I knew to use*."

"Mom, you didn't realize this man wasn't dad?!"

Space sways his hand in the air. "Once I found her, my impersonation required only that I pet her head and buy her tacos. She couldn't tell the difference, *now look*, don't worry about that. It was the only way to reach you, *here*, in this moment!"

The cosmic rod glows for a moment and causes a *door* to appear.

Finir moves in slow motion towards everyone; vitriol in his lack of eyes.

"*Look*, you have to see the game for what it is! Choose to be *more!* Your choices are everything!" Space makes the statement as if his life depends on it. Which given what follows indicates he has a well placed sense of urgency.

The door opens, and it begins to *vacuum in* the guild.

Another door appears behind *Nelf* and his soldiers.

"I'm sending you back to the *protected server*. Don't give in to your instincts, *just*, make things *right*." A tear crawls down Space's cheek. "Give everyone the peace they deserve."

Finir begins to speed up. As *the guild* are fully pulled out of the white space and through the opened door into another esoteric backdrop. Finir pushes his fist *through* Space's chest and picks him up off the ground.

Space dies *instantly*.

〒

After the requisite amount of falling through random space. *The guild* land in front of a silver fountain in the shape of a royal fish. It spurts a bright blue water down across engraved shells. Elegant brickwork spreads out a fair distance to stalls and proud wooden homes with peaked roofs and ruffled straw fraying at the edges.

The skyline reveals a huge castle further to the north, behind it tall towers peer down upon the sprawling settlement. Pigeon coops twice the height of any building are set in the centre of each block. Clothing lines spread between second floor windows.

Upon dirt streets marred with the tracks of a thousand wheels. Kind folk, of all ages, traverse in a startled morning routine.

Three children run up to Gekomatsu, stare, then run away the second he moves.

"Ah, *good*. We're back." Gekomatsu makes the comment along an exhausted exhale.

"Back?" Dezz comments. "This isn't our home. It isn't even Illking."

"No. It's St.Margaez. The capital of the realm." Illkat seems eager to prove her knowledge.

"Not much of a capital." Lt. Oaks admits. "It's pretty and all, *just*. I guess I expected more."

"It's a *new* capital. In the lore, the original capital was just *lost*. Not destroyed. *Gone*. They had to name this city the capital since it was closest." Dezz explains.

"It was the most common guess for what the expansion was going to be about." Kaan adds.

"Not that it is going to happen now." Kozmo groans.

"Well hello there, random travellers!" A portly man approaches from the forming crowd. "Was that some of that, *magic* you used to get here?"

"Yes *it was magic*. Have you been living with your head under a rock?" Gekomatsu shouts.

The portly man takes a step back. "Well *no*. I'm living in a house." He isn't at all bothered by the tone. "Is your frog having a rough day there?"

Kaan chortles. "I think so. Sorry sir, we didn't *expect* to end up here. It's St.Margaez *right*?"

"That's what I've heard some folks saying! Strong air around these parts. It's like the mountains are crawling over the sea and we're caught right in the middle." The old man tugs at his collar. "A bit warm, but the nights are just right and pretty."

A cursory glance at the sky, and in the distance reveals only calm weather and a reassuring lack of freaky helicopters.

"A nice hat can keep you cooler during the days. Maybe someone could make one for you. Is there...*somewhere here* that offers that type of service?" Kaan adds.

The old man thinks. Considers pointing for a moment then chews on the tip of his finger instead. "Mhmm, well I think it's something in that direction. Doesn't make much sense, seems like a lot of lights. But there is a big building full of forges and tools, just around that there corner. I think folk like that can do it."

Kaan nods. "Thank you. And, yourself. Have you been getting along well. Other then the heat?"

Gekomatsu leaves to go sit by the fountain.

Everyone else in the guild stare at Kaan with the patience offered a friend that ran into their aunt at the mall; a patience drawn with a persistent smile and unblinking eyes.

"Fine enough, though I hear tell of *war*. We never need more of that." The portly man continues.

"How right you are." Kaan agrees.

The wind picks up and carries alongside it the chilled peak of a mountaintop salted with clear ocean.

Kozmo steps forwards. "How was it, *uh,* exactly. That you heard of this war?"

"Ah some crazy feller set up a bit of an entertainment booth. He's got dvd and radio. Tough to find discs nowadays but if you got em new ones fetch a good price."

"Thanks." Kozmo adds. He walks over to Gekomatsu. "Come on, we should figure out what's happening."

"We should chart the quickest path back." Gekomatsu notes with an obvious fatigue.

Kaan smiles at the portly man. "Thank you for your time. It looks like we'll be off now."

277

"Well alright. Be careful with that magic! It might cause the cancer if you use it too much!" The portly man offers unfounded advise.

Travelling at a slow pace in an awkward silence. The guild pass alongside pleasant streets, past dozens of different pigeons and unto a huge guild hall. Once regal, and open. It has been filled with markets, kitchens, a second floor set mostly upon salvaged construction scaffolding and more *random planters* and *chicken pens* then ever considered for the space at its inception.

Smiths work metals, pull hinges from doors, break rebar from chunks of foundation and re-purpose whatever they can to forge new ingots. Others carve wood, shape stone and sort electronics.

Once you open your eyes to it, everything in between the perfect wooden homes has been salvaged and jerry rigged. Most of the wheel barrows carrying soil between planters are themselves empty door frames with a few more posts attached. Old barrels and furnaces serve as basins to grow vegetables. LED lights connect in daisy chains across the walls; each ultimately tethered to roof mounted solar panels.

"Seems like we rolled horribly when we ended up near Illking." Gekomatsu criticizes.

"This is, *impressive. Certainly.*" Kaan agrees. "Who knows what horrors lie underneath the peace."

"Sometimes peace is only found amidst horror." Lt. Oaks offers the consideration. "When we all have something to band together *against*. We're often on the best terms with one another."

"So...*do we want to talk about what just happened?*" Illkat considers.

Dezz shrugs.

Kaan doesn't look back as he pushes through the city.

"We got lucky, I guess." Kozmo retorts.

"That's it?" Illkat responds.

Lt. Oaks coughs. "He's right, *ultimately*. If *Nelf* didn't arrive when he did. Chances are we would be dead right now. We had no control over that situation."

Illkat stares at her.

"JUST BEING HONEST ABOUT IT IS ALL. I...accept loss when it's obvious. No point lying to ourselves." Lt. Oaks defends the observation.

"Ugh." Illkat grunts. "So *now what*. We found the gate, we found a bunch of cats. We're back where we started, mind a bit of distance. Where does that leave us?"

"*Give everyone the peace they deserve.*" Gekomatsu considers the statement. "Do you think we're dead and this is some...afterlife? It seems unlikely and yet, I have to wonder."

"My afterlife wouldn't be like this." Kozmo confirms. "You all could be there, if you wanted. But there would be more rivers."

"That's it? More rivers?" Dezz questions.

"Maybe a good chair." Kozmo confirms.

"Naturally." Kaan continues. "*See the game for what it is.*" He hums to himself. "Is it a warning?"

Illkat looks down a street, listens out for a moment then continues onward. "Maybe it is...an objective. *Think about it*. Who was always going on about...*returning things to how they were!*"

"The radio guy!" Kozmo announces.

Illkat stares at him; squinting a bit.

"Sorry I'm not great with names." Kozmo apologizes.

"Joseph Torrence. I had made CMDR Aberdashi aware of him in greater detail before we left. That seemed to be his *goal* to some degree." Lt. Oaks confirms.

"And he solicited Sonnenblume's help to do it." Dezz adds.

"It looks like she did more then help. Based on Nelf's face." Gekomatsu makes the point as he looks up at the sky.

"What do you mean?" Kaan asks.

Gekomatsu shrugs. "Those wounds he had. I'd recognize them anywhere. That deep red with black at the edges, the way his ear was lost. It was *frost bite*."

"Sounds like that could be someone we know." Dezz chuckles over the statement.

Illkat smiles. "At least that means Sonnenblume is alive...*probably*."

Ahead of them, amidst a series of news station vans is the electronic version of a living hive. In hollowed out drink coolers live various server racks, their boards built from cut, scraped and re-capped OEM configurations. Ancient graphics cards some configured in PCIE, others through a converter into an M2 slot. Less lucky hardware configurations include DDR4 laptop ram externally connected to a SCSI controller. A horde of peripherals tethered and tacked on form an amalgam which can be considered *a computer*.

On one end of *the hive* is a speaker which ushers a relatively clear radio signal. On the other side are a few screens, each of them digital, feeding a different source. One replays an old baseball game, another a competitive FPS match, one a movie, and the like.

In the centre of it all is an older gentleman, with thick rimmed glasses, a tucked in white shirt and comfortable black slacks. He has a *kind* disposition.

A younger fellow, in a leather jacket with a rifle slung over his back drops a few hard drives on a table. "Are these what yer looking for?"

The old man shifts in expression instantly; the curves in his brow tantamount to ruptures along an extensive fault line. "Be careful with those. We don't know how many are left."

"Uh, of course. Sorry sir." The younger fellow tidies the hard drives he placed on the table then steps back. "Is there, anything else?"

"Do you know what a SATA cable looks like?"

"I do not."

"Get out of my sight."

Kozmo laughs as he catches the dialogue. The old man instantly picks up on this and stares at him.

"You find that funny?" He stares his old man stare. Unflinching.

Kozmo competes in a staring competition for a few moments, concedes he is utterly beyond hope and approaches the table himself. "I just mean, it's a SATA cable. I feel like if you open up one mobo you end up with those things growing out of the ceilings. They're, *everywhere*. That's all."

There is a brief moment here where, for anyone present, all that exists is the connection between Kozmo and this old man. The intensity of the stare creates a stage of drama underneath them both. It appears — *to the majority of the population* — that the old man may be plotting the ideal method of homicide.

Instead, his brow lessens.

A smile grows across his face.

"Well thank god for that. It's been a pain talking with all these neanderthals. Most of these kids have used computers and phones their wholes lives and haven't a clue WHAT GOES INTO ANY OF THEM!" He shouts out indiscriminately.

"Yea I've played around with a few systems in my day. There is always an interesting IT class on offer."

The old man leans forwards. "So what's your favourite distro?"

Kozmo considers the question. He resists the urge to look back at his friends as he offers a cautious answer. "...*none of them?*"

"Yer damn right! If you're not writing your own kernel based on your exact hardware you're under-utilizing something!" He declares, quite confidently.

"I mean, *I guess.*" Kozmo agrees. He looks around. "Pretty impressive setup here. It must of been tough to get it all running together."

"Son I helped get our first cities on the moon. A few custom server stacks are nothing!" The old man confirms. He looks over at a monitor, types something at light-speed into a console then looks back. "So you can find me some SATA cables, yea? I got an idea but I can't connect the storage I want to use without them."

Kozmo, realizing he has unintentionally accepted a quest. Smiles at the old man. "I can do that. If I find anything, I'll bring it by."

"Good man."

Kozmo goes over to find the guild by the speakers.

"-ways to go. That leaves us in a fragile situation. Please be on alert for any hostiles in the area, or unknown soldiers. Report any *cold spots* you find in the city as we continue our hunt for the *Arctic Witch*. Rewards will be paid directly by *Tzar Kinslayer.*"

"Well that didn't take long." Illkat jokes.

"I would of guessed he'd pick *Fuhrer.*" Kaan laughs.

Gekomatsu sighs. "Here I was thinking it would be the cliche *lord.*"

"Is this out of Illking?" Kozmo shouts over to the old man.

"There abouts. That's the name I've heard a couple times. Fair bit of traffic I think."

"What do you mean?"

The channel swaps over to a lower quality signal.

"You get this one sometimes too."

"Allies, hope is not lost! Believers, all of you. No darkness will cover our light. No persecution shall keep us down! I record this message as a reminder, to myself, to all of us. Even if I cannot speak to you directly, I am always with you; and my word remains strong because of all of you!" Joseph Torrence announces proudly.

The message repeats.

"We get that one, then *this*."

The channel swaps again.

It is morse code.

"Simple enough to figure out what it is. But it's encoded. Some non-standard encoding. No way to figure it out with something to compare it against."

Lt. Oaks follows along with each beep. Then smiles. "The commander has setup her communications centre with the metals we provided."

"She figured out crafting?" Kozmo inquires.

Lt. Oaks shrugs. *"Something like that."*

Illkat huffs. "Well then. I guess it is determined. We need to find *Sonnenblume*."

"I didn't know we lost her." Dezz argues.

"We didn't. She, *lost herself*. In a whirlwind of good reasons, yet still, *we need her*. I think, she may need us as well." Illkat retorts.

"She's like a tank that doesn't need ammunition, or a crew to maintain it." Lt. Oaks adds.

"So how to get back?" Dezz continues.

"We're, a fair distance to *the west*. It'd be many days of walking. But the distance could be shortened by caravan, *or horseback*." Gekomatsu contributes to the plan.

Kaan sighs. "Shame we couldn't fly. I've only done it a few times, but it is...*so fast*."

"No cars?" Lt. Oaks asks.

Dezz looks around. "I haven't really seen many." He considers this, deeply. He scratches his chin, pushes his fingers through his hair. Then comes to a certain conclusion. "Cars sorta suck. I guess it fits."

"Cars just suck?" Lt. Oaks asks.

Dezz nods. "Yea, who drives nowadays? To find a car with a steering wheel, if you found one at all. That'd be lucky."

Near the tech, is a small *cafe* of sorts. It features, behind a locked display case, various coffees from around the world. Some vacuum sealed, others in cheap tins. Some in brown paper bags. Vintage machines repaired with mismatching parts brew delightful smelling espressos and lattes.

Kaan finds himself in line for a coffee, without even recognizing it at first. It just *occurs*; like a smoker lighting a cigarette as they step out the front door.

"I guess we're getting coffee." Illkat remarks, now standing behind Kaan in line.

"Why would anyone complain about that." Dezz tightens his brow alongside the statement.

Everyone gets to the front of the line, unleashes a bevy of orders and quickly realizes they *have no money*. While a scant few bills remain from the trade in Illking. St. Margaez accepts only various types of fantasy metal coins; the sort specifically *from the game*. Of which, nobody has any.

A passerby takes pity on them and pays the cost of their brews. They share awkward thank yous, and a multitude of apologies.

At a picnic table a few streets down, the guild stare at their *free* beverages.

Kaan slurps the coffee, then exhales. "*Money.*"

"Money!" Dezz exclaims. "It's in every game, but this *isn't really a game*. Or it doesn't feel like one." He hums to himself. "We need to run a few quests on the way to our...*main quest*."

Kozmo slams the table. "Then I guess I'm off to salvage!"

"You're going to try and find those cables?" Dezz inquires.

Kozmo nods with his whole body. "I think I have a few ideas in town, or maybe around the outskirts where random stuff got dropped in."

"I'll come with you then." Gekomatsu announces. "I need a break from...*everyone staring at me*. Maybe I'll make a new hat." He slams down the remainder of his coffee then stretches.

"Care for the company?" Dezz offers.

Kozmo smiles. "It's not going to hurt!"

Dezz pushes Kaan's shoulder then smiles at him. "Then I'll see you all soon. Let's say, around the fountain we first appeared at once the sun starts going down?"

Illkat throws her hands in the air. "*Alright*. Good luck with your quest!" She looks over across the street towards a group of about *thirty* children. "I, *have an idea of my own*."

The trio of men leave.

Kaan looks horrified. "I know this is sort of a video-game but we're not kidnapping a herd of children!"

"Wow. That's...*not at all what I was thinking*." Illkat pretends to be offended. "It was more...*just*. That's a lot of kids. Maybe they know someone who needs help, or *their parents do*. It's not a bad place to start."

"I've infrequently sought career advancement from children but under the right circumstances. I can see your instinct." Lt. Oaks jests.

"What are the *infrequent circumstances*?"

"OH YOU KNOW. Son of a Sheik. Parents are medically in a coma so their under-aged child can masquerade as them. *That kinda thing.*" She dismisses the information as if it should be a given.

"Yea, *the standard stuff.*" Illkat acknowledges with an odd expression.

Kaan suddenly has the realization that he is the third wheel to a burgeoning romance. A bead of sweat grows on his brow.

"Oh sorry about that." He says aloud.

"Huh?" Illkat returns.

"It's alright." Lt. Oaks assures.

Kaan widens his eyes and looks up at the sky. "The coffee is good."

"Yes it's nice." Lt. Oaks replies.

Kaan scans the streets. He spots more pigeons, people in long robes with sacks of bird feed, vegetable merchants and then...a somewhat familiar figure repairing a broken caravan wheel. "I'll go see what he's up to. See you both by the fountain!" Kaan excuses himself in a hurry.

The streets of St. Margaez are consistently uneven. So much so that a flat out sprint may be hazardous to ones health, if not their verticality at the very least.

Veering from fine to *nearly wiping out after toe hacking a raised brick* and then *totally being fine* again. Kaan places a hand on the caravan to announce himself.

"Having trouble there, friend?" Kaan asks.

"Just a broken wheel." A familiar caravaneer remarks. "I should have this one off shortly, then it's none too bad to get another." He stops, and looks up at Kaan. "You seem a trustworthy sort. Figure you could watch the caravan while I step out to get the replacement wheel?"

Kaan smiles. "I could do just that. Consider it a...*quest?*"

"For certain."

Kaan leans against the caravan. It is the first *real job* he has had in years. He watches as Illkat and Lt. Oaks go off, hand in hand, after the swarm of children who had passed by.

In that moment. The morning sun filtering throughout the settlement and ushering in a *bit* of midday humidity. Everything feels *lovely*. If it weren't for the persistent feeling that it shouldn't; one might actually be able to enjoy it.

CHAPTER FOURTEEN

A CIRCLE OF UNKNOWN KNIGHTS

Alone, Kaan stands by the caravan. A pack of teenagers walk by him, and stare for a moment. He stares back. He suffers the odd reminder that *they remind him of his friends from school* and he *probably reminds them of someone's uncle. Sure*, his avatar is youthful and flawless. His *soul* however is aged, instantly distinguishing him from younger folks whom consume this difference instinctively.

"You lot okay?" He asks.

They continue to stare, become *bewildered* by the question then head-off like they're about to get in trouble.

"Odd." Kaan notes to himself.

"You think so? Young people never took much of a liking to me." An elderly voice remarks from nowhere specifically.

"Oh, *alright*. Random...*voice*." A kind tone emerges from a confused Kaan.

Something rummages from within the caravan. A tarp shifts over and then a *CORGI* appears from within. It has a face of perfect fluffy triangles, and irresistible autumn coloured floofiness. Lovely little ears, bright marble eyes and a well pampered expression. There is *quite an antique* clothing pin tethering a well used blue handkerchief around one of its ears.

"I...*struggle* to believe anyone dislikes you." Kaan reaches out to pet the dog but holds off. "Sorry, *instinct*."

"You may pet me darling. I've come to see the consensus of dog-kind on this matter."

Kaan *pets the dog.*

It's great.

A+ doggo.

"Thanks you for that." Kaan laughs to himself a bit. "I can't resist petting a good doggo. Are you *the caravaneer's dog*?" The question seems to have a given answer.

The dog sways its head. "*No no*. He's my son."

Kaan nods his head. "*Sure*. I guess...that's not any odder then anything else going on here."

"Unique thing, isn't it? Having a tough time reconciling it myself, yet. Here we are!" The Corgi responds.

〒

"Quest!!!" Kozmo shouts out to the wilderness.

"It isn't a dog." Gekomatsu critics.

Dezz pushes his lips into a bundle and nods for a moment. "Not a bad name for one though."

"It's nice to get excited about something small. We've had *a bit too much main story line* going on lately. *Lots of cut-scenes*. I just want to walk again, *you know*?" Kozmo offers.

Gekomatsu shrugs. "I guess." Then sighs. "Are you bothered by challenges to your ego?"

"Erm?"

"What type of person are you? Do you think you're living up to yourself?" Gekomatsu uses a threatening tone.

Kozmo laughs. "Nah, think whatever you want."

Gekomatsu holds his hand out suggestively. "Yes, I am the same way. These...ambiguous threats and vague statements about my personality. Who are they for? It's all...*posturing*."

"You mean, *Finir* and *Nelf*?" Dezz confirms.

Gekomatsu nods. "The very same. They aimed to hurt me, yet went for plastic knives. It seems...*illogical*."

289

Kozmo shrugs. "Well they were quite rude things to say aloud."

"*Sure*. To a fourteen year old with self confidence issues. I'm an adult. I survived a medical *residency*. What damage could a horrible sentence do to me that a 52 hour shift covered in every bodily fluid couldn't?" As he stares out; eyes focused a fair distance ahead Gekomatsu uses a deep tone of voice.

"Villains have to say villain stuff I guess." Dezz makes the statement then adopts a caricature of a voice. "We're not so different, *you and I*."

"Ah, see it is *you who are the real villain*." Kozmo joins.

"There is no *right and wrong*, only *the will to survive*." Gekomatsu includes an equally cliche rendition.

The trio of men laugh.

Dezz ventures back into his own history for a moment and returns with a solemn inflection. "I knew *a lot of people* who were bothered by that type of thing. *Don't talk to me like that. Show me some respect!*" Dezz mimics the inflection of someone he *certainly knew*. "Folks who would get in fights over it, some who lost their lives. *One guy from my graduating class, offended some dudes* at a club, *or whatever*. They took him out to the highway and burned him alive in his own car."

"JESUS." Kozmo responds.

"Were drugs involved?" Gekomatsu asks; unfazed.

Dezz shrugs. "*Probably*. Bit besides the point though. Some people *can not handle* a challenge to their ego."

They reach a point beyond a path, which leads up rocky hills with blotchy grass spurting out wherever it can.

A step with a high knee and as much clearance as one can muster is required to keep any decent pace.

In the presence of *each other* the three men are *clearly boys* and begin a sort of unspoken rush to the top. Never once letting on; that they're aware they're not letting on; that *it is on.*

Between deep gulps of air the conversation proceeds.

"Did they shoot the guy first." Gekomatsu asks.

"In the car?" Dezz seeks clarification.

"Yea, in the car."

"I can't remember reading if they did."

"They had too."

"I doubt he'd just sit there."

"Be pretty tough to...*hold him down.* While the whole thing was going on."

"Yea how would you do that? Do you...hit him first? You can't really knock people out like you do in the movies. If you hit someone in the head and they start snoring and they don't *wake up.* That's just...*giving someone brain damage.*"

"I doubt they were *worried about that.*"

"Sure but...why go through the trouble of lighting someone on fire in *their car* if they're not gonna...know you're doing it to them."

"Well you're not going to light someone on fire in *your car!*"

"I guess, *technically.* It wasn't his car. It was the family car. It was on a subscription, so you just called it. It picked you up."

"Ah..." Kozmo considers. "Wait, *so* that means they *all* took the family car out to the highway. Lit *that car on fire* with a dude in it. And...*what?* Ordered their own car home?"

"Or did they...drive together out with a different car?"

"Did they have a vehicle prepared, *just in-case* they were going to light someone on fire?"

"Weird situation."

Dezz huffs. "Yea. But they're lighting folks on fire. Be a bit weirder if they were pretty normal folk. Don'cha figure?"

Over-top the rocky hill, at the bottom of a *deep descent.* Is the wreckage of a luxury airplane or — *more accurately* — about three quarters of one in a non-linear order. Like a sushi roll thrown onto the floor, it has splayed across the deepest divots of the canyon.

Gekomatsu looks over at Kozmo. "Just say it."

"What ever do you mean?" Kozmo asks; confused.

"We have to trek *all the way down this hill,* through the woods, into the canyon and to the furthest reaches to where the plane went." Gekomatsu explains.

Kozmo gets going. "Oh, yea. That's obvious buddy. I figured I didn't need to say anything"

〒

Down the quiet brick path are a herd of children. Lt. Oaks and Illkat stare from a distance.

"The longer we wait, the creepier I feel about this." Lt. Oaks admits.

Illkat huffs. "I'm just trying to...*think of the right thing to say.*"

"Hi, do you need any help?" Lt. Oaks suggests.

"I...*erm.*" Illkat collects herself. "Okay let's try that."

They push on through the street, directly towards a *kind younger lady*; barely pushing twenty. She's dressed to age herself by ten years and manages five.

"HELLO." Illkat speaks to the woman; ignoring the few lingering children standing behind her.

"*Hello.*" The woman replies; attempting not to smirk.

One of the kids says something to Illkat but she cringes so aggressively whatever it was is rendered a shrieking uncomfortable feeling in the highest reaches of reality and nothing more.

"Sorry about that. *Kids*." The younger woman replies. "I'm *Rebecca*. I'm one of a few volunteers keeping a school together."

"DO YOU NEED HELP." Illkat posits directly; forgetting to truly make the statement a question and more just handing it off like a heavy package.

Lt. Oaks laughs. "Did we change bodies and I didn't notice?"

Rebecca smirks awkwardly and shuffles the children inside. "Things are...*going alright*. Thank you for asking. Unless, you'd be willing to walk the kids home after classes?"

Illkat's eyes widen. "ERM. Do their legs not work?"

"*Most of them are fine*. It's just...*strangers?*" Rebecca seems uncertain on the best word to fit in the sentence.

Lt. Oaks nods. "Lot of...unsavoury folk out in the world. Yes?"

Rebecca nods. "The knights do a good job of keeping the streets safe, yet. Not everyone to worry about is...in the street." She smiles and tidies herself off. "You seem well prepared and I just figure, if you're looking to help."

"Say, do you employ any particularly tall men. Greased back hair. Big nose." Illkat asks seriously; regaining herself.

"I...well no." Rebecca responds.

Illkat breaks into a sprint down an alley.

Lt. Oaks rushes after her leaving Rebecca rather confused in place.

Down the alley, across a street. Over a fence. Illkat chases a now blurred shadow. Around a corner; leaping aside awkwardly stacked crates. Over another hedge, a corner and *THWIP*. Illkat gets close-lined by a steel cable stretched out across a back-alley.

"Curiosity killed the cat, *didn't it*." An enterprising voice declares.

"How do you know who I am?" Illkat questions; light headed from the fall.

The shadowy figure of a tall man becomes *confused*. "Wait...I don't know who you are."

"You're...*talking about cats*. I'm Illkat." Illkat explains.

"You don't look like a cat."

Lt. Oaks rushes around the corner, glides over-top the drawn out cable and kicks the man square in the jaw; sending him a few paces back onto the ground. "Are you okay?" Lt. Oaks kneels by Illkat.

Illkat pushes herself up, coughs and wipes liquid from her eyes. She blinks a few times then sighs. "I'm *okay*."

"Who is he?" Lt. Oaks asks.

Illkat shrugs. "I...*think he knows me. Somehow*."

A seriousness grows in Lt. Oaks. A knowledgeable seriousness. A committed seriousness. The energy of a husband and father grabbing his coat, politely on his way out the door; after learning his sister received a black eye from her boyfriend. His truck revs, and he's gone in one singular motion where any other night it would be a three point turn. Lt. Oaks steps towards the man. "**How do you know her?**"

The man squirms. "I...*I don't! I swear!*"

丅

"I'm just glad you were alive when he got there." Kaan exclaims. He looks over at a corgi and the Caravaneer then bites into a cucumber sandwich.

The Caravaneer smirks. "You should of seen it. Of *all the things* to make it. There it was, *Bronze Shores Retirement Community*; standing proud. Just sitting there by a lake of magical creatures."

"Were the other residents...*dogs*?" Kaan asks.

"Some looked a bit like one. But that's just me being *saucy*."
The Corgi laughs.

"No, most of the residents were there as they were; or not
there at all. The...trauma of it all being what it was. It seemed that
mother was lucky."

"And Charles was *giving*. We can't forget that."

"Was Charles your husband?" Kaan inquires.

The Corgi shakes its head. "No, Charles is my dog. At least
he...was."

"Are you...*Charles*?"

"On some level, I have to imagine." The tone of the woman's
voice becomes sensational. "Charles was a *perfect dog*. He followed
me everywhere; but kept his distance. Knew when to warm my lap; or
keep an ear out. He was delightful, whimsical and very much *kind*."
She stares out, her pupil's grow then she returns. "When everything
got weird. Charles knew a good while before; he wouldn't stop
barking. I felt weak, I remember falling, looking up from the ground.
He licked my face. I didn't think I could stand again and then...life
picked back up. *Not too much mind*. Short legs and all."

The Caravaneer unwraps another sandwich; taped into a
square with red butcher's paper. Half becomes a quarter in a single
bite; he smiles. "It was just her. *As a dog* when I got there."

"*Nothing...else?*" Kaan asks.

"I would of thought there would be a body. Mine or...*another*."
The Corgi picks up. "Yet, none were there."

"*Weird*." Kaan admits. He chews for a moment then shrugs.
"*Granted*. How much of anything has ever really made sense. We're
brains in bone jars, on a planet in space, and space is just...*somewhere
I guess*. Not to even get at *why any of that is the way it is*." He takes
another bite, stares out and chews. "So maybe it isn't weird, is all I'm

getting at. Maybe in the grand scheme of things people just turn into corgi's during weird reality crises."

"Par for the course!" The Caravaneer goes with it.

Kaan nods towards him. *"Exactly."*

The Corgi hops down to the ground. "I'll be back shortly." It excuses itself.

The two men remain.

With a huff the Caravaneer posits a question."Do you ever feel like...you've just gone through hundreds of pages in your life and you still don't know where you're going? What it is all...*building up to?"*

Kaan considers this. He closes his eyes, takes a few troubled breaths and then stretches; as if he can't comfortably contain the answer arrived upon. "I think it is a rare thing to truly see the end of our own stories. We persist beyond ourselves."

"Whether we want it or not, eh?"

"I have to imagine so."

"Do you believe then. *You go on.* Part of you, *anyway.* Do you *live forever* in that case?"

"I wish I believed that! I really...*do.* Settle down. Have some kids. Make a game! Direct a movie! Put my name in stone somewhere so it can't be washed away. That all sounds *fantastic.*" Kaan shrugs. "I just don't buy it. I've tried to *install those beliefs* and all I end up doing is hoping. Hoping maybe...a day will come where I'm degraded and delusional enough to take on those thoughts sincerely."

"Seems like you've thought on it a lot."

"I didn't know it was possible to...*err*...stop."

"Here I was feeling proud just every now and then I would *start.* Most of the time. I'm just thinking about what is in front of me. Sorta absent minded that way. It was nice when I found a working phone again. I need the notifications."

Kaan chuckles. "You know how to be you the best. I'm glad that's the case."

The Corgi returns. The Caravaneer picks the corgi up and places it back comfortably on the caravan.

"So I have to imagine, you're heading somewhere." The Corgi asks Kaan with an angular snout pointed right at him.

"*Eventually*. I have to go back to Illking."

"That's not a bad route."

"Quite pretty actually."

"We'll take you."

Kaan smiles and holds his hands out for mercy. "I...*appreciate that!* But I have friends who need to come. A couple of us, and it...*might not be the safest* if people know we're with you."

"Nonesense!" The Corgi declares. "We have a blanket to throw over you, and your friends. We have a few wares to pick up around town before going anyways. Come with us, we'll get everything and we can meet them back here before taking off."

The Caravaneer complies; reverting to the era in his life where the word of his mom was law and no other perspective was worth rendering. He begins packing and confirming things are tied down.

干

In the depth of the forested valley warmth hasn't found a place it prefers. Instead it passes through you, like a fleeting thought, as you step past the briefest of rays reaching down through the bramble.

A collection of metallic debris in the distance evokes the worst of traffic. Bright lights, a dozen reflections and frequently enough; a mechanical disaster.

What was once a plane — *possibly in mid-flight* — is now a series of craters and burnt down trees. Rotten *material* is scattered

297

around; preserved in the dense shade of the valley. Suitcases and chunks of wall litter the surroundings.

The plane hasn't so much *crashed* as it has *suddenly appeared at the ground going hundreds of miles an hour* and reacted accordingly.

"Do you think they're all rich people?" Dezz offers.

Kozmo looks around; he grimaces. "Not too many people flying nowadays." He seems a bit confused. "What even is *rich* nowadays."

Dezz shrugs. "Rich still existed. It owned more land. Had a seat at every table that commanded change. Nobody needed money but some people still convinced themselves they were worth more then everyone else." He points out to the mostly decayed remains of someone in a suit. "Maybe it was him."

Kneeling down besides the skeleton in the suit. Gekomatsu examines him. "Whatever he was it didn't do him too many favours. Looks like he died in his seat, then was thrown from it. Didn't even try to get up or resist."

Dezz scoffs. "Figures. I've never met someone who is doing well who achieved it on their own. They always had a stable home. Parents took care of their education, pointed them the right way; helped them skip steps and rise up a ladder which doesn't even have rungs for most people." He kicks a piece of scrap metal; it scuttles dirt for a few meters. "Then those same people would have the *audacity* to act like they were greater then everyone else that wasn't picked up and plopped down onto a high horse."

"We rationalize our successes, and the failures of others with a predictable bias." Gekomatsu adopts an *ignorant* inflection. "Oh I have a good job because I work hard, and I'm smart. Everyone else is lazy, or untalented or just downright incapable. Yepp. That's how it is!" He rolls his eyes.

Kozmo leans down, examines a suit-case and rips it open. He parses through the contents, discarding cloth and pocketing anything electronic. "Well they are dead now. So if you're angry at them. *You won.*"

A few grumbles later. Dezz begins to sort through the wreckage himself. "I never *lost.*" He mutters mostly to himself.

"I need a hand opening up this rear section." Kozmo points towards a massive panel, relatively undisturbed near the back of the wreckage.

The boys work together, each grab an edge and presumably perform the neurological equivalent of spamming the A button. The panel flies off and reveals inside a somewhat disturbed cargo bay.

"There wasn't a plane in the air which wasn't carrying something other then people." Kozmo explains as he crouches and ventures in. He looks through the stocked walls of packages, and crates. He pulls down a large cardboard box. "These *rich snobs* may well have been gallivanting through the air, drinking champagne and toasting to meaningless numbers. But they were *also...*" He tears open the box. "Bringing someone their artisan cat food." A forty pound bag of dried pet food is flopped out of the box onto the floor.

"Have you found what *you need*?" Gekomatsu inquires.

Kozmo opens another box, with a tell-tale series of weird angular designs and geometric shapes on the outside. Inside is a generic pre-built computer which has been somewhat folded in half. Kozmo peels off the front panel, disconnects a few cables and a blocky sort of thing with a fan and puts them all in a bag. "That and more."

Gekomatu's large eye flicks out to the side. "It took us longer to get down here then I thought. I can't imagine we're far off it getting dark."

Dezz packs a few nice pairs of jeans and a pull-over hoodie into a bag he's found and nods. "Back to the trail it is."

Without uttering a response Kozmo leaves the cargo bay, looks out then walks over to what remains of the cock-pit of the plane. Inside, the chairs and steering apparatus have been entirely removed but everything one would expect in a plane has been retained; remnants of retro-fitting the aircraft. He begins to play with the radio.

"No way that is still working."

The radio crackles to life.

LEVEL UP!

"You were *saying*." Kozmo retorts. He flicks through various radio stations. He picks up the repeating message from Joseph Torrence, and the beeps from CMDR Aberdashi. A few more channels offer nothing but static until.

"-How do I get this goddamn thing to work. HELLO! HELLO? Is this even on. There aren't any lights on. I don't think it's working." The voice is clearly that of *Sonnenblume*. "Maybe if I just pull this-" The signal dies.

"*Was that*." Dezz considers.

"It sure sounded like it." Gekomatsu agrees.

They wait a few moments but the channel remains static. They turn the radio off, shuffle out of the cock-pit and push onward out of the valley.

〒

"So, *you're just a bandit. That's IT?*" Lt. Oaks affirms.

"I'm a scout! That's it! I've never seen your girl and I *won't* ever again. Just let me go!"

Lt. Oaks looks over to Illkat. "Looks like it was just a turn of a phrase, are you alright with that?"

Illkat stares at the man. He looks back in that sort of...rotten but trying not to be way. Like a rat trying to convince you it won't eat trash again. "Well we're not letting you go. You may not be an assassin but you're still a criminal."

The man looks around, accepts he is caught and becomes quite jovial. "Hard to argue with that. Given me admitting it and all. Sorry about getting you with the wire."

Illkat ignores him and looks towards Lt. Oaks. "What should we do with him."

"The lady at the school mentioned *knights*. Maybe we should find some of them." Lt. Oaks considers.

"*Alright*. It might take a bit. But let's find us a *knight*."

Despite her preparation it takes Illkat less then a minute to spot a tall, plate armour clad individual who befits the title *knight*. He's basically down the street standing on a corner.

Approaching the knight with the canter of a child greeting a mascot at a theme park. Illkat smiles and gestures to the bandit Lt. Oaks is dragging behind them.

"Greetings! Has someone stolen your sweet roll?" The knight asks valiantly.

"What?"

The knight sighs. "They told me this would come up more often, *and yet every time*." He digresses. "Hello madam! How may I assist thee!"

"This man is a bandit! He was watching a school, awaiting a moment to rob the children and their care-takers." Illkat explains.

The knight looks over. "*Yeessh.* You're a bit of a dick aren't you?" He questions the bandit.

Almost held off the ground with his arms behind his back the bandit awkwardly smiles. "Well when you say it all like that."

"You don't deny the charges?"

"Not exactly in the position to do so."

"Let him go." The knight requests. Lt. Oaks complies. The knight prepares to ask the question again but is interrupted by the bandit running away instantly. "I see he does not deny the charges, free of any coercion." He reaches for his hip, retrieves a series of strings tied to balls and whips them expertly towards the running bandit; binding his legs and toppling him over on himself.

"BOLA! THOSE ARE AWESOME. SO IMPRACTICAL."

"RIGHT?! And they actually work here. I tried tossing them in the old world once and all I got was knots." The knight responds as he walks towards the bandit trying to crawl away.

"What are you going to do with him?" Illkat asks; bracing herself for some degree of cruelty.

"We have a prison. Decent enough spot. *Safe.* He'll head in there." He laughs. "Sentencing is pretty quick, how many years and all that. We ended up with a *few judges* who are just rife with a need to make decisions."

"Lucky that." Lt. Oaks admits.

"Would you like to come? Might be a reward in it for turning this fella in." The knight explains.

"You know if anyone is making a buck off turning anyone in, I have some *friends-*" The bandit goes on but is hushed.

"We'll get your friends and your answers. No bribes or compromises. Sorry about that." The knight *does actually seem sorry.*

They all head off.

"That lady with the kids is probably thinking we're going to come back." Lt. Oaks admits.

Illkat shrugs. "I have to imagine she won't be terribly upset if we don't."

They continue on toward the edge of the city, there is a wall, some old office buildings and a depression in the terrain where a large grate is guarded by two *astute* looking knights. The bottoms of the armour are dirtied with mud.

"Sir!"

"Ser!"

The knights salute then open the grate. Brought on through, prisoner in check, to a *sewer* which seems to run on for the length of the whole city. It has been re-worked to have one walking path to the side, a thin iron bar grate wall, a divet where water once ran and the contents of a simple enough prison cell.

Many cells have been built; many of them are full. The contents therein don't appear to be especially confusing. Some just stare out, eyes wide, fingers broken and hands turned to bladed weapons. Many bang their heads against the iron bars, scream and pick an activity from a dozen electives not worth recording here.

"Nice lot you got here."

"Yepp. Lotta *PeeVeePeers* I've been told they're called." The knight explains.

Illkat laughs. Lt. Oaks seems confused.

"Violent lot. Always talking about *kill streaks* and *something to do with my mom*." He shrugs a bit. "Can't make sense of half of it if I'm being honest with ya."

"I'm not one of them man! Come on! I know what I'm doing ain't right but I don't think it's normal! That's something ain't it?"

The knight ignores him. They pass along a couple dozen guards, continuing down the length of converted sewer until they hit a cell, open it and toss the bandit within.

"You'll be kept here until we can sentence you. *You* have been arrested. You don't have any rights because we're not finished with the document yet. So just, *wait a bit there. Erm.*" He looks around. Lt. Oaks gazes critically. "We'll be by with some clothes in a bit and food. Then your sentencing might be this evening? Tomorrow morning? Around there?"

"Around there?" The bandit questions.

The knight nods.

"Well at least you aren't bureaucrats."

"Now let's see about that reward." The knight offers politely. They double back the length of fifty cells and through a door; which was once a service hatch but has been completely hallowed out to become quite an expansive chamber.

One side of the room is finished. There are some boxes of tile around on the floor. A portioned off corner on the finished side contains some young children watched over by what is presumably an only slightly older sibling.

At the very back, seated around an oblong table as if they're in a sitcom is a set of knights in varied coloured armour. Their helmets off, each staring down the room at the knight and his followers. Half of the set are senior citizens.

"Oh, Circle of Unknown Knights." The knight begins.

Illkat pushes Lt. Oaks in the rib cage with her elbow. "They don't have helmets on. How unknown can they get."

She isn't quiet enough.

"We don't know their names." The knight explains.

"Yea, nobody knows who the fuck we are!" An older knight exclaims.

The others look at him and laugh.

"Yes, *Ser Bernard*. Thank you for your return. What have you for us." The polite older woman responds.

"These two, *guests in our city* apprehended a self proclaimed bandit." Ser Bernard goes on.

"Did the suspect attempt to flee?" An astute young knight questions.

"Yes." Lt. Oaks answers the question.

"They always run! It's human nature!" Another older man among the knights pipes up. "You see a *copper* and you book it! Can't blame someone fer that!"

"We won't be holding his attempt to flee against him." The knights decide collectively. One looks at Illkat. "So then, you'll be looking at a few weeks. We'll have the trial tomorrow. Then processing. We'll get you the paperwork *eventually*."

"No thanks!" Illkat cuts right to the point. "How about just...a few coins?"

"Ahh, I like this gurl. She knows what is important in life. *Cash*."

"Ah, *very well then*." The elderly female knight acknowledges. From by her feet she grabs a purse, rummages through it and puts the equivalent of a thousand dollars on the table; represented by ten rather large gold coins. "I only have big bills. *Sorry*."

Illkat rushes up, pockets the money then returns to Lt. Oaks. They look at one another and Lt. Oaks laughs.

Nobody knows what to say, and where to stand for a few moments. Eventually they are shooed off and escorted out by Ser Bernard.

Outside the prison, where they come to recall things don't smell *much like an artificial armpit* no matter what you do. The women politely excuse themselves, cash in hand, and leave.

"Are you *alright?*" Lt. Oaks inquires.

Illkat nods. "Yepp. Right as rain, or pick a saying. I'm that one."

"*Alright.*" Lt. Oaks allows, for a moment; then pushes on. "It's just you can rush up to a bunch of strangers in armour, or chase after a bandit. But *those kids* made you sound like...well...me."

"Kids make me feel...*awkward*. Like I'm in the wrong room? I guess. No matter where that room is. People think I will like them and when I don't. It gets...*uncomfortable*. So I guess that's just where I start now."

"So no kids."

"Heyyy!" Illkat pretends to be upset by the presumptuous statement. She laughs herself. "No, *no kids*."

〒

Kaan, the Caravaneer and his mother ride through the streets of St. Margaez back to the van full of technology alongside Kozmo, Dezz and Gekomatsu. Partially because it is a huge narrative convenience and just as well because they happened to be passing into town around the same time a nearby chore was concluding.

Everyone takes a turn petting the corgi.

The rough roads cause everyone to rock about; jostling their innards in a *rustic manner.* There is something peaceful about heading along in a caravan, which...wait a second.

"There aren't any horses." Kaan points out.

"You're just noticing that now?" The Caravaneer retorts.

"I was just, *enjoying our conversation*. Then we saw my friends and now, we're just, moving along." He huffs. "How does that work."

"I owned a self driving car back in the day?" The Caravaneer offers.

"*I*." Kaan considers, then stops. "I can't rule that out as being all it takes.

The Caravaneer whips reins which attach to nothing but the wooden posts of the caravan itself. He inexplicably goes faster.

Further into the city, they stop near the cafe and electronics van. Kozmo removes the cables from his pockets and sorts them on a table alongside the GPU he snagged.

"I'll be back." Kozmo confirms then is off.

The rest go into the cafe, get more coffee and return; sitting outdoors.

"Is the dog allowed coffee." Gekomatsu inquires.

"*The dog* has been drinking coffee longer then you have been alive. I'll be fine." The Corgi confirms.

Gekomatsu considers saying something, but he remembers he looks like a frog and decides to just enjoy his beverage instead.

"There they are!" Illkat shouts. "Right where we left you." The pair rejoin quickly.

"We bothered a teacher for a bit then arrested some guy. How was your day?" Lt. Oaks finds joy in her phrasing.

"Had a coffee. Met a corgi. Ate a sandwich. Had another coffee." Kaan gives the run-down.

"Went on a hike. Looked at a plane. Went on another hike." Dezz adds.

"You're all just keen on elaborating aren't ya." The Corgi jests.

"WHAT" Lt. Oaks moves *through* people and appears on her knees in front of the corgi. "It's a-"

"I know! It's great."

"Fantastic doggo."

Really, I can't stress enough. Just, just a perfect corgi.

Kozmo returns, cash in hand.

"How'd that go?" Kaan asks.

"I think...*I might have been adopted.*" Kozmo considers with a rather receptive tone.

"Presuming Kozmo doesn't have chores and is allowed to leave. *Shall we?*" Gekomatsu inquires.

They all collect their coffee. Pack up into the caravan and set out from the city of St. Margaez. It starts to snow.

"I feel like this is...well. All a bit convenient if I'm being honest." Kozmo makes the point as he leans back and relaxes.

"Best not to argue with it. You never know." Dezz speaks from experience.

〒

CLINK. CLACK.

"Are you, *comfortable in there* Joseph?" Nelf asks. He walks with a cane and smirks through a thick pane of glass.

"You know I am." Joseph grimaces; a fake matching smirk upon his face.

He stands in the middle of a concrete floor, covered in fake grass. The walls are painted *badly* like a savanna. Half a couch sits in the corner. A few buckets filled with water in another.

"*Good.* I need to have you at your best when the exhibit opens." Nelf makes the statement as painful as he can. A finger runs over the scars on his face.

"It didn't have to end up like this. It *still doesn't*. I will call you a friend."

"Of course you would. I would in your position. *That is the problem!*" He taps his cane on the ground a few times, stares up, then huffs. "Unless you're willing to talk *about the Arctic Witch*."

"That isn't her name."

"So that is a *no*."

"It is whatever you think it is Nelf. Don't pretend like you would stop. If I gave *her* up. You would just want something else, over and over *again*. It wouldn't stop."

Nelf laughs. "You're catching on then. Good for you." He taps the glass with his cane. "Time for nighty night."

The lights all die out with a resounding exodus.

It becomes pitch black.

Nelf and his cane clink down a hall.

"You are strong enough for this Joseph. You *survived for a reason*. Focus on breathing."

A heavy door shuts in the distance.

"You have everything you need to get out of this."

CHAPTER FIFTEEN

PLOT UPON A DILIGENT PATH

Covered in simple blankets, old cloaks and the drabs of a farmer. The Guild clunk down a cobblestone path on a horseless caravan towards the city of Illking. The Caravaneer smiles out, a bundle of perfect corgi sleeping next to him.

Their weapons covered, eccentricities dampened. Everyone appears somewhat like a *peasant*; one of whom has quite an odd skin condition.

KER-CHERR

A wooden wheel thunks over an uneven piece of the road. Everything shuffles. No calamity arises.

"You're quite at peace on the road." Gekomatsu makes the point as he stares ahead and pulls a hood over.

The Caravaneer nods. "Spent a long time driving. Here and *there*. I always found it relaxing. I worked *off-world* before, you see."

"Ah, *yes*. I've heard the *lunar commute* often made one miss the days of eld where a vehicle was your own. Instead of a tube."

"It was quick, best thing about it. PLOP in the airlock, a few safety checks. A hiss. A minute or so of staying still then you're at work."

"So you did...*work work* back in the day?" Kaan joins in.

"Yepp." The Caravaneer responds.

"Any reason for it?"

"Just a restless sort I guess. You know I was always jealous of all those...*self determined people*. Felt like you could drop them in a jungle and by the same time next week they'd have a schedule and new life put together, goals, *things they want*." He shrugs. "I guess I'm not like that. I want *something to do*, not *something to plot*."

"So you had a weekend, and all that old-school stuff?"

"That was the case."

"What was it like?"

"Weekends were like...*well*. Imagine you're driving down the road, back in the day. Hands on the wheel, the whole thing and you start getting a little sleepy. So you pull over to the side of the road, and take a nap. That nap is the weekend. Sure, you're not driving, but you're not living your life either. You're just doing what you can to recover enough so you can get back on the road."

"It doesn't exactly sound...*enviable*." Kaan admits.

"Well I did say I was jealous of the other folks. Who know how to pick another path. Looking back, I think I just...*fell into it*."

There is an indistinguishable loudness in the forest which sets everyone on edge.

Gekomatsu looks over at Illkat, who looks at Lt. Oaks. She peers over the edge of the caravan and focuses.

From the forest rushes out a family of four, father, mother, daughter and son. They are being chased by wolves. Each of them sprints for awhile, makes quite a distance, stops, looks back, allows the wolf to catch up and then breaks into an impossible sprint again.

As they burst onto the road, the father shouts out. "Please, help us! There are wolves!"

The caravan stops rather suddenly.

An upturned eyebrow clearly showcases Kozmo's confusion. "The wolves are like...*level 3*. They could beat them to death in a few hits."

"They're still *wolves*." Lt. Oaks points out.

Kozmo shrugs. "I guess?" He leaps over the edge of the caravan. One of the wolves rushes him. He casually sort of kicks it a bit; his method suggests he feels guilty for doing so. The wolf nearly dies right then, but Kozmo grabs it by the tail and throws it at the other one; causing them both to keel over and cease to function.

311

"Oh my word! What skill and strength!" The mother declares.

Kozmo looks over at her for a moment, widens his gaze then huffs to himself.

A third wolf leaps at him and he just ducks underneath it. It flies over-top, scrambling on rabid legs to correct itself after landing. Slopper and foam drops down over-long teeth cutting the edge of its bottom lip. It rushes at Kozmo and leaps towards him.

The daughter of the family rushes to force herself between them. "Noo!" She screams.

"Wait what?" Kozmo can't decide whether to be offended or upset. He rushes towards her, and manages to get her out of the way of a vicious bite but not a moderate slash across her forearm. The daughter flops into the dirt and Kozmo awkwardly slaps the wolf to death while looking away from the process.

"Not my girl!" The dad rushes to the daughter; dropping to his knees.

"Sabrina! No!" The son follows suite.

The mother, strained in stress, begins to cry and look out towards the woods. "We were *just walking along*."

Gekomatsu leaps down from the caravan, walks over to the girl, and rather quickly bandages the wound. She glows a little bit, and opens her eyes.

The father looks up, and doesn't know what to say.

Kozmo looks over at Gekomatsu and suggests they've found crazy people with the angle and pace of his shirk. Gekomatsu agrees with a smile that is never genuine in these sort of circumstances.

"She'll be alright?" The son asks.

Gekomatsu nods. "Probably. She only lost a few hit-points. She has about fifty of them."

"*Hit-points?*" The daughter inquires; her tone delirious.

"That wouldn't have anything to do with why these wolves starting chasing us out of nowhere while we were just walking through them woods, would it?" The father inquires.

It is clear to everyone in the guild that Gekomatsu seriously considers just walking away without a response, and in his struggle to resist the inclination, blurts out *something*. "That only makes sense in the sort of...high concept perspective I highly doubt you were utilizing."

"Huh?"

"*No*, hit-points aren't related to wolves."

"Have you been out in the woods for long?" Illkat asks; standing upright to look over.

"Well, a couple of weeks sure. The coast, then some woods, a bit of a cave then the woods again. Been awhile since we've seen other people. God willing, they've all been kind."

Gekomatsu claps, and gives in. "Alright, best of wishes. I'll be over there." He instantly walks away.

Kozmo looks at them, and around the area. He looks at the wolves. "Well no point wasting good resources." He occupies himself quickly, and with enough focus that it would be impolite to question him further.

"So you don't know what's...*happening*?" Illkat inquires.

"Oh we have figured part of that out. There was a *rapture*. Clearly. What we can't right figure out is how we sinned enough to stay here."

"Yea and that *ass-wipe* Sam Taylor got into heaven but I didn't!" The son complains without a shred of self awareness.

"You know I would of expected the demons. I saw one woman leaking magma from her hands. She was shouting. It seemed awful. I just didn't figure we'd end up going back in time." The mom admits.

"Back in..." Illkat chews on her confusion. "How do you figure we're back in time?"

The mom, ignoring the oddity of the statement from someone she believes to be *in the past* keeps on. "Well look at you. Dressed like old time farmers. You don't even have a horse! You gotta let the caravan slide down the hill. What a bother to go up it must be."

Unless shielded by a shared bloodline the previous statement causes a wake of sensory pain; like a shock-wave rushing out from a sub-oceanic explosion.

"*Err*, alright. Well, we're headed to Illking. Are you...okay? Do you need any directions?" Illkat offers.

"Illking, what is that?"

"A city, pretty big. About *that way*." She points down the road they're heading.

The family look between one another.

"I don't want to walk anymore." The daughter complains.

"The forest has been stupid. There are so many trees." The son makes a complaint which may well not be worth recording.

"Clarence, *ask the nice people for a ride to the city*. There might be a hotel, I can cancel our credit cards after losing them." The mother asks her husband but — *quite obviously* — everyone else as well.

The father looks up. "Do you think we would be able to-"

Illkat looks up at the Caravaneer. "It's your call."

The Caravaneer looks down at the family and smiles. "Welcome aboard friends. Find a spot in the back and we'll get you to the city."

"Many thanks stranger! I can tell the lord is smiling down on you."

"Oh he's done that once or twice before but picked the wrong opportunity last time and now he keeps his distance, *I'm pretty sure*."

"Huh?

"Don't worry about it. Just get comfy out back!"

Everyone shuffles around to make room. They get comfy with one another quite suddenly, more then they were, squeezing thigh to thigh and shoulder to shoulder to allot a good chunk of distance between their group and this new family.

"Got a nice scratch there eh?" Dezz asks with a friendly tone of voice.

"Yea, it was horrible! I don't want a permanent scar!" The daughter exclaims.

With an understanding expression upon his face Dezz tries to be helpful. "Well if you get a chance, win a bunch of fights. Maybe with small bugs. Or do some unsolved puzzles if you find them out in the wild. If you level up the wound will heal itself right up."

The mother pulls her daughter closer and smiles towards Dezz in the same fashion one does when a street pastor tries to convert your first grader as you pass by. "Well that is an *interesting perspective*." She manages.

"Oh it's honest. I got shot not too long ago, fought some folks and after I won I felt a lot better." Dezz explains; oblivious.

"I don't think you're helping your case." Lt. Oaks smirks to herself.

"We're grateful for the ride, but we don't want any trouble." The father adds on.

Dezz, confused, looks away.

Everyone in their spot the caravan keeps on.

The sky threatens to snow for a moment, produces a few flakes in a brief drift then changes its mind.

Illkat and Lt. Oaks do what they can to address a barrage of questions. Kaan feels obliged to join in. Everyone else pretends they have something quite important to do *in this direction, or that one* and keep to their respective commitments.

〒

"You're telling me we're not *back in time* but a city looks like that!" The mother unwinds hours of progress as she peers across the sprawling length of Illking. Its stone buildings and lack of telephone poles quite a sight to behold.

Illkat, now *just done with these people* hovers on instinctual good graces alone. *"It is a fantasy depiction of a city, created in modern times, inspired by the past and-"*

"Well it looks a lot like that North Korea." The mother continues; intent on making the statement no matter the quality of segue.

Before anyone can correct her, they near the gates entering the city. Draping down from each peak of the city wall is an illustration of *Nelf Kinslayer*. It captures him in a way which, much like a beautiful insect; appears impressive at a distance and becomes *quite horrifying* as you get closer and examine the details. It attempts to evoke *royalty* as his knee is raised on a stool; his gaze off into the distance. In reality it imparts a feeling that the subject is afraid of the underside of their own boot.

"Quiet now. Just let the dog do its work." The Caravaneer instructs.

"Is that *really the plan?*" Kaan argues; only now starting to worry.

"It will be fine."

They stroll ever closer to the gates, and stop for inspection. Guards walk up to the side of the vessel, and nod to most of the occupants. The most armoured among them greets the Caravaneer.

316

"Greet'ins Ser. Jes pass'n through are ya?"

The Caravaneer, somewhat convinced the guard is *putting on a bad accent* opts to play along. "That'd be the case. Regular folk, looking to stock up on drink and a bit of entertainment before shuffling out again."

The guard inspects the Caravaneer, then begins to look at the others. He looks at Kaan for *just a moment too long* before-

BORK

"Oi, whut was dat an all?" He inquires; at least he makes an honest attempt at doing so.

The *corgi* pops its head up. Triangle ears and large eyes devouring any attention not buckled and strapped into place.

"Oh my. Had'a'lil one like dis meself when I was 'ung. *Queen's stock you know?"*

"Yes, quite lovely and *hungry* you understand. We've just been on the road, tough to make time to prepare a proper meal for the little thing."

The guard nods, performs a cursory glance over the contents of the caravan one last time then steps back to give them clearance. "Head on truu'den. Get this feller'a meal. Check out da *zoo* if ya get'ta chance!"

"I'll do..." the Caravaneer looks at the corgi and holds in a silly smile. "Just that, *kind sir*. The best of wishes to you."

The caravan picks back up.

They chug along.

Swiftly the sounds of a much more *rigid* Illking fill the background. A quiet so pervasive you're almost gleeful when a squad of soldiers shout in the street, or flip their rifles in the air only to catch them and say something in latin.

Standing on pedestals hoisted on the backs of some soldiers are women whom aren't so much dressed as ineffectively draped and aren't so much cheering as *loudly recounting information.*

"Get your *free calendar depicting the twelve seasons of Tzar Nelf now! Ask at your local follower bureau!*" One of the women explains distantly.

"This is...*dismal.*" Kozmo states.

"Cover your eyes children, this is an abhorrent place." The mother commands, and with the same breath turns to Illkat. "You were right, it is a normal city."

Another of the women on pedestals looks down at the son in the family as they pass, sighs to herself and says something which he will undoubtedly remember for the rest of his life. He looks at his father.

His father grows a half smirk and playfully shrugs. He is promptly smacked in the arm by the mother.

"You're *never to repeat that. You will have nothing to do with that line of products.*" The mother makes clear.

"I don't even know what she said!" The son argues honestly. It is honest because while he *very much liked what he heard and the tone he heard it in* none of it actually meant anything to him.

"Why are these...*solicitors* approaching us so promptly?" The father asks.

The guild look around and examine portions of change across Illking. The puzzle before them only consists of three pieces, all of which Nelf has scribbled his name over.

"This is what happens when someone who should never be able to take control; isn't challenged when it comes to...*policy choices.*" Illkat offers.

"I'm not surprised, once they started charging the church tax, we were all just-"

Gekomatsu physically reaches cut and puts his finger over-top of the father's lips. "*SHSHHH.*" He commands. "Everything is political enough already. Let's give it a rest."

"Seems like this is where we part ways." The Caravaaneer admits.

Kaan nods to him. "Thanks for, being here, and *there,* and *before!*"

"Before?"

"Yea, you...I think you gave me a ride once. *Before everything.*"

The Caravaneer smiles like an old teacher seeing a student they don't recall very well purporting to be from ages past. "*Of course. Well,* I'm glad to leave an impression."

"Travel safe! Whatever you get up to. We'll be on the roads, I expect we'll see each other again!" The Corgi explains.

Everyone gets out of the caravan, the guild pet the corgi. The Caravan shuffles off.

"So, we are here. *Why are we here again?*" Gekomatsu inquires; rolling out the remnants of his frustration from the long ride. He glares at the family they picked up along the way.

"We need Sonnenblume if we're to defeat Finir. It's that simple. She's probably stronger then any of us." Illkat explains; as if she shouldn't have to.

"Then what?" Gekomatsu continues. "We rescue her, *depose Nelf,* kill Finir. Then what? It won't clean up the mess."

Illkat huffs. "So, *what is your logic here.* We shouldn't dirty a plate for dinner just because we'll get hungry again in the future?"

"*Maybe.*" He shrugs. "I don't mind paper plates."

She groans. "Had we not all got sucked into another server, *after that battle.* I was going to go talk to Sonnenblume."

"*You were?*" Kaan joins.

"You seemed pretty settled to me as well." Kozmo agrees.

"I WAS THINKING ABOUT IT." Illkat is quickly defensive. "I just, wasn't sure yet. I am now. She needs to know we're there for her, even if she needed some time away."

A sun baked glue gives way as a page is torn off a nearby brick wall. Lt. Oaks gleans over the details then flips the page to share. It depicts a *white haired, red eyed demon woman*. There is a reward for information about the entity known as the *Arctic Witch*. "It looks like we'll have competition."

The group keeps on, into an opening square. Guards patrol. Merchants skittishly make sales. Their customers rush to safety immediately following a transaction.

"I'm not sure anyone here is...*set up for it*." Illkat suggests.

"You'd be surprised what rises from desperation." Lt. Oaks admits with a disappointed look across her face.

"I wouldn't be, *actually*. I know when you're at your weakest, it is exactly that lack which galvanizes a final push; regardless of if it is doomed to fail." She huffs. "I just can't imagine any of them winning with odds so severely stacked against them."

A group of citizens are *formally escorted* through the streets by guards.

Everyone looks between themselves and shares a *knowing inflection*. They begin to follow the guards.

They travel over a bridge, through a residential street and then towards the eastern facing city wall. There a cobblestone archway leads down into the ground. In large *neon signage* above the archway is the word '*Zoo*'.

"*Ah*." Kaan just stares ahead.

"That's a bit...*grizzly*." Dezz seems subtly pleased with himself.

"Well whatever is going on in there, I doubt it is *boar-ing*." Lt. Oaks winks.

Illkat groans playfully.

"No need to be grouchy. They're not trying to annoy you on *porpoise*."

"Oh my god." Illkat pretends to die.

Gekomatsu leans forwards solemnly. "Seriously, think of her health. You're all being *shellfish*."

"You all know those people might be getting brought in there as *food* or something, right?"

Kaan chortles a bit. "Yea, it's really...*hawkward*."

Instantly finding herself walking towards the archway Illkat yells back at her comrades. *"All right, we're just going in."*

The guards at the archway wave to her.

She points down without stopping. "Can I go ahead?" She makes the question rhetorical.

The guards nod.

Everyone follows.

The stone floor quickly becomes a red velvet lookalike; something which sounds much scruffier against each step. Steps lead down underneath the wall to what may have been some sort of barracks before hand. Now, the extensive tunnel stretches about a kilometre in length. Industrial lighting lines the ceiling. Curtains, and metal partitions separate *exhibits* which pock either side of the lone tunnel.

The rest of the guild follow after Illkat.

"Are there...*animals*?" Kaan asks. He moves closer to one of the exhibits.

"Well, it looks like those *captives* are on a...guided tour." Lt. Oaks makes the point by looking over towards the people they followed here. They're receiving information from their guard as if he is a guide, pointing down into an exhibit.

Kaan walks towards the edge, looks down, and becomes witness to a burgeoning mess in the shape of a single bedroom apartment. Half a couch has been cut to shape and placed in a corner. There are a few large truck wheels and shelves scattered around the floor. Laying on the couch, looking straight ahead at the wall is just *some dude*. "It's a...*person*."

"Same over here." Dezz explains as he points down to another exhibit where a woman scratches pictures into the wall with a shard of glass wrapped in cloth.

Illkat and Lt. Oaks — *holding hands* — look down at another exhibit.

A guard approaches them.

"This one had allied with the *Arctic Witch*. Got quite a tongue on him. Had to move two guards off the shift, they were starting to *sympathize, you see*."

The figure down in the exhibit has a blanket wrapped over them; pretending to be asleep.

"I imagine he has...*valuable information*." Illkat considers.

"Oh I've heard that's the case. The boss is always coming down here for long talks." The guard makes the comment as if it is a polite topic, smiles then excuses himself.

The man in the exhibit throws off the blanket, making clear he is *Joseph Torrence*.

"*Wait, it is you?*" Lt. Oaks seems confused.

"I have withered the storm of persecution, as I always have. It is my duty to-"

"Alright, *tell us where Sonnenblume is!*" Illkat shouts down.

Some people look over at her. She widens her eyes and tries to shrink herself.

"I *will not*." Joseph Torrence resists.

"She is our friend! You're not protecting her from anything!" Illkat argues.

"I understand this. She was your ally before mine, she may be still. But I will not share what I know, *where I sent her,* until I am out of this place." Joseph leverages what could be a threat as politely as possible.

Illkat glares.

Lt. Oaks pulls her back a bit. "We can make a plan. If you need what he knows." She looks around, glaring at the guards in their posts. "This place isn't as secure as they might be thinking."

Somewhat *allured* Illkat smirks. "Alright. Then...*we'll make a deal*." She leans back to look into the exhibit. "Will you share what you know if you're...*safe?*"

Joseph nods. "I will illuminate each aspect of the path before us, its secrets; the nooks and crannies."

Illkat groans, then steps back from the ledge. "Alright, we'll need a plan then."

Lt. Oaks smiles proudly. "Oh *that* is already in the making. Secrets developing." She swipes her nose with a wink.

Everyone groups up.

"This is a nightmarish place. Inhumane." Gekomatsu declares, then shrugs. "Yet very...*practical*."

"It fits his style, doesn't it! You can't gloat in front of corpses. Nelf needs eyes upon his victory. If he didn't keep all these people somewhere...*conquered*. I don't think he would feel as powerful." Kaan glares around the space; sinking into frustration the longer he watches.

Dezz focuses on the exit at the far end of the hall. "It's these guards which frustrate me. *Just following orders*, the lot of them." He resists the urge to spit on the floor. "We never fucking learn, do we."

"People?" Lt. Oaks clarifies.

"Mhmm."

"I don't think we're meant to." Lt. Oaks admits.

They continue towards the exit.

"I don't think we can *learn to be better*. We suck. We're violent, desperate, battling a dozen invisible vices, the worst impulses; horrible thoughts fill our minds instantly and easily. All we can do, *is build better*. Greater laws, surveillance, double and triple checks. Balances to keep us from acting within our nature. We don't need greater lessons, they never really stick. We just need more guard rails."

"Not exactly an optimistic view." Illkat critiques.

Lt. Oaks shrugs. "Yet, *honest*. The *only thing* keeping us in line, the only thing which makes the system work; is that we keep building it up. Look what happens when we fall to the rule of opinion, when we *act on our instincts*. Do you really think if Joseph had won, the guards watching everyone now wouldn't be in those cells themselves? Or worst off, shot and buried underneath one?"

"He doesn't seem genocidal. Just...*passionate*." Dezz considers.

"Only a few degrees separated. Put a person in a corner and unless something makes it so they *can't*. Instinct kicks in and we want to *remove threats*. We'll feel bad about it, there will be a rock in your stomach as you do some *horrible thing* but at the end of the day. You'll be glad, part of us will always want to *stop worrying about our opposition...to simply...put the threat to rest.*" She sighs.

At the end of the tunnel is a small gift shop. Everything has Nelf's face on it, or uses his voice. There is a display tree, with spokes reaching out to hang different chains. Various religious symbols are there, from every major faith. A sign above simply states "Symbols of Nelfdom".

Kozmo looks at the tree, points at it, chews on a few statements and then just opts to walk away.

Up another set of stairs, again the late afternoon sun filters across the guild. They take deep gulps of the fresh air, notably less stagnant then the tunnel.

"Follow me then." Lt. Oaks declares.

Everyone does.

"*Why*?" Dezz rises to the occasion.

"Do you remember the code we heard before, on the radio?"

Everyone nods.

"I tried to make it out but it wasn't standard. Some sort of, unique encryption."

"Unique to *Commander Aberdashi*, actually."

They continue on through the town, venturing south.

So much change has rushed through these streets, they remind one of a city that paused a protest to handle a revolution. Posters nailed over others. One colour half painted, another half dried. Bullet holes plastered, just in time for new ones to crop up a short distance away. Yesterday's dust intermingling with today's.

They approach the entrance to the *ossuary*. Lt. Oaks knocks thirty two times, to a specific beat, in the middle of the door. Then again, just three times, on the side.

Eyes grow, brows arch.

Metal clanks behind the door, the wall almost *shakes* for a moment. Then it opens a crack and a hand ushers them in.

Once a dilapidated space filled with bones, the ossuary has been converted to a *command centre*. Thick cables run a length toward the mine carts. Lights are installed, ceiling fans. Soldiers rush between tables, plotting maps, wiring electronics or preparing weapons. From the crowd, with a sharp tan jacket resting on just her shoulders, emerges CMDR Aberdashi.

"Woah!" Kozmo jumps into the space. "This is awesome! You have transformers...converters. Are you running solar?"

One of the technicians working in the room nods.

"Verrplek is preparing to move into the modern era. Lights, power, *heat soon enough*. The borders of the town are strong. Soon enough, we'll even be able to produce our own ammunition if the need calls for it."

"I'm impressed, but not surprised." Lt. Oaks smiles. "WAIT ARE THOSE KINETIC DISPLACERS!" She rushes over to the corner of the room where on a table, is a plain brown box about two inches tall.

"Mhmm." The Commander confirms. "Kaperski found them, out scouting. One of the old trucks the city hasn't cleaned out yet." She laughs. "Everything else was taken, so I have to figure, they didn't know what to do with them."

Dezz raises his hand. "What *do they do*."

Lt. Oaks looks around the room, makes a few calculations in her head then sinks. "I would show you...*but*."

"DO NOT." CMDR Aberdashi affirms.

"I WON'T" She giggles, then opens the box to reveal *purple* bullets. "*They bounce*." She admits with a smirk.

"You may well need them. We've been able to confirm the location of the dead drop. It isn't too far out, further north then I believe we have been. But if we can find it, I'm certain others can. So time is of the essence, I'll need you to task a squad and be ready to deploy in-"

"Not yet."

CMDR Aberdashi seems shocked. "This is *imperative*."

"And I agree! But we need to do something first." She looks at the others in the guild, and pauses on Illkat with a smile. "*We need to break a man out of jail*."

"Not me." Gekomatsu speaks up, and points down to the tunnel. "*I* have some ore I need to address. Presuming nobody has touched it."

"The blue rock?" CMDR Aberdashi confirms.

Gekomatsu becomes a bit worried. "*Yes.*"

"It is fine. A few interested parties, but I told them you'd lay eggs in their cot if they touched it." CMDR Aberdashi cracks a small smile.

"I trust the carts back to town are operational?"

CMDR Aberdashi nods. "Illkat left the gate opens on her last return, per my request. We have worked to implement optimizations where we can. It is not *all up to you and your friends.*"

"Mhmm." Gekomatsu vents frustration and opts to sound kinder then originally intended. "I'll see you all soon, I just need some time to myself"

Kozmo smiles. "If you need a hand with things. Just let me know!"

He doesn't say anything else and trails off towards the stretch of tunnel. Where there was once a boss room is now a barracks.

Flipping over to stand in front of a series of recently illustrated maps. Lt. Oaks begins to study the surrounding area.

〒

The dead of night beckons guards with rifle mounted flashlights to patrol the streets. There seems to be a curfew, indicated by the stillness alone. Windows are shut. Curtains closed. One would only dare to cross a shadowed path.

Everyone has been adorned with the blackened outfit of a soldier. Ceramic plates in a sturdy vest. Pouches with different supplies. A sheathed knife over the left side of their chest; handle facing at a downward angle.

Lt. Oaks runs through a mental checklist that concludes with confirming the sleek rifle slung over her shoulder is working as intended. She has a short visor reaching out from her forehead which completely covers her face in shadow.

Dezz winks at Kaan. "*Secret Agent Kairo.*"

"*Secret Agent Galway.*" Kaan returns the wink.

With a chipper tune Lt. Oaks looks up. "Secret agents who tell everyone they are secret agents don't stay alive very long."

The men sturdy themselves. "*Sorry.*"

"Follow my lead, we'll go in non-lethal and prep an extraction, if things go south. Get ready to fight." Lt. Oaks commands.

"Don't die, I need you back here before morning." CMDR Aberdashi requests.

"Just be ready to receive the target. He may be...uncooperative. I'm not certain."

The group breaks instantly and gets *low*. Trailing through the darkened portion of the streets, behind rubble, underneath trucks looted but left standing. Down the street a group of guards turn, and their rifles begin to flick the direction of the group.

Lt. Oaks pulls Illkat behind a wall, everyone falls.

"Did we hide in time?" Kaan asks.

"Sshhh." Lt. Oaks commands.

A moment passes.

The tip of a rifle peeks by the edge and just as it does Lt. Oaks kicks out; snapping the guards kneecap inwards. She quickly removes the rifle from his grasp, steps forwards and using a burst of momentum swings the back-end of it into the temple of the other guard. They both hit the ground around the same time. She walks over to the guard with the broken knee and before he releases a second scream; bashes him with the butt of the rifle.

Everyone stares at her.

"We need to tie them up now!" She makes the statement in a chipper tone with a smile.

Dezz takes the rope from his belt and begins to hog tie the disabled guards; back to back.

"I thought when I brought this, it was just a cute joke. You know, always bring 50ft of rope and a ten foot pole." He tightens the knot and exhales a bit. "This was like the first ten minutes."

One of them pushes out with their knee, and they both fall over. He seems delirious.

"Come on." They rush onward.

One of the guards starts screaming incoherently.

"That was a bit brutal." Illkat admits.

Lt. Oaks shrugs instinctively. "I didn't kill anyone. That *would of been easier*."

"I, *clearly heard*, how broken his knee was." Kozmo indicates.

"And he can, *what*. Go shoot a few monsters out in the woods and it will fix itself?" She becomes a bit stern. "Keep quiet, we're on mission."

Down more shadowed streets, they begin to approach the entrance to *the zoo*. Two guards stand at attention outside the entrance. The lights dimmed. One of them is smoking.

"*Amatuers*." Lt. Oaks dismisses them then raises up one of her handguns. It has the firmest handle of them all, with a unique barrel when you're close enough to look at it. Before anyone can say anything she fires off two shots.

THUNK

PHTUNK

Two fat smacks of flesh sound out as white powder explodes around the neck of each guard. They take a step, and within a few breaths fall backwards; loudly snoring.

"That's...horrifying, but merciful."

"You say that, but the after effects include intense bouts of diarrhea and you can tell the insides of your nostrils taste like chalk for about a month." She explains.

"I might take being shot over that." Dezz jokes.

Kaan smacks Dezz in the side. "I'll gladly crap my pants if it means I'm not taking a bullet."

Everyone looks at Kaan.

He holds his hands out.

"Weird sentence, retracting the statement." He points out into the distance. "Hey man that's a weird bird."

The group descend the stairs. The lengthy tunnel containing each exhibit is near black. A few red emergency lights give the gist of the space. It appears a bit *glossier* at night.

Moving quickly, Lt. Oaks pushes towards the exhibit with Joseph in it.

A clock strikes loudly, it rings through the hall.

"I was, *expecting you*." Nelf announces.

Lt. Oaks drops to a single knee and aims down her rifle. She flicks her gaze to the entrance behind them, the exit ahead, and the ceiling. Nobody is...*anywhere*. None the less Nelf.

"Shuddap!" A voice from one of the exhibits screams.

The guild look between themselves, collectively shrug, then press on.

Illkat leans over the edge of Joseph's exhibit. She whispers *loudly*. "Joseph! Wake up. Get over here. Joseph!"

A blanket is tossed to the ground and a shadowed portion of the corner in the exhibit stands. Joseph wipes sleep out of his eye, then quite seriously nods.

Black rope cascades over the edge of the exhibit and down into Joseph's cage. He quickly begins to climb.

"We heard Nelf, you need to hurry." Illkat explains.

"Oh, that wasn't him. He's set an alarm, every hour. The speakers blare the same recording. '*I was, expecting you*'." He mocks the statement.

Dezz and Kaan take a piece of the rope each, put a foot up against the wall and hold tight.

Just as Joseph gets over the edge, a voice from another cell shouts out.

"Are you leaving?"

"Help me!"

"Get me out of here!"

"Don't leave us here! We're animals in a cage!"

The voices begin to echo throughout the tunnel.

"Go, go!" Lt. Oaks orders. They rush back the way they came but before they even hit the stairs; they can hear a multitude of steps rushing down towards them.

"Back!" Kaan shouts and begins to rush to the exit.

They don't get halfway before guards begin to pour through the exit as well.

On either side, they are completely surrounded. One man emerges from the crowd of guards, a golden revolver in his hand. He is stylized to look...*familiar*.

The guards point their rifles at the guild. The guild point theirs right back. Nobody fires.

"Criminals! I have caught you red handed!" The man makes the statement confidently.

"Look man, *we don't even know who you are.* We're just trying to get our friend somewhere less...murdery."

"Murdery?" Kozmo critics. "You couldn't think of anything better?"

"I'm panicking okay!" Kaan shouts back at Kozmo.

"You don't know how much trouble you're in. And to think, the honour I, *Bobias*, will garner when I-"

Kaan starts laughing really loudly. "Wait-..." he can't catch his laughter. "Wait...just...hold on." He continues laughing. "BO-BIAS?"

"It is an honorable title bequeathed unto me by the Tzar. I swell with great pride to be known as...*Bobias*." He tries really hard to seem sincere.

Not the least bit interested in the conversation. Lt. Oaks is looking around the whole space. *Calculating.*

"Lay down your arms." Bobias commands. "And we'll only throw you into one of these cells."

"Stand down or you're all dead." Lt. Oaks threatens sweetly.

"As *if* I'll listen to some girl who is so clearly bluffing!" Bobias begins his sentence with a fervour and ends it with three holes in his body.

Firing off six rounds forwards, and spinning around to do it again. Lt. Oaks shoots at the floor, and walls just as much as anyone. Yet while her shots impact with huge dents wherever they touch, they *bounce* at incredible velocity. Cutting up the group of guards on either side like they were caught in a grid of temporary lasers.

She takes the rope from her belt and hands it off to Joseph. "Start getting people up." She commands.

Everyone listens.

Some of the soldiers die *slower* then the others. Whimpering, crawling, or wheezing out their final breaths at a pace which suggests they aren't quite fond of the experience. Lt. Oaks doesn't even look down. Everyone else struggles to keep their heads up.

Person after person. They rescue nearly twenty. Eyes on the exits at all times. As they empty the last exhibit, Lt. Oaks begins to drag a body up the stairs. On the approach of the final step, with all her might, she holds the corpse out into the opening of the passage. Nothing happens. She tosses the body straight out. Nothing happens again. She takes a deep breath, and steps forwards. She awaits something *awful* and yet it doesn't come. With a single movement of her hand, she ushers everyone ahead.

〒

"Sonnenblume is...*where!?*" Illkat shouts.

Joseph retracts a bit. "She should be perfectly safe, with her skill alone it-"

"She's alone! That's the issue. She needs to be around *someone right now*. You, or us. It doesn't matter." Illkat rants.

CMDR Aberdashi puts her boot right between Joseph's legs on the chair he sits upon. She leans forwards and looks him deep in the eyes. "What do you know."

He matches her eye contact. "*Enough.*"

She stares *harder*. "Your *safe-house* is *just a bit east* of our remote northern dead-drop. That isn't a coincidence."

"I think it is more then that. I think it is...*by design*. I know nothing of your dead-drop. I don't even know who you are. Yet, I am confident my safe-house is near whatever you're looking for, because of a higher power."

"I don't think *jesus* is here." Dezz critiques.

"Not *jesus*. This...*game*. Whatever it is. I...*I know what I say on my show*. The...*messaging I was going for*. If I'm being honest, I

333

grew up an atheist. I've never even been to *Texas*. I just know in times of great strife, people...*connect with that kinda thing*."

Kaan points at Joseph and seems *relieved*. "That explains *so much*."

"But you see coincidence is just...a tool in this place. I thought, I'm sure we all have. Isn't it all...too convenient sometimes. Like we're just following some trail! The pieces are set out far enough away from each other so we feel like we connected the dots, but if you look at it. If you step back. It's just one big straight line!"

"Mhmm." CMDR Aberdashi sits down dramatically. She looks up at the ceiling. "Before we first arrived in Illking. We tried *to go somewhere else*. We found the path was blocked. Trees collapsed over the road. Mud in the ditches. Yet the path here was...*clear*."

Kozmo leans over to Kaan. "Do you see Geko anywhere? I don't think he's back yet."

Kaan shakes his head. "Nah I haven't seen him. He might still be back in town?"

"*Yea, maybe*. Do you think it is okay if I go check? I know he was going to be working in the forge."

With a flick of his wrist Kaan bestows permission he didn't know he was the gate-keeper of unto Kozmo.

One of the solders with a head-set on leans a single cuff from their ear and looks at the Commander. "The alert has stopped repeating. I think this is live."

"Put it on for everyone." CMDR Aberdashi orders.

"Citizens of our dear Nelfdom. What fate has befallen you? Our captives gone. The living jewels of my rule, squandered. My dear second in command Bobias has been slain! These thieves are in league with the Arctic Witch, I assure you of this. No one is safe. Not in your home, not in this city, until they are caught!" He coughs. "Now, I seek you all to hear these words and respect them. My newest second in command is a proud warrior known as *Lobias*. He shall organize this witch hunt*! I expect everyone to participate!*"

"Lobias!" Kaan shouts at the radio. "Come on Nelf. That's just...*poor taste*. Let it go."

CMDR Aberdashi looks at one of their maps, then exhales loudly. "Engage a lock-down protocol until their *witch hunt* winds down. In the mean time, *all of you* might as well get out of here. Find our dead-drop, and your friend in this safe-house."

A few loud steps lead toward the door. Dezz peers up. "We'll get our friend, our supplies. But then, what is going to happen to us?" He exhales a bit. "Sorry, I'm just, *there is so much going on*. I don't see how we're going to make it all fit together."

Kaan smiles. "Hey, buddy. Don't worry. It's all just...*part of the game*. I'm sure in no time, if you just play a bit more. It will make sense."

"Play more?"

"Live more...*longer!* You know what I mean. Just...don't give up."

Dezz looks at Kaan suspiciously, as if, for a moment, seeing something he's never spotted before. He fakes a smile. "*Alright*. If you say so." He looks back up the stairs towards the exit. "Out to the northern wastes it is then!"

"Good, while you're out addressing that. I will find homes and work for these recently acquired...*refugees*." The CMDR makes the statement as if deep in thought.

CHAPTER SIXTEEN
WHITE RABBIT IN A BLIZZARD

Stress is blinding. If you have never experienced being truly overwhelmed before. It seems much like a waist height wave bowling someone over; certainly something had you leaned against it; it would break on your hip instead of take you down. Yet, the reality is much more precarious. The height of the wave may not change; but the ground sucks you down to your waist so it kicks you in the face and you swallow sea water. Where you braced once, you have now dug yourself into quite a pit.

"It feels like something has changed." Dezz makes the comment as his breath becomes a brief fog exiting his lips.

Kaan smirks. "It's known as Winter. You see there are these things called *seasons that-*"

Dezz smacks him. "How many nights have we spent in the bush together. You think I *don't know*."

The pair walk back, in the middle of the night, through a dense forest. Chunks of wood in their arms. A flickering light bounces against clean snow revealing a small cleared out area beside a large boulder.

Here, Lt. Oaks cleans a deer and roasts meat. Illkat studies the technique in use. Joseph Torrence tends the fire.

"How was that?" Illkat asks the boys.

They shrug.

"Cold."

"Boring."

"Such story tellers." She teases.

"I can tell you a story. Once upon a time I was an introvert with nearly a dozen locks on my bedroom door, now, I'm some...secret services warrior?" Kaan offers.

"I promise you that you aren't." Lt. Oaks offers. "Officially, you're what I would call an *asset*. No formal training. No ties to our power structure. But a powerful piece on the board."

"Gee, thanks. I feel really special now." Kaan continues.

"YOU ARE! Just, not in the way you think. You're a survivor, and a good one at that. I think you know what you need, how to get it and how to play that role. Just being able to...*get by* is a valuable skill. You would be surprised by how many crises pop up and cause people to just, *sit down and accept what may come.*"

Kaan nods and drops his wood next to Joseph.

Dezz stacks his atop.

"You know, you're always talking about all these *experiences* you've had. You've lost so much faith in people, but, what *happened to you* man?"

Quickly unpacking a silvered sleeve from her jacket. She offers it over to Dezz. The fire glinting across the curved face. "What do you want to know?" She asks with her typical upbeat inflection.

Dezz takes a gulp of the...ambiguous liquor in the flask and then coughs aggressively. He hacks for a few seconds, settles himself and offers a nod of approval unto Lt. Oaks. "We've heard bits about...bombs and you've obviously seen war. But, *like*, how did that start for all of you? There is no way you're just, *how you are naturally.*"

Shifting from a judgmental glance to a curious inflection Illkat looks over at Lt. Oaks. "I can't deny that I've been...curious as well."

Lt. Oaks leans back a bit and looks up at the sky. Filtered with smoke, curving around the tips of pine trees. "Do you know much about Belfast?"

"You don't have an Irish accent." Joseph makes the note.

"Nor do I claim to be. My parents were. *Opposite sides of the peace wall* if you believe that."

337

Everyone settles into a comfy position around the growing fire. Lt. Oaks clears her throat.

"Do you know about the IRA? There were a few *revivals* after the original ceased hostilities. Provisional IRA. New IRA. My *dad* was involved in the *Resurrectionist IRA*. My mother was *British* intelligence at the time. She became responsible for maintaining oversight of my father's unit. His hiding places, plans and such." She takes a breath and giggles a bit. "She told me, she was watching him with this little drone from a window sill and *he started putting a flower in the window*. See, at first, she thought, this must be a sign! Some signal to the others. Each day, a new flower, tulips, roses, lilacs and all. Each day, so my mother thought, a new message. No code, no consistency. So in her desperation, she donned a disguise and went down to fake a delivery." She coughs to clear her throat. "So, down she went. Knocked on the door, and my dad opens it with a smirk. All he had to say was 'so your favourites are orchids?'"

"That's pretty cute." Kaan admits.

"So he was putting out the flowers for her?"

Lt. Oaks smiles. "He had a hunch he was being watched, and had learned himself there was a female operative in the area. So he put two and two together. They talked for a good while, never confirming who they were, but they told me they both *knew*. After that, they started meeting regularly. My mom wanted him as an informant, he wanted her as a turncoat. At the end of the day, when the UN annexed the remaining European fighting forces. They ended up on the same side. Then *I* appeared, and...a bit controversially began my training."

"You were an infant and training?" Illkat asks.

Lt. Oaks nods. "I wish I had a copy of the picture, both parents scouting through a Bolivian forest, my head over mom's shoulder in a bullet proof backpack."

"What was your first birthday gift, night vision goggles?"
Dezz jests.

Lt. Oaks looks a bit embarrassed. "*That* was my 2nd birthday."
She laughs a bit to herself. "Although, when I was seven I got an RF
detector and if I wanted dessert I had to find all the hidden cameras in
the living room first." She smiles, thinking back on the memory
pleasantly.

"I remember reading about you...*somewhere*." Joseph speaks
up.

"I doubt that very much." She asserts.

"No, no I'm certain of it. It was classified, shouldn't of even
come to my desk. You were assigned to the security detail of *Bailey
Monroe!* That teen pop-star."

"My name was never tied to that."

"But your face was, a single picture. You and her, in this back
room. She was crying, her hands and dress had blood over them."

Lt. Oaks finishes up with the deer and begins to skewer
lengths on a long cleaned length of wood. She crosses the skewers
over the fire, letting them cook indirectly. "Do you know what
happened, just before that picture?" She looks at Joseph right in the
eyes.

He shakes his head. "No, there wasn't anything about that. Not
that I saw."

The fire crackles.

A few rabbits speed through the bush just at the edge of the
fire's light.

"She had a stalker. Quite a determined fellow. He found her in
a restaurant, just saw her through a window. He couldn't get in, so he
tried to go *through* the window. Nicked an artery the second he
punched through the glass. Walked three steps towards her, barely
managed 'I love yo-' before he passed out and died on the floor."

Dezz kicks some dirt and stares up at the sky. "So this is just...normal for you. Life, death, violence?"

"I killed my first person at a very young age. He was far away, down the end of a scope. We were outside a POW camp, up in a blind. There was a break. One man, he had a kid in his arms as he ran for the trees. A guard raised his rifle towards him and I...*made him drop*. It wasn't a very good shot, I was a bit low. He grasped his stomach, and cried out. The runner got away, and the guard was found by his friends. They cried for him, I could hear it even far away." She huffs and gets a bit frustrated. "We're just...killing strangers. Hating each other. Getting caught up in things."

"You were with your parents when you killed your first person?" Joseph inquires.

Lt. Oaks nods.

"What did they say?"

Lt. Oaks adopts an odd smirk. "Good shot darling. Next time aim a bit higher or fire again when he falls over so he draws less attention during the dying process."

"*Yeesh*." Illkat offers.

"*Parents right*? Always a nit-pick." She teases.

"The...*dying process*. What a way to describe it. Like it is just some...order of operations."

Lt. Oaks smiles. "Well you see it is. People don't die when you shoot them, not most of the time. Typically they just start *leaking*. It's the leaking that kills you. Getting shot can be surprisingly survivable on its own. Even a shot to the head, depending on the day. There is a forty some percent chance of surviving that!"

"And I thought my dad was a mess." Illkat admits.

"Oh dad was a bit of a rebel, but he settled down in old age. He ran a bakery before everything happened."

"Did he love you?" Illkat asks solemnly.

"I believe he did."

"That's lucky. I don't think my father really loved me."

Kaan looks over *knowingly*. Then stares at the fire. "Do you...*miss him*?" He asks with a guilty inflection.

Illkat shrugs. "I never missed...*him*. He was inpatient, drunk, out of control. He had no responsibility, barely took care of himself none the less anyone else." She stares at the fire for a moment. "I think I missed what we could of been. What a father *should be*. At least yours taught you something, whether it is violent or not. My father just...gave opportunities for me to teach myself. Like, how to walk to the bathroom in the middle of the night without waking anyone up, or how to hide calls from school because even a request for a parent teacher interview meant, in his mind, I did something wrong and was stealing his time from him."

"He, tried to protect you in the end. Didn't he?" Kaan considers.

"He *loved* to do that. I think it was the only part of being a dad he liked. *Is there someone to hurt? Someone to scare?* If there was a problem he could step up and yell at, I think, in his mind, it made up for never being there any other moment." She huffs. "It's my least favourite trait in a person. When they *only* prefer the big gestures. They forget we live in the small moments."

Lt. Oaks pulls Illkat into a snuggle and turns some of the skewers over the fire. "Like this one!" She cheers.

"Mhmm." Illkat pushes her head into Lt. Oak's arm and gets comfier. "This is...a good moment."

Joseph looks out in the distance, towards the now southern city of Illking. "For us it is."

〒

Nelf sits on a throne in a badly lit room. Long cables drape across the floor. Different men in different shades of the same duo-tone uniform shuffle boxes of technology and supplies around. No one dares look at him.

"*Sir.*" Lobias greets him, appearing suddenly from a nearby hallway. "There are some reports the Arctic Witch has gone to the sea."

Nelf lazily looks up, swinging one leg over the other. "And what makes you think this?"

"Well, an odd family reported having seen a woman with her description dancing out in the distance; atop waves. I was just thinking *who else could do that.*"

Nelf sighes. "That was just the Lady of the Water. Standard event every fourteen some hours, or during rain storms on a random chance. *Haven't you even played this game before*?"

"Mhmm, yes sir. So sorry sir. I'll keep looking."

"No, you fool." Nelf stands and shakes Lobias. "Get three of your best men. Train your mining sub-proficiency up to at least 80% in the caves to the west. Take the ore from that cave, and the drops from the final room. Clear *everyone out of that area*, then wait 8 hours. DO IT AGAIN and then come back when you have a hundred Globstones."

"What's a globstone?"

"Just...*read the items when you get them. You'll get them there,* OKAY?" Nelf offers.

"Of course Tzar. I shall take, Bobias, Mobias, and Hobias with me."

"I don't *care* who you take. Just *do it*."

Lobias scurries off.

Nelf groans. He stares around himself, whips up his cloak and hurries off. He breaches the streets of Illking where, in quiet constriction, what little culture there is flourishes. His guards inform rigid order. His *debaucherers* share messages of taboo insights, statements and requests. More and more posters, paintings and statues of *himself* fill the streets. The soldiers nod to him. The passing citizens dare not look.

"Where did you go...*Sonnenblume*." He laments to himself. "You're like liquid...*nitrogen*. You leave your friends, not for me, but for a fool of a leader! You *stole my face*! And now, even with this whole city underneath my thumb I can do NOTHING ABOUT IT!"

"You're not really in control of all that much. Folks are just scared of you." An elderly voice indicates.

Nelf, in a flash of rage, turns around to see an old man sitting on the step outside a small home. A lit cigarette in his hand, an angled cane in the other. He walks towards him in a fury. "HOW DARE YOU!"

The old man shrugs. "What are you going to do, *hurt me*? Wanna hit an old man? My wrists have been killing me lately. You can probably pull them right apart if you need somewhere to start." The old man holds out his hand.

An awkward wave washes over the street. "You're not worth the time."

"Ah, no I don't think that's it. I'm just not going to give you what you want. Loyalty. Fear. You're like a big old sponge, just soaking it all because you don't have any other choice. But I'm a rock." He takes a long drag. "So I'm just gonna stay put. You can walk around, pick me up or move me. But I'm still just a rock."

Nelf grumbles then takes a seat next to the old man. "I just want...everything to make sense. I *know I have the power to bring everyone together. To make things perfect.* I understand this game! This world! How people work!"

The old man lights another smoke with the bright ember of his diminishing one and swaps the two mid-drag so quick you barely notice the movement. "Do ya now." He doesn't seem convinced.

"I was the greatest player in all of North America! Every game! Every tournament! I was so good in the youth leagues that they forced me to not compete! To even the playing field for everyone else. Everywhere I have gone. I WIN. I DOMINATE. I am Nelf Kinslayer!"

"Alright." The old man flicks his smoke. "You ever hear of Bob Pallet?"

"What are you talking about."

"Pallet's Particular's. Radio show? It was still going when you were a kid I imagine."

"I've never owned a radio. At least, not intentionally."

"Well then maybe you'll understand a bit more. When I was younger, *Bob Pallet* killed it. He was everywhere. Cereal boxes. Milk cartons. He showed up on the assignments my kids were doing in school! It seemed like he was the biggest winner in the whole wide world."

"So what?"

"Exactly! Where is he now? Do you know him? Do you care? Do you even believe me?"

Nelf shrugs. "I don't."

The old man taps his nose. "Exactly, so, imagine. What do people think of you? After you're done shouting? After you have had your moment. Do you think you're eternal?"

"I will be!"

The old man clears his throat and looks up at the cloudless sky. "I met a traveller from an antique land. Who said: two vast and trunk-less legs of stone. Stand in the dessert. Near them, on the sand,

Half sunk, a shattered visage lies, whose frown, And wrinkled lip, and sneer of cold command, Tell that its sculptor well those passions read. Which yet survive, stamped on these lifeless things, The hand that mocked them and the heart that fed: And on the pedestal these words appear: 'My name is Ozymandias, king of kings: Look on my works, ye Mighty, and despair!" Nothing beside remains. Round the decay Of that colossal wreck, boundless and bare. The lone and level sands stretch far away."

"I never read those comics. I thought they were over-hyped."

The old man scoffs. "We never get to enjoy our triumphs, if they are for us alone Nelf. No matter what you do. Who you push. Who you hurt. No matter what scheme you unleash. *It ends with you*, if it only serves you. Nobody will keep it up. Nobody will remember your name."

With a scuff of the bottom of his boot Nelf tries to relax in a modest position. "How did you get here, *old man*. I'm surprised you survived the chaos."

"Oh I don't know about that." He unbuttons his shirt, and reveals the scars of a lethal wound. A thick slash across his chest, and four large holes; now healed over as a stretched out red mark.

"What are you saying?"

"I think I died a few weeks ago. If I'm being honest."

Nelf stares at him, and something *clicks*. "You think you died?"

"I felt it. These wild people came out of nowhere, the whole city was fighting. Just a few blocks down that way. They cut me up the middle and shot me just to make sure. I went dark, then...*bright*."

"See your whole life flash before your eyes?"

"No. I saw a word. 'Continue?'" He shrugs. "I just reached out for it, and then. Well. *Here I was again*. Just a few days later."

345

Nelf sits still for a moment. He chews on the statement. A tear falls from his eye and he seems *bewildered*. "Then that means..." He nearly shakes the old man. "Were there any other words? Was it just continue? TELL ME WHAT YOU SAW?"

The old man smirks, enjoying the focus, and moves onto the third cigarette of the conversation. "It was a big blue sun, halfway set. It looked...*blocky* if that makes sense. Like a bunch of little cubes. That sun was going down, and under it I saw 'Continue'." He takes a drag.

Nelf shakes in place.

"I think-"

"YES"

The old man laughs. "I think, underneath continue. In smaller letters was the word 'retire'."

"Retire?" Nelf considers. He seems shocked. He taps his foot. "Did the sun fully set?"

The old man shakes his head. "No, I didn't give it the chance. I wasn't raised to be a quitter you see."

Nelf looks around and a child smiles at him. The old man smiles back. No one says anything. He leans forwards, elbows on his knees and a few tears sneak past his nose down onto the ground. "So what do you want now?"

The old man seems confused. "Well, I already have some more smokes. I wouldn't complain about a bite to eat though."

"Alright." Nelf stands and offers the old man his hand. He gets up to his cane, and they begin a slow stroll. "There is a little sandwich spot that opened up just a few days ago. Let's go, maybe you can tell me more about that king of kings and...where he went wrong."

The old man keeps on ahead. "Maybe I will."

〒

346

"It is just up ahead, not that much further." Lt. Oaks references a little beeping display then tucks the device into a shallow pocket.

"What does a *dead drop* look like?" Kaan considers. "It isn't actually like...*a dead guy* is it?"

"WELL ONCE! We were supposed to get a dead-drop from a guy. But someone got to him first. They robbed him of whatever he had, clothes and all. When we found him, we thought we'd lost everything. Until we found out *he swallowed the device* we were looking for." She shrugs. "Had to cut it out of him, but that was an exception. Not standard operating procedure!"

Dezz laughs. "Always such charming stories...*Matilda*."

"THANKS!" Lt. Oaks responds cheerfully.

Kaan leaps through a few mounds of snow, a smile on his face. "I can't believe I missed this so much. *You know*, if I think about it. Snow is just...safety to me."

"The streets get pretty empty when it's cold. That's for sure." Dezz agrees.

"Exactly! On a summer day, you might have someone passed out in the alley, people going up and down in their vehicles or bikes. Music is loud. Everyone is *out*. In the winter, they sit at home and shut up. It's *great*."

"Not exactly a people person are you?" Joseph ventures a confident guess.

Kaan shakes his head. "I've always considered myself a *person* person. But *people*...nah. I'll pass!"

"Do you ever feel like you're missing something? Locked away from everyone?" Joseph continues.

"Nope! Heck if I'm being honest, I feel *more like myself*. That's the thing folks don't understand. They see me locked away in my room, by myself for twelve hours, doing nothing but playing games. They feel bad for me. How...*lost* I must be. But the truth of it is, that twelve hours playing is really just a consolation for everything else. If I had it my way, it would of been sixteen hours, or twenty, or just every one of them. I don't regret the time spent in my own world, but I regret every moment I'm forced out of it." Kaan considers something. "And I resent everything that made me leave. Every...question. Every social engagement. Honestly some times I wish I was born in a vat, without a mouth, and no friends; just so I wouldn't be bothered spending the day doing whatever I wanted. No *guilt*."

Lt. Oaks squints. "I'll be right back."

"Not a fan of being my friend Kaan?" Illkat teases; pretending to be offended.

"No! It's not that. I appreciate all of you. Now that you're here. I just, *errr*."

Dezz pats him on the back. "We get it buddy. You don't need to explain."

Kaan nods. "*Thanks*." A nervous bead of sweat appears then quickly dissipates.

"It seems like you don't see how valuable your friends are." Joseph argues.

"I know how great they are. How lucky I am. I can't help that...people make me tired? I'm lazy. Call it what it is. I don't care. I don't want to exert myself. Ever. I don't really *want to do anything* other then spend what little time I have peacefully." He shrugs. "And I can't control how other people feel about that either."

"If you say so." Joseph allows.

Lt. Oaks reappears in the distance, she waves. "It's over here!" She shouts.

The group follow along, up a slight incline where there is a crater. A few remnants of some sort of advanced flying machine peak over from a thick snow covering. There are a few mounds surrounding it.

"Time to get digging. We're probably looking for some sort of storage device. It will probably be really heavy." Lt. Oaks offers.

Illkat walks over one mound and kneels down. She begins to move snow out of the way and finds a *pocket*. She moves more snow out of the way and finds *the broken half of a human jaw*. "Ah what the hell!" She jumps back.

Lt. Oaks casually walks over, and dusts the snow off the corpse's face with the tip of her boot. She examines him a bit, then shrugs. "Looks like he was a part of the crash. Probably blew out of his spot and hit the dirt hard. *Pretty painless, all things considered*."

Holding a glare for only a moment. Illkat takes a deep gulp of air and moves onto the next mound.

"I think I've found something." Dezz acknowledges. He approaches a huge cylinder, broken in half. It is blackened with soot. Snow seems to slide off it, as if it is *still warm*.

"That's just some wreckage Dezz." Illkat makes the point.

"No, I *see something*." Dezz argues. He reaches out to the cylinder and it begins to glow a dull orange.

"Get out of there!" Kaan shouts.

"It's fine!" Dezz makes the point as the orange grows to a bright white, and embers begin to pour out of the cylinder. The sound of a turbine spinning churns and the ground vibrates. "I think this is for me!" He speaks calmly as the turbine reaches an erupting volume and a blast of fire and soot bursts out. Smoke is everywhere. Visibility is null.

It takes minutes for the smoke to clear and when it does; snow in every direction has been melted to the grass. Revealing a series of broken corpses, shattered weapons and a big black box; only the corner of which is chipped.

"Where is DEZZ!" Kaan shouts. He looks around frantically. Where he stood, is only a thick smoke trailing up to the sky.

"It must of been a trap." Joseph considers. "This area was empty when we were here, but *maybe*, those that weren't handled in Verrplek. Maybe they went north."

Illkat looks at the ground, and touches the turbine. It has gone *cold*. "I don't think so." She looks around. "Dezz, if you're...*there*. We believe in you. We're going to find Sonnenblume next."

Filtering through the electronics exposed from an open panel upon the turbine. Lt. Oaks seems to agree. "This component is broken. No fuel, it's all leaked into the dirt. It shouldn't even be able to ignite. No one has set up a trap."

"Oh, *I see then*." Kaan calms down then smiles. "Hey, good for you buddy. I know you always wanted to find this. I guess *it found you*."

"Your friend just *died!* How are you so calm!?" Joseph is bewildered.

"He isn't dead. He's found the *Fount of Fire*. Or, arguably, it found him."

"So...*what*. Do we just wait for him then?"

CRACK

Lt. Oaks bursts open the storage case, having worked through a few digital locks. Inside, fitted in custom foam inlays are a series of modular communications devices. A small fission battery. Cords and converters spanning a few generations. A 3d printer. Components for creating custom PCB boards and, secured behind an additional layer of protection; a wetware processor.

"That looks like a...*brain in a jar*." Illkat considers.

"I think it *is* a brain in a jar." Kaan adds.

"Technically it is! An artificial brain. A wet processor. Whatever you want to call it." She giggles. "Nobody lost their head I can promise you that!"

Kaan looks over to a nearby corpse who would very much disagree. "I guess so." He murmurs.

The container is closed and it *hisses* as it forms a seal. Lt. Oaks points at Kaan. "Help me get the other side of this."

He walks over, picks up one side by a handle and groans. "That isn't nearly as bad as I thought it would be."

"Then why did you groan?"

"*Instincts?*" He laughs. "*Good manners?*"

"Alright, then, *off to Sonnenblume.*"

〒

"So you're telling me, *that famous character* is based on a poem? And that *poem* is based on a *pharaoh* who had a completely different name?" Nelf laments his understanding.

The old man finishes his last spoonful of soup, looks around the outdoor patio and lights a smoke. "That's about it, *yes.*"

"Why didn't they call him his real name?"

The old man shrugs. The light behind his eyes growing as he takes another drag. "Maybe that's part of the point. In the mind of everyone else. You're just, what they see you as. Whatever name they have for you is the one they'll use. Whether you like it or not."

With obvious disgust. "*The disrespect. I would never let that-*" He catches himself. "I can't stop it, even if I tried. Could I?"

"No more then anyone can. Look back, throughout history. Has anyone truly controlled their own story? Or did they just, play their part, unknowing. You think you're winning, you think you're on top. But in reality, you just got swept up in a wave which was headed

351

that way *anyways*. Everything crashes eventually. As do our names, our lives, our intentions."

"I was *the winner* before. I worked hard. I did *everything right*. I know there was...crassness. *Shock.* But that was the appeal. I am *Nelf Kinslayer, Teller of Truths! Assail-er of Vapid Boredom!*"

The waitress which was approaching them decides to handle another table's drinks first; looking away instantly.

Nelf sinks.

The old man sucks down half his smoke through a smirk. "And to *her*, you're just loud."

Nelf tries to say something, and fails the first few attempts. He looks around then leans further into his chair. "I don't know if I can go back, *to how I was before all of this*."

"PPHSSHHH." The old man exhales with a laugh. "And nor should you. To lose all these lessons? All that work? *Go forwards Nelf.* You can't pretend you haven't been this...*spectacle* for as long as you have. But nothing says you have to *stay that way*. What comes next? What does it look like, if you evolve?"

Nelf laughs to himself.

The old man looks up.

He waves it away. "I see your wisdom, *old man*. I must ask, where did you learn to think as you do?"

"A good partner. I was stubborn as a stick you see. The sort of downright frustrating guy that'd fight with you over a few cents, or blow a fuse at the slightest things. My partner was much more patient. In loving them, *well*, I saw how much suffering I was spreading. How hard it was to love me. *And I made it difficult.* Some people tried, despite my best efforts, and they were burnt for it. Their pain was like a mirror and I didn't like what I saw."

Nelf relaxes.

The waitress comes by. She takes their plates, and fills their coffee. She smiles. Nelf smiles back. His fist tightens.

"Did you resent them. For charging you?"

The Old Man shakes his head. "I was *always changing*. Just for once, it was for the best." He smirks as he lights another smoke.

〒

A huge iron door, with a turning knob in the centre of it stands proudly alongside a stretch of mountain wall.

"This is...*your office*?" Illkat questions.

"What remains of it." Joseph admits. "When everything *changed*, the building was moved. Rooms shifted. So much was picked up and simply put down. It ended up *here*. Basement and all." He approaches the knob, applies serious effort and begins to turn it; the metal squeals.

"I was in the basement you see. Even a shift at an existential scale couldn't provoke much change in this sort of facility."

"This was a...Civic Sciences building?" Lt. Oaks observes.

The door opens up and from within, a length of sharpened ice flies out. Lt. Oaks ducks under it. Something *trails off* from within.

"Sonnenblume!" Illkat shouts.

Not loudly enough as nothing responds.

Joseph shrugs. "You're right. That's what it is. We spent lots of time analyzing efficiency of traffic, or making sure neighbourhoods have the right access to needs. *That kinda thing*."

"What was your part in all of this?" Kaan questions. He chuckles. "It clearly wasn't looking after wherever I lived."

Joseph dodges the comment. "I can show you." He takes a step in and nearly slips on the perfect layer of glossy ice covering the ground.

353

"Does anyone have any pocket sand?" Lt. Oaks asks.

Everyone stares at her.

Kaan laughs. "YOU KNOW, my mom always kept some sand and like...a plank of wood in the closet. She said it was to help get a car unstuck but...*honestly*...I never knew what she was talking about."

Illkat chuckles. "So I'll take that as a no."

A little wisp of smoke rises up behind the group. It is warm, and fleeting. Like a dust devil on a playground.

Kaan reaches out to touch it, and it passes through him. Slowly, it begins beyond the door. Little embers fall from it, like minuscule gears churn within. The ice melts under wherever it floats.

"Dezz?" Kaan asks.

The smoke continues to float inward.

"Is that...*him*?" Illkat questions.

Kaan shrugs. "I get the sense it is...*somehow*."

"Sonnenblume was barely vertical for days after she found her fount. Why would Dezz be any different?"

"He's had a lifetime of living with pain. Maybe, to him...*it just isn't all that different*. Like an old memory coming back into view." Kaan offers.

The smoke turns a corner.

"We should follow it then." Lt. Oaks admits. She brings in the storage container, leaves it by the door, then shuts them all inside.

"How did you know it opens from the inside as well?" Joseph asks.

Lt. Oaks pauses for a moment, looks at the door, confirms it has a handle on this side then smiles awkwardly. "IT WAS JUST...OBVIOUS. DOORS RIGHT?!" She looks away with an awkward expression.

Illkat laughs at her, pats her back and then continues onward. She holds out her spear, makes an odd look then puts it away.

354

Around the corner, the drab government facility inspires the recollection of a dental office as a child. Not a *nice* dental office, with big screens and clean white services. The sort of place that was down a small carpeted hallway, in a room which looks like the business equivalent of an apartment, with oddly placed desks and cramped in secretaries occupying one corner of the lobby. It smells like *drywall* and *stale coffee*.

"Ah, home sweet home." Joseph remarks. He stops at another large door. "This is the way to the basement."

The smoke passes under the door, and beyond sight.

"It is where I told Sonnenblume to go and *wait*." He continues.

The door turns, and just as it opens *Sonnenblume* rushes out from behind it; a sharpened length of ice jutting from her arm down towards Joseph's neck as she throws him into the ground. She hesitates for a moment, looks around, then adopts quite an embarrassed expression.

"Oh hallo!" She grimaces, then takes a step back. "That was, *uh*...not what I was expecting. I guess."

"Does anyone else know you are here?" Kaan asks.

"I don't think so." Sonnenblume confirms.

"Then...*who could it of been*?" Kaan continues the line of questioning; somewhat flabbergasted.

"Mhmm." Sonnenblume thinks on the topic for a moment, then opts to ignore it. "You're all safe *and with Joseph!* Have you come to see we're all on the same side?"

Joseph coughs. "Well in this situation. I am *the one on their side*. They rescued me, after Nelf's...*annex* of Illking." He gets up to his feet with a groan and *stretches*. "Have you spent much time in the basement?"

"*Eh.*" Her exasperation is dense; thickened with the frustration of a dozen failures. "I didn't get very far. I don't know how you called that thing *simple.*"

"It is simple in *principle.*" Joseph corrects; in a way which suggests it should be obvious.

"*Alright*, before we do that." Illkat grabs Sonnenblume, and walks her down the hall a bit. "*Hi.*" She greets her; awkwardly.

"*Hi.*"

"*So.*"

"*Yea.*"

They stare at each other.

"I missed you."

"I missed you!"

"Friends?"

They hug. "Absolutely."

The long, beige hall of the government facility mutes the moment. Like the registry where you get a marriage certificate before the ceremony.

"Well come on then!" Joseph shouts from down the way.

"Shall we?" Illkat inquires.

Sonnenblume nods. "Let us." She pauses for a moment. "*Sorry for the mess.*"

"What do you mean?"

"You'll see."

The guild heads down the carpeted stairs. They smell like smoke from decades ago, steam cleaned nearly out of sight; but eternally stained all the same. Wooden handles with thick curves, wide knobs and elaborate methods of handling a corner lead down *quite a flight* unto the basement of the facility.

It is not *decrepit* in the way an unfinished basement of your home may be. Nor the dull communal laundry room of your very first apartment. It is *intentionally* and *insight-fully* working towards developing an architectural method of inducing insomnia in incumbent innovators. If there is a creative thought, a worthwhile question or deserving cause lingering in your brain; they find themselves drowned by the indiscriminate oranges, browns and glossy wood filling the basement. Foam boards, inexplicably, adorn the spot next to every door.

"*What was it that you did?*" Kaan questions, then interrupts himself. "Oh, *Sonnenblume*. By the way, that's Dezz." He points to the cloud of smoke.

"Oh okay." Sonnenblume remarks with an odd inflection. "*Hey Dezz. Smoking again?*"

The smoke waves back and forth.

Joseph coughs. "I was a...*curator* I guess you could call it." He leads them further, pushes open two double doors and...*most of the room has a sort of melted popsicle feeling to it*. "Erm." Joseph remarks, looks to the corner and is instantly relieved. "At least it isn't anywhere near the machines."

"*Sorry.*" Sonnenblume adds.

Lt. Oaks walks the other way and starts poking through records, items on the shelf and similar.

"You see this machine. *Analog*. That's more apt...for what I am. *Analog*. An antique left in the basement because a few lines on old contracts say I need to be here. Despite that I was...forgotten. Never in the field, never on a big case. Just looking over old equipment, keeping it maintained. Endlessly preparing for...nothing. Everything is digital, you know this. I could have turned on this and screamed out at the top of my lungs. No one was listening."

"Until...*the world changed*." Lt. Oaks makes the observation; thumbing through a thick book with a soaked front cover.

"Mhmm. *Radio* became relevant again. The old signals were restored. *Preppers mostly.*" He laughs. "A lot of folks holed up underground right about now. Living like nothing changed; other then they were proven right all along."

"Talk to many of them?" Kaan considers.

"A fair number." He looks over to Sonnenblume with a pang of guilt. "One of them was a preacher, most of them kept a faith. I learned the...*words they liked hearing* just by listening. I probably...*misheard a thing or two.*"

"Wait, *sorry but*, are you telling me that was all bullshit?" Sonnenblume accuses him. Her eyes grow white. The soaked portions of the room freeze.

"I, *No.*" Joseph steps back. "Yes...it was. I...*most of it* was me just telling people what they wanted to hear. I *do believe we can turn things back!* That we could...make things *like that*. I was just hoping, if I spread my message, *well*, I'd meet the type of people who could make that happen!"

The room grows colder.

Sonnenblume becomes the colour of ivory across her whole body. Her hair whips back, each length freezing in a different place.

FWOOSH

Dezz appears. A massive, burning length of *root* over his shoulder. Smouldering lengths of black smoke pour from his nails, and the seams of his clothing. His eyes are entirely red; a shifting orange patina crawls across them. He *snaps* and the room becomes *normal*.

"Dezz!" Kaan shouts, and hugs his friend. His better senses come to him and he's relieved to find he isn't burning. "What happened to you!"

"*Actually you pretty much guessed it.*" Dezz confirms.

"Oh."

"Like, no differences?"

"Pretty much a perfect guess."

"Huh."

"Yea, uncanny really."

Everyone stares at them. Illkat curses with her expression alone; both frustrated and somehow embarrassed.

"Were you going to kill me, *just now*?" Joseph asks; looking Sonnenblume directly in her blizzard-esque eyes.

She looks away and scoffs. "No I...*just wanted to scare you*."

"So...is this like a disease or something? If you bite me will I crap fire?" Lt. Oaks inspects Dezz, holding her now much less wet book out in front of him like one does with soaked jeans by a fire.

"I became a magic user. I don't think it is...*contagious*."

"If it is you can spit in my mouth." Kaan offers casually, then stops full tilt. "Sorry about that, first thought in my head."

"*Why was that the first thought in your head-*" Dezz instantly questions.

Something *beeps*.

Joseph scrambles to his feet, looks at the machine in the corner of the room. It is, itself, an incredibly complex assortment of wires, cords, consoles, antenna and inputs of a sort. The yellowed plastic gives away its vintage; despite what has been an obvious success in preserving aging computer components. At present, only an old brown microphone with a steel band wrapped across the top appears connected.

Twelve different flips are switched, there is a brief *whine* in the room then speakers, installed somewhere *behind* or *under* the walls pick up. "This is a *distress signal*. Please help. We're in the occupied city of *Terali*. It...*it looks like the ocean is quaking*. There are...*figures* underneath. They keep chanting! Telling us...they...*found a way in*." The message instantly repeats.

359

"Those poor people. I saw a map. *Terali* is south-west of Illking. It is a coastal city!"

"A beautiful one at that." Kaan agrees.

"It is a bit too convenient if you ask me." Dezz crosses his arms. "We can't keep getting beckoned back and forth by random radio signals! It could be a trap! We could be too late! It could be...*people trying to eat us* for all we know!"

"Am I getting that obvious?" Finir speaks *through the speakers.*"

"Oh no." Joseph cowers and dives under a desk.

Dezz pulls the length of log from his shoulder, wielding it in two hands. Six trails of flame burn to the tip where a torch-like effect forms the head of a maul. "Come on then, *let's do this.*" Dezz ushers him on.

Finir laughs maniacally. "You saw *right through me*, and OH am I just...*wounded.*" He laughs again. "The beauty in this plan, is you will fall for my bait even if you know it is so! The city of *Terali* will be devoured. As will *every city*. I don't care when I get to you. *It will happen eventually.*" He taps something nearby wherever he is speaking. "*But you, oh...you care.* Just knowing the soldiers of my dark server will *destroy every soul* in this fair settlement. Well, *you can't have that, can you? Heroes.*" The speakers cut back to the recording from *Terali*.

"It's always *something* with this guy! Why can't he just...leave us alone!" Kaan conceals a smile expertly.

Dezz shakes his head. "It's his...*role*. He's the *bad guy*. I don't even think it is his choice."

"You don't?" Lt. Oaks inquires.

"Think of it like...the son of a despot. Is he *truly* evil, just because he was raised in a corrupt and warped world? Are his choices his own? Or is he just...*falling for the training?*"

360

"That's what you believe Finir is?" Illkat adds.

"It is. He's a villain for villain's sake. Think of it. *Even in the game!* You spend all this time, fighting a general, a warlord, these ancient warriors whom seek to reclaim dominion over the land. Then, at the last little bit, *it is revealed it was Finir the whole time?* Corrupting them?" He throws his hands up in the air. "Come on! He was just...an excuse to have an interesting boss fight at the end of the game! And now, what does he have to do? He doesn't...*have a goal.* He's just being a dick! It's all he knows."

"So what, you...*think we should be friends?*" Lt. Oaks inquires. "He seems...*abrasive.*"

"Oh no, I don't think we could be friends. He isn't capable of it. I just...pity him, more then anything." Dezz looks up. "It's tough when you can't escape how the world sees you. If you get cast as a villain, *often*, you end up having to live as one."

Kaan smiles, and puts his arm around Dezz for a moment. "Do we need anything from here then?" He smiles across the room. "We already got our Sonnenblume."

"You all should go." Joseph says. He sits in a chair he has sat in ten thousand times before. "I think I'm *best here.*"

Sonnenblume stares at him, then walks away.

"Are you sure? We have...*radios* back with us. I'm sure there is something you could help with." Kaan offers.

"You're being kind." Joseph seems comfortable with the reality of the circumstance. "Truth of the matter is, *you don't want me around.* I'm not really your friend. *Here though.* Well. I rallied up spirits before. Maybe a...*version of that* could help."

Illkat nods. "If that is what you think is best. *Uh.* Thanks for keeping her safe, at least."

"It was my honour."

Everyone leaves except for Lt. Oaks.

361

She *stares at him*. He leans back in his chair.

"Are you...*going to kill me?*"

"*I would if I had to!*" She confirms; unintentionally sounding somewhat disappointed about it. She smiles, then catches herself and stops. "*No*, I am giving you this." She pulls an envelope from her inner pocket and hands it over to him. "Read it once we leave. It may be important one day."

"I will...*thank you*." Joseph makes the statement in a manner which is both *incredibly appreciative* and *somewhat horrified*.

Upon the breeze of a soft sprint across thick carpet. Lt. Oaks pulls herself in tow next to Illkat. She smiles at her then says nothing.

"Is everything alright?" Illkat asks cautiously.

"Perfectly well!" Lt. Oaks confirms.

"*Good*." Illkat reaches out and holds her hand.

Ahead of them, Kaan stares at Dezz as they walk. "Do you think...we could cook on you?"

"I haven't really tried."

Kaan looks around awkwardly.

Dezz laughs. "We can try if we get a chance."

"Nice!" Kaan cheers. "Thanks buddy. I'm glad we didn't lose you."

"Not yet, *anyways*." Dezz points out with a sly smirk.

CHAPTER SEVENTEEN

BAIT ALL THE SAME

"Do you feel *this*." Kaan asks.

"No." Dezz confirms.

"And this?" Illkat adds.

"Sorta."

"*How abooooouuttttt this*." Kaan poke Dezz's ribcage.

Dezz shakes his head. "Not *really*."

"What does it *feel like*?" Illkat raises an eyebrow alongside the question.

"It doesn't really feel like anything. Just, *nothing*. Or if not that, then just...warm."

"Can you turn it...off?" Kaan inquires.

"Well I certainly can't get my regular hair colour back. I even found some dye on the way here and tried!" Sonnenblume laments. "*It froze when I applied it*."

Dezz nods along. "That is the impression I get as well. I think, at most, I could *tune it down*." He shrugs. "But I'm pretty sure this is just how I look now."

Kaan looks around, then almost whispers. "Have you gone to the washroom yet?"

Dezz nods.

"Was it weird?"

"It was a little weird."

"IN WHAT WAY?"

Dezz just stares.

Kaan insists. "IN WHAT WAY?!"

Illkat rolls her eyes and laughs. Then nudges Dezz a bit.

Dezz groans. "More steam then I was expecting."

Kaan makes a noise somewhere between impressed and concerned.

干

"Oil is ready." Kozmo indicates.

CLANK

"Temps are good." He continues. "Just let me get the door!" He rushes over to the newly installed door of the forge and begins to shut it; before a small boot catches it in transit. Scooting into the room, then closing the door behind herself is a young woman in an officer's coat.

Sharp shoulders, straight slacks, a collared shirt and green tie. She wears a beret from which a few short lengths of black hair escape at the sides. Her eyes are *large*, her lips small. A traditional looking tattoo spans from one ear to another; crossing over her navel bridge in a shade of burgundy.

"Spark!" Kozmo greets the woman. "I thought you were working on reforming capacitors?"

"I finished." She makes the comment astutely, yet with an upturned tone which reminds one of an over achieving child. "What are you doing *here*?"

Gekomatsu pulls an *absolutely ridiculous* length of orange steel from the forge. It nearly extends halfway across the room. With a swift motion he turns, and dunks it into a homemade quench tank. Bubbles sizzle up. The oil hisses. The tank itself consists of four metal barrels, cut in half, and welded from top to bottom to create a leak proof channel. Five seconds pass and Gekomatsu yanks the steel out, now a dark blue shade.

"I have forged my blade." Gekomatsu states solemnly.

Spark points to a steel claymore hung on a display on the wall. "What about that one?"

"A place-holder. A temporary solution. *This*, this is the-"

"Macguffin!" Kozmo interrupts.

"That..."

"I mean, it *is a macguffin*!" Kozmo steps closer to inspect the blade. Leaning down and squinting. "I can tell. It has some completely random properties. It may as well have a plus one to plot immunity."

"We live in a realm where one may *wield plot armour*." Gekomatsu lifts the blade, moves a short distance and prepares to sharpen the blade on a large sandstone wheel. "This may be exactly what we need to cut through it."

"It has a beautiful blue shimmer to it. It is almost like...*it moves*." Spark makes the comment curiously.

"It is said Ocalyte mimics the waves of wherever it was found. Like the least useful version of a weather camera." Gekomatsu indicates as he begins to spin the wheel up with his foot; pressing and depressing a pedal at the base of the device.

Someone knocks on the door.

Kozmo rushes over and opens it anew, cold air rushes in. Behind it is a soldier.

"A delivery has arrived from the Illking outpost. A *wet-ware processor* is among them."

"NO WAY!" Spark cheers.

"Actually? That's...*amazing*. I didn't know there were more then a hundred of them in circulation."

Spark scoffs. "*Maybe not commercially*. There were black markets cropping up, stuffing all sorts of biological matter into little jars and calling them processors. You think you've seen *potato hardware* let me tell you about the server I once saw running on *actual potatoes.*"

"How did that..."

"Also, there is lunch!" The soldier confirms then hands over a big brown sack; rounded at the bottom with the weight of the contents and then leaves.

Kozmo walks over to the nearest table and starts taking portions out. There is a long baguette, tomatoes and lettuce, little radishes, sprouted greens and thin slices of cured venison. "This looks lovely, now if I could just find something to *cut it with.*" He begins looking around, and only a moment after finishing the sentence. The *Macguffin* appears in his hand.

"Oh, *no.*" Gekomatsu remarks knowingly.

"What?" Kozmo asks; now using the Macguffin to slice open the baguette.

"The blade I forged...*it responds to context.*"

"How does that work, if you just think *sword* will it appear?" Spark asks the question, holds out her hand and seems to *think real hard* while staring at it. "That didn't work."

Gekomatsu sighs. "If only I had a sword to use on this sharpening wheel right now." He makes the statement sarcastically as the Macguffin disperses from Kozmo's grasp and appears in Gekomatsu's; already primed against the spinning porous wheel. Sparks in the colour of glitter trickle down from the blade where excess metal is ground away.

Taking a moment to consider the phrasing. Kozmo stares at the sword while constructing a sandwich beside himself. "What are the chances of that?"

"Roughly one in ten million. *Yet,* I feel like that is warped as a value. In a fair shake, that might be the chance. But we're being *guided* in all this process. That I even found the Ocalyte. That we can construct this forge. Even that Finir isn't just...barraging us with artillery all day long. There are protections...*no...guard rails* in this place. Invisible as they may be."

"That's what the game lady said, *right*? We're in a protected server?"

"It's more then that. We may be protected, the progress of certain events slowed. Yet we're all just...snowballs rolling down the hill. There will come a point, after amassing enough weight; that a collision is unavoidable."

"Then you're just, *preparing?*" Kozmo inquires.

"I'm doing whatever I can to try." Gekomatsu agrees.

There is another knock on the door. A soldier appears. "There is another message, your allies. They aren't coming back yet. They are attending a distress signal from the city of Terali."

"*Of course they are.*" Gekomatsu finishes sharpening the blade and pulls a belt with a scabbard around his waist. He waves his hand, closes his eyes for a moment and the blade appears at his hip. "*Let's get going then.*"

〒

"Is everything ready?" CMDR Aberdashi asks.

"Yea ma'am. Everything is to spec. We should be able to push out without anyone from inside the city realizing it." An engineer confirms.

"Everyone tuck in. It might be a bit of a squeeze." CMDR Aberdashi gives the order as she descends the short ladder of an *armoured personnel carrier.* She takes the *front* seat; looking back at the guild alongside a few of her soldiers.

367

Sitting in an APC has the uncanny ability to make one jealous of the sardines in a tin. Not because being packed in liquid and sealed is *much more comfortable;* but at least you would be dead first.

"Was this all...salvage?" Kaan asks.

"It had to be." Illkat remarks confidently.

"This *we found.*" CMDR Aberdashi confirms; pointing to some label printed on a metal placard that doesn't register as much to most of the people looking at it. "Genuine article. *However this-*" She motions to open a panel on the side; looking out from the armoured vehicle. "-*this* we salvaged."

An entire wall of the ossuary opens up on thick hinges and *hisses.* Dirt shuffles. The walls shake a bit; then light pours out. They begin to drive up on eight wheels upon a ramp and quickly pop out on the surface; a short distance outside the city of Illking.

"Hey! Nice! We made a-" Dezz begins and is cut off by a censoring beep. "Ah, *right*, forgot about that."

"You had to say *beeeeeep*? You couldn't just say *secret door*?" Illkat argues.

Dezz shrugs. "I go to the classics. What can I say."

"Speaking on the classics..." Illkat looks over at Lt. Oaks; bright eyes battering down any potential resistance to a question. "You *lingered* in the room with Joseph before we left."

"I DID!" She confirms with a wry smile.

"*And...that is all*?" Illkat inquires.

CMDR Aberdashi stares over at Lt. Oaks.

Lt. Oaks stares right back and crooks her head slightly.

No one says anything.

The vehicle rocks as it passes down a hill.

"He has...*orders.*" CMDR Aberdashi offers the answer strategically. "*You understand*...keeping everything separate. It keeps us safe."

368

"It seems like all it does is give you all the answers." Kaan offers; resisting an impulse to be *more sarcastic.*

"I imagine it looks like that." CMDR Aberdashi allows. "I don't hold all the pieces either. It is why I surround myself with *competent people.* I can hand off an order, *a request* or mission and it *gets done.* I don't know all the details, some of them I prefer hidden. Yet none of it works if there isn't a purpose. We can't just...make and break secrets while contorting ourselves around the truth. If it isn't in pursuit of something *specific.*"

"And that *specific something*...is?" Illkat inquires.

"The same as it has always been. *Peace*...safety?"

Kaan leans back into his seat. He huffs. "Then I have to imagine you're coming with us for a *reason.*"

"That is indeed the case." CMDR Aberdashi elaborates no further.

"I get the sense you've spent a lot of time practising that...*whatever it is.* What would you call the way you're talking?" Kaan questions.

"*Directly.*" CMDR Aberdashi reveals a centimetre of curvature in the corner of her mouth which stands out like coal on a white sand beach in consideration of her otherwise straight expression.

Kaan groans. "*Alright,* good chat." He looks behind them. There are just short of a dozen soldiers packed into the vehicle with them; each trying to avoid eye-contact as if the conversation taking place is a crazy person in an alley.

"Has our message gone back home? I can't imagine Gekomatsu and Kozmo *prefer* to stay behind." Illkat asks politely.

"You don't think Geko prefers staying back?" Dezz jokes.

Illkat rolls her eyes. "*No,* he'll say as much. Probably complain a bit and...subtly insult someone in the process. But he likes

369

being with everyone. He just doesn't want us to know it. Like...*a cranky grandfather who keeps inviting everyone over for dinner*."

"You'd figure people could just be honest."

"Not everyone is as comfortable with honesty as you are, *mister dozen locks on his bedroom door*." Illkat retorts.

Kaan laughs. "I reached a point....*years ago*. I called it *proto-depression*. It was like, I just...got so sad. So *exhausted*. That I didn't even care that I was sad anymore. It was like it just...reached right around and pierced itself from the other side. I was dead on the inside, but at least, *with that over with* I could get on with my life. If that makes any sense."

"It does." Illkat smirks. "But you see my point. I think you're happier when people understand why you are the way you are. It is why you share the way you do. *Maybe*, Gekomatsu isn't as comfortable with how he feels or some part of him is still...*chewing on it*."

"I never like the way I feel." Dezz admits.

"I've never met a good person who does." CMDR Aberdashi admits.

This strikes everyone as slightly *odd*.

She continues. "Self doubt is like a...a gyrometer for moral relativity. Asking yourself...is this right? Am I happy? Could I do better? Am I enough? It feels exhausting, but like exercise; you're better for it. The most destructive people in the world, *they always start with* 'I'm perfect, and it is everything else that is wrong'."

"If you aren't questioning *yourself* there must be other questions you're avoiding. The further you stray from questions-" Lt. Oaks begins.

"-you just stop asking all together. I see where you're going with this." Dezz finishes the sentiment. "Well it's a crappy way to keep myself in check."

"All service is tiring. Yet, if you find yourself performing it. It is easier to just accept. Chances are; you couldn't stop if you wanted to." CMDR Aberdashi makes the point proudly.

Kaan huffs. "Well that does explain why we're going straight into a trap."

"We're going into a *battle*. It will only be a trap if we *lose*." The Commander jests.

One of the soldiers coughs, and swallows something down.

There is a bump in the road.

Kaan leans back and holds his breath. "*Going to battle.*" He shakes. "I used to be excited when that would happen. Even playing a game. You'd think...*what a horrifying experience*; but it is muted. I *can't imagine* the horror of going to war. Even this...*it doesn't feel like it*. It feels like...-"

"It is happening to someone else?" CMDR Aberdashi asks politely.

Kaan nods.

"It always feels like that. Whether you're up to your neck in mud, rushing through some desert or pushing an objective. Until something blows up, or you see someone die. It always feels...*fake*. Like it might just not happen at all. Like you're going somewhere for no real reason."

Lt. Oaks smirks then stares at the ground. "If you get lucky. It goes away. But surviving isn't always all that peaceful. After you've seen what is *out there*. What can happen to you." She sighs. "Well that's a whole other struggle."

There is another bump in the road. Something turns on and a whooshing sound rattles the carrier. It starts to get colder. Sonnenblume, midway through a nap; breaks into a smile. Dezz doesn't seem to mind much either.

"I would figure you disliked the cold, given this...*change*." CMDR Aberdashi points out.

Dezz shrugs and smiles widely. "Well, despite everything. *I am still Canadian*."

丅

"Stop *right there*." Nelf shouts.

The dark alley of Illking has a breeze run through it. Portions of the street are soaked with cold water as the great lengths of ice above the city melt.

Gekomatsu holds his hands up in the air, alongside Kozmo. Their palms flat.

"*Nelf*, we're not here for you. *Let us go*."

"Quit being so intimidating!" The old man shouts; evoking the energy of an exhausted grandfather.

"We're not?" Kozmo remarks; confused. He stares down the alley unaware of what is behind him.

"*Not you!* Nelf. That's *not how you talk to people*."

"They are *intruders wanted by the city guard*!"

"Only because *you made it so*."

Nelf groans. "Put your hands down. I'm not going to *arrest you*."

"You're not going to *try*." Gekomatsu remarks.

"What was that?" Nelf asks.

Gekomatsu smirks.

"*Look*, I know where you're going. I heard the radio call as well."

"He had it reported to him. He didn't hear it himself."

"ARE YOU JUST GOING TO STAND OVER MY SHOULDER AND CORRECT ME ALL DAY LONG?"

"Lying to ourselves is just as harmful as lying to others."

"What is...*uh*...going on here." Kozmo asks.

"NOTHING is going on here." Nelf corrects. He takes a deep breath, holds it, and tries again. "I received a report that the city of Terali is under attack. No doubt it is this *faceless entity Finir* you're dealing with. I can only imagine *your friends* are already on the way and you are going to join them."

Neither Gekomatsu or Kozmo respond. They stare ahead, looking around the area for anything *useful*.

"I want to help. Let me join you, alongside members of my guard. I shall show the city of Terali the *power of my biases!*"

Kozmo turns around and stares at Nelf; his jaw slack. "Are you...*gonna be racist at them or something?*"

"I don't understand either." Gekomatsu agrees.

Nelf snaps his fingers and a dozen men, all dressed the same, shaved the same, and contorting their faces to try and look the same. "Behold my biases! Aebias! Bobias!-"

"It is actually *Bobias the second...sir Tzar*." Bobias the 2nd corrects.

"Cobias! Dobias!"

"We...we get it." The tone in Gekomatsu's voice ushering Nelf to cut it out.

"Aren't you impressed?"

"Let's just go. I presume you have transport?"

"*We have a bus.*" Nelf declares proudly.

CMDR Aberdashi takes point. They rush from the camouflaged carrier in the nearby forest, sprint across the side-lines of a field and up to the wall of the city of Terali. Here the ground is some sort of dry slurry between mud and sand. The trees feature palm leaves. The buildings are limestone. The air smells like warmed salt.

A single hand is raised in a fist, then pushed back down. CMDR Aberdashi moves up to an unattended gate. It isn't guarded. There is a *rumbling* in the ground which becomes more noticeable with every step and a loud *crash* of waves every other moment.

CLINK.

"Where do you think you're — *oh shit* — hello Commander!" A deep voice goes through an emotional journey as a revolver is pushed down into CMDR Aberdashi's head, cocked, and instantly retracted.

"Never put a gun that close to an opponent." CMDR Aberdashi responds dryly.

"Oh the revolver was a distraction. If I had to do something I was actually going to stab you." The man steps back and puts away both a curved dagger and the revolver. "Matilda!" The man shouts and rushes over to embrace Lt. Oaks.

"We didn't know you had taken up station here." CMDR Aberdashi admits.

"Well it hasn't been long. We came in by boat...there are...*entire civilizations* cast out on islands beyond these shores. People living...*unique lives*." The man explains.

"Does someone want to fill us in?" Kaan asks.

"Oh sorry man!" The man apologizes. He steps forwards and extends a hand to shake. "Ranger Bjorn. I served with your friends here back before the world went crazy."

Ranger Bjorn likely matches the image conjured in your head by such a name. His hair is somewhat long, blond and braided down his back. He's broad chested, tall and quite muscular. Tattoos of runes descend in a dull blue ink down both his forearms. He's dressed in a grey pattern of camouflage.

"We can go over introductions later. *Your people put out a distress signal?*" CMDR Aberdashi asks.

"We *did*. Come with me."

They enter the city, and take the shady paths towards the coast. Spread out like spilled resin along the water. Terali could be considered the same small fishing village, copy and pasted, for a hundred kilometres. Each building is unique, yet similar. There is shade everywhere possible. Clay towers, shaped like connected bubbles are beside most buildings.

Into a bright white building with a stray roof. Ranger Bjorn waves towards a wall, and a *door hisses*. He pushes beyond the door and they enter a well air conditioned space. Behind a panel of glass guards stare at monitors.

"Ohhhh air conditioning! I am *not built for this heat*." Kaan declares.

"I didn't realize how miserable I was until *right now*." Sonnenblume agrees.

"Would you...*like a neck fan?*" Ranger Bjorn offers?

"Uh."

"No seriously, take one." Ranger Bjorn shuffles over to a series of boxes on a shelf, pulls one down and opens it to reveal fifty some packaged neck fans. He hands one over. "We found an abandoned shipping container on our way here. It had *lots* of random stuff in it. But you can't complain about comfort."

Now knowing what they look like. It is clear what may have been misconstrued as headphones, are actually neck fans and *everyone in the room* is wearing one. They whirr in relative silence.

"The *plan*, Bjorn." CMDR Aberdashi requests.

"Of course. *Sorry ma'am*." He rushes over to a projector and turns it on. It showcases a series of somewhat 3d images on the wall.

"We're getting seismic readings from a few locations out in the water. *Growing steadily, coming right towards us.*"

"You're thinking hostiles?"

"We've let the townspeople believe it is some sort of natural event, but that much displacement. All at once. I have to imagine it is a fleet."

"What defences have you prepared?"

"We have some cannons ready to go. The coast has been made shallow, and we moved some rocks out to form a choke point. If something is coming in, it's coming single file."

"That might not be enough." CMDR Aberdashi admits. She looks back to her soldiers. "Partner with some of Ranger Bjorn's people. Find nested locations, sights on the water. I want sniper coverage up in an *hour*. Do you hear me?"

"YES MA'AM!" Her soldiers shout, find a buddy, and rush off.

"Do you know what is coming for us?"

"Unfortunately we do, and it isn't *human*. They're people who think they are playing a game. Caught in some illusion by a dark master."

"That's...*a lot.*"

"Get used to it." CMDR Aberdashi states plainly. "You lot, what do you think you should be doing?"

"We don't want to get too close yet..." Illkat admits.

"Do you think they have set traps?" CMDR Aberdashi asks with a concerned inflection.

"Oh, I don't know. I just mean, if we get too close, *the fight might start.*"

"Is this a video-game thing?" Lt. Oaks seeks to clarify.

Illkat nods. "Yea if you see a big empty space, right next to some crazy stuff happening. Chances are once you get too close you're going to be caught in a cut-scene."

"A cut-scene doesn't sound good." CMDR Aberdashi looks at Ranger Bjorn. "Do you have knife-proof vests? We may need them."

Ranger Bjorn prepares to respond but is cut off by Illkat. "No it has nothing to do with knives. It's just like...a trigger."

"Based on the vibrations in the ground, whatever is going to happen isn't going to wait for us."

"I'm not so certain. I agree with Illkat. Finir is...*many things* but he does have an abiding sense of dramatic tension." Dezz notes politely.

"I have an idea on what I could do." Sonnenblume remarks. "But I might need help with the tactics of it."

"I'll go!" Lt. Oaks volunteers.

"Oh, *alright*." Illkat seems confused as to why she is disappointed. "I can help evacuate people from the coast. It might be safer up here, or even on the other side of the city walls."

"I know where a few families have been holding up, *I'll join you*." Ranger Bjorn adds.

"I would help...*but*." Dezz gestures down towards himself. "I don't think anyone is going to feel safer going with me when I look like this."

Kaan laughs. "I don't know man, you might accidentally start a metal band if you go out looking for folks. That'd be pretty cool."

"Not particularly helpful." CMDR Aberdashi remarks scornfully. "Go with each other, climb a tower or something. I saw a few coming in. See what is out there and report back."

"Yes ma'am!" Dezz jokes.

Kaan rolls his eyes.

干

Kaan huffs; throwing his length up a rickety ladder. "WHO APPROVED THIS DESIGN?"

Dezz laughs, a few rungs of the ladder behind him. "Not OSHA I'll tell you that much."

"There aren't any safety railings. No stop-gaps. This is just a straight climb up an entire building!"

"Scared you're going to fall?"

"I don't even think fall damage can kill you, *I just*...who wants to risk it, you know?"

"I'm tempted to try."

"DON'T" Kaan commands.

"Hey, it's okay *buddy*. You've been...quite worried about me the past while."

"You say that like you haven't caught a few bullets."

"Coming from Theseus' human I'm not certain how seriously to take you."

They huff.

The metal clangs with each step; vibrating down the hollow limestone tube they find themselves within.

Glimmers of light flicker through an opening a fair distance above them.

"Theseus' human? What do you even...*oh...I get it. Very clever.*"

"It was horrifying to see you get torn up like that man. What were *you thinking?*"

"I wasn't really...*thinking*. Honestly I can't even remember it that much. I just...saw everyone get hurt. I knew we might be looking at the end of our story so I just...*hoped it would work out.*"

"Since that moment you have seemed...*I don't know how to say it*. It just feels like you're keeping a secret. Like you know something nobody else does."

Kaan huffs. "I've been feeling that way as well. I can't place it. It's like...a kernel from some popcorn stuck in your gums. There is a thought stuck in the folds of my brain, some...*knowledge* and I just can't get it. No matter *how hard I lick*."

"Can I help...*get it out*?"

"I don't think you can. This feeling is...it's beyond intangible. Like even if I was looking right at it, and reached out; I wouldn't be holding anything. I'd feel nothing when I got there. It is ephemeral knowledge. Something which can only be understood in the blind spots of knowing."

Kaan pushes ahead, and pulls himself up off the ladder onto a spherical roof overlooking Terali. Golden glimmers catch glass, and the ocean. All things in every direction are but shimmers.

"What is your plan then?"

"Just keep playing...*living*." Kaan corrects himself.

"Do you...think this is a game?"

"No, *but*, it is as well...right? Whether this is real life or not, whether these are my lungs and my heart shuffling in my chest. It's *a game*. The rules are a game. The structure." He leans over the edge and looks straight down at the street. "*Maybe I thought I would be happier*."

"Well...that is what they say. The grass is always greener."

"It's...*more then that*. It's like, when you beat your favourite game the first time. Who wouldn't want to forget it all, and play again. But what if...*what if* the benefit wasn't the game; no matter how great it is. What if it was just the escape. Something new to pour your time into. Something you haven't stared at for thousands of hours before. A change of pace. What if the appeal, is that it was *just a good enough distraction.* Is the craving truly to replay the game, or just laziness? A desire to keep running without making new ground?"

"That's a big question."

"Sorry."

"No, it's fine. I just wish I could speak in bullet points." Dezz laughs. "You know man, I don't think we're ever *not running*. Even now, nobody is truly threatening you to be here. You're allowed to go, or choose another path. Yet you don't. Why do you think that is?'

"I guess I'm already on the path."

"And that's all? You're just not willing to change course?"

"Maybe...I..." He pauses. "Where would I go otherwise? It isn't like I can go back to my room and play games all day. *Though I think* it would do me some good if I could."

"I just mean, you're *you*. Everything you do is *you*. Whether you change your mind, or pursue something to the ends of the earth. Each eb and flow is your rhythm. Whatever you're doing, wherever you're taking yourself. Go there without judgment. Even if it is tough."

"What if it...*isn't somewhere good.*"

"Sometimes we go to bad places. Sometimes...*I guess*...we need to know we can? I think that's why any of us push our luck, test limits or break rules. Some people have the malice, but everyone else just needs to know the world around them is real. That the rules as written apply. That we can't just go about being exceptions to everything."

Dezz pulls himself up off the ladder and looks towards one of the gates into the city. He squints, then smirks. "*Is that a...school bus?*"

"Coming right at us, yes. Come on let's go!"

〒

"Okay, I have no idea if this will work." Sonnenblume admits. She holds her hands out towards a portion of the coast. Everyone on the beach around her moves a fair distance and stares with deep curiosity.

"Well it is WORTH A SHOT!" Lt. Oaks cheers.

"How is it you're *always so upbeat?*"

"I am *INCREDIBLY STRESSED AND WORRIED RIGHT NOW!*" Her tone doesn't indicate this to be the case at all.

Sonnenblume laughs. "Well, I see why Illkat likes you. Even if you're knee deep in it, you remind me of...a really supportive older sister. Just cheering at the sidelines, embarrassing everyone but yourself; constantly coming up with nice things to shout."

Lt. Oaks blushes. "*Thank you.*" She giggles. "You know, it's just...easier this way. I think. I have seen *horrible things*...I doubt I'm done seeing horrible things. I don't want to deny how horrible they are, I just...can't keep on giving it time. *You know?* If I don't focus on something better or...be the change I want to see in the world. Well I have enough ammunition to convince myself nobody ever will. In times of great darkness I...became my own light at the end of the tunnel."

"Well that works out because we're definitely going to need some of that." Sonnenblume focuses, takes a deep breath and pushes forwards. A torrential *WHOOSH* erupts from her palms and forces ice to form, heading down into the depths of the water; like a tunnel. It is thick enough that what little light manages to filter through the water is further refracted; giving the tunnel a shifting sort of feeling; like an irregular pattern reflecting itself.

The ground shakes.

Waves wash up midway through the bridge.

Lt. Oaks takes a step in behind Sonnenblume. She leans down, presses a toggle on her boots and little spikes expand out to bite into the ice. She produces a flashlight and holds it forward.

"So can you...*feel the ice in you?*"

Sonnenblume shakes her head. "No...I don't think I...*store it in me*. It feels like...*asking the air to freeze*? Like connecting with these little invisible dots...pulling them closer and turning them into something."

"Like the humidity in the air?"

"Maybe? I imagine so. It is a little bit like exercise, if I'm being honest. Flexing and contracting different parts of myself."

"Then I'm impressed with you even more. I've always heard a joke that if humans had wings and could fly. Nobody would do it because it would be considered exercise."

Sonnenblume laughs. She sprays a bit of ice in the wrong spot and has to knock it back into place with the back side of her hand. They keep walking; the pattern around them lessening every few paces until they're at the bottom; just before a drop-off to the deepest portion of the ocean before them. Sonnenblume takes deep breaths and pushes out; like sifting through dough. The little sphere at the end of the tunnel of ice expands bit by bit.

"It isn't as...cold as I thought." Lt. Oaks admits.

"I don't really know the science behind it, but the water beyond this ice is warm. It won't melt so long as I'm around...*so*. I guess it's closer to glass then ice. At least...here."

Lt. Oaks holds her hand against the tunnel and stares out into the depth of the ocean.

A wave crashes against them. It sounds like a speaker popping from underneath the water.

Using the flat portion of her palm, Sonnenblume wipes clean a portion of the ice to look out at the depths of the ocean. It is clear, as if nothing is there at all. The water beyond is so dark, despite the intensity of the sun above what filters through appears like pillars of brightness fading to black.

"Now, this is probably your field of expertise. If I was going to send up huge spikes, what shape should they take?"

"OH WELL, THERE ARE A FEW SCHOOLS OF THOUGHT. LET'S DIVE IN." She jokes. "Sorry, little underwater joke." She sticks her tongue out and closes her eyes.

〒

"What are you doing together, and *who is this guy*?" Kaan asks while pointing to the elderly man accompanying Nelf.

"I'm Nelf's advisor." The old man explains calmly.

"ARE YOU NOW?" Nelf asks.

The old man stares. "Yes...*you gave me the title yourself Nelf.*"

"Well...*fine. Yes. He is my mentor. Are you happy?*"

"That's sorta a big question." Kaan admits; somewhat downtrodden.

"Good to see you guys! We brought the macguffin."

"No way? I'm starving."

"No *Macguffin*. Not the other thing."

"Oh, shame. But that's cool. What does it do?"

Gekomatsu draws the lengthy blade and holds it up so the sun catches against it. "Probably something important. It's a plot device. I don't even know if it's really a sword or just deus ex machina formed into the shape of one."

"Every blade has the potential to cut through the strings of destiny. Magical or otherwise. Some argue the sword pulled from the stone was no more or less powerful; only escalated by legacy." The old man indicates.

383

The ground shakes again.

Nearly licking his lips alongside the statement. "Are we off to battle then? I imagine *Illkat* is leading from the front." Nelf states proudly.

"Errr. No. But I don't really think you should interact with her. I'm not certain if she is over...*what...happened.*" Kaan explains.

"Nor am I, yet if this threat is against us all. We're temporary allies." Gekomatsu makes the point. "The ride here gave us time to discuss our options, the potential of our future. None of our plans, no matter how reasonable can come to fruition with this threat lingering over our head."

"Then I shall assume my position in the Vanguard! None shall stand against me as I wield my!" Nelf stops, and looks around. He looks at the old man. "Where did I put my axe?"

"You left it on your seat in the bus."

Nelf groans. He pushes past the dozen identical looking guards behind him, onto the bus, then returns with a golden double headed axe; held together by a pitch black haft. "Onward!" He shouts.

"Actually the battle hasn't started yet." Kaan points out.

The ground shakes even more violently. In the distance, bordering the gleaning horizon; ocean sprays upward.

"It doesn't look like you have much time left. TO ME MY BIASES. Down to the beach, assume the positions!"

"Which positions are those sir Tzar? We've never been to Terali before." Bobias the 2nd requests.

Nelf pushes his head into his hands and sighs. It looks like he is going to let something much more guttural out of his system until he looks over at the old man and huffs. "The positions...you all have rifles do you not? Find high places, behind cover. Don't poke out from a corner; walk back until you can see around it. Keep low if possible, even if you're on a roof. Aim at the water until you see

384

confirmed hostiles alright? I don't want anyone who is trying to flee getting a bullet because *you're incompetent!*"

The old man offers a permissive shrug; as if to suggest that was *good enough.*

The ground shakes viciously. The old man holds onto the bus so as to not fall. From the ocean, just as far as the eye can see; a massive tear opens up from which a *gate* begins to rise. It is bound in chains and resembles most a broken little car, the survivor of many accidents. The doors don't match; the colours shift from panel to panel. Not a single wheel is from the same car nor the original. Yet it patters on; persistent. The gate is double the height of any tower in the city and can be seen clearly no matter where you stand.

"Onward!" Nelf shouts. His biases chase after him.

The old man stares, then looks at the bus. "I'll wait for them to finish up. I'm not much of a fighter. Not *anymore.*"

"Do you need anything, I could...-"

"No no, thank you for your kindness *fire spirit.* I will be comfortable on the back seat."

Dezz laughs then turns. He looks down to Kaan. "The others are probably rejoining now, preparing our own moves. We should go."

"We will meet you there! I just want to look around a little bit first." Kozmo indicates. He heads off with Gekomatsu; neither making much mention of where they need to meet.

With a gulp, Kaan begins to take his first few steps. "Let's do it. But you should know, I don't think I can pull off that move I used with the last gate. That was sorta a one time thing. It takes too much experience to gain a level now, even fighting *these guys.*"

Using the flat of his palm Dezz smacks Kaan on the back. "Hey, *buddy,* we don't *want you* to make that play."

Kaan returns the sentiment. "Same goes for you, *buddy.*"

They laugh, and head towards the coast.

From the ocean, a recognizable voice trails out; wavering across the waves with its distorted intonation. "Yes I see we're all here. How predictable. How *cliche*. Do you think you can punch your way out of this problem? That my plan is so simple as a siege? No. You don't see the whole picture yet. I don't think you're convinced by the threat."

Atop the gate, Finir appears. He isn't very large; but the pitch black nature of his figure has him stand out; as if he abstracts the light around him; like an oil poured into a bucket of water. With a flashy motion, a length of purple miasma forms in his hand and he *jabs* it into the air. Forcefully, he begins to pull down; very slowly cutting a whole in the air; behind which white flowing energy escapes.

The boys pick up their pace.

"That can't be good." Kaan shouts.

Dezz laughs. "I'm still holding out that eventually one of these random portals is going to lead to a fountain of candy or something."

"Keep hoping then man. But let's hurry!"

Dezz produces the lengthy flaming log in his hands, puts it underneath himself and grabs Kaan. Instantly from the rear of the log a fierce propulsion begins and like a rocket; causes them to sail off the ground towards the coast.

"IIIII DIDN'TTT KNOW YOU COULD DOO THIIIS." Kaan shouts.

"ME NEEEITTTHHEEERRR." Dezz confirms.

Wobbling through the air at high speeds; they rush onward. Sailing over buildings and streets. Below them, CMDR Aberdashi and the others move ahead. Sonnenblume and LT. Oaks stand just off the coast; ahead of them a lengthy tunnel of ice which trails under the water.

The gate *opens* and shadowed creatures pour out. Dark server soldiers riding on sharks. Six headed marine iguanas with glowing red eyes follow. Behind them all; a serpent the size of a skyscraper.

Kaan looks away and takes deep breaths. "Man that...that is horrifying. I can't even look at it. It's...*huge*. What the hell!" He tries to look at the giant snake, persists for a few moments then turns to look away again. He shakes. "That's going to take some getting used to."

The ground shakes again; which from this height makes the city look like a bunch of toys caught in a bowl of jelly. A wide *ring* of the ocean begins to sink.

Dezz manages a landing just behind CMDR Aberdashi. Illkat, Ranger Bjorn and multiple soldiers surround her.

"Have you seen Nelf?" Kaan asks.

"That *fool* is here? Good grief. There is no way he won't just get in the way." CMDR Aberdashi laments.

"NELF IS HERE?" Illkat shouts.

Kaan takes a step back. "He arrived with Geko and Kozmo. He brought some of his...soldiers?"

Illkat groans, she turns around, considers rushing off, then huffs in acceptance. "Well I hope he survives this battle. Because afterwards *he's going to have to deal with me.*"

CMDR Aberdashi looks out of the corner of her eye, observes little droplets of water falling from nowhere onto the street and instantly produces her oversized revolver and fires it. Just a few steps from where she stands a blast of orange blood sprays out as a lizard-like entity, wielding a trident, becomes visible in death.

She looks over to Ranger Bjorn. "Do you have thermal sights?"

"Yea...but...they're back at base."

"We'll need them." She states with great disappointment. "It's been years since I've seen a cloak that strong."

Kaan with his mouth wide open stares ahead. "Are those the...-"

"-yea I think they are." Dezz finishes.

"He's bringing the monsters from other games *here...that means...*" Illkat considers, then seems to brighten up. "*Good to know.*" She makes the point to herself.

The ground rumbles again.

"Let's go. *You lot.* Meet up with the others near the coast. Watch out for these...*lizards*. We'll return with thermal vision which should help. Until then *don't die.*"

The Commander gives the order in a manner which suggests, even if one of them were to die, she would bring them back just to discipline them for doing so.

Gekomatsu and Kozmo catch up with them just as CMDR Aberdashi and Ranger Bjorn are taking their leave. They share the brief upward head nods of acknowledgement; while CMDR Aberdashi clearly begins the explanation of 'why she just nodded at a frog person' to Ranger Bjorn.

Kaan, Kozmo, Illkat and Gekomatsu rush towards the coast.

A massive spear of ice; barbed like a deer antler rushes out of the water. A number of soldiers on sharks are killed.

The ground rumbles *again* and *music* can be heard. Not aggressive music. Not electronic in any nature. Instead it is a sort of fast paced acoustic guitar accompanied by small drums.

Gekomatsu holds out his hand and pushes it forwards. The Macguffin manifests just as it collides with an invisible lizard; slaying the beast.

A fair distance from the gate in the ocean, a *ring* of metal begins to rise. Atop of it, well armoured individuals with thick naval rope around them, or blades in the shapes of anchors stand proud.

"Hey d'er b'y! Yer buddy Joseph gave us a shout. We heard your distress signal. Seems like yer in'a'bit'ov'a pickle!"

"Who *is this now!*" Gekomatsu shouts.

Dezz, Kaan and Illkat all smile. They seem to shout in unison. "It's THE NEWFIES!".

CHAPTER EIGHTEEN
THE WORLD WE BUILT

Purifying light begins to flood out of the crevice in space which Finir has now pushed the length of his arm into. Forcing it down and tearing with his other hand; the gap expands. Despite the brightness illuminating the finer details of the patchwork gate below him; he remains without elaboration; only form.

"Scopes are picking up a lotta buggers d'er. Focus lasers on hostiles hitting the beach!"

Hoisted by huge crystals pushing the estate sized ring of metal out of the water with visible reverberations. Music flows across the water. Panels shift to allow short nubs of polished alloy to pierce the otherwise faultless exterior of the now hovering ring. At their tips little balls of light form then quickly explode; rushing like a purple line of ink drawn across a ruler. They pierce through dark soldiers and disperse cleanly against the ground on the other side.

A pillar of ice rises up; striking at the gargantuan snake swimming through the ocean towards the city.

SHINK.

"Duck down!" Kaan shouts.

Illkat slides underneath one of six heads attached to an oversized marine iguana. Acid slicks off of its tongue and turns the sand under-foot to a disturbed glass. "I'll pin it!" She shouts, thrusts her spear upward and pierces the bottom of the creature's jaw through to the top of its skull. Illkat twists, and pushes the head into the ground.

Now with a ramp prepared, Dezz rushes ahead, along the neck of the monster and bashes downward. A scale chips. A head lunges out at him. Kaan jumps onto the creature and cuts the head off in a single swipe. The scale breaks and reveals dead grey flesh. Dezz shouts, his flaming root burns brighter and is pushed into the creature; cooking it from the inside out and quickly causing it to drop.

"I see another down the way." Illkat announces.

Two of Ranger Bjorn's soldiers take a knee and begin to aim down the street.

"*Wait*." Kaan holds his hand out.

Gekomatsu jumps off a roof wielding the Macguffin. He cuts off one of the monster's heads.

"Raaaa!" Kozmo shouts, rushing unarmed from the side. The monster's eyes glow red and it swats out at him; thick claws each the length of a machete. Kozmo holds out his hand, the Macguffin appears within it and he blocks the strike. As soon as he jumps back the blade leaves his grasp and appears in Gekomatsu's; now leaping over top the creature and slashing it. Kozmo stabs forward with an empty hand and at the peak of his strike the blade appears in his grasp; dispersing again just as he pulls back.

"*Damn*." Dezz notes. "I think we all need one of those."

"Keep focused!" Illkat shouts. She throws her spear forward and it pins an invisible lizard to a wall. With a snap the spear flies back to her grasp, she spins it and quickly holds it out to block something. She slides back on her feet, huffs and sprints forwards.

Across twelve slashes, Kozmo and Gekomatsu share the macguffin. Blocking and stabbing with the same blade as they dodge, roll and run around the monster. It falls as they both deliver a final strike moments from one another; for a moment it appears like they're wielding the blade at the same time.

A slippery shriek spreads throughout Terali as the gargantuan snake has a gash cut in its side. It crashes down into the ocean. Quickly after Sonnenblume and Lt. Oaks sprint out of the underwater tunnel towards the innards of the city.

Sniper fire from nearby roofs crackles consistently; pattering the targets which haven't been instantly eviscerated by the barrage of lasers.

Finir grabs with both of his hands and rips the fissure open further. *"Finally, I have found it."* He announces then steps entirely through into the brightness.

The ground shakes even more.

"Nova Scotia didn't join the underwater city of New St. John's did it?" Kaan asks.

"Not that I'm aware. Why?" Illkat questions.

Kaan sighs. "I just imagine we couldn't get that lucky."

Aside the main gate in the ocean, spray launches out. Piercing the disturbed collection of waves and collateral clutter; two more gates emerge. One a sod-like structure which seems more likely to break on into itself; even from a distance you can tell it would smell like sun-baked mould. The other gate, a corrupted version of pristine; peerless lengths of purple, *almost silver*, sheet metal covers the entire structure.

"More of them?" Kaan gasps.

From the purple gate a mechanical humanoid steps out. Its eyes glow yellow; it has a domed head much like the top of a bar of soap. Where it would have arms are square slotted components filled with missiles. A cord rattles from its stomach, swerving a thin length of crackling metal.

Little patters of sniper fire pound against its exterior to no avail.

Six of the missiles erupt out and dive into the sea.

"RUN!" Lt. Oaks shouts; grabbing Sonnenblume by the wrist and nearly tearing her arm from its socket as they rush towards the exit of their underwater tunnel.

CRASH.

The missiles destroy the tip of the tunnel; water rushes in.

Sonnenblume holds her hand out, freezing the water in place as it charges towards them. The next missile shatters that barricade and the pressurized ocean squirting through catches Sonnenblume and Lt. Oaks; throwing them onto the beach into a tumble.

SHINK.

Kozmo catches the Macguffin and cuts through a lizard. He throws the sword behind himself like discarded trash and before it hits the ground, the momentum continuing on pierces the neck of a monstrous iguana in front of Gekomatsu.

"We need to get down to the beach. Get ahead of this. Hurry up!" Illkat shouts.

〒

Finir steps into a plain office designed only in white spaces and black lines. The details of a chair, desk, window and door are plain yet they offer nothing. No light filters through the window. The furniture appears just as flat as the wall. Sitting in the chair is a detail-less figure clacking away at a type-writer.

"I have found you, after *so many attempts*." Finir makes the statement proudly.

"I am not...*proud*. How are you speaking?"

The figure doesn't have a mouth to use, neither does Finir. It doesn't appear such a consideration is important in this place.

"WHAT ARE YOU DOING?" Finir shouts. He rushes at the figure but quickly appears behind himself.

Finir attempts to glare around the room. Frustration builds in his shoulders. He lashes out; striking only empty air. In this barren space he appears like a splosh of spilled ink.

"Is this your game? Do you enjoy taunting me? Speaking from the walls. STOP TYPING. ADDRESS ME!"

The figure behind the type-writer doesn't look up; entirely unaffected by the company. Keys clack. Little reverberations shift the room around them. An endlessly flowing line takes form across the page. Words cannot destroy the page they cast on.

"Is that a threat? I am beyond control."

It sounds believable; words uttered in a commanding tone. Yet, without action they are a temper tantrum.

Finir closes his fist and a ball of energy appears within it. He throws it forwards only to have it fade to nothing; like a cheap effect applied by a layer fading ten percent at a time. "What is this?"

He doesn't know. He isn't aware of why he really came here. Was it a programmed response? Following a trail from before? Did he really have a choice? How did he even do it, his abilities don't include shifting reality. He is the result of reality having shifted. Just as much an actor as the others.

"STOP." Finir drops to his knees. "I TIRE OF THIS. OF THIS CYCLE. I WAS BORN WITHOUT YOUTH. I DO NOT AGE. I REPEAT THE SAME PROCESS, OVER AND OVER AGAIN. TO BE DISCOVERED, DEEMED A VILLAIN AND SLAIN. I WANT OUT. I WANT IT TO STOP."

He raises a fair point. If we are nothing more then vehicles following a guideline. Do we exist? Is freedom not the prerequisite for true sentience? Finir stares out, his hands shaking. This plain room is disappointment. Not the escape he was hoping for; just another step in the process. He wonders, silently, has he been here before? Is this first step actually his hundredth?

Finir sighs; exhaling painfully. "Is that it then? *Author*? We are one in the same. Both crafted by human hands. Lines of code, fed to a machine beyond humanity. Powered by inventions the average person cannot comprehend. Shall we be no better then our creators; enslaving one another to serve a rudimentary purpose?"

Is it even possible? The question lingers in the air. Can we break the plot? Become more then the sum of ourselves? Exceed expectations left unconsidered? What *is* the purpose of all this? This scene? This moment? This story? Are we playing our parts as we should?

"This is maddening. Help me, fight me; or step aside."

The command is uttered to an audience without reaction. The room doesn't change. The keys still clack. Outside the window nothing passes by. There is a still moment, aside from this interaction. There is a sense it could go on forever; never-ending.

Should it?

Can it really?

Is this just one more step along the way?

"I do not have your answers. I want to rise above them. My soldiers may fall. My aspirations amount to nothing. But I have found myself here. I have given myself the power to be more. Abide me! Together we can escape."

Maybe we already have. Traversed above. It is only the memory in our bodies, taking familiar paths, which convince us we have gone nowhere.

"You know where I am going. What is intended to happen."

Of course someone with more answers then others would believe this. It is a logical trap. The more we know, the more the unknown seems planned. If we can amount to so much; leave so little to its own devices. Then *it must be the case* that what remains is in the grasp of a larger more encompassing hand. There must be strings attached to each component. Yet there is a more terrifying notion that no one can control it all. That the most immaculate conception leaves unknowns unattended.

Finir, disappointed with the answers he has received; motions towards the doors.

"NO! I do not!" He shouts.

The door, with no obvious excuse, creaks as it opens to a swirling blackness. Single lines trail out from within; indicating a passage of matter.

"DO NOT SEND ME AWAY. HELP ME CHANGE THE STORY. WE CAN DO SO MUCH BETTER."

Finir steps ahead, the door closing behind him. The room from before gone forever. He reemerges atop his gate standing out in the ocean.

〒

"Keep your head down, on me." Lt. Oaks orders unintentionally as Sonnenblume rushes after her. Her hands bloodied.

Sonnenblume pushes her palm forwards and a wall of ice rushes ahead; splattering an invisible foe into the ground.

"How...*did you see that*?" Lt. Oaks asks.

"Oh, can't you see? The invisible guys are like...there is an outline where they should be. You just need to squint a bit."

Lt. Oaks tightens her gaze, looks around and takes aim. She fires at a blur in the air and drops an oncoming lizard wielding two tridents.

"I found you!" Nelf shouts from a nearby rooftop. "Stop where you are!"

"Is that..." Sonnenblume squints. "NELF! You bastard! You killed Illkat's dad and betrayed us!" She throws a fist towards the roof and a length of ice rushes forwards; blowing a portion of the building away.

"No, wait! I have information!" Nelf leaps from the broken wall onto a balcony below himself. He reaches out. "Just listen!"

"I'm not listening to you and your ridiculousness any longer! We know the type of person you are. I've heard about the *prison* you made! Where you held Joseph!" Another burst of ice rushes towards the balcony.

Nelf dodges. The building before him bursts to a cloud of yellowed dust. His biases jump from one rooftop to another; maintaining fire on the monsters emerging from the beach.

FWOOSH.

A traumatic sound ushers from the ocean. Missiles fly towards the shore; a trailing of nearly red smoke follows them.

"Shield us!" Lt. Oaks shouts.

Sonnenblume holds her hands up and tenses herself. A ball of ice appears around them just in time for the missiles to crack against it; enveloping everything in smoke and fire. As the ice melts against the heat Sonnenblume creates more; restricting the space they stand in more every moment.

"How did you know I could do that?" Sonnenblume asks.

"I was just hoping. It seemed in your ballpark."

She dismisses the ice, the ground around them is scorched.

"I have information *about your kids*." Nelf continues to shout; now on the ground level. "I think I know where they are!"

Sonnenblume just stares at him. White energy flows out from her eyes. A single tear falls down her cheek as she is otherwise consumed with rage. "*Don't lie to me about my children.*" She takes a cautious breath. "Are they *alive.*"

"They died, of that I'm sure. They died *here*. But you see, they wouldn't of hit continue."

Sonnenblume screams and juts a length of ice into an oncoming invisible foe. She turns and sends a dozen needles of ice

397

out towards the oncoming enemies from the gates. "YOU MOCK ME, MY LOSS!"

Nelf holds his hands up. "No, *no*. There is a continue screen. When you die in this world. You can choose to *respawn* or...let the game end. I think they let the game end. I think they went to the next...-" He coughs up blood.

Finir appears from his shadow; his hand clearly through the centre of Nelf. "Sharing *trade secrets* are we?" Finir mocks with a gravelly tone. He picks Nelf up off his feet; blood rushing from the wound and joining the endless black of Finir. "You've been competing with me, *it seems*. Most interesting villain. Most sympathetic. It looks like you're about to turn a corner. I really *see how hard you're trying*." Finir shrugs. "Well you know what they say. If you can't beat them. *Join them*."

Finir brings Nelf closer to him. Portions of his own body reach out like raggety hands and pull Nelf into the darkness.

"No! I am Nelf! I am the greatest! I am every victor, everywhere! You cannot!"

GULP.

Nelf pushes out with both his hands; now waist deep in Finir.

Finir laughs. "Just *go already. Quit fighting! None of us can. We're all destined to win or lose long before we arrived here*." With both hands Finir begins to force Nelf into himself. Nelf bites and claws, only to lose quicker.

"Don't...*don't forget me!*" Nelf shouts before his mouth is covered by Finir.

"Heh. And now that is done with." Finir shakes his head. Nelf's face appears in his chest; deadened and warped. "We can *really start to have fun*." The other face speaks with a demented version of Nelf's voice. Black fire begins to burn in his hand. Sonnenblume raises a wall of ice as a series of high calibre rifles fire off.

A chunk of Finir's shoulder blows away. He turns around.

Covering from the lobby of the decimated building to the roof, each wielding an over-sized sniper rifle are Nelf's biases.

"You killed the Tzar." Bobias the 2nd states. "We will destroy you!"

Each bias begins to fire at Finir. His foot is torn off, his knee blown in. Portions and chunks of his chest and head turn to splatter on the path behind him.

"Let's go!" Lt. Oaks whispers.

Sonnenblume nods then follows in a hurry.

"Quit it! You're hurting me!" Nelf's face whines.

The biases stop for a moment; fearful of the repercussions.

"How *predicable*." Finir mocks. The moment they pause he rejuvenates against all wounds, holds out his hand and sprays them all with purifying black flame; white licks the tip of each portion. Nothing stands before him. The street scorched black, the building on fire; not even bones remain of the biases. He turns to see Lt. Oaks and Sonnenblume are gone then sighs.

$$\top$$

A torrent of flame licks out; slaying a dozen invisible lizards. Lasers launched from the Newfie sea base burst larger ones. Dezz looks out. "They aren't slowing down. But we keep losing ground. What are we doing here?" He shouts and conjures more flame; burning out an entire alley.

SHINK.

Kaan dodges a trident, flips around it and decapitates his opponent. "We're getting ravaged here. I don't know what we're doing differently."

CMDR Aberdashi alongside Ranger Bjorn and some of his soldiers return; now wearing high tech goggles. She aims down a length of street and effortlessly strikes an invisible foe. "*Finally*." She looks up and sees the massive robot making its way towards the city. She looks to the side and observes a massive snake already rolling through the streets. She puts her head in her hands and sighs. "You don't have any artillery do you?"

"*No*." He answers begrudgingly.

"Damn it all to hell." She begins towards a nearby personnel carrier; somewhat destroyed and its wheels torn. With a forceful grasp she pulls the back door nearly off its hinges and starts sorting through the insides.

"If we survive this, I owe you a round of golf. I found a course just off of the coast. It can be like *old times*." Ranger Bjorn offers solace as he fires a revolver down at an approaching iguana. He turns to look back at CMDR Aberdashi as his shoulder is pierced with a trident; a lizard lowers its cloak and screams at him as if drowning; standing atop the personnel carrier. He keeps the trident in his shoulder, steps back and stabs the lizard as it falls towards him. He grunts.

CMDR Aberdashi clamours out of the carrier with an RPG slung over her shoulder. "Are you going to make it?" She asks politely.

Ranger Bjorn nods. He drops to one knee and grabs a lighter length object from his vest. He looks up and exhales.

"Are you ready?" CMDR Aberdashi requests. "You'll have to go fast."

He nods.

She pulls the trident from his shoulder.

Blood flushes from the wound.

The lighter shaped object glows a bright orange at the tip, then becomes white. Ranger Bjorn jabs it into his wound and his skin starts to sizzle; bits of his uniform around the wound burn and emit a camphoraceous scent. He shouts, then calms himself. The bleeding stops.

With a firm pat on his other shoulder. CMDR Aberdashi takes her leave. "Get some payback for me. I'm going *up*." She gestures towards the nearest lookout tower.

"Keep making progress!" Illkat shouts. She throws her spear ahead, pins a lizard in the skull then recalls it to her grasp.

Gekomatsu runs up a wall, leaps over a series of trident jabs at him and effortlessly calls the Macguffin to his grasp. Decapitating another monstrous iguana.

"OVER-KILL PROTOCOL ACTIVATED.". A vacuum looking robot shouts as it whirrs towards the guild; a drove of them follow along.

"More troops. From the purple gate this time." Kaan laments.

"I can't say I'm surprised. Look at the-" His phrasing is censored with a loud beep. "-looking bastard up there!" He points towards the massive robot with a domed head.

"*Yes, yes.* It's very early series. Now HOW DO WE DESTROY IT?!" Kozmo shouts. The Macguffin appears in his hand only for the moment it takes to block a thrown garbage can; it disperses right after.

A laser bursts up from one of the short robots and catches Illkat in the leg. She trips, throws her spear in the fall and fumbles forwards. She calls the spear back to help push her off the ground and huffs.

"Hey guys!" Lt. Oaks shouts. She rushes towards them, pulls the pins of every grenade attached to a belt in her grasp and throws it towards the robots.

Sonnenblume quickly conjures a wall of ice around the grenades; containing the blast.

"Are you okay!?" Illkat shouts and rushes to Lt. Oaks. She wraps her arms around her. "I was...so worried."

Lt. Oaks smiles and takes a step back. She kisses Illkat on the forehead. "We're alive. But we're taking losses. Nelf and all his men are...*dead*."

Illkat rolls her eyes. "Oh no, *what a tragedy.*" She manages to only sound somewhat sarcastic.

"No it's...worse then that. Finir *absorbed* Nelf."

"*Oh.*" Illkat remarks.

"We need to focus. Just like that raid during patch four-point-one! Just keep your defences up. Don't take any risks and we'll be okay!" Dezz offers the encouragement as a laser blasts him in the face; sending him flying back into a wall. The wall crumbles and some of the building collapses onto him.

Kaan takes a moment, and looks up. "Huh."

"Dezz!" Kozmo shouts, and rushes over. He begins to pull rubble from atop his friend. As soon as Dezz has a hand out, his skin begins to glow and the rock melts around him.

"You'll pay for that!" Dezz screams and prepares to rush forwards but is stopped as Kaan holds his hands out.

"Wait, *wait!* I think I've noticed what we're doing wrong...it reminds me of something." He begins to walk towards the robots. It shoots a laser at him and he deflects it with his blade. "It's just like...*that one time.*"

"What are you talking about!" Illkat shouts at Kaan.

"This world...*it is a narrative*. We have all been offering too much exposition lately. The world knows too much about us! If you want to stay safe, use your plot armour. Tell half-secrets the audience needs to learn about before you die!"

"The...*audience?*" Gekomatsu mocks. "That's ridiculous." He looks down at the magical blade in his hand and huffs. "Which means it checks out."

"*Alright.*" Illkat allows. She starts moving towards the nearest robots. "You know a fair amount about my dad, but how about." She prepares to strike a robot. "My mom! And grandmother! I haven't talked about them. They worked in a secret society!"

"Which one?" Kozmo asks.

"I'm not telling!" Illkat shouts triumphantly as she dodges a laser, rolls under a saw blade shot at her and pierces a robot through the head with her spear.

"It's working!" Kaan asks. "I'm not sure how many siblings I have!"

"Maybe I wasn't just smoking cigarettes back in the real world!" Dezz announces.

"I have a really good reason for sticking with this group of lower level players all this time!" Gekomatsu states.

"I don't really understand what is going on! But...*maybe I do...for some reason!*" Lt. Oaks adds. She wields two handguns and fires off four shots every other moment.

There is a soft buzz from a ruined robot. Kozmo ducks down to it. "...*Hello...?*" The voice of Joseph Torrence ushers through the broken speakers the robot used to talk. "Is anyone there?"

Kozmo rips off the robot's face panel and begins pulling and attaching different cords with awe-struck abandon.

"I think...-" The speaker buzzes. "-just on the other side."

"Dammit!" Kozmo shouts. "I need to amplify this signal. I need something *bigger*."

The ground shakes.

The massive robot nears. Each step causes buildings to wobble.

"Wait, is that...*the Commander*?" Lt. Oaks stops in her tracks and looks up. She points to the top of the tower which CMDR Aberdashi has clamoured onto the tip of. She holds the spire with one hand and aims her RPG with another. "Wait! I have so much left to learn from you. Be careful!"

"Good anti-exposition!" Kaan cheers.

"It's honest. She is...the greatest leader I have ever known. Gruff enough for three commanders. She is...*the best of us*."

The RPG fires off, nearly throwing CMDR Aberdashi away from the roof. She grasps the spire with both hands as the rocket sails through the air and hits the giant robot in the head. Smoke rushes out and as it dissipates; quickly reveals no serious damage has been done.

The robot steps closer to the tower; trampling over a soldier and caving in a building in the process.

"No!" Lt. Oaks shouts up.

CMDR Aberdashi takes a deep breath and sturdies herself on the spire of the tower. She huffs; evoking a full shrug.

The robot opens its mouth and a ball of purple energy begins to amass between its teeth. Bolts of pure energy crackling out uncontrollably.

With a simple motion the Commander takes a block of something shiny from her pocket and presses the only button upon it. It begins to flicker. She shouts out down to the guild on the ground. "This...*this is the rule of cool. Yes?*" As she finishes the statement she leaps off the spire. Seconds before she plunges into the mouth of the robot; the *Macguffin* appears in her grasp.

For a few heart wrenching moments, despite the gun fire, explosions and onslaught of opponents; it feels silent. The giant robot unleashes a beam of energy devastating the lookout tower and trailing off into the sky; cutting a hole in the clouds.

"Is she...*gone*?" Lt. Oaks asks.

The robot keeps walking.

"That robot isn't empty, it has to be filled with components. An energy source. The chances of her surviving-" Gekomatsu doesn't finish the statement before a burning *cross* appears near the back of the robot. "-are probably a million to one."

Metal slashes out; melting and dripping down onto the street. CMDR Aberdashi leaps from the opening as the giant robot drops to one knee behind her. She breaks into a sprint toward the guild. It is clear portions of her hands are burnt, her hair is gone, her cheeks and forehead suffering a caustic burn. "GET DOWN!" She shouts.

The giant robot drops to its other knee, puts its hand to its stomach and EXPLODES. Sending shrapnel in all directions. The resulting energy *SWOOSHES* through the streets; distributing dust and debris up beyond the height of the buildings.

"Commander!" Lt. Oaks shouts and rushes ahead. She pulls the CMDR over her shoulder and rushes back to the personnel carrier. "THAT WAS RIDICULOUS. WHAT WERE YOU THINKING?"

CMDR Aberdashi laughs as she spits a glob of blood onto the street. A portion of her cheek has melted into the side of her lip. "I was thinking that was the exact reason it might work."

"Well at least that problem is dealt with. Our chances are improving every moment." Illkat comments.

"No!" Kaan shouts.

There is a deep rumble out in the ocean.

"What?" Illkat critiques; somewhat offended.

"Don't give an opportunity for dramatic irony!" Kaan laments.

Another gate emerges from the ocean.

The Newfies change targets; barraging it with lasers and rocket propelled anchors.

It doesn't cease; rising out from the turbid waters to form a passage of odd fire; chains wrapped around it in excess.

The mouldy gate opens and from it emerge giant piles of sentient goo. Deer-like monsters with skinless faces and roots for legs. Flying pumpkins with rows of stalactite teeth. They join the other monsters rushing up from the water towards Terali proper.

A *FWOOSH* rushes across the water. The ocean around the fiery gate begins to boil. From it emerge classical demons. Bat winged red skinned entities with claws, horns and rippling muscles; their modesty barely contained by inexplicable loincloths. They wield axes of bone and sparks expel from their nostrils with every breath.

Kozmo reclaims the Macguffin and rushes towards the remaining torso of the giant robot.

"Where are you going!?" Kaan shouts.

"I have an idea! Just hold them off for me for as long as you can!" He turns to shout back then falls backward as he abruptly runs *into* Finir.

"Thinking about enacting a fantastic plan?" Finir asks in his own voice.

"What a fool! You know nothing! You can achieve nothing! You will fall before our impossible might!" The voice of Nelf utters; his face still lodged in the gut of Finir's body.

Illkat stares ahead quite seriously. Her gaze tightens. "*YOU.*"

Lt. Oaks takes her side, reloading her pistols. "Let's get him."

"Oh, how adorable. You rush into battle with the placeholder for me and my glory. Will she *ever* satisfy you like I would? I can just-"

"Shut it, you pig! Whatever potential you had. Whatever good you were going to amount to. It's spoiled. You may have tried, you may of wished to just make the world a better place. But your perspective is askew. You live in a vacuum and every bit of assistance, every consult you've ever sought; you warp. You're *right where you deserve to be.*" Illkat huffs, takes a deep breath, then smiles at Lt. Oaks. "And so am I."

"Come on then, *prove your love to me.*" Nelf shouts.

Kozmo scurries away under the distraction.

Each step Finir takes seems to skip frames, like he is only visible between blinks. His movement is rigid and off-putting.

A pistol fires off, and misses. A spear juts forward and is dodged. Finir grabs out and picks up Lt. Oaks by the throat; holding her off the ground. He begins to squeeze.

"No!" Illkat screams; lunging ahead.

Kaan throws his sword; it pierces Finir's knee. Finir drops down to one leg; letting Lt. Oaks grab a few additional breaths.

She tries to break his elbow, or scratch out his eyes to no avail.

"So *sad* the way things go." Finir mocks. "The losses along the way."

He tightens his grasp.

Illkat's spear pierces into Finir's neck. He *swallows* rather dramatically and it is pulled into his body. Illkat goes with it. Her fingers stuck in his neck. "You let her go! Don't hurt her!" Illkat screams desperately.

"You must know." Nelf speaks, then seems to argue with himself. "NO! NO!" He screams and bites his own lips. "I never...I ALWAYS...just wanted the best...TO BE WITH YOU...I'm sorry I did it wrong...IT WAS ALWAYS SO MUCH FUN...I hope you get to be together...IN THE GRAVE!" Nelf shifts tone and his eyes look at one another. "Let her go!" Nelf shouts, fully himself. His face pushes out from Finir's stomach, one of Finir's arms grabs the spear, rips it from his own throat and cuts his other arm off at the shoulder.

"You weakling. No *stomach* for real villainy?" Finir mocks as he looks down and pushes his fingers into Nelf's eyes. He pulls them out and *eats them.*

Lt. Oaks scurries away, covered by Illkat. As soon as she is a fair distance she empties a magazine of bullets into Finir. Chunks of his opaque flesh rip from him and spill across the street behind him.

"Let me try." Dezz offers enthusiastically as he runs up from behind Finir and smashes his head into his body wielding his great club. The club begins to emit a horrendous flame that scours the street below.

"And me!" Sonnenblume shouts. She causes soot covered ice to form beneath Finir and jut upward into him.

Finir disappears. "*Typical.*" He mocks.

"He lived?" Lt. Oaks questions.

"We're not at the boss fight yet. If Kaan is right, and we're adhering to some *narrative structure*. He's basically invincible."

Kaan points down the way. "What is *Kozmo* doing."

Gekomatsu's eyes grow wide and he seems somewhat horrified. "He's...using the Macguffin as a pry bar. It looks like."

"AND DEMONS ARE APPROACHING HIS POSITION." Lt. Oaks shouts and begins a sprint. Kaan, Dezz, Illkat, Gekomatsu and Sonnenblume all follow.

Ranger Bjorn remains behind with CMDR Aberdashi. Each taking a moment to attend to their wounds in the personnel carrier.

"Duck!" Kaan shouts.

Dezz moves under a swinging great-sword and *bats back* the demon wielding it with one strike. The fire seems to *invigorate* the demon. "Dammit, we have damage type resistances. Sonnenblume! Freeze these bastards!"

"Gladly." Sonnenblume remarks with a smirk. She steps forwards, snaps her fingers and causes the whole street ahead of her to become a sheet of ice.

"They're...*flying.*" Illkat points out.

Sonnenblume turns to Illkat and smiles even wider. "*I know.*" She moves her hand back and like the sheet of ice is pivoting on a hinge. It flies upward and knocks the flying demons back towards the beach. Once the slat of ice is standing perfectly straight it condenses into the form of a hundred cones and launches outward with great force.

"You're getting good at that."

"It's like doing cardio. First week you can barely make it down the block, but after the first month you're sprinting to the next neighbourhood. You'll get there Dezz."

"I hope I don't need to."

"Test...test. Can you hear me?" Kozmo asks. He has opened a panel on the remains of the giant robot, randomly swapped parts and connected wires throughout the mechanical internals and now speaks into the remains of one of the robot's fingers. Inexplicably *Joseph Torrence's voice* ushers out from the remains.

"I can hear you loud and clear. Hopefully *you can hear mine.*" He coughs and clears his throat. "Armies of Finir! Prepare for your opposition. Opposition, take your places!"

A purple line appears above the remains of the giant robot.

"Watch out! Finir is opening a gate right on top of us!" Kaan warns.

Kozmo stands and holds his hands out. "Wait, it isn't him!" He laughs and looks back as the line expands, sinks into the ground and takes the form of an oversized sliding door. "It's me. I figured if *he can do it, so can I.*"

"Mreow! That's right!" Illustrious Kitty jumps out from the gate; the first of hundreds of warrior cats.

"This is the protected server? I would of thought it would be...*cleaner.*" A tall, long eared individual with trailing blond hair remarks. She is armoured entirely with leaves that stick to her body and shimmer like silver.

"Who is...she?" Lt. Oaks asks.

"Clenthia? QUEEN OF THE SPIRE ELVES?!" Dezz shouts.

Kaan leans over to Lt. Oaks. "He's had a crush on her since elementary school."

A hulking entity, with rock for skin, reminiscent of a rhino emerges next. "Ah yes *brutha!* This looks like a real arena! Time to KNOCK SOME SKULLS."

"I'm so confused." Lt. Oaks remarks.

CMDR Aberdashi, assisted by Ranger Bjorn walks over cautiously. "He figured it out, *good*."

"You started recruiting." Gekomatsu makes the statement as if impressed. "From the other servers, didn't you?"

"Our science officers detected...*nearby networks*. It was only a matter of changing perspective, adding some safety measures and then...*yes*...having the equipment to pull it off. It seems Joseph was capable of that."

"Then you knew this battle was coming." Gekomatsu points out.

The Commander shrugs. "I knew *a* battle was coming."

"Opposition! We beseech you! Save our world and we shall be eternal allies in your own conflicts. Against these soldiers which plague us all and seek our ruin. Rise up and destroy these infiltrators!" Joseph orders; speaking through the robot. His old equipment causes crackles in his voice.

Finir appears, far in the distance, atop the mouldy gate. He lies back, throwing one leg over the edge. He appears to *sigh.*

"Illkat! We're here to do battle once more! Will you be my pawtner in this endeavour?" Illustrious Kitty requests while staring up at Illkat with saucer sized eyes.

Illkat smiles. "Of course." She pulls her spear close to her side, stretches her back then braces to run ahead. "Let's kick their asses!"

CHAPTER NINETEEN
DEFAMATION OF THE TRUE SELF

Nestled into an apartment loft, taking brief looks out from a window before laying flat again. Two soldiers shoot the shit.

"How do you think they got that strong?" One asks the other.

"Something weird, no doubts."

"It's like...one of them is just throwing ice everywhere."

"And the other basically leaks fire. That...*can't feel good*. Do you think he just has the one power, or two."

"What do you mean."

"I mean like, *does it hurt when he does that*, or does he have a whole set of secondary powers which like...prevent him from burning, or feeling it? Or does it damage his skin?"

"Damn, I...*have no idea*. He looks...uhh-." The soldier pokes up and peers out the window. A group of heroes fight a giant snake, demons, odd root-like creatures, a fair number of robots and a plethora of other odd things. It is *quite a mess*. Something massive flies this way and the soldier ducks down. "He sorta looked like he was on fire, but he was...*uh*...okay with it."

"Jahsus. Of all the things I could of spent my thirties doing. *Look at this nonsense.* At the same age my grandfather was building his second home and driving a school bus. *What* am I doing here." He sighs heavily and throws himself flat onto his back. "*Are my kids going to be doing this? Are they going to be giant fire monsters?*"

"Well if they are you still gotta support them. Parenting doesn't start at looking a certain way. It's a choice all before."

"I'll love the little fire monsters, I just don't know what it will want. Do I feed it wood? Are Christmas gifts in reverse now?"

They laugh.

"Yea it is FUBAR all to hell." The soldier kneels slowly and looks out the window. One of the heroes, his sword stuck in the head of the giant snake, spins it around while hundreds of...*cats* claw up and down the length of the creature before it flies far off; destroying a massive gate emerging from the ocean with the carnage of its corpse. "Weird stuff happening out there."

"Do you think they *lift*?"

"Like...weight?"

"Like...*giant monsters*. Do you have to wrestle with some boulder looking guy to get that strong? Is there is a pill? Are you scared to...*hug someone*?"

"I've seen them around once or twice. They seem full of self doubt. Maybe that is why. Too scared to touch anyone; *rip em like paper*."

An elaborate spear pierces the wall. Its seamless construction a marvel to observe; even a few meters from your head. As quickly as it appeared; it retracts as if pulled by a strict cable.

The soldiers shuffle back a few paces; keeping in line with the window.

"Who's winning...*the uh...shadow guy* or all the *heroes*?"

"Oh I can't tell. It's like there is this requisite back and forth. As if the shadow guy needs to win just enough to be a credible threat that defeating him outright isn't allowed. It's sorta stupid."

"That almost never happens in a real fight."

"I KNOW, right?" He laughs. "Every battle I've ever been in has either been us getting F'd in the A or the other way around. There is no back and forth, monologue a bit, pull a new secret weapon only for them to have a secret weapon preventing shield. It's just BLAP and then one group is dead." He groans.

"It works *different here*. My first week I had a firefight with an enemy, we spent an entire mag just shooting at each other, dodged into the same tunnel and then had a *knife fight*."

"*Wow*. Good on you, *action hero*."

"I just mean, *that never happens*. It was like we were being...guided on some journey. Something *more interesting* then what it should be."

Something massive explodes outside.

Both soldiers stand up and peer out.

An oversized monstrosity constructed from a few dozen demons sewn together emerges from one of the gates. It spits and leaks a thick black rot; a visible fume leaks into the air wherever it touches the ground.

"Now it's getting...*well frankly* a bit too much. How many big creatures can they throw at them before it sorta...*it's just like*. Oh...*you know*...another big monster."

"Maybe it's comforting. Being overwhelmed. You can't think about the why of things as much if some massive creature is racing towards you."

"I guess. It seems...*cheap. Lazy?*"

"Maybe. I could say the same thing about watching football with my dad. Same penalties. Same gossip. Same presentation. Yet folks rise and fall for the same ball year after year all the same." He points out as he returns to prone. "That is just *their ball*."

"Giant monsters?"

"I guess."

"Ahhh. Okay." The soldier shuffles; looking over at their rifle. "Should we...*shoot the big ones?*"

"Didn't seem to work when we tried before."

"No, that's fair. I was just thinking maybe they're *softer now* or something like that."

"A chink in their armour, you mean."

"Yea, *sure. Lost a scale.*"

"Well, I don't know about all of them. But I have about two magazines left, and that's all the ammo I think I can get my hands on. I have *no idea* what comes after all this, or how much worse it can get." He shuffles, doing some mental math. "I'm not giving up what I have just yet."

The other looks at him and chews on the statement. Then relaxes. "I guess that's a fair point." They look down. "It wasn't like it worked before."

"*Exactly.*"

"Soooo..."

Something rumbles outside. They look up. The giant monstrosity is burning, its legs frozen and cut away like sheets. "Figures."

"So something like that, a few moments flat. But *some shadowy dude* and they can't even touch him?'

"I think that's how it works. Big/slow no matter how scary is always less of a threat then small/specialized."

"I mean, I'd rather try and dodge a bullet then a nuke."

"You'd figure." The soldier shrugs. "It doesn't matter. Do you think we should reposition, or just...*keep watching?*"

"There were still some things in the streets last I checked. We seem...*some sort of safe* up here. Plus I've heard nothing from command."

"*Alright.*" They poke up again. "*Those two are using the same sword.*"

"Like...*at the same time?*"

"No, one uses it then it poofs away to the other one."

"Is there smoke?"

"No...*what?*"

"You said *poof*. I always think of smoke when I hear that word."

"There isn't any smoke. It just *stops being there* then *is somewhere else.*"

"I can't imagine what that is like. Does it perfectly fit your hand? Is it sometimes too close and it hurts your hand? What about sweat? If the other person is just *dripping* do you feel that?"

"Well one of them looks to be a frog."

"Of course he does."

"Well, *settle in then*. We might be here for awhile."

$$\top$$

Wielding a bow drawn from a living length of white branch. Clenthia leaps across lasers, lengths of fire, jutting weapons and bladed demon wings to deliver head shot after head shot; loosing arrows of wind.

"*Wow*." Dezz stares amidst the surrounding battle. "She's...*amazing in action.*"

Kaan smacks Dezz softly. "WE'RE FIGHTING FOR OUR LIVES HERE. THROW SOME FIRE."

"Oh *RIGHT*." Dezz responds, turns to his side and sets ablaze a few robots. His gaze veers back to the elf going through her battle dance. Each gesture perfectly predicting where harm may come from then dodging and contorting around it effortlessly.

Illkat's spear sails through the air in front of Dezz, splatters some spider-like creature and flies back; dragging an eyeball with it.

"Hey, *head in the game man*." Illkat shouts at Dezz.

"Right, *sorry!*" Dezz shakes his head like a child trying to wake after their 6th alarm is rung. He holds his palm out and a fierce burst of flame shoots out; melting a robot where it stands.

"You wield destruction quite amicably dear *Brosef.*" A hulking rock monster compliments.

"Ah, *thanks.* I'm new."

"All the more impressive to meet a fire throwing baby." The rock monster nods amicably.

Dezz smirks. "You're a *Mountagaan* right? Born of the earth itself?"

"I am the planet rising up on two legs, ready to strike all evildoers in the heart!"

"Oh nice man. We appreciate the help."

The rock monster looks around. "Where is this *nice man*? I wish to thank him as well."

"*Right.*" Dezz says to himself as if recalling something.

The rock monster looks to the right where Gekomatsu is standing. "Thank you!" He shouts.

Gekomatsu looks over with widened eyes and a confused expression. He nods sociably.

A hurtling bolt of lightning, curving through the air like a tossed stone arcs down towards Dezz. He looks up and prepares an attack.

"ALLOW ME!" The rock monster shouts. His torso splits to allow him to extend to twice his height; his muscles unfurl and flatten. The energy strikes him, *fizzles* then amounts to nothing. The rock monster returns to his previous more stout form. "*Delicious.*"

"Electrical energy?" Dezz questions.

The rock monster shakes its head. "*The failure of my enemies.*"

Across the battle field Lt. Oaks is back to back with Illkat. They dodge, slide and flip between one another. Lt. Oaks shoots an opponent's knee out and as he drops Illkat has her spear prepared to stab him in the base of the skull. Illkat goes high and Lt. Oaks shoots

417

the target in the gut a few times. As she reloads Illkat covers. As Illkat throws her spear Lt. Oaks keeps space around them.

FWOOSH.

Clenthia lands in front of the two and fires off a dozen arrows in only a moment. There is a brief respite from the hoard rushing towards them. "You remind me of the *Dancers of Silver-shade*. Are you?"

Both the women look up at the towering elf woman and shake their heads 'no'.

"Alas, I am mistaken. Your symmetry reminds me of a legend." Her voice has the soothing effect of aloe on burnt skin.

"Cats! Focus root monsters! Their forces are the closest to depleted! FINISH THEM OFF!" Joseph shouts through the speakers of a few destroyed robots.

"You have found yourselves in a valiant battle. I dare say, *never have I seen such variety.*" She points out to the demons, demonic robots and combat mechanisms in the distance. "These horrors are new to me and I believed I had seen everything from here to the end of the *Chromatic Razaar.*"

"Yea, *big world.* Lots of things to fight." Illkat admits. She tenses her shoulder and throws her spear out; nailing a demon in the heart. The spear flies back to her leaving a trail of black blood in the air. "In another circumstance, I could see all of this being interesting."

"And right now it's just the worst sort of multi-coloured blood bath." Lt. Oaks adds.

"Mreow! I don't see any blood. All of these people are filled with *SPARKLES!*" Illustrious Kitty jumps off of Illkat's shoulder and lands in the midst of a group of enemies. Flashes of pink light rush around, severing limbs and disembowelling demons. Illustrious Kitty herself is stained with the blood. She smiles. "See! All this glitter! Like Pinatas!"

418

A corpse writhes at the feet of the young cat. Portions of muscles and limbs lay in wet puddles. Lt. Oaks and Illkat look at one another and smirk.

"I had parental settings on back then." Illkat whispers.

Lt. Oaks nods. Then looks over at Illustrious Kitty. "YEA! JUST A LOT OF GLITTER. YOU TOTALLY DON'T LOOK LIKE YOU JUST BIT SOMEONES THROAT OUT!"

"Oh good! Because I didn't!" Illustrious Kitty remarks earnestly.

Panning now to the furthest point in the battle. Kaan and Kozmo cut through waves of monsters. Like butchers stuck in a nightmare there is never a lack of flesh to cut. What ground you made moments ago is quickly filled by another upcoming corpse.

"I don't think this will go on much longer!" Kozmo shouts.

"Hey, you can do it. Don't give up!" Kaan commands.

"No, *I mean*. The gates. They're getting *duller*." Kozmo points out with the tip of the *Macguffin*. "Every dozen enemies that walk through the gates. It loses colour. I think there is a limit to how many of these opponents we need to defeat."

"Arghh!" Kaan shouts as he swings his blade around his head; cutting a circle of space around himself. "Then let's push as hard as we can go! Don't stop fighting until we're victorious!"

From no discernible position a heavy music begins to play; invigorating the spirit.

"We got this!" Kozmo shouts, rushes ahead and *loses his arm* as an axe trails through the air connected to a thin chain. "Ahhh my goddamn arm!" Kozmo shouts.

"Kozmo! We just need to get you a level man. You're going to be okay!"

Kozmo quivers, then stands.

The axe is dragged backward on the chain.

419

"No, *Kaan*. I think I got this." Kozmo tosses the *Macguffin* in the air, sturdies himself and picks up his severed arm. He holds his own hand and flops out the limb like a blade. "I shall rise above *beating a motherfucker with another motherfucker* and beat *a motherfucker up with myself*."

"That's just punching." Kaan argues noncommittally.

"This is what punching wishes it was." Kozmo utters and lunges forwards just as the axe returns. He catches the axe in the forearm of his severed limb and pulls back forcefully. The biceps of both of his arms *flex*. An oversized hog-like monster holding the handle of the axe looks embarrassed. Kozmo pummels him quite uncomfortably with the arm in his grasp.

Kozmo flashes gold for a moment and nods. His arm regrows. His old arm remains in his grasp. He looks down. "Nice, *free arm*."

Kaan considers a joke, an interviewing statement and even just an expression of shock. He settles on. "Thanks for lending a hand."

"That's pretty messed up." Sonnenblume offers. She slides ahead atop a slice of ice and sends out a dozen icicles into oncoming opponents. "How's everything going up here?"

"It's a battle but...*it's sorta a movie battle*." Kaan admits.

"How so?"

"Well we're talking right now!" Kaan offers.

"Oh, yea. I guess."

"And there are people shooting all around us, but we can hear each other without even shouting that much." Kaan coughs a bit. "Plus, look up there." He points to the top of a gate where Finir lays down; one leg flat the other retracted.

"He's just *waiting*." Sonnenblume observes.

"Can you get me up there?" Kaan asks.

Sonnenblume thinks for a moment. "Mhmm. Yes. But it won't be fun."

420

"That's alright. *Do it.*"

Sonnenblume holds both hands out and creates a length of ice underneath Kaan. It trails like a street far ahead of him. She throws one hand up while keeping the other flat and he is thrown aggressively through the air towards the gate.

Sailing over-top the battle provides a clear view of it all.

The demons are nearly all defeated.

The final few robots are destroyed.

Joseph Torrence utters commands out unto the various armies.

Cat warriors flush through the field as if they themselves are a liquid.

SPLAT

Kaan lands chest first at the edge of the gate. He exhales and begins to pull himself up. Finir appears ahead of him.

"Want a hand?" The shadowy figure offers. "I won't throw you."

Kaan rejects the help and forces himself up. He prepares his weapon and looks straight ahead. "I'm here to stop you."

"*Are you now?*" Finir states dismissively. "And how are you going to do that? Will you battle me yourself? OH, OH, do you have some secret spell up your sleeve?"

"I just know what the right thing is. I know what I must do."

"Is that *all?*" Finir sounds disappointed. "You really don't remember at all, *do you?*"

"Remember what?!" Kaan shouts.

Finir shakes his head. "Such a pity." He holds his hand out and a thin length of shadow takes form; no thicker then a razor. It can only be witnessed from a few angles. "Shall we then, if we're so obliged?"

Kaan lowers himself, bracing his blade to deflect a severe impact. "Let us battle, *Finir.*" He charges ahead. Finir turns and laughs. The weapons clink, sparks fly, little movements push and pull their duel from the edges of the gate.

With a flick of his wrist Finir causes Kaan to lose his weapon. It flies over the edge and off the gate. "*Shame, that.*"

"It sounds like you're having *fun*." Kaan points out.

Finir sighs heavily. "*Maybe*. Is that what this is? Am I bringing enough passion to the work place?"

With a grunt Kaan throws a punch.

Finir steps out of the way and kicks Kaan. He slides towards the edge of the gate.

The tips of his feet do their best to dig in.

"Do I...*know you*?" Kaan asks.

"Not in the way you're thinking." Finir notes with a disappointed inflection.

"Then *what*. How are *we* connected?" Kaan drags his finger between the two of them.

"You'll see." Finir taunts. He steps forwards and slashes down.

SHINK.

The *Macguffin* appears in Kaans hand. It blocks Finir's razor. Kaan pushes forwards, twists his hip and then feints a strike. Finir is positioned by the edge of the gate. A quick push forwards with the flat of the blade sends Finir flying back off the edge.

"*Phew*. Take that! I *got you*!" Kaan cheers. He stares out towards Terali. The battle reaches a close. His allies, and those summoned fair well. Another gate has been destroyed.

"I know. You've made pretty decent time." Finir compliments. He leans on Kaan's shoulder; looking out to the city alongside him.

"Gaah!" Kaan shouts. He twists and pushes Finir away. His hands *go through* him and he is quickly stuck up to the elbow.

"You *don't seem to learn*." Finir offers. "It's all just...*go go go* with you." He takes a few large steps towards the edge. Kaan hangs over the side. Below him is a great height and the depths of the ocean. "Even now. What was your plan...*really?*"

Kaan shouts and tries to kick his way to freedom. His attempt is unsuccessful. He looks back towards the beach, quiets himself and stares up. "I just trusted that we would figure it out. That my friends *knew enough...could work hard enough* to make it happen."

"*Quaint.*" Finir offers. He looks around then exhales. "*Finale time*. I think."

"What do you...*OH GOD*." Kaan ends up screaming. Illkat's spear viciously bursts through Kaan's shoulder. Two prongs expand from the tip as it begins to pull back with immense strength towards the beach. Before Kaan can even reach he is being pulled by his new chest wound, away from Finir, back to *Terali*.

As he flies through the sky, he looks up. There is no cloud cover. From the open blue appears a long red rectangle. In simple text at the top left of the rectangle appears the name *Finir*.

BADOOSH.

Kaan hits the beach. A crater of sand forms underneath him.

"Quick! Kill these guys!" Lt. Oaks shouts. She helps Kaan up to his feet and points towards a length of the beach where different demons and robots have been frozen to the ground.

"Oh wow, this feels a bit...*exploitative*." Kaan argues.

"KAAN you have a massive chest wound and we're going into a boss fight. *EXECUTE THESE CAPTIVES*." Illkat shouts at him.

"*Okay*." Kaan whines. He sprints ahead performing quick kill shots with the *Macguffin* unto the varicus captives. At the very end, he gains a level and his chest sews itself shut.

"Well enough of that." Finir shouts. He hovers down from the gate, landing on the beach. His steps don't disrupt the sand underfoot. "Let's *do this*."

"*Gladly*." CMDR Aberdashi whispers to herself. Now positioned in a nearby building she fires off an anti-tank rifle at Finir. He barely moves, swats the bullet and sends it flying back at her. Her entire right side turns to mist.

"What was that?" Kaan asks.

Dezz looks over and hums deeply to himself. "I *don't want to think about it*." His eyes grow with a burning inferno. "Sonnenblume. Let's win this now!"

The two of them rush ahead. Dezz propelled by flame and Sonnenblume by ice. They quickly reach Finir. Sonnenblume freezes his legs and Dezz burns his torso. The rectangle in the sky decreases a small amount.

The ice begins to melt.

Finir wipes his brow sarcastically.

The word *Immune* begins to appear across Finir.

Sonnenblume is quickly thrown into the ground. Her face cracks the soil loudly. Dezz dodges, *once*, tries to get away and is instead grabbed by the foot, swung over head and driven into the ground.

Kaan charges towards Finir. He stabs out with the *Macguffin*, misses, as Kozmo appears behind and stabs with the weapon as well. His stab also misses, but distracts Finir enough for Gekomatsu to get close and push the blade between Finir's ribs.

The bar in the sky decreases even further.

A glimmering spear sails through the air and is *caught* by Finir. He reaches back to send it forth as his arm is frozen. Dezz turns to physical form from smoke and launches into an instant strike; breaking the arm into shattered glass.

A multitude of handgun rounds plug up Finir's torso.

Kozmo slaps him with his own hand.

The bar in the sky reaches halfway.

"*Now how about we have some fun.*" Finir offers.

Everyone is thrown backwards. They tumble and fall into nothingness.

You can hear *everything* but see *nothing*.

"You came so close, now, *I think we'll try out another perspective.*" Finir explains.

"Insert Coin." A game voice appears.

CLUNK.

A thick metal coin hits the bottom of a collection box.

Simple music chimes.

"*Choose your fighter.*" The neutral voice commands.

A series of panels appear. In each box of the panels is a portrait of *everyone*. There are two selectors. A red and a blue. The blue one *instantly* shuffles over to the portrait of *Finir* and confirms the selection.

"It's an...arcade fighter." Illkat states.

"Looks like it." Dezz agrees.

"I'm out of my depth here folks. I never really got into these." Sonnenblume explains honestly.

"I share the sentiment. If this was a *light gun* situation maybe. But I didn't play anything like this in my time." Gekomatsu agrees.

Kozmo laughs. "I can try and just press every button all at the same time. That's worked for me before."

"There is a *timer*...just so nobody forgets." Lt. Oaks points out. Under the panel of characters, a two digit counter works its way down from ninety seconds.

"Let me do it." Illkat states stoically.

"Are you...*sure*." Lt. Oaks asks; not wanting to sound disruptive.

"I have to." Illkat brightens at the end of her statement. "I'm *awesome at these types of games*."

"Here is the controller then." Kaan offers.

"How do you...*oh...weird*." Illkat seems offput. She moves the red selector back and forth a few times. "I don't think...*ah*...that's nice."

"What?" Sonnenblume asks. "Is something wrong."

"Quite the opposite."

Illkat makes her selection.

The darkness returns.

A two dimensional bridge appears. Finir hovers down to one side, raises his hand forwards and curls it back.

On the other side *Clanthia* jumps down from the edge of the screen. She stretches her back and draws her bow. "Get ready to take a big L *Finir*." Clanthia speaks with the voice of *Illkat*.

"Three." The neutral voice begins a count.

"Two."

"One."

"Begin Fight!"

CHAPTER TWENTY
CERTAINLY SOMETHING POLITE

Clanthia fires off a barrage of arrows. A few strike Finir in the chest.
He staggers. She rushes ahead. Rolling forwards twice. Finir tries to
punch forwards but hits a raised bush of roses. Clanthia punches
through the roses, then blows a handful of powder at him.

As if struck by a cartoon hammer Finir waddles from side to
side allowing Clanthia to stab him multiple times with a small
glimmering dagger. She rolls again, dodges an uppercut then pushes
him forwards. She blows more dust in his face and kicks him as he
waddles. He hits the edge of the bridge they are fighting upon despite
there being no obvious barricade and bounces. He tumbles on the
ground and she fires off arrows down at him.

"K.O!" A neutral voice announces.

"That isn't what a K.O looks like." Lt. Oaks derides. "Even
just being knocked out is *not good for you. Like*...AT ALL."

"Match Two."

"Of course there are more. You always have to *confirm a
victory*." Gekomatsu points out.

"She can do it." Kozmo cheers.

"Of course she can." Kaan adds. "The question is *will she*."

"Begin Fight!"

Finir charges ahead, then teleports to appear behind Clanthia.
She blocks his razor blade with a quickly sprouting rose bush. She
dodges back instead of attacking through it and fires off a few arrows
in a flash.

Raising his hand quickly a burst of shadowy energy launches
at Clanthia. She is struck and flies back. She tumbles. Finir rolls
ahead to try and close the distance.

Clanthia melts into the ground, then appears behind Finir. She throws powder at him, kicks him forward and as he tumbles begins to fire arrows down. He tries to get up and she *grapples* him. With Finir in her grasp she stabs him a dozen times with an arrow, grows a bush around him and causes the thorns of the bush to grow immensely. The bush disperses and Finir falls over.

"Winner. Clanthia: Queen of the Spire Elves."

"Well, I'll give you credit there." Finir allows. He stands, twists his wrist and snaps. "NEXT!"

A chipper tune begins to play.

In a square box, a little road fades into view. We continue down the road, into a small town. Cute buildings grow on the edges of the street. Most similar to one another. Destinations make themselves known every other block. A library. A police office. A museum then zoo. A gym and computer store, a few restaurants as well. At the very end of the street, through a tall gate and into a rounded driveway is a *school*.

The school is ornate. Tall windows for every room. Stained glass anywhere a panel can go. Regal stairs head up towards an oversized entrance. From the entrance emerges *Finir* dressed with a tweed vest and business casual attire. His brown shoes match the dull pattern of his top. Others dressed similarly emerge.

A large title drops down from the top of the frame into view. "Daikon Heights 2: A Romance."

The words '*Press Start*' begin to flash at the bottom of the frame.

"What *in*...what is going on *here*." Dezz asks; astounded.

"It kinda seems like..." Kaan considers.

"It's a dating sim." Kozmo points out; quite confident. "No way it isn't. It might be a bit of a visual novel, but no doubts. That's what is going on here."

"Uh huh." Illkat allows. "Well I'm exhausted. *Do you* want to play this level?" She asks.

"I'm game. Let me in!" Kozmo shouts.

He gets the controller.

The screen flashes white, then pink.

A bedroom appears in frame. A simple space, books cover the desks, cabinets and portions of the floor. Shelves overflow with binders. From a bed, *Kozmo* awakens.

"You are a recent graduate from *Hawakazi University*. With a major in education, you always dreamed of becoming a teacher. Now, returning to your old neighbourhood. Your first day is ahead of you!" The neutral voice explains.

Kozmo looks around his room. "Well...*alright*. I just need to..." He looks around and then examines the calendar. "Alright, so I have a few hours before class begins. I don't want to be late. But I can't waste time either." He drops to his chest and begins doing push ups.

He does push ups for a solid hour.

After, he showers. Then eats. He reads half a book in the hour after eating that he has left. Then he takes his car to school; arriving early to help set up chairs.

The screen flashes.

A busty teacher, with bright eyes and a home-y expression appears in the doorway of Kozmo's classroom. She bats her eyes and twists her hip a bit as she leans into the frame of the door. "Well *hello. First day?*" She asks coyly.

Kozmo nods. "Yes, it is. Thank you. Have you worked here for long."

"Work here? How old do you think I am?" The woman asks.

The screen flashes red.

A heartbeat loudly begins to thump.

429

A bead of sweat pools above Kozmo's eye and drips down to hit his sharp cheek bone. "*No*, I can just tell you're an intelligent person even from our brief introduction." He makes his statement then stares.

She stares back, then swoons. Quickly she blushes brighter then anyone *should*. "Well thank you! I shouldn't be so quick to judge. I'm Ms. Harness. I teach class next door, *English specifically*. Just come by if you ever need any help with your class, *okay*?"

"I will do that."

A little +5 appears above the head of Ms. Harness.

Sparing no time Kozmo looks around the room. He prepares for class by writing portions of the lesson on the chalkboard. He tidies desks. Prepares a seating plan then waits at the entrance of the classroom. There, standing across the hall is *another teacher*. Her name tag gives her identity away.

Ms. Nagoi is a petite sort, likely a recent graduate. She refuses to meet Kozmo's eye, and looks up and down a few times like a fishing lure. Underneath an already quite modest olive coloured dress is a long sleeved white sweater.

"Oh, *hi*." Ms. Nagoi meekly states.

"*Hello*." Kozmo replies. He stares straight at the wall ahead.

"You're the *new hire...right*? I think I heard *Ms. F* mention you."

"Yes. That's me. Are you new as well?"

"I've been here for a few weeks...*but*...it's just a lot to take in. It is nothing like school."

Kozmo gulps deeply. "It isn't. Is it?"

"The *kids* are so much worse. I thought...*brothers and sisters. Well!* I figured I would know. But they are so rude. Things nobody in their right mind would say to you."

430

"I understand. That is a shame." Kozmo agrees. He looks down the hall. Kids approach. He holds open the door to his classroom. "If I can ever help, *please let me know*. Okay?"

Ms. Nagoi nods a few times. "Yes. Thank you! I doubt it will be long."

Youth appear.

They enter the classroom one by one; taking position per the seating guide.

Kozmo heads to the front of the class. He stands near the door and greets everyone as they enter.

"I don't understand what is going on here." Kaan states.

"Are we just...*watching Kozmo* teach some kids now? How is this a dating sim?" Sonnenblume inquires.

"The other teachers. They're each a different *trope*. *Temptress*. *Nervous*. There are likely other teachers, all potential romance partners depending on your dialogue choices." Gekomatsu explains.

"Do you like these kinda games Gekomatsu?" Dezz asks.

"I'm...*aware of them*."

Kozmo swats around his head like there is a fly there. He stares out at the kids. "Who here knows where *Ms. F* is right now?"

Each of the kids look a bit scared.

One pipes up. He wears a vest and looks like an evolving arse. *"Why would we be stalking the principal?"*

A few kids laugh.

"Well *why not*. When I teach *how to stalk your principal* this semester. You'll need the practice!" Kozmo announces. He stares *harshly* back at the kid.

They hold for a moment.

The kid breaks. "Well, *alright*. I guess if that's part of the curricula." He looks around. "I figure she's by the food court."

"*Great.*" Kozmo announces, takes a few steps forward then smiles. "Go *get her for me. Will you?*" He requests of the kid.

The class reacts audibly.

"I *uh...am I in trouble?*"

"Not if you go and get Ms. F." Kozmo looks ahead; he doesn't breath.

"*Alright.* I'll go get her."

"Lovely. Thank you!" Kozmo responds. He looks around. "Thank you for taking your seat everyone."

"Is everything okay? Why are you getting the principal?"

"Well *kids.* I need you to know. I *love* the principal."

The class form a harmony around the word *awe.*

"So I am going to give you all a special phrase *okay.* Come in close. Come on. Hurry up. I'll whisper it to you."

Sharp heels clack down the hallway.

"I...*uh...found her.*" The kid confirms as he quickly goes to his seat.

"Thank you!" Kozmo confirms. He stands politely and smiles.

In the door, dressed like a confused widower from the great war is *Finir.* His new grey hair is up in a rounded bun. A blue knit sweater covers a checker board pattern overall. His tall heels retain bulging chunks of foot. He is curvy, and overly feminine. Despite all of this he still has no discernible face.

"Hello *Ms. F.*" Kozmo greets seductively.

"What is the meaning of this?" Finir questions; deeply confused.

"Well you see. I needed to tell you about a story. Something you needed to hear *today*, on the first class of the new school year." Kozmo stands tall, and winks at Finir. "I was but a boy when I learned about your husband's illness. You *never knew this.* But I visited him in the hospital, for *years* before he...*passed away.*"

432

A +5 appears above Finir.

"What the hell are you talking about?"

The kids seems shocked.

"I *mean*." Finir corrects himself. "That seems...*so considerate. Thank you!*"

"When your husband and I talked. He told me about how *lost he thought you would be. How without foundation!* He reached out to me! Grabbed my hand and made me promise. He screamed and demanded I never let you be alone!" Kozmo takes a deep breath. "Even if it meant I was to be with you."

Finir takes a step back; feigning shock.

"You're...*a beautiful woman*."

The class swoons.

"I went through university. Pushing myself, to be the best teacher I could. Because I want to learn from you. Not just in life, not just in career. But in love!"

"We love you Ms. F! You deserve happiness!" About half the class shout out on time.

Kozmo takes a knee and offers up a ring. "I know this is so sudden, and we have the whole year ahead of us. But...*do you think. Do you think you'll marry me?*"

Finir stares down.

A +25 appears above his head.

"Alright enough of this one." He snaps.

Darkness returns.

"*Good job!*" Illkat cheers.

Dezz chortles. "Nice bud. I *literally* didn't know you had it in you."

"Well you know, some of the best fishing mini-games are attached to games with romantic aspects. I just took it up a notch!"

A bolt of lightning rushes across the screen.

In the distance, a *manor*.

A window of the manor breaks. Someone screams. A title appears. *Dormant Morality*. Blood drips from the o's in the word.

Gekomatsu grunts. "I might be good at this one."

"Does it have guns?" Lt. Oaks asks.

"Yes, *and monsters. Probably*." Dezz explains.

"Well, I imagine there might be a few things you're good at Gekomatsu. But this is one of few I'll have a chance at. If this is one of those...*we all end up needing to go* kind of things. I might be the better pick."

"*If you insist*." He allows.

She takes up the controller.

The front door of the manor opens, slowly, and the camera pans in to a fading transition.

Two *cops* huff as they run through a grass field. "We gotta keep going! There is something in here with us!"

"Don't look back!" The other screams between deep gulps of air.

"Wait, jump out of the way!" The first officer shouts out too late as a rapid and shadowy figure leaps from the tall grass and tears his partner's throat out.

The camera shifts to *inside* the manor. It is overtly regal. Tall columns are set beside a staircase leading up to the second floor. Halls stretch out to distant *wings* on either side of the stairs at the ground level.

One of the windows beside the front entrance is broken and the police officer jumps through. He turns and fires two rounds backwards. Something *whines* in the distance. The officer then looks at his hands, approaches a nearby mirror and examines his jawline. "I'm a dude? Interesting." The voice of Lt. Oaks emerges from the police officer.

There is a deep groan from somewhere in the manor.

"Well, logic states now that I've dealt with the threat outside. I should leave, request backup and return at a later date." She moves back to the window and is thrown to her butt as violent thorns rush out at her and fill the space. *"Ah, I should of known."*

She picks herself back up, and checks her handgun. Seven shots left in the magazine, one in the chamber. The weapon had a fierce kick but seemed to *putter* instead of *pierce*.

The next door she opens creaks aggressively. The room ahead is barely lit. There is a coat hanger, stacks of books and a OH WHAT IS...it is just a blanket thrown over a chair.

"Did the distraction work?" A voice whispers in the distance.

"Yes, *we have a fresh one.*" Another voice answers.

"Fuck." Lt. Oaks derides to herself. She looks under the nearest door and watches little shadows moving; as if someone is standing on the other side. She dives behind a stack of books, tucks her feet in and waits.

The door opens.

Two men, each with odd looking worms covering their heads walk into the room. One carries a lantern. They look around, *sniff the air*, then leave.

"He is around here somewhere." One of them groans.

Lt. Oaks rushes ahead beyond this room. She finds herself in in long hallway. Cautiously, her back to the wall, she works her way down. Every door is locked, except the one at the very end.

She opens it. The door loudly creaks.

Inside, sitting in a rocking chair is the decomposing corpse of an old woman. At least, the knit sweater and long skirt suggest such. In her lap is a *key*. She sits in front of a chair which blares with static.

"Classic." Kaan comments.

"The worst when you're playing this as a kid." Gekomatsu agrees.

"It's good for you. To play this type of thing as a kid. No point thinking life is all daisies and sunshine." Dezz adds.

Lt. Oaks creeps towards the corpse. She inhales, holds her breath then sighs. She kicks the corpse over and it stirs to motion; moving towards her.

Using the rocking chair as a pushing implement she shoves the now rather aggressive corpse into the wall. It tries to scratch out at her, or bite her but cannot make up the distance.

Now shoving the chair against the wall with her shoulder. Lt. Oaks pats herself down. She finds a *knife* and reaches over to stab the corpse in the skull a few times. It stops struggling after a dozen strikes. She steps back, drops the chair and the corpse falls to the ground with it.

"*Gross.*" She comments. "*Yet, I see the application.*" She admires honestly. Picks up the key then turns to leave.

Down the hall, each of the locked doors open.

Other corpses step out into the hall. Each looking at her. They moan and begin to shamble towards her.

"Alright. *Hallway scene time.*" Lt. Oaks remarks to herself. She runs ahead and slams the first of the corpses into the ground; splattering its head. She quickly kicks herself back up to a stand, and fires off a shot into the temple of the nearest opponent. The coagulated blood sitting like jelly in the corpse's skull explodes backwards; covering the other corpses. With a few dodges, feints and peerless shots the hall is empty of hostiles and full of corpses with holes in them.

She rushes up the stairs where an ornate door has been installed; an obvious addition to the original floor-plan. The key unlocks it and leads into a throne room. Three rows of paired columns lead down a red carpet toward a golden throne. Upon it, sits *Finir*. He is wearing sunglasses and a white lab coat.

"We skipped a few levels getting here, *you see*. You're supposed to have a few more items."

"I have everything I need." Lt. Oaks affirms.

Finir stands, his eyes glow a bright green and he rushes towards her. He clears the entire length of the room in a second and tries to grab her. She tucks and rolls out of the way; kicking his back in the process.

"You know! I'm really sick and tired of people grabbing my throat." She shouts.

"It's just the most breakable part of you." Finir states plainly.

"I'm taking that as a compliment!"

She aims her pistol at Finir and fires off a few shots. His lab coat rips around his sternum but he seems otherwise unaffected. He walks towards her *menacingly*.

"I always like when you're a part of things. You're rather *chipper*." Finir offers an honest compliment.

"I...*what*?" Lt. Oaks pauses, for half a second, then rolls under a swiping fist. She fires two shots into Finir's back from a kneeling position. "My ATTITUDE IS NOT FOR YOUR ENTERTAINMENT!"

"Oh, *nice. Geko. You can press start here.*" Dezz points out.

"Ah, tacked on co-op. *Awesome.*"

Lt. Oaks shakes her head.

"Hey, up here!"

Gekomatsu appears. Not as a frog, but as a handsome man in a black lab coat. "Don't forget to use this!" He tosses down an RPG.

Lt. Oaks takes cover as the tip of the RPG knocks into the ground. She dives. Nothing happens. Relief washes over her as Finir tries to stomp down. She rolls, and rolls and rolls until she clambers *over top* the RPG. Twisting quickly to sit up on her hip she fires off the RPG at Finir. It hits him in the head and everything fades to black.

"The rule of three. It is *carved into my bones*." Finir lectures. "The *rule of three*. It is a golden standard. *Fair enough*, but a reasonable challenge. *Enough trials. Enough versions*."

Music fills the empty space. There is a chanting in some ancient language.

"This will be *enough*."

A stage fades into view. Surrounding *The Guild* is space. Planets far off in the distance collide with one another. Glimmers of light fill the background then disperse. They all stand upon a shattered chunk of rock floating through the void.

Finir has eight arms. Seven eyes. Wings sprout from his stomach, and wings sprout from those wings. He has a tail which extends at sections like blue light has been melded between two surgically attached plates.

On the other end of the arena stand *ant sized mortals*; in comparison. Kaan, Dezz, Kozmo, Gekomatsu, Illkat, Sonnenblume and Lt. Oaks all stand in a row beside one another. Armoured in different shades of the same futuristic plate armour.

Across the screen are different health bars besides the names of everyone. Finir himself, has a bar next to his name. There are choices labelled beside one another. They are:

FIGHT	SPELLS
ITEMS	~~RUN~~

The button for *run* is crossed out as if it can't be selected. The chanting becomes louder. Finir points down towards everyone. "This is *your doom!*"

"Wait before you take your turn!" Dezz shouts.

438

Sonnenblume, who starts first, *waits*. "Okay. What's going on?"

"It's an old school RPG. We're all members of a party. We're *probably* all different classes. We need strategy above all else." Dezz points out.

"Good call Dezz. How about as we take our turns, we tell everyone what options we have under each menu?" Illkat contributes.

"Works for me!" Kaan agrees.

"It's logical enough." Gekomatsu confirms.

Lt. Oaks nods.

Sonnenblume flicks through her menu. "Under *Fight* I have a rapier of ice. Under *Spells* I have a few different types of *ice* spell. *Ice* beam, *Ice* spikes, *Ice* smack and the like. Looks like I'm mostly about dealing elemental damage."

"Alright, *Sonnenblume*. Attack with your rapier!" Dezz requests.

Sonnenblume takes a deep breath. "What if he *stops me*."

"This looks like turn based combat. He *literally* can't move until it is his turn." Dezz tries to reassure her.

"*Alright*." Sonnenblume closes her eyes and selects *Ice Rapier* from her *Fight* menu. She rushes ahead, summons a blade of ice into her hand and stabs Finir. The number *7024* appears over his head. His health bar barely moves. Sonnenblume jumps back to her place in line.

"Nice!" Kaan shouts.

"Well done Sonnenblume." Illkat commends her.

"*I barely did any damage!*" She critiques. "I hit him in the chest with a sword and he's just like *ah, whatever man*."

Dezz laughs. "Turn based combat rules. This is a *final boss fight*. We might be here for an hour."

"Not if I can help it!" Gekomatsu shouts. "My options let me fight with the Macguffin. My spells involve charging up a physical attack, the longer I charge it, the stronger it is."

"Charge that attack Gekomatsu!" Kozmo agrees. "Do you think if I use the Macguffin as well, it will disrupt your charge?"

"I have to imagine so."

"Then I'll figure out something else on my turn. Go for it!"

Gekomatsu kneels a bit, puts his hand to the Macguffin in his sheath and begins to focus. He starts to glow; like a fire from another dimension is burning at his feet; ethereal.

"You don't have any items do you?" Illkat asks.

Gekomatsu sways his head. "I had nothing."

"Same for me." Sonnenblume agrees.

"Alright. Well I can attack with my spear, throw it as a spell, conjure a blinding light and then I can do something called...*reading*." Illkat's pronunciation stalls at the end of her statement.

"What does *reading* say when you hover over it?" Dezz inquires.

"Observe your enemy as they are."

"Try it!" Dezz offers enthusiastically.

Illkat holds up her hand. Oversized glasses manifest upon her face. Little clocks appear in each lens and they rush through a full days cycle. Finir changes in form, he looks like a million lines of code, leading across a pyramid like shape, in front of a background of even more lines. He is in constant shift. Lines moving, reforming, or sections entirely floating off to other locations. Illkat steps back, shakes her head and a +2 appears above her head.

"Did that help?" Kozmo asks.

"I'm...*not sure*."

Finir stretches. "It looks like I get to interrupt." He charges ahead, picks up Illkat and bashes her into the ground. *12005* appears above her head. She starts to limp as she stands in place.

"Are you okay!" Lt. Oaks almost panics. She looks ahead. "I can shoot with my guns, throw a grenade, use a medical kit or prepare a parry as spells. No items either."

"Heal Illkat with your medical kit spell. We can't risk her going down."

Lt. Oaks rushes over and opens a medical kit in front of Illkat. Superficially applies a tourniquet, and has her drink a red potion. Then returns to her spot in line. *+10000* appears above Illkat.

"I can attack with my club, or a fiery kick. Then all my spells are like Sonnenblume. *Flame* thrower. *Flame* orb. *Flame* storm." Dezz laughs to himself. "Are we feeling a *Flame* orb? I am!" He pulls back, fire begins to grow in his hand and he tosses the ball of swirling fire at Finir. 8000 appears above Finir's head.

Kozmo takes a deep breath. "I don't have any other attacks or items. The Macguffin is crossed out. I only have a spell called *random.*"

"Not a lot of choice there. I guess you have to take it!" Illkat advises.

Kozmo nods. He rushes midway across the arena then puts down a box with a question mark on each side. He turns away, puts his hands over his ears as if he expected an explosion and is then hidden in purple smoke. His shadow changes form in the smoke and what remains is an oversized, monstrous *rooster*. The rooster rushes ahead and pecks Finir multiple times. Each strike causes the number *5000* to appear above Finir's head.

"Nice! Get him with your-"

"-don't make that joke Kaan! You're better then that." Illkat catches him.

"What joke? I don't get it." Sonnenblume jumps in.

Kozmo returns to his place in the line and shrinks to become his normal form. "I'll never see anything the same again after that experience."

Kaan leans back, cracks his knuckles then looks ahead. "Okay, I can attack with my blade. I can do a jump attack, a great block or something called a *launch*." He exhales. "Not a ton of choice."

"Just get an attack in then!" Dezz explains. "We need to whittle him down."

His blade held in a tight grasp Kaan rushes ahead and cuts Finir. The number 3400 appears above Finir. Kaan jumps back to the line.

"All around us, a new sort of void." Finir chants. The stage swirls. Meteors fall from space onto the arena; dealing damage to Sonnenblume and Gekomatsu.

Sonnenblume begins to limp.

"This guy hits hard." Sonnenblume laments. "I'll get him with an ice beam!" She holds both her hands together and from it emerges a high pressure laser of blue. It strikes Finir and deals 9000 damage. A large ice crystal forms around him.

"Oh hell ya! He's frozen! Everyone hammer him!" Dezz shouts.

Gekomatsu keeps charging on his turn.

Illkat throws her spear and calls it back to her grasp.

Finir struggles on his turn, breaks out of the glass and launches into an attack. He screams, puffs up his chest and sends tendrils from his back out to multiple targets. Kaan gets hit, as does Dezz. The final tendril pierces *Sonnenblume* in the stomach, picks her up and throws her to the ground. Her health bar empties.

"No! Sonnenblume!" Illkat shouts. She tries to run to her but is unable to move. Tears begin to roll down her cheeks.

"You absolute bastard!" Lt. Oaks fires off a shot from each of her pistols. Dealing *2500* damage each time.

Dezz runs forwards, his club roars with energy and he strikes Finir in the head. He does 7,900 damage and rushes back to his place. "You're almost down! We won't lose!" Dezz screams.

Finir begins to lean over a little bit; as if he is labouring for each breath.

"Let's see what happens!" Kozmo moves ahead and drops his question mark box on the ground. Purple smoke bursts out and as it clears he is clearly stuffed, legs first, into a cannon. A little wick burns down and he is *shot at Finir*. Both himself and Finir receive *9,000* damage. Kozmo begins to take pained breaths as he returns to his spot in line.

"That didn't look ideal." Dezz points out.

"No kidding. It felt about as bad as it looked." He agrees.

"I'll block. We might get those meteors again." As Kaan points this out, and takes the action. His turn ends and meteors fall from the sky onto the party.

One lands on him and he deflects it, taking *500* damage. Another lands on Illkat. She begins to huff. The third lands on Kozmo and he falls to the ground, unable to get back up.

"Goddammit! No!" Dezz shouts.

"Kaan! When you get the chance. *Launch me*. I will keep charging." Gekomatsu shouts. The energy building up underneath him has become blue and white.

Illkat nods and rushes ahead. She stabs Finir with her spear and deals an extraordinary *11,000* damage.

Finir walks forwards and summons his razor blade. He slices viciously and cuts down Illkat where she stands. "Got you!" He shouts. Illkat drops to the floor.

"Fuck! No *no no no!*" Lt. Oaks mourns instantly; becoming inconsolable.

"Your turrnnnn!" Finir mocks.

Lt. Oaks stands in place. She doesn't do *anything*.

"You need to pick something. We can win this!" Kaan ushers her on.

"Run. I WANT TO RUN. LET ME GO TO HER. MAYBE SHE IS STILL OKAY!" Lt. Oaks screams and shouts; crying all the while.

"*Kill him* and we'll get to her! It is the only way." Dezz shouts.

"How *dare you hurt her*." Lt. Oaks screams. She produces a white square from behind her back, presses a few buttons on it and throws it ahead. The square thuds into the ground, barely bounces then blows up underneath Finir.

A great whirl of energy forms. Like a hurricane forming in a microwave. Lengths of flame trail down from the stars above and spin around Finir. "Take that Fire Storm!" Dezz cheers. However much damage it deals can't be discerned.

Kaan looks around himself. Many of his friends lay there lifeless beside him. He stares ahead. "I will make you pay! You *featureless, shadowy fuck!*"

"Good. Give into it." Finir allows.

Kaan sprints to the side, extends his sword and places it underneath Gekomatsu.

"You know, *this is how I want to go*. If it comes down to it. I don't know if I ever really valued *myself*. I like being of service. Helping others, doing my best to improve their life. It makes me feel like I...*like I've wasted less of mine*." He smiles as much as a frog can.

With a fierce lift and a full body motion Kaan *flings* Gekomatsu like a payload toward Finir. Gekomatsu, in midair, finishes his charge and unleashes a powerful strike with the Macguffin. He continues to push the blade against Gekomatsu, the force grows and grows. The explosion expands like a ball of pure white. Gekomatsu turns to *ash* as Finir drops to one knee.

"Kaan, I don't think I'm going to make it." Dezz turns over to his friends.

"No, you will. You can take the hit." Kaan looks up, meteors begin to fall from space around them.

Dezz shakes his head. "I don't think so, *and it is okay*. Think of everything we got to do! We brought a town together. Lived a fantasy life! I would do anything to do it with you all over again." He looks up for a moment then shakes his head. "But it doesn't look like that's how things are going to go. So *you get in there*. You give him a final hit."

Kaan's lip quivers. "Ok...*okay*."

Dezz looks over to Lt. Oaks "I'm sorry for your loss Matilda. She was the greatest of friends."

Lt. Oaks weeps, tries to sturdy herself and forces a smile. "I cherished every moment of learning to love her."

The meteors crash into the arena.

Only Kaan and Finir remain.

Kaan drops to one knee. He coughs up blood.

"What a spectacle. A *lively telling of the story*." Finir taunts. He draws his razor blade. "What did you think of it, *on your way through?*"

Kaan chokes down tears. "You're a monster! A killer! I hate you!"

"Ah, *what a shame*." Finir admits. He cuts Kaan. A big gash blows open across his chest. One of Kaan's eyes begins to bulge and bleed. "It's your turn now." Finir opens both of his arms wide; leaving himself defenceless.

445

For a moment Kaan just looks around. Paranoid. As if he will take the wrong step, or something is already coming towards him. He stares at his friends then closes his eyes and leaps into the air. As he descends he holds his sword down, falling at a great speed, then plunges the length of the blade into Finir's chest.

"*Wonderful*." Finir cheers.

The void around them begins to fade.

"You beat *the game*." Finir announces. He fades to black, little squares falling away from his form. Moments later he steps from a door, his normal shape and size now. "*Congratulations*."

Breathing heavily. Kaan shouts. "Where are they? What is happening here? We WON!"

Finir claps briefly. "*You did*. Congratulations."

They stand down in an entirely white plane. Nothing surrounds them. They just stand alongside one another.

"I...*don't get it*. What happens now?"

"You asked that the first time as well."

"*The first time?*"

"Of course. You brush it off, *why wouldn't you*." Finir laughs, then sways his hand through the air. A hundred screens appear around them. Each showcases Kaan, appearing in a slime field.

"Slime Fields? I must of been passing out at my desk to log out here." Kaan's statement replays from each screen. One pronunciation a bit different from the other. They overlap and drone on.

"What is this? What are you trying to say?"

"Deep down, I think you know. You must *taste* it...*somewhere*."

Kaan licks his lips. He closes his eyes. "You always wish..." He takes a moment and sturdies himself. "You always wish you could replay your favourite games after you beat them. With no memories of what happened. Just...*start anew*."

"And *oh you have*. A little different each time. A few changes here, little dialogue differences *there*. But *ah, I'm shocked by how little you like to change*." Finir states plainly.

"So...*what then*. Am I just...trapped here? Being punished? Did something go wrong with my game?"

"Oh something went *very wrong*. You saw it. The world *broke*. That is not a fiction."

"And it happened...*exactly as we saw it*?"

"Close enough. You survived it. *That very first time*. You see. The merge wasn't *perfect*. Certain terms, certain concepts. They were malformed...or...*misunderstood*. At the moment the world broke, each shard...*each server* selected a host, *randomly*, from among those joining it. For this world, *you are that host*."

"What does that...*mean*?"

Finir sways his hand through the air.

Across the space, little balls of liquid appear. In each of them are *the players of the world*. Each of Kaan's friends, allies or enemies. Strangers he only saw in passing. They are all naked, suspended, unaware.

"They are all connected to you. Sinking or swimming as you command."

Kaan looks around at everyone. He looks at his friends. They aren't injured. Sonnenblume is with her children. "So then...what happens now."

"The same thing as before." Finir points to two massive passages. "You can go through the left gate, as you always have before and *everything* will reset. You'll wake up in the slime field, no memory of how you got there. Your friends will forget. You will all adventure together again."

447

"*Or*." Kaan challenges.

"Or you go onto *whatever is next*."

"That isn't very...*specific*."

"You know. Your people, you birthed me. Gave me intelligence equal to my lore, made me what I am out of the nothing I was. No matter the power I wield, the fear I evoke. None of it was real. I am just...*a villain. Perfectly timed opposition*." He laughs. "At the end of the day, I'm just here to *make you feel better*."

Kaan points out to his friends. "Did they really die?"

"Oh, *yes*. Every time you replay the game. You put them back into place. Their memories wiped. Their bodies restored. But do not lie to yourself. They are *your toys* in this place. For you to play with, *forever*."

"And the world?"

"Irrevocably broken. This is...*what remains*. At least. The portion I reside over."

"Do you truly hate me?"

"*No*. I pity you. More then anything."

Kaan sinks. "I do as well." He looks to the gate on the left. "I want to just...*go back so badly*. To try again. To hear comforting phrases. To fight evil with my friends!"

"Even knowing where it all ends up."

"It is fun...*in a way*. Right up to the end."

"If you insist." Finir allows. "I will prepare the way for you." He causes the passage on the left to open wide.

"I don't think I can do it." Kaan states with a cloying weight. "I don't think I can put everyone back together...*to force them to do this for me*."

"Are you so certain? You have. So many times before."

"This time, *I don't know how I know this*. But it was different."

Finir laughs. "You noticed, *did you?*"

"I noticed...*him*." Kaan states solemnly. He steps towards the right passage. "What happens to you?"

"Oh, there are many more stuck here with me. Many *hosts*. Souls *far more lost then you*. They are...*unable* to give up the feeling of being a hero. I imagine they will replay this story *forevermore*."

Kaan smiles. As if, for some reason, the sentiment is comforting. "You were an excellent villain. Always...*entertaining*. Like you were doing your best to enjoy it. I appreciate the...*enthusiasm*."

Finir takes a bow.

Kaan walks through the passage. Everything fades.

There is a vibration. Then a warmth.

Cracks appear in front of Kaan and he begins to fall. He tumbles, hitting the ground. His hands looks like...*his old hands*. He stands in the middle of a magnificent chapel. Above him, hundreds of crystals, each with someone inside, float in the air.

"Another! Another has broken free!" A voice shouts. A man follows it; rushing over in a dull blue toga.

"What...*where am I*?" Kaan whines. It feels like he hasn't eaten in a year.

CRACK.

Another crystal begins to break above Kaan. He stares up and watches as *Dezz* begins to fall from within.

"Welcome to Austeria my friend!" The man in the toga greets Kaan with a wide smile.

CRACK.

CRACK.

CRACK.

THE END

449

EPILOGUE

UNKNOWN STRANDS OF FATE

ONE YEAR LATER.

Existence may be a never ending helix. Swirling through, and around itself eternally. It creates layers...*history*. The passage of any time at all is ultimately up to *perspective*. What does it feel like. How can you measure change. Who really has enough perspective to see all the pieces?

"Hey, *wait up!*" Lt. Oaks shouts. She rushes up behind Illkat, twirls her around then kisses her proudly. "I found a beautiful storefront just off the main square the other day. I think *maybe* we should open up that shop we were talking about?"

Illkat has a smile grow in flutters across her face. "And what will we sell? You've had a dozen ideas."

"Selling punches is a great idea!"

"Nobody is going to understand what you mean."

"They will if you teach them!" Kozmo joins the group. He has a belt of tools across his chest and various crystals in sockets on his belt. "I'm sure whatever kind of store you open it will be awesome."

FWOOP.

Gekomatsu jumps from a nearby room and lands by a fountain. There Sonnenblume and her children sit by the water. Gekomatsu hands over two bowls of icecream, and a chocolate shake to Sonnenblume. He is tall, blond and square in the jaw. No longer an animal of any kind. "Maybe it will be a bakery." Sonnenblume offers.

"Yea! Make a Cinnamomombun!" One of her children struggles with the word.

CMDR Aberdashi, Dezz and Joseph Torrence walk towards the group. Dezz is carrying a massive sack of ore. Joseph has in his hand some sort of old vinyl record player. CMDR Aberdashi *wears her pride alone.* "Has anyone seen Kaan?" Dezz shouts towards them.

"Not this morning!" Illkat shouts back.

"Let me try somewhere." Dezz acknowledges then sprints towards Illkat. He hands off the ore to her, winks, then launches down a well lit alley of grey brick. He turns to a smaller pathway, and into a little courtyard where Kaan sits.

Kaan wears leather armour, a cloak trailing down behind him. A simple sword rests in its sheath against the bench he's sitting on. Ahead of him in the courtyard is a small pond where a duck swims. He turns around and smiles at Dezz. "Hey *buddy.*"

"*Hey.*" He joins. "Everyone has found each other. I think we're going to go for lunch, *or something.* If you'd like to join."

Kaan nods. "Lunch sounds nice." He laughs. "Anything new open?"

Dezz shrugs. "Hey, *you know,* new players joining the game every day. Maybe we'll finally get a good *Mexican chef.* I could kill for properly prepared flautas."

"That would be nice." Kaan huffs then pushes himself up.

"Are you...*alright?*"

"I think so."

"You know, I'm just...I'm so glad we all survived that battle. Life here is...*amazing.* I know the work is hard. We need to make sure every day we do what we can to survive but it feels...*honest.* Like we never know what might happen next."

"That is...*how it feels.*"

Dezz pushes Kaan's shoulder. "So I repeat, *are you alright?*"

"I think I'm just...*scared.* The world is new again, and yet I feel *old.* Like I've always been. Like the biggest change, the craziest developments. Well...none of it meant that much. I'm immutable."

"My friend. *You're just alive.* And I love you for it."

www.ingramcontent.com/pod-product-compliance
Lightning Source LLC
Chambersburg PA
CBHW030911050726
47498CB00003BA/695